THE SUMMER
THAT MELTED
EVERYTHING

TIFFANY McDANIEL

ST. MARTIN'S PRESS  NEW YORK

THE SUMMER THAT MELTED EVERYTHING. Copyright © 2016 by Tiffany McDaniel. All rights reserved. Printed in the United States of America. For information, address St. Martin's Press, 175 Fifth Avenue, New York, N.Y. 10010.

www.stmartins.com

Designed by Steven Seighman

Library of Congress Cataloging-in-Publication Data

Names: McDaniel, Tiffany, author.
Title: The summer that melted everything : a novel / Tiffany McDaniel.
Description: New York : St. Martin's Press, 2016.
Identifiers: LCCN 2016003510| ISBN 9781250078063 (hardback) | ISBN
    9781466890343 (e-book)
Subjects: LCSH: Teenage boys—Fiction. | Families—Fiction. | Small
    cities—Fiction. | Heat waves (Meteorology)—Fiction. | Suspicion—Fiction. |
    Ohio—Fiction. | BISAC: FICTION / Literary. | FICTION / Family Life. |
    GSAFD: Mystery fiction.
Classification: LCC PS3613.C38683 S96 2016 | DDC 813/.6—dc23
LC record available at http://lccn.loc.gov/2016003510

Our books may be purchased in bulk for promotional, educational, or business use. Please contact your local bookseller or the Macmillan Corporate and Premium Sales Department at 1-800-221-7945, extension 5442, or by e-mail at MacmillanSpecialMarkets@macmillan.com.

First Edition: July 2016

10 9 8 7 6 5 4 3 2 1

My dad, Glen, is comet-tailed nights and what the screen-door lizards sing.
My mom, Betty, is a jazz song played by honeysuckle trumpets and honey-
suckle vines.
Dina, my sister, is water-hose rain on green grass and butter mints at noon.
Jennifer, my sister too, is dandelion stars and infinite firefly skies.

All told, they are my summer. This book is for them.

THE SUMMER
THAT MELTED
EVERYTHING

I

Of Man's first disobedience, and the fruit
Of that forbidden tree whose mortal taste
Brought death into the World

—MILTON, *PARADISE LOST* I:I–3

THE HEAT CAME with the devil. It was the summer of 1984, and while the devil had been invited, the heat had not. It should've been expected, though. Heat is, after all, the devil's name, and when's the last time you left home without yours?

It was a heat that didn't just melt tangible things like ice, chocolate, Popsicles. It melted all the intangibles too. Fear, faith, anger, and those long-trusted templates of common sense. It melted lives as well, leaving futures to be slung with the dirt of the gravedigger's shovel.

I was thirteen when it all happened. An age that saw me both overwhelmed and altered by life in a way I'd never been before. I haven't been thirteen in a long time. If I were a man who still celebrated his birthday, there would be eighty-four flames flickering above the cake, above this life and its frightening genius, its inescapable tragedy, its summer of teeth that opened wide and consumed the little universe we called Breathed, Ohio.

I will say that 1984 was a year that understood how to make history. Apple launched its Macintosh computer for the masses, two astronauts walked the stars like gods, and singer Marvin Gaye, who sang about how sweet it was to be loved, was shot through the heart and killed by his father.

In May of that year, a group of scientists published their research in a scientific journal, revealing how they had isolated and identified a retrovirus that would come to be called HIV. They confidently concluded in their papers that HIV was responsible for the acquired immune deficiency syndrome. AIDS, as the nightmares say.

Yes, 1984 was a year about news. It was the year Michael Jackson would burn for Pepsi, and the Bubble Boy of Houston, Texas, would come out of his plastic prison, be touched by his mother for the very first time, and moments later die at just twelve years of age.

Overall, the 1980s would prove industrious years for the devil. It was a time you couldn't just quit the horns. Satanic cult hysteria was at its height, and it stood tall. Fear was a square that decade so it could fit into our homes better, into our neat little four-cornered lives.

If a carton of milk turned over, the devil did it. If a kid showed bruises, he'd be put in therapy immediately to confess how his own parents had molested him around a bonfire while wearing black robes.

Look no further than the McMartin Preschool investigation, which started in '84 and ended with fantastical allegations of children being flushed down toilets and abused by Chuck Norris. While these allegations eventually would be flushed down the toilet themselves, that time of panic would always be remembered as the moment when the bright, bright stars could not save the dark, dark sky.

Breathed's own devil would come differently. The man who invited him was my father, Autopsy Bliss. Autopsy is an acutely strange name for a man to have, but his mother was an acutely strange woman. Even more, she was an acutely strange religious woman who used the Bible as a stethoscope to hear the pulse of the devil in the world around her.

The sounds could be anything: The wind knocking over a tin can. The clicking of rain on the windowpane. The erratic heartbeat of a jogger passing by.

Sometimes the things we believe we hear are really just our own shifting needs. Grandmother needed to hear the spook of the snake so she could better believe it actually existed.

She was a determined woman who pickled lemons, knew her way around a tool box, and raised a son by herself, all while earning a degree in ancient studies. She had the ancients in mind when she named her son.

She would say, "The word *autopsy* is a relative of the word *autopsia,* which in the ancient vernacular of the Greeks means *to see for oneself.* In the amphitheater of the great beyond, we all do our own autopsies. These self-imposed autopsies are done not on the physical body of our being but on the spirit of it. We call these ultimate examinations the autopsy of the soul."

After the summer ended, I asked my father why he had invited the devil.

"Because I wanted to see for myself," he answered with the definition of his name, his words doing their best to swerve his tears lest they be drowned on impact. "To see for myself."

Growing up, my father was the wood in his mother's lathe, held in place and carefully shaped over the years by her faith. When he was thirteen, his edges nearly smoothed, the lathe suddenly stopped turning, all because his mother slipped on the linoleum floor in their kitchen and fell backward with no parachute.

The bruises would come to look like pale plums on her flesh. And while not one bone had been broken, a spiritual break did occur.

As Dad helped her to her feet, she let go of a moan she'd been holding. Then, in a giddy woe, she dropped her knees back to the linoleum.

"He wasn't there," she cried.

"Who wasn't there?" Dad asked, her shaking contagious to him.

"As I was falling, I reached out my hand." She made again the gesture of that very thing. "He didn't grab it."

"I tried, Momma."

"Yes." She cupped his cheeks in her clammy palms. "But God didn't. I realize now we're all alone, kiddo."

She took the crucifixes off the walls, buried her Bible in the infant section of the cemetery, and never again poured her knees down to the ground in prayer. Her faith was a sudden and complete loss. Dad still had the fumes of his faith left, and in those fumes, he found himself one day walking into the courthouse, where his mother was getting reprimanded by the judge for unabashedly vandalizing the church—the second time.

While Dad waited outside her courtroom, he heard voices a few doors down. He went in and sat through the trial of a man accused of pulling out a shotgun at the coin laundry, leaving bloodstains that couldn't be washed out.

To Dad that man was the devil emerged and the courtroom was God's filter removing that emergence from society. As he stood there, Dad could see tiny breaks in the courtroom wall. The holes of a net through which a bright, warm light shone, pure and glorious. It was a light that made him want to stand and shout *Amen* until he was hoarse.

While his soul had before paced back and forth from doubt to belief, on that day in the courtroom, his soul settled on believing. If not in everything else, then at least in that filter, that instrument of purity. And the handler of that filter, in Dad's eyes, the person who made sure everything went the very best of ways, was the prosecutor. The one responsible for making sure the devils of the world are trapped by the filter.

Dad sat there in the courtroom, hands shaking, his feet swinging just above the floor they were too short to reach. When the guilty verdict came, he joined in the applause as he smelled a whiff of bleach that he associated not with the janitor in the hallway but rather with the filth trapped by the filter and the world being cleaner for it.

The courtroom emptied until only Dad and the prosecutor remained.

Dad sat on the bench, wide-eyed and waiting.

"So you are who I heard." The prosecutor's voice was like a pristine preaching to Dad.

"How could you have heard me, sir?" Dad asked in pure awe.

"You were so loud."

"But, sir, I didn't say a dang thing."

The prosecutor laughed like it was the funniest thing he had ever heard. "And in that silence, you said it all. Why, you were as loud as shine on chrome, bright and boisterous in that silent gleam. And such loud boys will grow to be loud men who are meant to be in the courtroom, but never—no, not ever—as the ones in handcuffs."

That was the moment Dad knew he himself would become a handler of the filter. And while his mother never regained her faith, he kept his in the courtroom and in the trials of humanity and, most important, in that filter.

They said he was one of the best prosecuting attorneys the state had ever seen. Yet there was something unsettled about my father. Handling the filter did not prove to be an exact science. Many times after winning a case, he would escape from the applause and congratulatory pats on the back to come home and sit quietly with his eyes squinted. That was how you knew he was thinking. Squinted eyes, arms folded, legs crossed.

It was on one such night that he uncrossed his legs, unfolded his arms, and widened his eyes, in that order. Then he stood, rather certain as he grabbed a pen and a piece of paper. He began to write what would end up being an invitation to the devil.

It was the first day of summer when that invitation was published in our town's newspaper, *The Breathanian*. We were eating breakfast, and Mom had laid the paper in the middle of the table. With morning milk dribbling down our chins, we stared at the invitation, which had made the front page. Mom told Dad he was too audacious for his own good. She was right. Even the atheists had to admit it took a fearless man to audition the existence of the Prince of Darkness.

I still have that invitation around here somewhere. Everything seems so piled up nowadays. Hills all around me, from the soft mounds of laundry to the dishes in the sink. The trash pile is already waist-high. I walk through these fields of empty frozen dinner trays and beer bottles the way I used to walk through fields of tall grass and wild-flowers.

An old man living alone is no keeper of elegance. The outside world is no help. I keep getting these coupons for hearing aids. They send them in gray envelopes that pile like storm clouds on my table. *Thunder, thunder, boom, boom*, and there the invitation is under it all, like a bolt of lightning from the sky.

> *Dear Mr. Devil, Sir Satan, Lord Lucifer, and all other crosses you bear,*
> *I cordially invite you to Breathed, Ohio. Land of hills and hay bales,*
> *of sinners and forgivers.*
> *May you come in peace.*
>
> *With great faith,*
> *Autopsy Bliss*

I never thought we'd get an answer to that invitation. At the time, I wasn't even sure I believed in God or His antonym. If I had come upon a yard sale selling what was purported to be the true Veil of Veronica beside a bent Hula-Hoop, well, I was the type of boy who would have bought the Hula-Hoop, even if the veil was free.

If the devil was going to come, I expected to see the myth of him. A demon with an asphalt shine. He'd be fury. A chill. A bad cough. Cujo at the car window, a ticket at the *Creepshow* booth, a leap into the depth of night.

I imagined him with reptilian skin in a suit whose burning lapel set off fire alarms. His fingernails sharp as shark teeth and cannibals in ten different ways. Snakes on him like tar. Flies buzzing around him like an odd sense of humor. There would be hooves, horns, pitch-forks. Maybe a goatee.

This is what I thought he'd be. A spectacular fright. I was wrong.

I had made the mistake of hearing the word *devil* and immediately imagined horns. But did you know that in Wisconsin, there is a lake, a wondrous lake, called Devil? In Wyoming, there is a magnificent intrusion of rock named after the same. There is even a most spectacular breed of praying mantis known as Devil's Flower. And a flower, in the genus *Crocosmia,* known simply as Lucifer.

Why, upon hearing the word *devil,* did I just imagine the monster? Why did I fail to see a lake? A flower growing by that lake? A mantis praying on the very top of a rock?

A foolish mistake, it is, to expect the beast, because sometimes, sometimes, it is the flower's turn to own the name.

2

. . . a flower which once
in Paradise, fast by the Tree of Life,
Began to bloom

—MILTON, *PARADISE LOST* 3:353–355

I ONCE HEARD someone refer to Breathed as the scar of the paradise we lost. So it was in many ways, a place with a perfect wound just below the surface.

It was a resting in the southern low of Ohio, in the foothills of the Appalachian Mountains, where each porch had an orchard of small talk and rocking chairs, where cigarette tongues flapped over glasses of lemonade. They said the wooded hills were the fence God Himself built for us. Hills I always thought were the busiest hills in all the world. Busy rising and rolling and surrounding.

One hill could be a pine grove, quick to height and like steeples of the original church. While on another hill, you'd find meadows where grapevines hung on the edges like fallen telephone wires you could swing on with the sparks.

Sandstone was as mountain as the hills got. The sandstone rocks all seemed to remind folks of something, and so were given names like the Grinning Ass, Slain Turtle, and Betting Dragon. You could see images in any of the rock formations. More than that, you could find fossils of the past residents, like lizards and them bugs with all those ridges on the sides.

The rocks were especially outstanding on the sides of the hills where they would ledge out and cliff off with mossy turns. The trees would grow out on those ledges, their roots dangling between the crevices of rock. We all called them roots Praying Snakes. There was just something about the way they slithered across the rocks and dangled like they had a chance.

Summer in Breathed was my favorite season of all. Nothing but barefoot boys and grass-stained girls flowering beneath the trees. My favorite summer sight was those trees. Whether up in the hills or down around the houses, trees were Breathed. Some were old, and they squatted, clothed in heavy moss and time like they were enduring Neanderthals who should not still exist. Others were timelessly modern, smooth and lean and familiars to twine.

Trees were Breathed, but so were the factories—plenty of factories making everything from clothespins to camping tents. There was a coal mine at the eastern side of town and a rock quarry at the western. Fishing and swimming and baptisms could be had in the wide and deep Breathed River that eventually met up with the Ohio and from there the great Mississippi with all its fine strength and slipping song.

If you drove anywhere or walked anywhere in Breathed, you did so on lanes. Never streets, never roads, but dirt-laid lanes that each had their own story. Paved roads were something other towns did. Breathed hung onto its dirt, in more ways than one. Not even Main Lane, the main artery of the town, had been paved, though it was lined with trees and brick sidewalks that fed into brick buildings.

From Main Lane, the town unfurled into lanes of houses, and eventually lanes of farms, the farther out you got. Breathed was the combination of flower and weed, of the overgrown and the mowed. It was Appalachian country, as only Southern Ohio can be, and it was beautiful as a sunbeam in waist-high grass.

It was a good town for a boy to have come of age in. There was a small movie theater, where I had my first kiss while E.T. flew in front of the moon, and a pizza parlor with arcade games I would play until my eyes hurt from the bright, flashing screens. Most days, though, were spent on the tire swing over the river or tossing a baseball back and forth with my brother. In these moments, the gild receded and life was its most naked bliss.

What I've just described is the town of my heart, not necessarily the town itself, which had an underbelly that knew how to be of mood with the mud. Just as in every other small town and big city, the women cried and the men knew how to shout. Dogs were beat, children too. There weren't always mothers to bloom identical to the rose, and more often than not, there was no picket fence to paint.

Yes, Breathed was the scar of paradise lost, and beneath the flour-and-butter drawl, there was the town's own sort of sibilant hiss on the wind, which made you quiet and made you sense snakes.

They say I was the first one in all of Breathed to see him. I always wondered about that. If maybe I wasn't the first one to see him, but just the first one to stop.

As I walked, I could hear the song "Cruel Summer" blaring from a boom box from the open windows of a house that smelled like rhubarb pie and Aqua Net. That was the strange collision of the decade and our small town. A crash of gingham curtains and spandex miniskirts.

Everything seems neon lit when I look back at that time, like the tracksuits that made color exhausting and the parachute pants that gave all the boys who wore them airplane eyes. Sometimes I'll even remember an old man in greasy coveralls and instead of mechanic's blue, I see them bright yellow and glowing. That's the art of the '80s. It's also the damage of it.

Perhaps because they belonged to me, I will say that the '80s were as best as any time to grow up in. I think too they were a good time to meet the devil. Particularly that June day in 1984, when the sky seemed to be made on the kitchen counter, the clouds scattering like spilled flour.

That morning before I left the house, I had glanced at the old thermometer on the side of the garden shed. The mercury was at a comfortable 74 degrees. Added to that was a breeze that made fools of fans.

I was on my way home from Papa Juniper's Market with a bag of groceries for Mom when I came upon the courthouse and saw him standing under the large tree at the front.

He was so very dark and small in those overalls, like I was looking at him through the opposite end of a telescope.

"Excuse me." He held his hand out toward me, but did not touch. "Sorry to stop you. Do you have any ice cream in that bag?"

He had yet to look at me.

"Naw, I ain't got no ice cream."

I thought he should have asked for a pillow. He looked so tired, like he came from nights spent being jerked from brief moments of sleep.

"You can pick some up from Papa Juniper's. It's just back that way." I turned with my finger pointed back, though we were not on Main Lane, so the store was no longer in view and what I ended up pointing at was a woman walking blistered and barefoot with her red heels in her hand.

"I got some chocolate." I patted my jeans pocket.

He twisted his mouth off to the side like a blown-off curtain. If I would have let him, he probably would've gone days like that.

"C'mon." I passed the grocery bag from one arm to the other. "You want the chocolate or not? I gotta get home."

"I really wanted ice cream." It was then he looked into my eyes for the first time, and it was such an intense stare, I almost overlooked his irises, as certain and green as the leaves. The stare broke only when he turned his attention to the birds above.

I looked at his ribs, which were exposed by the cut-out sides of the overalls. I could almost hear the hunger gnawing on his bones, so I reached into my pocket for the chocolate. "You best eat somethin'. You look all . . . deflated."

My fingers sank with the chocolate, like I was holding a small bag of juice.

"That's odd." I set the bag of groceries down to open the wrapper. The chocolate oozed and dropped. I said the first thing that came to mind: "It died."

"Dead, you say?" The boy looked down at the chocolate splattered on the ground.

"Well, it's melted. Ain't that death for chocolate? It ain't even that hot."

"Isn't it, though?" He tilted his face to the sky, the light illuminating the green in his eyes to a yellowed shade as he stared at the sun the way every adult in my life up to that point had warned me not to.

"Isn't it, what?"

His eyes fell slowly from the light to me as he asked, "Isn't it hot?"

My sudden awareness of the heat was a *pop,* the way the bubble joins the water in a boil. I felt lit, a change told in degrees, steadily climbing upon my internal thermometer. From a distance, maybe I was a car with its headlights on. Up close, I was flames burning up.

The lukewarm past had been overtaken by the scalding now. Gone was the perfect temperature. The breeze. All replaced by an almost violent heat that turned your bones into volcanoes, your blood into the lava that yelled their eruptions. Folks would later talk about that sudden onset of heat. It was their best evidence of the devil's arrival.

I wiped my forehead with the back of my hand. "This heat, it puts sweat on the skull. Where the hell has it come from?"

He was looking across the lane. It was then I saw bruising on his collarbone, though fading one blue shade at a time.

I swallowed, suddenly conscious of my thirst. "Whatcha doin' here in front of the courthouse anyways?"

"I was invited."

"Invited?" I squinted like Dad. I went on like that until a man humming "Amazing Grace" continued past us on the sidewalk. The man glanced back at the boy but never stopped his humming, though it did slow to a more concerned pace. Meanwhile, I chewed at my already short nail. "Who were you invited by?"

The boy reached into the bulging front pocket of his overalls. He worked around the bulge to pull out a folded newspaper.

My eyes darted from the invitation on its front page to him. "You don't mean to say that you're . . ."

He said nothing, neither with words nor with face. I could have pushed at him until the day's end and never got anything of a telling expression.

"Are you sayin' that you're the devil?"

"It is not my first name, but it is one of them." He reached down to scratch his thigh. It was then I noticed the denim was worn at the knees more than anywhere else. Over top of the wear were layers of dirt, as if kneeling were all the time for him.

"You're lyin'." I searched his head for horns. "You're just a boy."

His fingers twitched. "I was once, if that counts."

If looks were to be believed, he still was just a boy. Something of my age, though from his solemn quietude, I knew he was old in the soul. A boy whose black crayon would be the shortest in his box.

I reckoned he came from even farther out in the country, where outhouses were still in use and your nearest neighbor was the field you planted.

At that moment, I felt compelled to look at his hands. I thought if he was the devil, they would be singed, charred, somehow influenced by fathering the fires of hell. What I saw were hands experienced in plucking chickens and in steering a tractor over a long haul of ground.

The clock in the courthouse tower behind him began to chime the hour. He glanced back at the clock with its white face, like a plain dinner platter. Atop the roof of the tower stood Lady Justice, poised on the balls of her feet. If it wasn't for that clock and statue, the place of court would have been just a large wooden house with a wide wraparound porch scattered with rocking chairs and dirty ashtrays. This was what law and order looked like in Breathed. A house with a termite problem that made the gray boards like stewed wood.

The boy's eyes fell from the clock to the tree in front and its smooth bark and pointed leaves lining the length of the pale gray branches.

"They call it the Tree of Heaven," I told him. "It's some sort of ail . . . ailanthus, Dad calls it. He says they should never have planted it here."

"Such a name as heaven, you think everyone would plant one in their living rooms."

"You could plant it in your livin' room. It'd sure grow outta carpet. Them things grow anywhere. And they just keep growin'. It's a pest."

"Peculiar that a tree named after paradise is a pest."

He spoke all his words in the burdened and slow pace of a pallbearer in wartime.

"Where your folks at? C'mon, I know you're not the devil."

From the pocket, he pulled out the bulge, which was a gray pottery bowl with five dark lines of blue circling it. It was followed by a spoon inscribed with LUKE 10:18: I SAW SATAN FALL LIKE LIGHTNING FROM HEAVEN.

"It's a real shame you don't have any ice cream. I have everything for it." He held the items close to his chest.

"We might have some at the house. Ain't no point in you standin' here. Don'tcha know the courthouse is shut on Sundays?"

"Is it Sunday?" He held a tightness in his dark brows that stretched to his elbows.

"Yep."

For what felt like a very long time, he made a quiet study of me. I picked up the bag of groceries and held it like a shield to my chest. Finally he asked, if it was indeed Sunday, why I wasn't in church.

"Never am." I shrugged. "Dad will go. He don't make a regular thing out of it, though. He says the courtroom is his church." I leaned in as if whispering were the only way to say, "My dad is Autopsy Bliss."

He too whispered, reciting the last bit of the invitation: "With great faith, Autopsy Bliss."

I made room for a man and his limping dog. Once they passed, I stepped closer to the boy. "You're really Satan?"

"Yes."

"The big man Lucifer?"

He nodded his head.

"The villain of the story?"

"I didn't say that."

"If you're the devil, then you're the bad one. That's just the way it is. Well, come on then."

"Where to?"

"To meet the man who invited you."

3

FROM THE LOOKS of it, his overalls were his only wearing. Was that a year's worth of dirt on the strap? The cuffs of the pants? How long did it take to fray the denim like that? To lose the button? To rip that hole by the knee, the biggest of them all?

The only spot not worn was the seat. Did he never sit down? Too busy getting that dirt caked into the thread. That dust settled into the pockets. In some areas, the denim was so thin, you could see his skin lifting like shadow through the thread-baring weave.

He didn't walk like other boys. There was no bounce, no thrill of movement. I could see him low and deep, peacefully wise below the grass line of the cemetery.

His skin reminded me of when I had been woken by high-pitched screeches outside my window. I rolled out of bed, pressing my face into the screen. It was too dark to see anything, but I knew the birds were close from their battle sounds and the whooshing thud of their wings.

The next morning, a feather lay on the ground beneath my window. It was black on the tip, but the closer it got to the quill, the black began to gray into an almost hurting brown. I thought it a sore color for a feather to have. When I saw the boy, I thought it made for even sorer skin with its reddened tinge.

Once we came to the residential lanes, I watched him as he carefully studied everything from flies on roadkill to a tangle of barbed wire rusting in a field. They were poems handwritten by nature to him, and he was as fascinated with them as I would've been about a ticket to the World Series.

"How do you say this place?" he asked.

"Whatcha mean?"

"I mean, the name of the town. How do you say it?"

"Oh, well, most folks think it's pronounced like the past tense of breathin'. You know, like you just breathed somethin' in. But it's not like that at all. Say *breath*. And then *ed*. Breath-ed. Say it so the tongue don't recognize such a large break between *Breath* and *ed*. Breathed."

He repeated after me.

"Yeah, just like that."

I knew by looking at him, he was the type of boy who got up with the sunrise, already tired, and worked until the sunset, shrunk to the bone. He knew the resilience of a seed, and the vulnerabilities of it also. The blessing of a full field and the destroyed hope of a barren one.

I wondered how many times those dirt-crusted fingernails had tried to pry growth from a drought. How many times those small hands had thrown buckets of water from flooded plains. He knew how to jar and can vegetables the way I knew how to play *Mario Bros.* We were in the same world, yet to me he smelled of rocket fuel.

"Your eyes . . ." I stared at his irises, never having seen such a dark yet sparkling shade. They were like July foliage in the sun. "They're so green."

"They're leaves I took as souvenirs from the Garden of Eden." He said it so certain, I couldn't doubt its truth.

A truck backfired. Or maybe that was just what that group of kids sounded like as they came bursting from around the corner, nearly knocking the boy over. At first I thought his hands were up in order to catch his balance. Then I realized he was reaching out to the kids. Each sleeve or arm that came close enough he tried to grab hold of but couldn't. They were passing him by as if he should know better. As if he should know he could never be them. Joyous and free and in pure bliss.

There was someone in the group falling back, calling my name.

It was Flint, always Flint. The boy with Coke-bottle glasses and one eye lazier than the other.

"Hey, Fieldin'." He ran in place as the others kept forward. "We're goin' out to the river for a swim. You comin'? Mason swears he seen an alligator in there."

"Ain't nothin' but a longnose gar." I shook my head, unimpressed.

"I told 'im." He wearily shrugged his shoulders while his bare, dirty feet continued to pound the ground as he looked from me to the boy. "Who's the cricket you got with ya, Fieldin'?"

The boy was looking up, his wide eyes as seemingly edgeless as the sky he tilted to. His mouth slightly opened in dazzled wonder. What drew those wide eyes? That dazzled wonder? Why, nothing more than a hawk. Just something to glance at for most, but to him it was something more. The way he looked at it made it almost holy, a sort of flying cross. The moment spiritual. He could have sat down on a lawn chair and turned it into a pew.

"This is, um, well"—I grabbed the back of my hot neck—"it's the devil."

Flint stopped running in place, though his arms took longer to slow down to his sides. "What's that you say?"

"He's the devil."

Flint scratched his temple like his own dad was prone to do in situations of deep figuring. "Let me get this straight, Fieldin.' You mean to tell me that this here little tick is the devil? The one come to answer your pa's invitation?"

"That's right." I pulled my words close. They seemed less silly like that.

Still his laugh came. Hard and bumpy like the gravelly path that led to his trailer park. He took a step closer to the boy, clicking his tongue the way one would approach a potentially skittish pony. The boy lowered his eyes from the hawk.

Flint smiled small, like a tapping at a door. "Hey."

The boy stared back, no tell on his face. Flint didn't need more than that.

"Wait'll I tell the fellas." He pushed his thick glasses up on his nose and took off, his bare feet kicking and lifting the road dust into little clouds that hung long after he'd gone, like swarms of gnats.

"Ain't no goin' back now. Flint will make sure the whole town knows who you say you are, so you better be prepared to be just that."

The boy nodded.

"C'mon then. We're almost there." I pointed to the KETTLE LANE sign before us. "My house is at the end of here. There's an actual kettle buried somewhere on this lane. They say if you find the kettle, you can drink your way to immortality. If I find it, I'll let you have a sip."

"No, thank you."

"Don'tcha wanna live forever?"

"I'm the devil. I am already forever."

Any further conversation was doubted by the start of a John Deere in the nearby yard. Instead of trying to compete with its blaring rumble, we continued down the lane in silence.

The lane was drenched in sunlight. The trees put their shade down in the large lawns of the large houses that made up Kettle Lane.

The first house on the lane belonged to our neighbor, Grayson Elohim, and was part of an inheritance from Elohim's banker father.

As we came upon the orange-red brick, we saw Elohim eating on the porch. His feet, too short to reach the floor, hung barefoot. His lunch consisted of macaroni salad and a raw onion sandwich. No meat would be found on his table. At that time, he was the town's only vegetarian. I used to think this put his sharp teeth to waste.

He ate at the large, dark dining table on his white porch every day for all his meals. The heavily polished table was set for two, with a yellowed lace tablecloth, while a radio in the background played violin. He'd go through the gentlemanly motions of dining with his wife in mind.

At one time he had been engaged, but his fiancée drowned in 1956. Though her body was recovered from the Atlantic and buried in Breathed, he lived as if she were by his side and not low and deep and slowly disappeared by the soft power of the worms.

He showed me her picture once in his red leather scrapbook. A tall woman with lines like string, a very white string at that. As far as loveliness goes, she had something like it. Enough to be far too lovely for an ugly little man like Elohim.

He was named Grayson, for being the son with the gray eyes. In his porridge-lumped face, his gray eyes gave possibility to his high-rising forehead and low-hanging chin. He wore his ashen hair long and slung in a low, limp ponytail. He had started balding in his late twenties following the sinking of the *Andrea Doria*. By '84, and in his late fifties, he was completely bald on top, except for this strange growth of hair that grew above his forehead like a limp horn. He turned it into two by parting the meager strands, wearing them long to the corners of his mouth.

"Hey, Mr. Elohim." I threw my hand up.

"Why, hey there, Fielding." He spooned more macaroni salad onto his plate.

When I turned to introduce the boy, he was gone.

"Over here." The boy's hushed voice came from the other side of a nearby tree.

"Who you talkin' to, Fielding?" Elohim stood up from the table, craning his brief neck in the tree's direction.

I did my best to urge the boy out, but still he stayed behind the tree.

"I thought you come by yourself." Elohim cleaned his teeth with a toothpick. "If there's anyone else, you come on out now. I don't like hidden things."

The boy wouldn't budge. Not even when I tugged his bony arm. When I asked him why he looked so afraid, he nodded toward Elohim.

"You 'fraid of 'im 'cause he's a midget?" I asked quiet enough so Elohim wouldn't hear me call him anything other than short. "He won't harm ya none."

The boy chewed his lip. "You sure?"

"He's never hurt me, and I've known 'im my whole life. That's sayin' somethin', ain't it?"

"Come on out," Elohim called. "I won't bite."

I smelled a whiff of urine as the boy took a small step, still holding tight to the trunk of the tree.

"Can't see ya." Elohim wiped his mouth with his napkin.

After a deep breath, the boy stepped out from the trunk completely, though he had stuck his arms inside his overalls and seemed to lose his neck as his chin stayed pressed to his chest. It was as if he were trying to retreat into the overalls, which were wet between the legs.

Elohim gasped the Lord's name as the napkin fell, landing flat from the wadded ball it'd been in his hand. It was then I saw the still-fresh reddish brown stains on its white fabric.

I looked up and into Elohim's gaping mouth, his particularly sharp canine teeth showing like icicles below a roofline. "You okay, Mr. Elohim?"

"I don't know yet," he whispered. On his way to the porch steps, he walked on the napkin, picking up some of the red-brown stains on his bare foot. "Who did you say this was?"

I cleared my throat and introduced the boy by naming him the devil.

"Fielding, I didn't quite hear ya correctly."

"I said devil, all right." I shifted the bag of groceries to my other arm as Elohim drew down the porch steps, slow and at a slant like he was walking in a large gown he had to be careful not to step on the edge of lest he fall.

I turned and watched a stray dog sniff its way into Elohim's open garage, where it peed on the tire of his white convertible, an Eldorado from 1956. When I turned back, Elohim was in reach and the boy was so close to my side, our arms were touching. He pointed toward a rusty can, which was out of place by Elohim's clean porch, asking me in a whisper what it was.

"Mr. Elohim's can of pop, mashed potato chips, and some sort of poison. What type of poison you say you use again, Mr. Elohim?"

"Poison." He grunted, his eyes hard for the boy.

"Poison for what?" the boy asked.

Another grunt from Elohim. "Coons."

A squirrel leaped over to the can. I quickly hissed to scatter it away.

"Wrong animals gonna eat the poison, Mr. Elohim."

He ignored me and instead jutted his sagging chin toward the boy. "Well?"

"Well, what?" The boy had taken his arms out from his overalls as he stood a little taller.

"You've nothin' to say?"

"What would he have to say?" I shrugged. "Before I forget, Mr. Elohim, I won't be able to help ya build that chimney this Thursday. My brother's got a baseball game."

Elohim chewed the air in his mouth, the gray in his eyes filling out to the corners like smoke.

"You all right, Mr. Elohim?" I watched the sweat get low on his lumped face.

"Mind your own damn business, Fielding." Realizing his sudden anger, he apologized as he rubbed his eyes. "It's just too hot. Shouldn't be this way yet." In a milder tone, he asked, "You get a chance to read those pamphlets I gave ya, Fielding?"

Elohim's pamphlets were notebook papers full of his vegetarian thoughts. Things like, animals live a horizontal life while we live a vertical one. According to him, this means when we eat something horizontal, we risk falling down:

It's like putting a river in a skyscraper. The river is horizontal while the skyscraper is vertical. They are two forces working toward opposite goals. Nothing good will be accomplished. Eventually the skyscraper will shift ever so slightly and start to lean and all because it feels the river pushing at its sides. If the river is not drained, it will keep pushing and pushing against the sides of the skyscraper until one day the skyscraper leans so far, it falls and becomes what it was never meant to be. You can never succeed in what you were never meant to be.

These were the curious ideas of a man that spoke more to the fears of the man himself than to any dietary philosophy.

"Well, did you read 'em or not?" He was asking me, but his eyes were on the boy.

"I did read 'em, yes, Mr. Elohim. Thank you." I looked down because I could still taste that morning's bacon. It was then I saw the smear of reddish brown on his wrist.

"What is that red stuff?" I pointed to his wrist. "It was on your napkin too."

"Hmm? Oh, it's barbecue sauce." He quickly licked it away.

"What vegetable you put that on?" I looked over his head to the table, a fly circling the gray bowl of macaroni salad.

He didn't answer. He was slowly lifting his heels off the ground, standing as tall as his toes would allow. All the while, his stare with the boy was something solid, as if their eyes were impaled on the same thorn.

The boy stood taller himself and seemed a little braver. Even his urine spot was no longer a failing, as it was nearly dry, especially in that heat.

Elohim had been an authority on the porch. From there, he could look down on us. But in the yard, standing in front of us, all three feet seven inches of him, we had the advantage of height and were looking down on him. It was as if this was confidence for the boy who knew short men shrink in the shadow of the still-growing adolescent.

"Do you have any ice cream?"

The boy's question caused the muscles in Elohim's neck to go to rope.

"To be honest, it's because of the ice cream that I'm even here." As if he could not smile, the boy licked his lips.

"I don't have no ice cream." Elohim's hands balled up into fists that shook at his sides, his voice shaking with them. "I have none. Did ya hear me, Fielding?" He turned to me. "I have no ice cream. Anyone want to check my house, they most certainly can." He looked worried someone was going to take him up on the offer.

"You look like the type of man to have a freezer full." The boy seemed an inch taller than he had stood before.

"You are mistaken."

"I must be."

"You better watch out, boy." Elohim reached up to stab his finger into the bruises on the boy's collarbone. "Watch what you speak. You keep sayin' you're the devil, and one of these days, someone's gonna believe you. Then whatcha gonna do? You're either gonna be the leader of their belief or the victim of it. Both are dangerous things."

Elohim *goddamn*ed his way back toward his porch.

"Where you goin', Mr. Elohim?" I called after him.

"Gotta check on someone."

"Someone, Mr. Elohim?"

"Something, Fielding, I said I've got to check on something. Now, you get on outta here. And take your snake with you."

"I'm sorry about your fiancée." The boy's words were soft as he looked up at the birds flying overhead.

"How'd you know about his fiancée?"

Elohim took not a step toward the boy but a step back. If I had doubted any fear he might have had in seeing the boy, there was no doubting it in his backing stride. "It all comes out now, does it?"

The boy dropped his eyes to Elohim. "It's a miraculous thing, how a ship floats. Always a tragedy when it sinks. So many died. Your love among them. For that, sorry just doesn't seem enough to say, so I won't say it but I'll mean it just the same. I want you to know, water is not so bad to die in. I assure you. At first it burns in your chest—"

"Burns?" Another trembling step back from Elohim.

"Yes, you feel fire in water."

"Fire?" Each step Elohim took made him sound so far away.

"Yes. Fire. Then it goes out. The water puts it out. You don't feel the rest. It's just a slip into a sunset death. It's what I've taken to calling drowning. I've spoken to many drowned souls, and they all say they've seen bursts of colors surrounding a very bright yet falling light. Doesn't that sound like a sunset to you?"

"Is what you're tellin' me supposed to comfort me?" Elohim backed up the porch steps. "You tellin' me that my heart burned—"

"Just for a moment," the boy carefully interrupted. "She burned for just a moment."

"And it was a moment too long. You need to burn to feel just how long it was for someone like her. How would that be? To burn?"

If a look could start a fire, it would have been the one Elohim gave before stomping into his house. The way he slammed the door sounded a lot like the start of a war.

"You shouldn't have told 'im all that." I sighed and started walking away. "It was like you were throwin' her bones in his face. You gotta learn how to talk to folks better or they're really gonna start believin' you are the devil. How'd you know all that stuff anyways?"

"Even in hell we get the newspaper. And those obituaries—well, I don't know who writes them, but they are awfully descriptive, almost terribly so. Sometimes all you want to hear is a name, not the direction their blood took after leaving the vein."

Was he serious? In other boys, I would've been able to tell. There would be a spark of mischief in the eye, a started smile, a half cock to the head. He was none of these things. He was tired eyes and a yawn, after which he watched the birds fly above.

As we continued down the lane, we passed the Delmar house, where the daughter stood in the front yard, leaning against a large oak. She had a pen and *Alice in Wonderland* in her hands. She raised her eyes to the boy as we passed.

"She's got a fake leg," I whispered to him. "The left one."

The mannequin-stiff leg was paler than her own skin. Attached to it was a black flat. Not real, just part of the plastic. I always wondered if she hated not being able to change her shoe. Always being the girl in the black flat.

Because she wore long dresses to hide the leg, she was immediately taken out of the catalog culture. No miniskirts for her. Her body was not clung to by neon lights. She was never without a buttoned sweater, while her loose and wispy dresses dated her in old-fashioned florals and muted colors. Seeing her in those dresses made me think of lace and lavender and radio theater.

She wasn't thought to be the prettiest of girls. Her hazel eyes were a little too aslant. Her wrists were a little too bony. Her freckles were a little too much. She had a sedateness about her that most girls her age didn't have. You'd never find her reciting the lyrics to Van Halen or hanging a poster of the latest crush on her wall. You looked at her and knew when she went to bed, she'd rather be blowing out a candle than flicking a light switch. Modernity was lost on her and died in cobwebs in the background to her old-fashioned grace.

"What's her name?" The boy looked as if he could've taken her hand right then and there.

"Dresden Delmar."

His wave came slow. His hand starting first on his stomach, then sliding up to his chest, his neck, until his fingers rolled out from under his chin and his hand was finally held up to her. Because there was no actual waving motion, it looked as if he were showing her something on his palm.

She quickly ducked behind the book, doing her best to tuck her red, frizzy hair behind her ear.

"Is she shy?"

I shrugged my shoulders. "I've seen her 'round school. I think I might've had English class with her. I know she doesn't talk much. Sits in the back, things like that."

She quickly disappeared around the tree until he could no longer see her. Then he said how her hair reminded him of the color of leaves in the autumn.

"Red and burnt by an October oven."

And then he smiled for the first time, and she peeked around to see it.

4

MY KNEES KNOW I'm a praying man. The broken dishes, the empty beer bottles, the hole in the wall the size of my fist, all know I am an unanswered man. Why is no one answering me?

It's been seventy years since I've stepped foot onto Ohio soil. The closest I've ever been back was fifteen years ago, when one night I stood on the West Virginia side of the West Virginia and Ohio border. I cupped my hands around my mouth to distance my voice over the Ohio River that formed the border as I yelled for everyone I used to know. Hell, I even yelled my own name.

I frightened some birds, heard the river flowing down below, but the biggest reply of all was silence. No one yelled back to me. No one said, *Hey, we're here in Breathed. Come back now. It's all okay. You can come back. It is just fine.* I waited for all the familiar voices to say just this, but I am the unanswered man. I am the inside of silence.

What is it they say about home? You can't go back again, right? So find a new one, Fielding. I've tried. I've lived all over. In apartments, in houses, in an abandoned gas station for a short time because I liked the way the sun hit its pumps, but I've never had a home again. They've all just been places. The place I'm at now? It's a trailer park called King Cactus.

There are no kings, there are no queens, there is just the unraveled, trying to live. When I first saw the place, I winced and remembered the blood of the beetles. They would swarm Ohio, especially in the autumn, when they would cluster on our window screens, squeezing into our homes, where they would collect in the warm lampshades or crowd around the ceiling fixtures like a pilgrimage. When frightened or smashed, the beetles secreted a pungent odor with their blood. It is that bitter, yellow blood that the trailer park reminds me of and why I knew I would spend the remainder of my life here.

I could afford better, but what's the damn point? There's no spouse to be disappointed by this failing trailer. There are no kids or grandkids to care about the overturned milk crate I use as a step to my front door. There are no friends who will be stopping by and thus leave me embarrassed by my lawn chair furnishings or the piles of this life shaping hills as tall as the direction allows. It's a waste of time to live better when you've got no one to care for and no one to care for you.

I've been here in Southern Arizona five years now. For all the trees we had in Breathed, here there are saguaros. For all the grass, there is sand. For all the hills, there are rocky peaks, and for all the hollers, there are canyons. There is no river or pond or deer drinking hole to be found. There is an aboveground pool. The last person who swam in it came down with some sort of parasite. I thought at first they said he came down with paradise, so I took a swim myself, diving down beneath the empty beer cans floating on the surface but finding nothing but a dead snake in the bottom.

Did you know that the hottest desert in all of the United States is right here in Arizona? The Sonoran Desert. I call it The Son That Ran. I suppose it's that running son that has made me settle here. It's a different heat from Ohio, though. Dry. Less humid. But as long as it makes me sweat, I don't much give a good goddamn how the flames ripen.

There has never been great wealth in trailer parks, but King Cactus, with its royal moniker, seems particularly spent. It certainly is a far cry from the house I grew up in.

Kettle Lane ended with my house, a big square thing of brick in a tepid brown. At each side, a Victorian learned conservatory full of wicker and vines. It was a house that sat proud, seemingly thrilled by its own existence and the ivy creeping up its sides.

Dad was kneeling in the freshly cut yard with our dog Granny. They were both looking at the small snake Dad held in his hands.

I hollered to Dad, but he didn't hear me. I was about to call him again, but the boy grabbed my arm and urged me to wait.

"Let's see what he does with the snake."

"Why?" I shrugged out of his hot grip.

"You can tell a lot about a man by what he does with a snake."

Dad allowed the small snake to slip turns through his fingers until Granny barked. The snake hissed toward the sound as Dad stood. He walked to the back of the house, keeping the snake rather close to his chest before releasing it into the dense woods bordering our back-yard.

"Well?" I turned to the boy. "It wasn't nothin' but a harmless snake anyways. Looked to be a garter."

"A snake that could harm you, you don't have much choice to kill. You wouldn't be able to leave a cobra in your sock drawer. But a snake that is no threat will greatly define the man who decides to kill it any-ways."

"Weren't you a snake once? If you are the devil, that is."

"I've been called a snake, yes. But haven't you ever been called something without having actually been it?"

I shrugged my shoulders and hollered to Dad until he turned from the woods.

Suddenly the boy started laughing. I looked down to see Granny licking his toes and told him her name.

"Why do you call her Granny?" He went to his knees and started scratching the sides of her neck.

"Any other name but Granny would be too young for her. She was born old and gray. Besides, don't she look like somebody's granny?"

She stood no taller than our shins. A shaggy mutt with a rickety bark that sounded like a horse and buggy. She had the habit of squinting her eyes like everything was too far away even when it was right in front of her. She always seemed to be searching for her glasses, but like any granny, she couldn't quite remember where she'd put them last. She'd look up at you, seeming to ask, *Do you remember where I put them?*

Her fur, more like hair, was longest at the back of her head, where it rolled and swirled and looked like she had it tied in a bun. It was hard not to see her in a schoolmarm dress, a brooch glistening at her collar, a crocheted shawl over her shoulders.

She barked and nuzzled up into his neck until he fell back with her tongue lapping his cheeks, her tail wagging over him and his laughter. At that moment, he was just a boy. That laugh was so innocent, you felt like the worst it had ever done was to love a falling leaf.

I look back and think of all the ways he wasn't the devil in that moment. The devil would break a dog's neck, not cradle it in his own. The devil would have a mouth comparable to a crate of knives, not a mouth with teeth that held the curves of marshmallows. I think of all the devils I've seen in my long life. I know now how brief the innocent, how permanent the wicked.

I looked toward Dad, still walking from the woods, on the way occasionally stopping to look up at the sky as if it were asking something of him and he was listening.

My dad was a tall man and I always thought remarkable, like somewhere a stained glass window was missing its center. He was like that, centered, responsible to a fault.

He was only forty-nine that summer, but his forehead seemed older, like it was recycled from some centenarian who had lived a hundred devastating years. The wrinkles were long, seemingly circling all the way around as an unofficial equator. The only thing longer were his fingers, which were tall and grasslike when his hands were up. Perhaps that's why his palms were always a bit moist. They were the wetlands and his fingers the bulrushes that grew at the edges of them.

Him being an attorney meant tailored suits, always three-piece for him so he could tuck his tie into a vest.

"That way," he'd say, "it'll never catch on a branch and play noose."

Even when he wasn't working, he was formal. He wasn't the kind for jeans with, say, a ball cap and tennis shoes. It was always ironed trousers, gleaming cuff links, and polished oxfords.

I always thought he had too demanding a job for someone like him. We are all sensitive to a degree when it comes to the great terrible things in the world, but he was torn apart by them.

Some cases affected him more than others, like the one with the little girl who was beaten to death by her addict parents. He'd stare at those bloody crime photos over and over again, long after he put the parents away. Then one day he said he was going out.

He drove a few miles outside of Breathed to a roadside bar and said the types of things you should never say to a biker gang. He was bedridden for six weeks. When I asked him why he did it, he used his one good hand to write *I wanted to see for myself* on a pad of paper because his mouth was wired shut.

His jaw would heal, as would his swollen eyes, cracked ribs, and broken kneecap. The bruises would go on their way, the blood would stop lifting to the surface, and his arm would eventually come out of that cast. But he'd still have the scar at his hairline where the beer bottle had been broken. He never tried to hide this scar. He'd brush his thick brown hair back so there'd be no chance of not seeing it. He did just this as he strolled between me and the boy.

"I feel like someone forgot to tell me just how hot it was to be today." He removed his suit jacket and draped it over his arm. He kept his back to us as he looked toward the house. "And who, may I ask, are you?"

The boy didn't answer, so Dad turned to see why, his blue eyes squinted.

"He's the devil, Dad."

"Now, Fielding, it isn't polite to call someone the devil without just cause."

"I'm callin' him the devil 'cause he is the devil. Or so he says. Go on, tell 'im." I gave the boy a gentle push toward Dad.

The boy stood there a moment, digging his dirty toe into the ground before confirming in a washed-out voice, "It is true. I am the devil."

The grasses at Dad's palms fluttered as he tried to recall ever seeing the boy before. "Where are you from, son?"

"Originally, I am from the above. But now, well, now I'm from the below. Fallen there."

"Fallen? *Salinero v. Pon,* is it?"

"What's that?" the boy asked, not used to Dad and his court case references.

"Oh, *Salinero v. Pon?* Well, it was a case where a man fell from a window, and all because weight was removed. Will you argue like him, I wonder?" he asked the boy in all seriousness. "That the reason you fell is because someone removed your weight?"

"I wish my defense could be so easy," the boy answered in the same seriousness.

"Mmm-hmm." Dad thrust his hands on his hips. "I'm going to tell you right now, son, I am prepared to believe you, no matter how outrageous it may seem. I am the one who wrote an invitation to the devil in the first place. It would be lousy of me not to believe my invitation has indeed been answered. I did think I had prepared myself for every devil imaginable. Not one of my imaginings looked like you, though."

We all three turned to the back porch, where Mom was hollering for Dad.

"What's goin' on, Autopsy? Who's that boy?" She hovered her foot over the porch steps but would never take them.

"You boys stay here." Dad shook his head and muttered about the heat as he left.

Meanwhile, the boy hadn't stopped staring at Mom. "What's her name?"

"Stella. If you wanna see her, you'll have to go to her. Porch is the farthest she'll come."

"Why?"

"She's afraid of the rain."

"It's not raining."

"Naw, but it might start."

He looked up at the blue sky, knowing it would not rain.

"What's the date?" He dropped his eyes back to the porch, where Mom and Dad stood talking.

"June twenty-third. Why?"

"The days . . . they've been blurring together."

"Just hang a calendar on your wall."

"The walls of hell are not like other walls. I tore a picture of the ocean out from a magazine and hung it on my wall once. An ocean is a good life place. Everyone always seems happy there. And for a moment, I was happy with my picture, but then the blue sky turned gray. The waves, once calm, took a turn to rage. Then came the screams. As I looked closer, I saw the screams came from men drowning in the water.

"All I wanted was a picture of a good life. What I got was a reminder that there is no good life for me. That was the last time I hung anything on my walls. Imagine what would happen if I hung a calendar."

I shook my head in awe of him. "Say, what are we supposed to call ya? I mean, we can't just call you the devil all the time. Ain'tcha got a nickname or nothin'?"

He rubbed his palms until I thought he was going to start a fire. "I suppose you can call me Sal."

"Where'd that come from?"

"From the beginning of Satan and the first step into Lucifer. Sa–L."

"All right. Sal. I like it."

Dad called us to the porch, where I informed him and Mom of Sal's name.

"Welcome, Sal." Dad placed his hand on Sal's shoulder before saying he was going into town to speak to Sheriff Sands and would be back shortly. By his orders, we were to stay with Mom, who held out her arms toward Sal, waiting for him to come up the porch steps, where she could yank him into her.

"Welcome, welcome." She had a drawl like raw vegetables. Hard. Rooted. Not yet ripe.

"You know who you're huggin' right now, Mom?" I sat the groceries down on the porch floor and leaned back into the rail as she smothered Sal in her bosom.

My mother was always in dresses then. I don't think I ever saw anything else in her closet in those days. Her nylon hosiery was as pants as she got. I think because she was always in the house, she was doing her best to be that quintessential housewife. The one in the styled dress that fell full-skirted under her always-worn apron. That day it was the plum gingham apron that she'd made herself with her own chicken-scratch embroidery.

"Oh, he ain't the devil. He's too short." She kissed his cheeks, leaving her wine-colored lipstick smeared there.

She had that tendency to be overaffectionate. It was almost like a nervous tic. It was the staying in the house that did it. She thought if she loved you enough, you'd never want to leave her, and then the house wouldn't seem so lonely as it could be to her at times, when it was just her and the vacuum.

"Mom, what does bein' short have to do with it?"

"There are some awful tall men who go to hell." She released Sal to adjust her shoulder pads. "Just look at Cousin Lloyd. With all them tall men, the leader of hell is gonna have to be tall or else all these tall men are gonna be lookin' down. No one much respects things they look down on."

Just then my brother Grand pressed his face into the screen of the back door, his skin popping small through the net of wire.

"That's my older brother Grand," I told Sal. "No doubt you recognize him?"

Sal shook his head.

"Hey, Grand, come out here and meet the devil so he can recognize you."

"The devil, eh?" Grand opened the screen door and stepped out onto the porch. "Hi, Дьявол."

"He's always in the papers." I smiled with everything I had at my brother. "They say he's gonna go pro."

"Pro at what?" Sal asked.

"Baseball. He's the best anybody has ever seen."

"Easy, little man." Grand put on his team ball cap, lowering its lavender bill. "You'll raise the hopes so high, I'll never reach."

Grand had a vernal face of clean, almost transparent skin, like freshly washed windows. His appearance was his own, but he got there by first taking after Dad. Hair dark brown like a wet branch. Eyes blue like the hill fog. His thick brown brow proved a thoughtful underlining to his forehead, upon which stretched a lone wrinkle, deep for his age.

Something about his eyes made me think of Russia. Perhaps because they were so large, the largest country in the world of his face. Then again, knowing what I know now, maybe it was because his eyes were so like *matryoshka* dolls, hiding the real him within boxes of lacquered mystery. You'd open one box and find another just the same. No matter how many boxes you took away, there was always one more.

Because I told him his eyes were Russian, he decided to learn the language and would at the most unexpected times drop Russian words in a saline accent Tolstoy would have praised, for an Ohioan at least. It was because of this habit we kept a Russian-to-English dictionary on the coffee table within easy reach.

I often found myself opening that dictionary and trying to learn all that foreign. Mom and Dad didn't bother with learning it. It was enough for them to be able to look the meaning up quickly, if at all. But for me and Grand, the foreign was something we had an innate desire to learn.

"Kind of young to be the devil, ain'tcha?" Grand smiled at Sal.

Grand was traditionally handsome. His hair was not worn long and loose like mine or his friends'. His was short and tight like that of a father in the 1950s.

I think about the way the world wanted him to be. As classic as a front porch post. Clean direction, straight up and down. But really he was as wild and as twisting as the honeysuckle vines. Bending and exploding in uneven wonders. Moveable and crooked, crossing in awesome curves and beautiful bends.

As far as small town fame goes, my brother was a star. The boy who always did what was expected of him in every aspect of his life. He looked like a heartbreaker, so he broke hearts. He looked like a brain, so he never missed making the honor roll, and he looked like an athlete, so he became the one Breathed pinned its Major League hopes to.

As fate would have it, Grand was born with an arm for pitching with a precise windup and an acceleration and follow-through that everyone said would get him to the Majors.

His forkballs and curves were guaranteed strikes that palsied the batter into a trembling swing. In the games of light rainfall, he would throw a God-given spitter the ump wouldn't be able to shout illegal on. His cutters might've been a swarm of midges, for the bats hit the air more than those pitches, while his four-seam fastballs were always food for the catcher's mitt.

Grand was the very meaning of his name. I wanted to be just like him. There wasn't a sport I was really great at, but I could climb. That was why Elohim asked me to join him on his jobs. He'd seen me climbing the tree in front of his house. As I was climbing, one of the branches broke beneath my foot. I was quick and fell only for the second it took to find another branch. I didn't panic. I merely accepted the fact. That particular branch was gone, and I had to find me another. It was because of this that Elohim said I had the feet of a steeplejack.

"Where you goin'?" Mom gently grabbed Grand's arm.

"I got baseball practice." He leaned in for a kiss. "See ya later."

"In time for dinner?"

"не пропустите это для мира." He took his smile close to her ear, where he whispered the translation, "Wouldn't miss it for the world."

I looked at his shoelaces and their reddish brown staining. He saw me and tipped his ball cap before jumping to the ground from the top porch step. And I smiled, as in love with my older brother as any young boy could be.

"It's volcano weather 'round here." Mom slung her head back, trying to toss her long black hair. As usual, the ends were tied up in her apron strings, looking like a tail at her backside. A tail Dad would've come up behind and tugged, if he'd been there.

While Grand took after Dad's brown hair and blue eyes, I took after Mom. Our hair, in its rib-cage shape, fell in a blackness that wisdom calls night. Its winding way was a narrative of the hills, it was the snakes swimming the river, the crow strapped with worms. Dad called it *scared hair,* the way it curled up into itself at the ends.

This scare would fall to my shoulders then, as it would for the rest of my life, as it does now. Though in youth it was described as swept by the wind, now, in its white and dark gray staying, it is merely disheveled, falling across my shoulders like claws settled in. As is my beard, like a talon on my chest, but I like to think it is my best Walt Whitman.

I tried to count my moles once. The same flat ones she had and which she called chocolate chips. When I was a real small kid, I actually believed the moles were chocolate chips and that if she stood too close to the oven, they'd melt away, so I'd tug on her apron strings and she'd laugh as I led her from the heat.

There was something smeared about our eyes, mine and Mom's, like contact made with ink before it has had the chance to dry. In my youth, such eyes used to look exotic. Now they're just something tired.

"So." Mom lightly clapped her hands once and turned to Sal and me. "Where would you boys like to go first? We can go to Chile, Egypt, Greece, New Zealand. And all in one afternoon."

She led us into the house, which she had arranged and decorated as invertebrate versions of the nations of the world. Mom herself had never been anyplace but Breathed, so she based her countries on what books told her and what photographs showed her they were like. Because of this they lacked the culture of the traveler and instead held true to that glittered optimism of the one who has yet to travel beyond the picture on the postcard.

She showed Sal room after room, quietly and with only her nylons swishing. The rooms verged on the gaudy, with trinkets, paintings, bright wallpaper done up in the countries' colors and floras. Fabric was imported. Wood was country specific. The most expensive items were special ordered over the phone, the cheaper charms straight from catalog. She did hire carpenters, painters, artists, any and all who would carve for her the Taj Mahal in our dining room table, Saint Basil's Cathedral in the fireplace mantel, the Great Wall in the crown molding.

Making a world proved to be expensive, and had there been only Dad's income, we would have lost more than the respect of the rooms. But Mom was the daughter of the tennis shoe king of Breathed, and after he died she became the sole heir of Breathed Shoe Company, with the factory located just outside town.

"Folks say I shut myself up, never seein' the world, but I ask ya how can anyone see as much of the world as I see on a daily basis?" She spun in the middle of Spain.

"But they're not the real places." Sal's statement brought her to a sudden stop. "That Machu Picchu in the other room is smaller than a shrub. Don't you want to see the real places? The real world? Feel the sun on your face as you marvel at the pyramids? Feel the rain while on top of the Eiffel Tower?"

I nudged him with my elbow. "I told ya she's afraid of the rain."

Mom dropped to the floor, crossing her lanky legs beneath the billowy skirt of her dress. She propped her elbows up on her knees and held her face with a sigh while the shadows of the room lengthened out toward her, making her one of them.

"What's the matter with her?" Sal looked on.

"I'm fine." Her whisper crippled her words. "You boys go on, have your fun. Don't worry 'bout me. I've a whole world 'round me. Why shouldn't I be fine?"

"C'mon." I tugged his arm. "I'm starvin'. Let's make some sandwiches."

"I don't want sandwiches." He groaned like a true kid as I pulled him into the kitchen. "I want ice cream."

"Oh, that's right." I let his thin arm go. On my way to the freezer he asked about Mom's fear of the rain.

"Oh, um . . ." I tossed around the frozen vegetables, looking for any ice cream. "Don't know, really."

"You've never asked her?"

"Oh, man, I forgot the groceries on the porch."

"I said, you've never asked her?"

"Well, yeah, I . . ." I saw the box of frozen fish sticks. "I think it has somethin' to do with a fish or swimmin' or somethin'. I don't remember."

"You don't remember why your mother is afraid?"

"We've got Popsicles." I pulled the open box out of the freezer and peered inside. "Grape is all that's left."

I offered one toward him. He shook his head and asked again about her fear.

"I told ya, it has somethin' to do with a fish." I flung the box back into the freezer.

"But you don't know for sure?"

"No, I don't. Lay off it."

"If I had a mother, I would know for sure why she was afraid."

"Don'tcha have one?"

He shook his head low.

"I don't know if that's true, Amos." Dad stood in the doorway of the kitchen with the sheriff beside him.

"Why'd you call him Amos, Dad?"

"I'm not Amos, sir." Sal looked from the balding sheriff to Dad and then back again.

"You sure fit the description. Best start to come clean now, sonny." The sheriff crossed his arms over his bulging stomach, his leaner days having been lost.

"Really, I'm not."

"You said he matched the description. What was it?" I had asked Dad, but the sheriff was the one to answer, "A boy of thirteen. Black. Wearin' overalls. No shoes. A runaway been missin' for two months."

"Is that all the description?" I looked at Sal.

"It's enough, ain't it?" The sheriff was the type of man who spit aggressively when outdoors. It was a great strain for him to keep from spitting when indoors, and I saw this very strain as he cleared his throat.

"Well, what about his eyes? Do they say if this Amos has green eyes?"

The sheriff looked annoyed with my questioning. "Listen, Fieldin', they don't say nothin' 'bout eye color, but I've no doubt that there boy is this missin' Amos." His big lips pushed out in a sigh as he looked at Sal. "Your folks will be here tomorrow mornin', rise and shine or rise and dull—either way, this little lie of yours will have run its course.

"In the meantime, since we've no holdin' cell for little boys in our jail, me and Mr. Bliss think it's a good idea for you to roost here till your folks arrive. Hear me, sonny?" The sheriff had hung onto the Arkansas accent of his roots.

"You can stay in my room, Sal."

"He can stay in one of the spares." Dad patted his tie, which was safe in his vest. "He probably wants his own room to himself."

Sal looked up at Dad. "If it's all right, I'd like to stay with Fielding."

"I don't know." Dad rubbed some tension out of his shoulder. "It's so terribly hot in here, isn't it? Where's your mother, Fielding? I should talk to her."

"Somewhere in there. I think Madagascar. Or was it Spain?"

"Well, if that's all, Autopsy, I best be goin'." The sheriff adjusted his belt, the sweat marks beneath his pits looking like gigantic ponds. "Got a call on the way here about Grayson."

"Mr. Elohim?" I glanced at Sal. "What about 'im? We just saw 'im."

"Ah, that midget's all kinds of crazy."

Dad cleared his throat. "They like to be called *dwarf,* I think. Or maybe *little person.* Course, that makes them sound less than, doesn't it?"

"First we lost *ni*—" The sheriff quickly stopped himself from finishing the word while glancing from Dad to Sal. "We lost the N-word, and now we're losin' *midget.* Next thing ya know, we won't be able to call people ugly. It'll be *appearance impaired,* or somethin' political like that."

"What'd Mr. Elohim do?" I asked again.

"Well, apparently he went into Juniper's and took all the ice cream outta the freezers and from the back storage. Threw it in a pile in the middle of one of the aisles and used his big propane torch, you know the one he clears brush with, to set fire to it all. Store was unharmed, as the large exhaust fan in the ceilin' sucked up the majority of the smoke. But I hear melted milk is everywhere."

"So all the ice cream?" Sal slumped. "It's all—"

"Been put to death." The sheriff's laugh sounded like a shovel scratching sandstone.

"Will you arrest him then, Sheriff?" Sal was as serious as they come. "Arrest Mr. Elohim for murder?"

The sheriff simply smiled, his crooked teeth small and gray. He shook Dad's hand and hollered a farewell to Mom on his way out of the house.

"What a day." Dad stepped to the freezer, grabbing out a Popsicle. "It sure is smoldering, isn't it?"

Sal sat at the table, removing the bowl and spoon from his overalls and placing them in front of him.

"You still, uh, keeping that thought going?" Dad stood slurping the grape Popsicle, already melting. "That you are the devil?"

"I am the devil."

Dad held the dripping Popsicle over the sink. "Prove it. Prove that you're really him, really the Lord of Flies. Go on. Show me your horns."

"I've never had horns. That's always been something made up to decorate my story and clog my chance not to be a beast."

"Well, what about your wings? You were once an angel, right? Wings can't just be decoration of that story. So where are your wings, Lucifer?"

"The moment I fell, my wings wilted like roses left too long in the vase. The misery of the bare back is to live after flight, to be the low that will never again rise.

"To live on land is to live in a dimming station, but to fly above, everything sparkles, everything is endlessly crystal. Even the dry dirt improves to jewel when you can be the wings over it.

"To be removed from flight is to be removed from the comet

lines, the star-soaked song. How can I go on from that? How can I be something of value when I've lost my most valuable me? Land is my forever now, my thoroughly ended heaven. No sky will have me, no God either.

"I am the warning to all little children before bedtime. Say your prayers, be done with sin, lest you become the devil, the one too sunk, no save will have him."

Dad stared in wonder, as if in the presence of a poet and his pain. "How old are you again?"

"I can show you what is left of my wings." Sal stood and unbuckled his overalls as he turned around to reveal two long scars on the edges of his shoulder blades.

"No matter what form I take, the scars take it with me. I turned into an earthworm once and they turned into it with me." He rebuckled his overalls and sat back down.

Dad laid the dripping Popsicle in the sink before taking a seat at the table. "You can change into anything you want?"

"Not anything with wings. I'll never have them again."

"So what we see before us now, it isn't really you after all?"

Sal sighed so light, it was almost hidden if not for the slight raise in his shoulders. "What you see before you is what lost reflects when it looks into a muddy puddle."

Mom turned an electric fan on in the next room. The battle between heat and home had begun.

I spoke next. Dad was too busy. His eyes were trying to help his thoughts find the seams in the boy before him.

"What about this Amos?" I asked. "Sal?"

He nodded his head. "I know about him. I met him."

"Where?" Dad sat up.

"It smelled like . . . cinder blocks." Sal looked down at the bowl and spoon. "I'd like to wash these, if I may?"

Dad nodded as he tapped his fingers on the table, clearly in a hurry to put the puzzle before him together and solve the mystery. "I'll give you this, son, you are convincing, but I got a feeling when those parents show tomorrow morning that you will be their son. A very imaginative son, but a son nonetheless."

Dad left, saying he was going to check on Mom.

As Sal washed the bowl and spoon, I stared at the wing scars on his back, following his blades of shoulder. No one could be blind to the scars' near perfect sameness.

"I wish I could fly." I said it more to myself than to him.

The spoon clanked against the sink's side and he flinched. "Has your father ever thrown you up on his shoulders? Carried you around?"

"Sure, when I was a cricket."

"Then you've felt what it feels like to fly. It is being carried by something that raises you up while at the same time promises to never drop you."

"Well, if that's the case, then when you flew I guess you knew what it's like to be carried by a father."

He stopped washing the bowl, the running water the only sound. He turned it off, and in its place of rushing, he came slow to say, "And yet why is it I stand here not knowing just that? Knowing only the feeling of falling, the blood dripping like red feathers down my back."

5

The hell within him

—MILTON, *PARADISE LOST* 4:20

OLD MAN, WHY do you buy so many rolls of aluminum foil? For my sins, I answer, to make them beautiful.

I write my sins on a piece of foil and place it on the ground with a rock on its corner so the foil doesn't get carried off. Then I go away from it. Go a distance from it because then, from afar, the sins become beautiful silver things that catch the light of the sun so brightly, heaven is left in want.

I tried. Let it be said I did try. When I was twenty-nine I jumped out of a plane over the sweeping canola fields of North Dakota. Before I got on the plane, I placed my sins amongst the blooming yellow crop. A bullet here, a gun over there, a few baseballs scattered throughout. Really, they were all melted candles. Isn't that what sin is, after all? Life given too much flame? The devil's at the wick, and the wax heads south.

Just before I jumped from the plane, I promised myself if I landed on only the yellow blooms, I would take it as a sign of my ghosts allowing me peace. With that peace, I would no longer suffer in the worst shadow of the snake. I would stop skinning peaches. Cease all mad damage. I'd bring an end to splintering my knuckles against picket fences and running chainsaws through rows of American corn.

I'd sweeten my heart. Be gentled by the small of a lover's back. I'd no longer scrape my spine against cinder blocks nor cannibalize myself in perfect bites. I'd get rid of my stash of horns and keep hell out of the honey. I would learn how to say June, July, August, September without scream and as one word. Forgiveness.

If, however, I were to land on one of my sins, I promised myself I would go on with the punishment and the guilt and let the final fangs in to do all their damage. I would stay the shape that best fits the coffin and accept the terrifying permanence of my crimes.

As I readied to jump from the plane, I looked down at those bright yellow fields. Sal once said there was no yellow in hell. That was why I picked North Dakota during its canola season. Those yellow fields gave me my best chance to land in heaven.

As I jumped from the plane, I tried to see my sins, if not to somehow steer away from them. Maybe that was cheating, but who doesn't choose to fall well when such a choice is to be had? I had no say, really, in where I landed. All I could do was trust the fall.

When it did finally come to an end, it was a bumpy landing, a little facedown, a little rolling. Had I landed on one of my sins?

Nothing beneath me. Nothing trapped up in the dragged parachute. I laid it out flat so I could see. I retraced my tumble. The ground clean, too much yellow to be hell. I tilted my head back to the sky and smiled for the first time since 1984.

"That was a real nice landin'. I say, a real nice one."

I turned to a voice and the man it belonged to standing by the road, his car just parked there, the door still open.

"I saw you comin' down." He pointed to the plane as his shaggy graying hair dripped over his sunburnt forehead. "Pulled over to watch. It was a good fall ya had. Was it scary?"

"Just the landing."

He took a few steps into the field as he looked up at the sky, at the plane circling overhead. "I always thought I might wanna do somethin' like that." He lowered his eyes back to me as I turned to pull in the parachute. "Say, what's that you got on ya?"

"What?" I looked down at myself. "Where?"

"On the back of your pants there. Here, I'll get it." He stepped closer and plucked something from the back of my pant leg. "Now, what in tarnation is this?" He held the smashed candle up in his hand.

"My sin," I answered from the back of the cave that had suddenly swallowed me. "That is my sin."

And so it had been decided I would not be set free from the prison or its bars like eternal candle wicks, burning any chance of escape. All I could do, all I have done, is to sit with the flames, sleep with the heat, smell the burn of flesh filling the urn one ash at a time.

I think about that first night they came to look at Sal, and I think maybe it was beautiful from a distance. The way a flooding river is. Maybe the knuckles, some tapping, some banging at our door weren't so loud from far away. Maybe the faces pressed into our window screens looked like hung pictures. The hollers asking if they could see, maybe they sounded like songs out on the edge. Yes, maybe it was beautiful from far off, but up close it was a crowd. It was a noise. It was drowning under flooding waters.

That first evening, our house swelled. They came to see the devil Flint told them we had. They'd look at Sal, pat him on the head, be a bit disappointed.

"Just a little boy. That's all. Just a boy. Though dark as the night, ain't he?"

"Yeah, but look at them eyes. You don't normally see that color in 'em. Maybe we shouldn't say he ain't the devil just yet. They're just so green."

Staying outside through all of it was Elohim. I waved for him to come in, but he just took a step back. I still remember the way the gold band gleamed from his ring finger. In his mind, he was a husband, and just in case anyone doubted it, he was going to look the part. Hell, he was going to live the part.

When he got letters or sent them, he put in a *Mrs.* beside his *Mr.,* and when he hung clothes on his line to dry, one could not help but notice the dresses and bras. Perfume and lipstick sat on the vanity in his bedroom, and the strands of his fiancée's hair from the last time she brushed it on Kettle Lane were fossilized in bristles. He was surrounded by a woman who wasn't there. He was one half of a relationship that did not exist.

Just as I was about to go out to Elohim, a man bumped into me on his way in the house. With his cowboy hat and spurs, he looked like a man sure of the saddle. He had a Polaroid camera in his hand and a cigarette in his mouth. I told him to put it out before he went into the house. He silently took my picture, though he did nothing to the cigarette as he stepped through the front door, adding to the rest of that crowd consisting of our friends, neighbors, and strangers, like the woman in the bright red dress with showy purple flowers who nearly knocked over the vase in the entry hall with her wide swinging hips and rear like a bag of apples.

There was a man who when he bent low to look at Sal, showed the part in his hair and the dandruff there, like shavings of pearl. He was pushed to the side by a woman in a rhinestone belt. She wanted a good look at Sal, and she didn't want anyone in her way. The man in the cowboy hat took her picture, maybe only to remember the woman who chewed her gum as if her jaw was about to be undone from creation.

There was just something about that woman. The ponytail rising out of the very top of her head like a mushroom cloud. The awful stare of her eyes. A shiny viciousness as if when the wolves saw her, they turned and ran the other way, fear putting their tails between their legs.

I felt like telling the sheriff he should go through her house. I was certain he'd find bottles of tampered Tylenol, potassium cyanide, and a scrapbook of newspaper articles from 1982.

As she looked down on Sal before her, she suddenly stopped chewing the gum. Her thin lips settled like a single bleed across her face. The old acne scars like embedded wreckage.

She cleared her throat, and in one easy go of it, she asked, "Is God a nigger too?"

The gasps of the women were like bright cries. Things that knocked their shoulder pads out of balance and put runs in their hosiery right then and there. My mother included. Some of the men shoved their hands into their pockets and looked down at the toes of their shoes. It was their best natural stance. The braver ones looked directly at Sal. Stepped closer to him even. Waiting as one ear for his response.

He hadn't so much as flinched.

If the woman had expected to sword him, she was mistaken. His elegance so apparent, even in the filthy overalls. Maybe in his own wounded thoughts he could not give such chance to dignity, but before us he stood as tall as he could. His chin raised. His eyes upon hers not in anger but almost in pity, as if he already knew her eternity was to writhe in flames over and over again.

It was at this time Dad finally made his way from the back of the room. Pushing through the crowd to stand between the woman and Sal.

My father's fists were clenched so tight it was almost as if his fingers had melted and all that remained were his palms. A layer of sweat seemed to cover him completely. His face so red, it looked like candy. Like one of those fireballs you get out of the machine with a quarter.

He was yelling at the woman, asking her how dare she use such language in his house. She started chewing her gum again. Unchanged by his voice shaking, by the near-to-something mist in his eyes. In fact, she smiled. A smile that had eaten things before.

Angered even more, he lowered his head and shook it, trying very carefully not to lose himself. "You listen to me, you ignorant hill rat, you take yourself and your hateful mouth and get out of here."

The flames in my father's eyes burned toward the crowd. They had been getting on his nerves ever since their arrival. The way their shoes dirtied the rugs. The way their smoke grayed the rooms. The way they came to look at Sal like a thing on exhibit.

Dad was telling every one of them to get out of our house. I'd never seen my father so angry. Years later, I would find myself dog-earing a page in a book about the ocean. On the page a painting of gray, wild waves. I have since torn that page out of the book and set the painting to frame by the side of my bed. I suppose it is a painting of my father from that night he raged like waves in a storm.

After herding the last of the crowd out the door, Dad slammed it, and sighed into himself, "We haven't even had our dinner yet."

Not used to shouting, he sounded hoarse as he asked what was for dinner. He dropped down in his chair at the table, tired and looking like he'd just come in from a two-day shift in the mines.

"Those people, my God," he muttered as Mom brought in the meat loaf.

"Well, we can't have a man on fire at the dinner table. You'll scorch my tablecloth. We must extinguish the flames." She told him to close his eyes. Then she used his glass of water and her finger to lightly drop the water on his eyelids.

As tiny streams of water slipped down his cheeks, he opened his eyes and she looked deep into them as she smiled and said, "Not a fire for miles."

She kissed him on the forehead before returning to the kitchen to bring out the mashed potatoes, green beans, and rolls, while the rounded skirt of her dress reached and whispered to the tablecloth as she passed. She had changed from the afternoon into a bright yellow dress, and Sal couldn't help but stare at her as she floated about the table like a motored cloud.

"What is it, Sal?" She tightened under his watchful gaze, holding her hand to her flat stomach as if the problem were there. As if it could be anywhere in her tall, narrow frame, wide only in the pads at her shoulders.

"Your dress." He raised his hand as if he was going to reach out and touch it. "It is just so yellow."

She apologized, looking as though she really meant it. "I can go up and change." She held her arm toward the stairs, her bracelet all dangle below her thin wrist.

Sal looked almost worried. "Please leave it on. It's such a pretty yellow. There's no yellow where I come from. There is a lot of black. A lot of brown. But none of those colors like yellow. I mean truly yellow. There are yellow things, of course, blue things, purple things. But they are always black first and therefore never anything more."

"I'm home." Grand came in, dropping his ball bag down to the floor. His hair was wet. I inhaled its peppermint smell as he passed.

"What's the deal with this heat? We could barely practice. Had to take a cold shower at the school. We all did. You should've seen the sweat goin' down the drain." He pulled his chair out, opposite me and Sal at the table, and sat down. "Ah, Mom, why'd ya make meat loaf and potatoes? It's a million degrees outside."

Mom made sure to give him an extra-large pile of potatoes that steamed even more.

"Tell us about where you come from, Sal." Dad grabbed a roll. "You sound like you might be from up north. Cleveland? Close to there, are you?"

"He's from the south, Dad. You know. Hell." I opened my can of Pepsi. "What's hell like, Sal?"

He pulled at his bottom lip. "What do you want to know?"

"Everything. Like, who's there?"

"Cousin Lloyd is definitely there." He reached for a roll. "What he did to those little boys was horrible."

Mom was standing at Sal's side by then, about to serve him a slice of meat loaf, but upon hearing about Lloyd, she gasped, causing the fork in her hand to turn downward and drop the slice onto Sal's leg.

"How'd you know about what Lloyd did?" She pointed the fork at him.

He was silent for a long time, staring down at the meat loaf on his leg, its hot juices oozing into the thin denim of his overalls.

"I asked you a question, young man." She continued to point the fork at him. "How do you know about Lloyd?"

He looked up at her. "I know the sins of everyone who comes to hell. That's part of my misery. To know and feel theirs."

"Autopsy?" Mom turned helplessly to Dad. "How does he know about Cousin Lloyd?"

Dad squinted his eyes. "I suppose he could have looked it up in a newspaper. When Lloyd was charged with the pornography, it was in the paper."

"Oh, yes." Mom sighed as she stabbed the meatloaf on Sal's leg with the fork. "That must be it. You silly boy. You had me scared there for a minute."

"But I didn't look in any newspaper," Sal tried to tell her, but she was already convinced as she plopped the meat down on his plate. He stared at it like it was his cross to bear.

"What about Walt Whitman?" Grand asked as Mom reprimanded him for using the tablecloth as a napkin. He apologized to her and asked Sal again about Whitman. "We're reading him in English. 'Song of Myself.' Is he in hell?"

"Walt Whitman?" Sal was on his second roll. "He's not in hell."

"I'm surprised. I mean, he writes well enough. I celebrate myself and sing myself and all that, but I heard he was into other guys." Grand's voice went off to the side, like crumbs on a counter being wiped away.

"What does that have to with hell?" Sal shrugged.

"I mean, don't all fags go to hell?" Grand asked it so casually, he might have been asking if there was any more pop.

Dad grabbed his forehead. "What is with all this language today? There is to be no more of it in this house. Do you hear?" He pounded his finger down into the table until the nearby gravy boat shook. "No more words that say something about our own ignorance. Grand, are you listening? Look at me. You are not to say that word again. Grand?"

"All right, Dad. Geez."

"And not one of you is to use the N-word that horrid woman said tonight to Sal. I swear I wish people were forced to make a list of names and recite them every time they use that word.

"A list of the names of every black man, woman, and child hated, beaten, killed for the color of their flesh. It should be law—by God, it should be law—that if you say that word, you must then say their names.

"No one wants to say one word and then realize it means so many more." He picked up his glass and took a long drink of water, after which he apologized to Sal for the woman's wrong. "She was a piece of shit."

"Autopsy." Mom was sitting down in her own chair by then, opposite Dad's at the table. She was smiling. She knew, as we all did, that when Dad spoke profanity, which he so rarely did, it came out funny instead of bad.

"Well, it's true." He propped his elbows up on the arms of the chair as he leaned back. "Sometimes this world is like red fences in the snow. There ain't no hiding who we really are."

Sal leaned back in his own chair, propping his elbows up like Dad. While Dad had been talking, Sal had been listening carefully. Later that night he would say to me, "I've never met a better man than your father. Compared to him, it's as if all other men are homeless dogs that bed in the mud."

"Was Walt Whitman the one to write about the road less traveled by?" Mom used her napkin to dab her sweat.

"That was Robert Frost," Grand answered.

"And he was gay?"

"No, Mom, Walt Whitman was the"—Grand glanced at Dad and swallowed the word he was going to say—"the one who wasn't into women. Or so they say. But if he's not in hell, maybe he was straight. Ain't that whatcha said, little devil?" Grand looked across the table at Sal. "That Whitman's not in hell?"

"Homosexuality is not flammable. You can't burn by it alone." Sal was helping himself to another spoon of green beans.

"Well, they do say it is a sin." Mom held her glass of ice water to her cheek. "Like my momma used to say, when you play in the thorns, you ain't gonna get nothin' but scratched."

"Hmm-mmm." Dad scrunched his brow as he buttered his roll. "I think it's more of a psychological disease. Just something a little off in the mind. They could probably fix it with a little determination."

"Then there's this new sickness goin' around." Mom clicked her tongue in sympathy. "I feel bad for 'em, I really do, but some say it's God punishin' 'em for their lifestyle. Maybe He is, punishin' 'em, that is. I mean this sickness is from that moment of 'em comin' together. It makes ya think maybe God is tellin' 'em to stop comin' together. Maybe He's tellin' 'em to stay apart." She patted the sides of her neck. "Lordy, this heat has a fury, don't it?"

Grand leaned to one side, as if the chair he was sitting in was teetering on an edge and he had to shift his weight to keep from falling over. He asked me to pass the salt, though he never actually used it once I gave it to him. He just held it so tight, before setting it down.

"Sal?" Dad lightly drummed his fork against his plate. "I'm interested, if you are the devil, that is, what is hell like?"

Sal quickly swallowed his mouthful of potatoes and briefly wiped his mouth before saying hell is a hallway of doors.

"And behind each door is a suffering of the individual soul. One door I opened was to a man sitting in a desert. There was nothing scary about it. There was blue sky. White fluffy clouds. Rose-colored sands. There were no snakes hissing at him. No scorpions about to sting. The heat nor the sun was a threat. A thornless saguaro shaded him, and he was neither hot nor thirsty, as he had a full canteen by his side, would always have it full and by his side, no matter how much he drank. To someone else, that empty desert might have been paradise, but to that man it was absolute hell.

"Another door opened to a woman in lipstick and a dress that would cost the farm. She was sitting in a room full of flowers and tea and those little frosted cakes. She was holding a beautiful, gold-fringed blanket, cradling it as if it were wrapped around a child. You could hear the child, hear him crying, hear him laughing, hear him sleeping even. But never was he seen. All she could do was to stare into the empty blanket and will continue to do so even after grief becomes a word too small for the feeling.

"Another door opened to a day. The third Wednesday in an October. It was a country festival, the Pumpkin Show, they called it, where thousand-pound pumpkins were being judged and autumn leaves were confetti in the air. No one was crying. No one was sad. No one was noticing the man whose hell this was and who stood in the middle of the largest pumpkin pie ever baked and screamed. He screamed long. He's screaming still, but no one hears him but himself . . . and me.

"People think hell is about flames and demons, but I employ no demons. There are fires, yes, each door burns. I've started none of these fires, not even the one that burns my own door. And just as I cannot put out my own, I cannot put out theirs.

"I have tried. I've carried buckets of water to these doors, but the more water I splash on the flames, the bigger they get and I have to turn away in the throbbing torture of it all. I am not the ruler of hell. I am merely its first and most famous sufferer turned custodian with the key to the gate in my back pocket."

Mom sighed for us all. "You're such a sad little boy."

"That ain't what I thought hell would be like at all."

"What did you think it would be like?" Sal turned to me.

"Don't know. I guess I thought demons. I thought proddin' with cattle rods. I thought just a lot of blood. The way you describe it, it's even more frightenin'."

"You know where the name *hell* came from." He crossed his hands on his lap. "After I fell, I kept repeating to myself, *God will forgive me. God will forgive me.* Centuries of repeating this, I started to shorten it to *He'll forgive me.* Then finally to one word, *He'll. He'll.*

"Somewhere along the way, I lost that apostrophe and now it's only Hell. But hidden in that one word is *God will forgive me.* God will forgive me. That is what is behind my door, you understand. A world of no apostrophes and, therefore, no hope."

6

Our torments also may, in length of time,
Become our elements

—MILTON, *PARADISE LOST* 2:274–275

A COUPLE YEARS ago, a woman sold me a time machine at a yard sale. It looked like an ordinary window. The wood spiked along its sides, a result of it being hastily and carelessly removed from the house it once sat in. The glass was filthy, and tape was placed over the hairline crack in the bottom pane.

"I could tell by lookin' at ya that you got some business needin' to be done in the past," she said, her faded American flag scarf flapping in the breeze. "Lucky for you, that there winda only opens to the world we done had, and I'll let it go for what it costs to buy a six-pack. You ain't gonna find time travel cheaper than that."

"Does it really work?" I asked.

She spoke kindly, if not with some pity, "What we doin' here, mister?"

I scratched my chin through my matted beard. "You're selling me a time machine."

"You don't have a problem with that?" All her wrinkles seemed to be pulled up with her arched eyebrow. "I got a cane over there you might like. Got some shampoo too. When's the last time you washed this hair of yours?"

She redirected her hand to fan her face. "I hate this damn heat. I mean just look at this ground beneath us." We both looked down at the cracked earth. "You know another town 'round here has gone completely dry. Everyone in it had to pick up and move away.

"I remember a postcard of Arizona I saw when I was a little girl. Beautiful blue sky, some flowerin' cactuses. It was the type of place you'd wanna drive your convertible in. A good life place. Turned out, it ain't nothin' but another hell." She glanced from me to the time machine. "What year is it you're headed to?"

"1984."

"Of all the junk I thought I'd be sellin' today, I never thought I'd be sellin' a time machine."

After I'd given her the money, she mumbled with just a bit of grief, "You know it's not a real time machine, right?"

I nodded and started to drag the frame back toward my trailer.

When I got home, I used Grand's old pocketknife to carve *May 1984* into the sill.

If I was going to travel back and see my family, I had some cleaning up to do. I went inside the trailer and slipped out of the pajama pants I'd been wearing for the past few days, along with the T-shirt stained from canned spaghetti. I brushed my teeth, showered, and trimmed my hair and beard. Hell, I even bothered with deodorant. I figured time travel would be sweaty.

While I was putting on my tennis shoes, laced but not tied with Grand's old shoelaces, I heard the shattering from outside. When I got out there, I saw the neighbor boy standing by shards of glass on the ground. He had a baseball in his hand. The one he throws to his dog.

"I didn't mean to break your winda." He hid his eyes under his ball cap. "I'm awful sorry, Mr. Bliss."

The ball had shattered the top pane. It was my foot and tennis shoe that shattered the bottom one. The anger came, and a kick was the least I could do.

Over two years have gone by, and the boy still apologizes every time he sees me. I know it wasn't a time machine. And yet, when I later crawled through the gaping hole of the gone window, there was a brief moment in crossing the sill I almost believed I would come out the other side to a neon light and in that I could save everything.

I had yet to know what having Sal in our lives would mean, so that first night me and him spent together in my room, I was excited to have him, though I was hot as hell as I kicked the blankets off to the floor and fell back, sweating on the sheets.

Sal was lying in the large window bed, lined with cushions and pillows, where I would sleep myself during past summers when it was especially hot because I could press my face against the cold glass of the pane. I told Sal he could do the same, but he seemed at peace with the heat, lying with his blanket up to his chin and choosing a pair of my pajamas that were long sleeved. Mom had tossed his overalls in the washer after dinner, not saying anything about their stale urine smell. She told me to share my clothes with him. It would be a while before I saw him in those overalls again.

"This heat is humongous." I kicked the air. "How we gonna sleep?"

I reached over to my bedside table and turned the fan on high, directing it so it'd blow on my face as I lay there with my arms folded behind my head, staring up at the ceiling, which was painted as the jungle top canopy of the Amazon rainforest.

My bedroom was Brazil, and in it an anaconda coiled around a branch, scarlet macaws were painted in flight on the walls, and leaf frogs were carved on my bedposts. Mom had made her Brazil more Amazon than anything else, though there was a little Rio de Janeiro on my double closet doors that when closed formed two halves of Christ the Redeemer.

"Fielding?" Sal spoke over the hum of the fan.

"Yeah?"

"Do you like Mr. Elohim?"

"You know what a steeplejack is? It's where you fell chimneys and build steeples, do things like that. It's all roof work, is what it is. And he's teachin' me the art. He's a nice guy. Hey, Sal? I've been wonderin'. I mean, if you're the devil, you've met God. What's He look like?"

"What do you think He looks like?"

"Like a cotton swab, thin and white with too much hair on His head and too much hair on His feet. Wouldn't that be funny? A cotton swab? Kind of makes ya think twice 'bout stickin' a Q-tip up your nose, don't it? Though, thinkin' 'bout it now, maybe if we left a swab in our ear, we'd start behavin' a little differently. Havin' God inside our ear just might make us all, I don't know, a little . . . more."

"Also make you a little more deaf with only one ear whose hearing is not sacrificed by a plug of cotton." He leaned up on his elbow as he asked me to tell him about a day. A day I felt loved.

I turned in the heat, thinking, but not thinking long.

"January seventh of this year. It was my thirteenth birthday, but that didn't stop the sore throat or the coughin'. I had a forehead of lava. I had to stay in bed. Suck back that horrible cough syrup."

I did my best hacking cough, feigning to fall out of bed until he laughed.

I stayed sitting on the floor, up against the bed, as I told him how Mom came in with a bowl of chicken noodle soup.

"She didn't give it to me. She sat it right here on the floor. Then she went out and Dad came in with a bowl. He did the same damn thing she did and left without a word. When Grand come in, I asked what the hell was goin' on but he didn't say a thing, just sat his bowl down beside Mom's and Dad's.

"This was how it went, them bringin' in bowl after bowl of chicken noodle until there were thirteen. Dad laid saltines so they floated on top of the soup and so Mom could stand a birthday candle up on each cracker. It was Grand who lit the wicks.

"Mom said it was the birthday cake for boys who are sick. 'So get out of bed and get down here with us to make a wish quick,' Dad said, 'before the candles sink.'

"You know what I wished for, Sal?"

"What?"

"To be sick for every birthday. That day, I felt loved."

He looked down at his chest as he said, "Then you already know."

"Already know what?"

"What God looks like."

He pushed his blanket off to the side and stood to kneel by the window bed, his elbows up on the cushions, his palms together. I climbed back up into bed and switched the fan to low so I could hear him. I laid back and closed my eyes.

In his earthy voice, his prayers sounded like the haymaking I heard one time when passing a field in harvest. The *cling clang* of sharpening the scythe's blade. The sharp scythe swiping and cutting the grass in crunching whooshes. The rake coming softly but scratchy as the cut grass is gathered and rolled into bales. Bales to be kept back and saved in the very seconds that had made them.

7

MY DREAMS THAT first night were of long hallways and burning doors. By the time morning came, I felt burned myself. I lay there in bed. My eyes closed and the fan, a poor help on my face.

"Those people are here."

I looked up at Sal. The window behind him putting his edges in light.

"What people?" I yawned.

"Amos' people." He tugged at his shirt. It would be a while before my bright, clean clothes looked natural on him. He was more field than town. More old soul pasture than adolescent attitude.

He left as I threw on a tank and cut-offs. When I got downstairs, I found him in the kitchen with Mom, Dad, the sheriff, and a man with mechanic hands holding a woman who was still wearing her maid's uniform from last night's shift. She kept shaking her head at Sal, crying that he was not her Amos.

"Yours." Sal was offering the bowl and spoon to the woman.

"They ain't mine, honey." She blew her nose, the gold crosses shaking at her ears.

As Sal set the things back on top of the counter, Dad whispered to

Mom, after which she took me and Sal into the living room, where she turned up the television. We sat on the sofa, listening to the San Francisco lovers on *Phil Donahue* talk about the shock of testing positive.

A few minutes later, Amos' parents were driving away in their rusted Chevette while Dad and the sheriff returned to us in the living room.

"I was certain he was gonna be theirs." The sheriff tucked his thumbs into his belt loops. "Well, hell, I'll continue the investigation. Let ya know what I come up with."

Dad brushed the sweaty strands of his hair back. "He can stay with us in the meantime."

"I won't put you good folks out like that." The sheriff looked about to spit. Only the rug stopped him. "He can stay in the jail."

"That boy in that dank basement?" Mom shot up from the sofa. "With drunks and thieves and rapists and murderers? He'll come outta there all lessoned up in sin."

"Now, Stella, I'd put 'im in his own cell. I ain't stupid, ya know."

"Like hell you ain't. Your bright idea is to put a boy in a basement. I thought you were dumb. I didn't know you were son-of-a-bitch dumb."

"Stella." Dad winced.

"We all know why Dottie left you," Mom continued. "Ran off with that well-to-do fella. If you ask me, she should've done it years earlier, instead of stayin' with a small dick like you. She told us all. Called ya pinky pants behind your back."

She started taunting the sheriff with her pinkies, the sweat shining on her forehead like bad stars. When she began to choke on her laughter, Dad was quick to pat her on the back.

"Calm down, Stella. For Christ's sake, breathe."

"Oh God—" She caught her breath. "I'm so sorry I said those things. I . . . the heat." She swept the damp strands of her hair back, unable to meet the sheriff's eyes. "It's just the heat. I didn't mean it. I'm so sorry."

"My apologies as well, Sheriff." Dad aired his collar. "I think it's safe to say Sal is wanted, and he can stay here until something more permanent can be decided upon. And again, I'm so sorry for what has been spoken here."

You could feel the sheriff's anger take over the room. Almost like a whooshing past your face. A sort of entity that felt like it could have peeled the wallpaper off the walls and broken the crystal.

"I best be goin'." The sheriff straightened as if he were being asked to show how tall he really was. Then he quietly nodded at all of us, very slowly at Mom, before leaving with his hands clenched at his sides, only the pinkies left out like small horns.

"Well, that was very sudden, Stella." Dad checked his tie once more.

"I'm not used to it bein' so hot. None of us are. We're not prepared for a heat like this. I can just imagine the things that'll be had from here on out. We best get cool, and soon. We're all in a volcano of trouble. I feel it."

"Calm down now, Stella." Dad cleared his throat. "I think I'll go . . . I think I'll take a walk to the cemetery. I'd like to talk this whole situation over with Mother." He turned to Sal to clarify. "My mother has passed. But she always had a way of clarifying the distinctly strange. I think speaking with her has the great possibility of enlightening me on this matter we have before us."

"The cemetery is a million miles away." Mom wrung her hands. "You'll be gone forever. I was plannin' on makin' lentil stew. You have to boil lentils, Autopsy. You know how I feel about boilin' things, all them bubbles poppin' up. It's like rain in a pot. And now we won't be havin' lentil stew, 'cause you won't be here to boil it. You have to stay."

Dad tugged on the tail of her hair until she smiled.

"I won't be gone long." His long arms wrapping around her was like being somewhere in a wheat field.

"You'll be gone forever. Once you start talkin' to your mother, I become a widow." She broke the embrace and bit her fingernail hard enough to chip the polish. She frowned at this and more as she said to him, "If you must go, then go, but before you do, bring me my canna for the day."

Breathed envied Mom's cannas, which were tall, tropical flowers done up in colors with familiar names like red, orange, yellow, peach. Yet they weren't familiar at all. They were the colors of the other side of a journey to another world.

The job of caring for the cannas was left to me, Dad, and Grand because even though the cannas were just a few feet from the house, Mom never risked the rain. She gardened from the back porch, using us as her hands. We were her reach in the outside world. She told us when the cannas were dry and needed more water. We'd get the hose and give them a drink while she followed through the motions with us, feigning to pull the hose across the yard and then to stand still with her hand up and moving side to side like she was spraying something more than air.

She examined their growth through binoculars, looking out for insects or other damage. I remember the year the leaf rollers came, a great pest that rolls the leaves of the cannas in order to pupate inside them. Mom instructed me from the back porch to cut off the infected leaves. She held a pair of scissors and cut with me. Then she handed me flour to sprinkle on the remaining leaves as prevention, keeping some flour for herself, which she sprinkled all over the back porch.

Every day she asked for a canna. I suppose to feel the petals, the leaves, the roots, allowing her to feel somewhat responsible for them.

"What variety today, my love?" Dad pulled her back to him without much difficulty.

"Oh, I'd say Alaska." She tilted her face to his and softly wiped the sweat from his cheeks. "Alaska will do for today. Perhaps it'll cool me down."

"In that case—" Dad kissed her wet forehead. "—I shall get enough Alaska for all of us."

The Alaska variety has a yellow middle surrounded by white

petals. Pee in Alaskan snow, that's what I said as I took the flower from Dad.

"Not pee." Sal frowned at me. "It's your mother in her yellow dress and she's twirling in the Alaskan snow. In the white rain."

"I'm off now. You boys be good." Dad carried his own flower tucked under his arm as he walked out the door.

Mom watched him go as if he were a feather falling off her wing. "Well"—she turned to us—"what say you boys run down to Juniper's for me. Get some lentils."

"You don't have any, Mom? I thought that was what you were makin' for dinner?"

"Well, my love—" She licked her palm and tried to lay down my cowlick, the same as hers. "—I can't make 'em if I don't have 'em, now, can I?"

"Mom, stop." I swatted her hand away. "Give me some money so I can go."

"And may we have enough to buy ice cream?"

"Mr. Elohim flamed all the ice cream yesterday," I reminded Sal.

"Hmm, I wonder why he did that." Mom reached into her change purse. "I'll give ya some extra so you can getcha some chocolate bars."

"C'mon." I grabbed Sal's arm once I had the money. "Maybe Mr. Elohim didn't burn all of it. Maybe they had some hidden in a back freezer."

When we came upon the Delmar house, Sal stopped and stared at Dresden, who was once again standing against the oak in her yard, this time with *To Kill a Mockingbird*. Sal waved and softly called her name. She held the pen in her hand tighter and the book higher, though her freckled forehead and her light eyes peered above the page at him.

"Tell me something about her, Fielding."

"Her dad split a few years back, so it's just her and her mom, Alvernine. Alvernine's one of them fancy-pancy ladies and sexy as hell. She's consumed by bein' Miss Perfection. She wouldn't like you." I smacked a sweat bee away. "Though, maybe if ya gave her a rose. She started a club on 'em."

"Is Dresden in the club?"

"Naw. It's just society ladies, like Alvernine. Why you care so much about this girl anyways?"

"Even a devil's heart isn't just for beating." He gave Dresden one last wave. In response, she hid her face completely behind the book, her frizzy hair sticking out around the cover like red static.

Sal glanced back at her before we left, but his attention was soon placed on the birds flying above.

Papa Juniper's was on Main Lane, which was a long lane of stores serving as the main route of business in Breathed. Storefronts of wide windows, brick façades, and that summer, flowers and plants wilting in the heat. The soaring elms lining the lane shaped a canopy not unlike a vaulted ceiling, giving rise to the lane's nickname, the Cathedral. A nickname not just for the ceiling the trees gave the lane but also because the trees were said to be blessed on account of their escape from the Dutch fungus that had obliterated most of the nation's elms.

In 1984, there were no big-box stores or outside commercial influence. The businesses were Breathed born and bred. Main Lane was a place you could buy books, furniture, music, condoms, a brand-new refrigerator, and finish it all off with a haircut at Chairfool's barbershop or a meal at Dandelion Dimes, named so by the founder who, in the late 1800s, would accept a yellow dandelion head as payment equivalent to a dime.

Juniper's, with its whitewashed brick and little blue juniper berries painted on every one, was the only grocery store. Down from it was the butcher's, and down from there a bakery called Mamaw's Flour, which every Fourth of July would bake the largest blueberry pie. It sure looked nice, but wasn't much for taste.

If you needed dressing, there was Fancy's Dress Shop for the ladies. Contrary to their name, they did sell pants, though they never brought them to the house when Mom called up and said she'd like to go shopping. They would come with their hangers and garment bags, laying the dresses out, knowing just the kind she liked. She'd go over them, point to this one and that one, eventually buying them all, I think because she felt they went to an awful lot of trouble, bringing the store to her.

Across the lane from Fancy's was the Burgundy Toad, which is where Dad bought his suits and ties, among other menswear, with little burgundy toads embroidered in the labels. While Fancy's and Toad's catered to the older shopper, the young ones could find the latest fashion at Saint Sammy's. Though the sign out front had last had a face-lift in 1954, you could find the latest acid-washed jeans there.

Sal glanced at the mannequin in the window with her purple bikini printed with little neon hearts as me and him passed Saint's on the way to Juniper's. Once inside the market, we found all the ice cream had indeed been melted. In the aisle where Elohim had torched it, the concrete floor was left cracked by the heat.

What I knew of Elohim's punishment for the act of vandalism was that he was to pay for the ice cream, the cleanup, as well as patch the cracks in the concrete.

Because the exhaust fan in the ceiling above had carried out a good deal of the smoke, very little residue remained on the food around. Being as it was burned in the canned food aisle, the cans merely had to be wiped.

When we saw one of the workers passing through with a mop in his hand, we asked him if he was sure there wasn't any ice cream left undiscovered in the back.

"It all burned. We expect a shipment by the end of next week. You can check back then." He perched his pimpled chin up on the mop handle while he stared at Sal.

"Well, where's the chocolate bars and candy?" I looked at the shelves, which were covered in thick brown smears.

"All of it melted, just started oozin' out all over the place. Ain't got to cleanin' all of it off the shelves there yet. Basically anything that can melt, has melted. I mean, the freezers, you see." He gestured off to some bags of ice and various other perishables stuffed into the freezers. "I managed to save all that, but the rest ain't nothin' but somethin' that once was."

"You still got lentils?"

"Oh, sure. Those are some heatproof bastards there."

With the lentils in hand, me and Sal left Juniper's.

You could hear the whispers around us.

"There's the devil."

"He don't look like no devil to me."

"They never do."

"Didn't Grady meet the devil once?"

"Naw. Not face-to-face. Just presence-to-presence. Shucks, we all got that goin' for us."

In front of the yellow-painted brick of Dandelion Dimes, we ran into Otis Jeremiah with his pregnant wife, Dovey. Otis worked at the tennis shoe factory. He was usually the one to come to the house to update Mom on production.

"Hey, there, Fieldin'." Otis grabbed my shoulders as if he were testing the strength of them. He always finished with a disappointed look that said I should exercise more.

Otis himself was one of those guys you thought they based video game soldiers on, with his prizefight biceps and log-laid abs. Every day you'd see him running around Breathed, doing his miles in a shirt cut off to his chest to go with his short cut-offs, so tight, cling wrap would've been looser. He was the only man I knew who wore shorts shorter than the girls' and more belly shirts than a toddler. Every day he wore this workout gear, even when he wasn't working out, which made him seem underdressed in those places without dumbbells.

He was a sweaty sight to behold, with his permed mullet kept back from his pyramidal face by a red, white, and blue sweatband that matched the bands on his wrists, like some sort of signature of Captain America. His striped socks stretched over his wide calves. His bright tennis shoes whitened daily. Forever loyal, Otis wore only tennis shoes that came from our factory. Our trademark was a large eye made of thread and sewn into the back of each shoe. Eyes in the backs of your heels was an image Grandfather had decided upon when he founded the factory.

"You know, Fieldin', I've come up with a new shoe design I think your momma is really gonna love. Square shoes." Otis moved his fingers in an air square, his pumped-up chest showing like cleavage beneath his neon pink tank.

"Square?"

"Now, hear me out. Ain't square things easier to store than misshapen things like the average shoe? That's why we store 'em in shoe boxes 'cause the boxes are square. But if the shoe itself is square, there'd be no need for the box. We could cut costs right there."

Otis was the town kidder. Nobody ever smiled quite like him. His smiles were something that captured you, that took possession of you, that dared you to feel the joy. Above all else, his smiles were his big white teeth, almost even squares, they were. That was why Mom used to call his smiles *the sheets on the clothesline*.

"If you made square shoes, there'd certainly be a lot of people tripping."

"What?" Otis chuckled at Sal, surprised at the loss of the joke. "Say that again."

"Tripping. Square things on your feet means four corners will have the chance to be successful in eight different ways of making you fall."

"Well, I . . ." Otis trailed into his thoughts, which you knew were all square falls.

"How far along?" Sal gestured to Dovey's belly, as rising and as round as one of the hills surrounding us.

"Just over six months." She giggled with a slight pig snort.

Dovey was as consumed by physical fitness as her husband. While being pregnant kept her back from the more strenuous activities she was used to, she was still the local Jazzercise instructor and wasn't without her spandex leotards and leggings, even while pregnant, which made for a whole *snake swallowed the world* bit.

"Say"—Otis pointed his finger at Sal—"you're the boy they all been squawkin' 'bout to be the devil?"

Sal confirmed with a nod.

Otis grinned. "Well, whatcha wanna give me for my soul?"

"Otis." Dovey grabbed the bulge in his forearm.

"It's all right, sugar-sock, this kid ain't nothin' but two legs of human."

Dovey wasn't so sure.

"May I touch your stomach?" Sal held his hand up.

"Uh, gee, I don't know, kid." She leaned back, but Otis grabbed Sal's hand and placed it on her stomach.

"There ya go, kiddo." Otis beamed. I doubt there's ever been a prouder father-to-be.

Sal closed his eyes, his hand tenderly cupping her roundness. "It feels like the seven millionth hand."

Dovey stared at Sal's hand as she asked just what the seven millionth hand was.

Sal began to speak about a staircase between heaven and earth, and as he did, his words were a little deeper, a little bleaker, a little more crafted to the haunt of what it means to speak fine.

"It is called the Staircase of the Fallen, and it is the way down from heaven for those who are too wrong to stay. Like me.

"You may look up, but the staircase is too high above and too far to see from here. Just floating there by itself like it's been stolen from home and somewhere there's a house missing the way upstairs.

"It's a mean thing, falling down steps, it's a thing to matter the most. And as I tumbled down this staircase, I felt every step, all seven million of them. The steps are too there not to be felt, they are too edged not to sober you to the errors of your fray. The pain is smart enough to poet out a space, where bruises are verse and rhymes are moans over and over again.

"It's a terrible thing for an angel to fall, because you cannot survive it by wing. The flight you had before is just a bird magic you'll never have again. How brief the feather to the angel who discovers discontent. After all, isn't that what my fall was? My discontent to just be in place, never to change from the one suit of my life. But I was tired of being the obedient son who cheapened his own self by farming his father's commands. I wanted my own life. I wanted my own good life.

"God is no fool. He has made the fall a touching torture, for with each step, there is a hand that reaches for you in that good, old-fashioned, second-chance sort of way. You reach back and hold tight to it because to do so is deciding to believe that by holding on, you can survive being let go of. But no matter how much you beg, no matter how much of yourself you give to the chance, you are let go of. That is the undeniable torment of the fall. For such a divine event, it's a rather ordinary agony. To have hope raised, only to realize there is no hope to be had. Hope is just a beautiful instance in the myth of the second chance.

"When I came to the last step, the seven millionth step, the hand that reached for me was unlike the others. It was a five-finger shape and yet it was more. As if it had shaped clay before and gone numb from long hours of creation. It was a hand that brought *God* to my lips.

"The other hands had always known they were going to let me go, and in that, they were merely cruel. But that seven millionth hand was a hand in the midst of a choice. Would it let me go or would it pull me up? Would it re-feather me? Would it forgive? Would it call me *son* once more?

"The hand's first existence was that of warmth. Its second was that of dignifying my hope by holding my hand tighter than all the others.

But above all else, the hand existed as that of pure love. I could near all the hearts of this world and never come near being loved like that again. That was how I knew the seven millionth hand was God's.

"As I dangled there in the sky from His hand, I knew He didn't want to let me go. But I also knew that if He did not let go, He would be ruined by holding onto me. So in that choice, I let go of Him. I had to, for His sake. I had to fall as the Devil, so He could stay the God."

Sal opened his eyes, and it was like several rains coming down his cheeks at once. He looked up at Dovey and told her that touching her belly was like holding and being held by the seventh millionth hand.

"Because above all else, it was love. It was love, and that is what I feel inside you now."

Dovey wiped her cheeks and smiled as she gently laid her hand upon Sal's. She was about to say something. I thought perhaps sing a lullaby to him, but the shout kept her from it.

"Devil!"

Elohim was pointing at Sal from across the lane, his arm looking like a trembling sword. "He'll make you ill, mother-to-be. His touch is the layin' on of the end. It is death."

With tears still in her eyes from Sal's story, Dovey yanked his hand from her stomach. "Don't—don't touch me."

I had never seen a woman look so frightened as she wrapped her arms around her belly. It was as if that whole moment between her and Sal had never happened. I suppose when the life of your child is threatened, you don't hesitate. When someone shouts *devil*, you shield against the horns.

As Elohim continued shouting, Dovey quickly turned to take a step, but the toe of her tennis shoe caught the uneven brick in the walk.

All those years of exercising and that experience of jumping up in the air and landing so agile and safe had abandoned her. Falling will do that. It'll dumb your landing, your ability to catch yourself. Her hands flew up in the air as her back arched and her belly led the way down. It hit first, her belly, in a dull sound as it pushed in on contact with the hard brick. Her face down after, smacking against the brick in a sickening thud.

A woman shrieked about the baby. I didn't know who, because I was like everyone else, looking at Dovey and the blood on her face. I'm not even sure where it was all coming from. It started at the top of her forehead, but that could've just been the spread from her gushing nose. All I know is that she wore the blood like a mask, and it dangled in drops from her chin before falling down to her stomach, where it landed in the half-moon shapes of broken thumbnails.

I heard someone shouting for the sheriff, for the doctor, for God. Dovey just sat there, her hands anxiously gripping her stomach as if trying to feel the baby's heartbeat with her fingers.

Otis looked lost. He kept looking down at his muscles as if to say, *Come on, do something.* But they lazed in their size. He suddenly looked as if he regretted ever lifting a dumbbell in the first place. They had not prepared him for what to do for a fallen wife and child. They had not prepared him to keep that from happening, and at this he frowned into his abs.

"Help her up, Otis," someone from the crowd ordered. It was his job, they said when someone tried to do it for him.

He squatted down as if preparing to perform a dead lift. With his arms around Dovey's hips, he lifted her up. She was still gripping her stomach. I don't think she even realized she was being raised. The blood from her nose kept at it as if it had been waiting a long time to gush. She looked at Sal, a bit drunkenlike. Then her eyes widened in that mask of blood.

"I know what it feels like now." Her front tooth, loosened in the fall, flopped against her lip like a piece of tissue. "I know what it feels like to fall from the seven millionth hand." And then she laughed. She laughed delirious and sick and sad. Self-shattering through sound.

"Dovey." Otis' leg muscles tightened as if at any moment he was going to have to run away from her. "Please, Dovey, stop laughin' like that."

She did stop, though I preferred her laughter to the screams that followed.

Over and over again, she was already fearing the worst. Otis led her away, saying the doctor would check her out and that everything was going to be just fine. She didn't believe a word he said.

As one organism, the town watched Otis and Dovey until they disappeared around the corner. Then in near unison, the town turned back to me first, then Sal.

"I seen him push her," a voice came like nails on a chalkboard. *"Pushed her down."*

"Yeah, he did. I seen it too." Raspy and so sure.

Elohim was still shouting, hopping from one foot to the other, yelling about devils and death. He smiled when the crowd took a step toward us. Another step. Another smile. Fists were bunching up at sides until knuckles went white. Necks were being cracked. Men were pushing up their sleeves. Women flung their purses up into the crooks of their arms, getting them out of the way.

I watched as one woman tied her feathered hair back out of her face while the man beside her shot his arms out from his shoulders the way a boxer walks to the ring.

Mom had been right. The heat was making people behave on their most terrible side. Maybe it even gave them the confidence to act foolishly, rashly, without real reason. Hands in such heat bloom to fists. Fists are the flora of the mad season.

"He didn't do nothin'." I realized I was trembling. "Just stay back. Y'hear?"

"He pushed her down." A small voice from a small old lady who spoke for them all when she pointed at Sal and said, as soft as a hill flower, "He's bad."

"Just stay back. I'll tell my dad on y'all. He's Autopsy Bliss, in case some of you don't know. He's a lawyer, and if you do anything, he'll put you in prison."

"Devil." One of them pointed not at Sal, but at me.

"But I'm not—"

"Devil."

That wasn't what was supposed to be part of my life as Fielding Bliss. No one ever said you've got to prepare to be hated. You've got to prepare for the yelling and the anger. You have got to prepare how to survive being the guilty one, even in innocence. And yet, there I was, sharing the horns with Sal.

I remember how a kid no more than seven started practicing his punches. His mother patted his head. "That's good, son. That's real good."

Friends, neighbors, my fellow Breathanians were advancing on us. The only time I'd ever been truly scared in my thirteen years was when a five-foot black racer chased me out of a field after I got too close to its eggs. The crowd was like that racer, rising up on its tail and hissing at me and Sal.

The light was letting go, and it was violence's chance. The closeness of that very violence surged through me like an overwhelming disturbance that chilled my blood, a seemingly impossible feat in that heat, but that's how scared shitless I was.

I tore open the bag of lentils and poured them into my hand. I threw hard, and while the lentils fell, I grabbed Sal's hand—so sweaty I had to grip twice. Our hands eventually slipped from each other's as we ran as fast as we could from the open, hungry mouth that had taken chase.

The young girls were the first to fall away, followed by the women whose heels wouldn't let them go any farther. They threw these heels at us like loose, sharp teeth as they hollered for the men to keep on, keep on and tear us to pieces.

"Make us proud," they insisted, some still in aprons smelling of home.

Me and Sal dodged the honking cars on the lanes before sticking to the yards, running in between houses and through the spray of a water hose and a man watering his oleander. My legs ached. A cramp was coming on in the right hamstring. I looked back. The crowd had gotten smaller. The older of the men had stopped, clutching their chests in a line like a heart attack parade. My own heart was thumping so badly, I looked down and thought at first I was bleeding from the chest, soon realizing it was just sweat and water from the hose soaking through my red T-shirt.

Our pursuers dwindled until all who remained was an eighteen-year-old from Breathed High who was OSU bound on a track scholarship. Dressed for Breathed track, in the school's dark purple and lavender tank and shorts, he jumped over fallen logs and fences like hurdles, took turns with the ease of straight tracks and was sprinting to the finish line of our heels. I wanted to keep looking back, stare the cheetah of the Midwest in the eyes, but Sal kept screaming to just keep running.

I could feel the boy's breath on the backs of my calves, and just when I thought he was going to reach out and grab us, I heard a scream and the squealing of tires. I turned and saw the track star bounce off the hood of a DeLorean, his sweat flinging from his forehead as he flew up into the air, seemingly touching the sun.

The driver was out of the car quick. I could hear him asking the boy to wiggle his toes as Sal pulled me away. I could hear the boy saying he couldn't, *oh God,* he couldn't wiggle his toes.

Just before we crossed into the woods, I saw the red lights of the sheriff's car.

"That boy." I bent over and grabbed my knees, feeling I might get sick. "You know he has a track scholarship. To OSU. I wonder . . . I wonder if . . . Oh, God."

"C'mon," Sal tugged my arm. "We best get lost for a while."

We climbed up the nearby hill, running until we were deep in its cover of woods and could no longer hear the siren.

Sal caught his breath against a tree. "Where should we go?"

"I know a place. Follow me."

We jumped every time a twig snapped, every time a wild turkey gobbled, every time a hawk squawked like a scream, fearing they had found us out. He chewed his lip until I thought he would chew it down to his chin.

I was so out of my head, I got lost. I couldn't stop thinking about that boy enough to remember direction. We must have passed the same deer drinking hole three different times. Eventually I sobered from worry enough to find the overgrown pasture up on the side of the hill. Past it was a pine grove that led by an old abandoned schoolhouse and from there to the tree me and Grand had built a house in.

"This is mine and Grand's secret place." I climbed up the slats hammered into the wide trunk. "I've never brought anyone here before."

I paused on the slats, glancing down at Sal climbing up behind me. "I hope her baby's gonna be all right. Did you see all that blood? Sal? I saw her belly. I saw it push in when she hit. I've never seen anything like it. Have you?"

He nodded he had. I turned back to the slats and climbed the rest of the way.

"And that runner." I paced the spacey boards that made up the floor while Sal leaned back against the tree trunk continuing its growth up through the middle of the house. "I can't get the sound of the tires squealin' outta my head."

He stared at the two red handprints on the wall. "If this is yours and your brother's place, why'd you bring me here, Fielding?"

"Ain'tcha like me and Grand? I mean maybe you and me ain't brothers, but I mean we ain't just friends. We're in this together now. They weren't just chasin' you, Sal. They were chasin' me too."

On the floor was a wooden crate with one of Mom's afghans draped over it. I threw the afghan off as I said, "There's too many people confused 'bout what they think happened back there. They got it in their damn heads that you pushed her. Hell, they think I pushed her too. We've got a right to protect ourselves against that confusion, don't we?"

He came and nudged the crate with his toe as I sat down, happy to be closer to the floor I thought I was going to collapse down to at any moment. My hands were still shaking, little vibrations as if they were being chewed on by gnats.

When I pulled the revolver out of the crate, Sal took it from me by its ivory handle.

"Cool, huh? Me and Grand found it in the attic a few years ago. We never did tell Mom and Dad 'bout it. Parents get . . . worried 'bout guns." I opened the chamber to show him the bullets inside. "It's only missin' one."

He closed one eye and peered down the barrel of the gun.

"Sal? Was that true back there, 'bout the staircase 'n' all?"

He looked deeper into the barrel and then held the gun up, aiming it at the wall behind me. "It's true."

"What'd you mean when ya said you were discontented with the one suit of your life?"

I thought for a moment he was actually going to fire the gun, but he slowly lowered it to his lap as he asked, "Have you ever tried on one of your father's suits?"

I shook my head.

"You will one day."

"Are you sayin' that's all ya did? Was try on one of God's suits?"

"I just wanted to try it on. See if it fit me or one day might." For the first time, he seemed more sweat than skin. "The thing about trying on your father's suit is that if you wear it outside the closet, you are no longer merely trying it on. You are wearing it. Some may think this is you trying to replace your father."

"Did ya step outside the closet, Sal?"

He nodded. "But only because there were no mirrors in the closet and I just wanted to see how I looked. That was all. I just wanted to see how I looked in my father's suit." He lowered his eyes to the gun. "It didn't fit."

8

Melt, as I do,

. . . . .

. . . bliss on bliss

—MILTON, *PARADISE LOST* 4:389, 508

In lieu of family and friends at the dinner table, I've piled laundry in the chairs to avoid the emptiness. Still it's not easy to dine with dirty jeans and stained shirts. Yesterday I tried something new. I had dinner at the VFW. It was my first time there with them veterans of foreign wars.

When I walked in, they leaned back in their chairs and nodded sympathetically, like I was one of them. Maybe that was because of the service uniform I was wearing and had bought at the thrift store down the road.

As soon as I sat down at the bar, a guy attached to my side, asking what war.

I pretended not to hear him. He smelled like a dog fight. Sweaty. Bloody. A little scared.

When the bartender came, I placed my order for a beer and the BBQ ribs meal.

"I asked ya what war were ya in?" The drunk beside me took a swallow or two of his beer.

"The *big* one." I sipped my own beer the bartender had just served.

"Yeah, the *big* one." The drunk's eyes got even glassier. He knew exactly what war I was talking about, even if he didn't.

"Hey, I forgot to ask for your card." The bartender had returned. "Your membership card."

"This is my membership card." I tapped the uniform.

"Amen." The drunk threw back his beer and asked for another.

"You're over your limit, Gus. Look"—he turned back to me—"I gotta have the card."

"Leave 'im alone." Gus slapped my back, a little too hard. "He was in the *big* one."

The bartender looked from Gus to me and waited. I picked up my glass of beer in case he was going to try to take it away from me.

"I don't have a card."

"You're not a veteran?" The bartender slung his towel over his shoulder and leaned onto the counter. "We only serve veterans."

"I'm a veteran. Just not of the United States Army or Navy or whatever the hell this is." I pinched the uniform.

"You said . . ." Gus slurred. "You said you were in the *big* war."

I finished the last of my beer in a great gulp. "I was."

"He's my guest." Gus kept turning his glass up to his lips even though it was empty. "He don't need no card if he's a guest of someone with a card. And ain't ol' Gus here got a card?" He flipped his card out from his pocket. It was creased until his name had faded.

The bartender shrugged and returned to wiping the counter.

"You ever kill anybody?" Gus perched his chin on my shoulder and wobbled on his stool. A few more, and I'd be wobbling with him. Two old birds singing on the same old wire.

"Yeah." I wiped my mouth on my sleeve. "Yeah, I killed someone once. Hey, can I get another?"

The meal was shit. Made me miss my frozen dinners. Damn Gus, who ended up passing out when I was midsentence and before he saw me, beers later, coming to blows with three silver-haired Iraq War veterans, one in a wheelchair. I can't make my fists like I used to, but I still got the punch. Bartender and a couple of the other young ones had to break us up. Not sure what started it all, but I never am.

As I stumbled from the VFW, bloody and bruised, I thought of Dovey. Her care went beyond the resources of Breathed's doctor, so they sent her up to the hospital in Columbus to monitor the baby. That's where they took the track star too. He finally made it to OSU, though it was the hospital instead of the track. He would be there for months but not as long as he was in the rehabilitation center. He'd never walk again.

Later I'd hear he rolled his wheelchair off a train platform while wearing his old lavender and dark purple track uniform from Breathed High. Sometimes the only thing left to do is to flee the life and hope that after we've fled we're spared the judgment of dying wrong.

He must have been something like thirty-six by then. I sent his mother lilies for the funeral, unsigned. Would have sent them to his widow, but he never married.

An apology to him was on my lips as I sat down on the sidewalk, not even half a block away from the VFW.

"Hey, buddy, you okay?"

A passerby. I flipped him and his nosey dog the bird.

"Fuck you too, buddy."

Finally left in peace, I tried to lie down. Couldn't, though—on account of the heartburn brought on by the barbecue sauce in that shit meal. As I sat up, a sheriff car went driving by. Partly the night, partly my drunkenness, but I saw Sal looking out the window at me just as he'd looked that June morning when Sheriff Sands drove him away.

Sitting there on the sidewalk, feeling as certain as any drunk man can feel, I reached for Sal, screaming his name. I was convinced I was seeing him with his face pressed against the glass. I somehow stood up and stumbled out into the road. The sheriff was nearing the turn and by it would turn out of my life.

I picked up a handful of small gravels from off the pavement.

Winding up like I was on the mound, I pitched them, just as Grand had taught me. They pinged and bounced off the car's trunk, causing the brake lights to flash red and the tires to squeal to a stop. When the sheriff got out, he did so cussing and with his hand on his holster.

"Now, you just take a step back onto that sidewalk there. You hear me? Goddamn it. I said take a step back. That's good. Now, why you throwin' rocks at my fuckin' car like that?" He used his flashlight to shine on the trunk. "Could've broken my damn winda out, you old fool."

I stammered as he shined the light into my eyes.

"Been drinkin' tonight, have we?"

"Just a little, sir."

"You know you've pissed yourself?" He shined the light down.

"Couldn't find the bathroom, sir."

"Says the man who's just had a little. You look like a caveman, all that hair, all that beard. You used to be in one of them rock bands or somethin'? Can't let it go now? You still have to look the part, don'tcha? If I was you, I'd get myself to the barber and only drink coffee from now on, you understand?"

He was so close, I could smell coffee on his breath. I knew he could smell the beer on mine. I closed my mouth and didn't breathe. I got light-headed as he asked if I was driving home.

I shook my head. My lungs tightening, about to burst.

"How you plan on gettin' home?"

My answer was a sharp intake of breath.

"You drivin'?"

"No, sir."

"Ain't you too old for this shit?" His hand dropped from his holster. "What's that you got all over your beard? That red stuff?"

"Barbecue sauce."

He shined the flashlight down over the rest of me and my thrift store uniform. "You were in the armed forces?"

"I was in a war, yes. It was me." I stabbed my finger into my chest.

"It was me who stopped the war." I made my hand into a gun and whispered a bang. "That was me with the gun."

He lowered the light down to my tennis shoes. "Your shoelaces are untied."

"I know."

"Weird-lookin' color for shoelaces."

"They're my brother's, sir. They're my brother's shoelaces."

"What's that brownish color on 'em?"

"Dried blood."

He sighed as he clicked off the flashlight. "I should take you in."

"Yes, sir."

"Public intoxication. Public stupidity. Public stink."

"Wouldn't be my first, sir." I held out my wrists, ready to be cuffed.

"I'm on my way home myself." He turned to leave. "Ain't got no desire to take you in and do more paperwork tonight. You get home, old timer. I don't wanna hear you killed no one. I said get home. What are you doin'?" He stepped back around his car to see me lowering myself to the ground.

I burped and he threw his hands up at me. Mumbled something like *jackass* before he got into his car and drove away while I sat there and closed my eyes, remembering Sheriff Sands and how he said Breathed wasn't safe for Sal anymore.

Dovey's fall and the track star's accident were a few days gone when the sheriff came to our house, telling Dad it was being said Sal had a hand in those tragic accidents.

"I like to think we take care of and solve our own problems," the sheriff said, "but I don't want that boy in danger. I think you agree."

When Sal was told he would be leaving, he put on the overalls he had arrived in. Dad said he didn't have to do that. Said he wouldn't even be leaving until the next morning, but Sal wouldn't take them off.

When I woke in the middle of the night, I found him downstairs, scribbling a small tangle of ink in the corner of the reproduction painting of *The Great Wave* in the room we knew as Japan.

"What you doin', Sal?"

"Leaving something for you to remember me."

These remembrances he left throughout the house, from a cut in the sofa's skirt to a page torn in the Russian-to-English dictionary. Little cuts, tiny slashes, small scribbles that wouldn't be seen unless you were really looking. Looking for the curtain to have the tiny hole in its valance or the rug to be missing its seventh fringe. Things taken away. That was how he saw his presence. It would be how his presence would be proved in the end.

The morning he left, he took our names from us. I was not a field growing life. Grand was not Grand. He was just some guy throwing a baseball in the background. Mom and Dad was just the foot and the step standing side by side, and the house was just a square with four sides for all of us but not one for him.

He looked up at Dad with the type of disappointment people never forget. "You invited me here, Autopsy Bliss. Your invitation, it was why I came. To see for myself. I felt wanted. But it was a lie. You lied to me, Autopsy Bliss. You all did."

He got in the front seat with the sheriff before Dad could say anything. I don't know what Dad would've said. Neither did he. Later we heard him walking through the house, rattling off cases one after the other. That was coping to my father.

Not more than forty minutes later, and Dad was getting a call from the sheriff, who was out of breath, saying Sal had escaped.

I thought Sal would leave Breathed, go find another Fielding, another Grand, another Dad and Mom who would take him in as their own. But as the day changed to night, I lay in bed feeling like I was just waiting for him to return. How could he not? With little parts of himself still there. In the torn page of the dictionary, the cut sofa, the corner of the painting. Pieces of him coming together into the center we all revolved around.

I didn't hear him calling my name at first, not over the hum of the fans. Finally I heard his nails scratching at the screen of the open window, his face pressed there.

"Let me in, Fielding."

I didn't dare go for a light as I got out of bed and quietly removed the screen.

"How'd you get here?" I stepped back as he came in over the sill.

"I climbed up the ivy."

"No, how did you get here? I thought you left with the sheriff?"

"I'm good at escaping." He wiped his dripping forehead on his forearm, Breathed's unofficial gesture of that summer.

"But how'd you do it?" I replaced the screen as he ignored my question and instead said he was thirsty.

"Ain't got a glass up here. Get a couple handfuls outta the faucet."

He frantically shoveled the water into his mouth, ending by splashing his face, while I sat on the edge of the bed, waiting for him to tell me about his daring escape.

"Elohim." He wiped his mouth and sat down beside me. "He flagged me and the sheriff down. The sheriff got out to talk to him. Elohim said how it was wrong for the sheriff to be driving me out of Breathed and how I should stay. He said he would talk to people. He promised he would keep Breathed a safe place for me."

"But . . . Elohim hates you. Why would he want you to stay?"

He shrugged. "While they were talking, I slipped out the sheriff's open door."

Headlights suddenly lit up the dark room. We hunkered down over to the front window, where we saw a car driving up to the house. I didn't see it was the sheriff until he got out and spit.

"Fielding."

Me and Sal turned to Dad, standing in the open doorway, the sweat on his face glistening in the moonlight.

"Dad? How'd you know?"

"It's all right. I had a feeling he might come back here, so I sat up waiting. I saw him crossing the yard."

Sal shrank into the darkness of the room. "What's going to happen now, Autopsy?"

Dad placed his hand on Sal's shoulder. "I'm going to talk to the sheriff. You boys wait in this room. No more running off, you hear?" He squeezed Sal's shoulder.

Like good shadows, me and Sal snuck downstairs to listen outside Dad's study door, which hadn't closed completely in the latch, allowing us to hear the sheriff.

"The woman at children's services has said that if he returned here after his escape, it meant he felt safe amongst y'all and it'd be more psychologically harmin' to take him away and place him with a different foster family. Accordin' to her, he's in a fragile state at the moment. Possibly abandoned in the first place, so he's fearful of losin' another home."

"Is that true?" I whispered to Sal.

He placed his trembling finger to his lips.

"She says as long as you're able to provide a safe and healthy environment for the boy, then she don't have no problem with his stayin' here for the time bein'. She knows about the accidents but not to the extent of the boy bein' thought responsible. And after the promise from Elohim today, I feel no need to elaborate on the details with her.

"Folks only started believin' those things about the boy 'cause of that midget in the first place, and if he swears he'll turn things around with their thinkin', then so be it. Lord knows why he suddenly wants that boy to stay. For the sake of calm, I'll have to think nothin' of it, though I'll keep my eye on Elohim. I advise you to do the same.

"I told her you and Stella are very willin' for Sal to stay here. I assured her you're a respectable family. She likes that you're a lawyer 'n' all. She's gonna be payin' ya a visit in a couple days to check things out. I suspect she'll look 'round the house, ask y'all a couple of questions, so I'd make sure Grand and Fieldin' are here if need be. If she deems it all proper, you'll be granted temporary custody of the boy."

Suddenly the study door was yanked open the rest of the way. Me and Sal slowly raised our heads to see Dad shaking his and looking down at us.

"Go on up to bed, you two. I'll be up in a little while."

He made sure we climbed up the stairs before returning to the sheriff.

"So?" I asked Sal once we were in my room.

"So what?" He fell back in the window bed.

"I mean ain'tcha happy you're stayin'? You're lucky Elohim stopped the sheriff."

"I don't need Elohim. I'm the devil. No one tells me when to stay and when to leave. But it sure is nice to be wanted. I tell you, Fielding, it sure is nice to be wanted right in this very place."

9

Where all life dies, death lives, Nature breeds,

.   .   .   .

These yelling monsters

— MILTON, *PARADISE LOST* 2:624, 795

SHE CAME IN a large black car with candy bar wrappers all over the passenger seat. Her breath smelled like Butterfingers. Her shirt had coffee stains. Her gold bracelets dangled over the clipboard and her fake nails, in radioactive green, scratched the paper as she put the little checks in the little boxes. She was children's services, and she spoke mostly to Mom and Dad. She did ask me and Grand things like, *Do you get along with Sal? Would you mind him staying with you for a while? Is there any reason his staying would be a bad idea?*

Yes, we answered. No, we said. And if there were any reasons, we couldn't think of them. We fibbed on that last one, but Dad had said we were not to bring up Dovey or the runner with the gone spine.

She and her clipboard went through the house, wanted to see where Sal slept, things like that. At the end, she gave Dad and Mom some papers to sign. Temporary is what the papers said, though Dad still kneeled in front of Sal and said he was one of us now.

"Did you know that before you came along, Sal, our four-person family was too small to own our name?" Dad held up the piece of paper he'd written our name on so he could illustrate his point. "I had the *B*, Mother there had the *L*, Grand had the *I*, and Fielding had the *S*. But this second *S* here has been waiting to be claimed this entire time. You, Sal, you are the last *S* in our name. You are the wholeness of our family."

So we were, suddenly a family of five, and June wasn't even over yet. By that time, sweat lived on us, leaving our skin stuck between the sensation and the response to that unbearable heat. While the sweat dripped, dropped, and flowed, it seemed at times to press upon us like dry twigs threatening to spark.

Owing to that longstanding advice on how to stay cool, an aerial view of Breathed would have captured a town of pastel seersucker and beige linen. No one wore anything heavier. There were those who dared to free themselves of clothes altogether and nap quietly bare on the banks of the river or stretch out in their backyards with the garden hoses. At first those who went naked tended to unintentionally build fences of young masturbators, but soon orgasms, even the most triumphant ones, became too minuscule a wage for the labors of the hand in such a roasting heat.

At that time, not many homes, especially the older ones like ours, had central air, so we had air conditioners sitting bulky in windows for rooms like the living room and the kitchen.

Even with air-conditioning, we relied on electric fans. We had a couple stored in the attic. Dad bought more at the hardware store before they sold out. He did then what others did, which was to drive to the surrounding towns to buy what fans they had. Fans became the statement of our house and their steady hum-buzz was like living in a beehive. To influence the temperature of their flow, Dad would place bowls of ice water in front of their blades, which brought a cool, though not cold, relief.

Even now, I sweat from that heat. People think it's Arizona that makes me sweat, but it's always been Ohio.

Did I tell you the neighbor boy brought me over a fan the other day?

"I just thought you looked awful hot," he said as he set it up on the table. "Do ya like it?"

"It's not going to help."

"Sure it will. And I got somethin' else that might help ya."

He ran out of the trailer, returning minutes later with a cane.

"I just worry you're gonna fall down. I used my allowance to get it. It's not new. I got it at a yard sale, but I think it'll work just fine."

I slapped the cane down to the floor. There is nothing more angering than being told you're old, and nothing tells it quite like a cane.

"Don't you know I was friends with the devil once?"

As if that will make me greater than just another old man.

"I'm awful sorry, Mr. Bliss. I just thought it'd help."

Good intentions slapped down to the floor is a hard scene to come away from. I sighed and did my best.

"Listen, kid. My shoelaces are untied. That's why I look like I'm about to fall. No cane can ever help me with that."

"But, Mr. Bliss." He looked down at my bare feet. "You're not wearin' any shoes."

"That doesn't matter. The laces are still untied." I pointed down at the old pair of dirty tennis shoes on the floor.

"But how can they trip you up if you're not even wearin' 'em?"

"Because those laces are everything, and when everything gets untied, you don't stop tripping just because the shoes are off."

He stepped over to the shoes, where he bent down and ran his fingers over the eyes threaded into the backs of their heels. "There's somethin' on the laces." He grabbed hold of them and looked closer.

"Blood," I answered as if I were carrying armloads of it, exhausted by that very thing.

I thought he would let go of the laces. Instead, he tied them.

"What do you think you're doing?" I found myself not stopping him.

"I'm tyin' them. So they won't trip you anymore."

It was the kindest thing anyone had done for me in years. It was so kind, I had to sit down.

After he tied both shoes, he stood and walked around the trailer, staring at the photographs of chimneys and steeples framed on the walls.

"That one over there was one I did in San Francisco," I told him from my lawn chair. "That one beside it is from a small town called Sunburst—that's in Montana, in case you don't know. The big one there is from Baton Rouge, and—"

"You haven't got any pictures, Mr. Bliss."

"What do you call those?"

"I mean you don't have no pictures of family. Of friends."

"They are my family. They are my friends."

"I'm sorry, Mr. Bliss." He lowered his eyes. "I didn't mean to make you sad."

"I'm not sad, for Christ's sake."

"Do you want me to leave?"

"I should kick you out. The disrespect you have for your elders. I'm a man, goddamn it, you respect that."

He stood there, watching me scratch my chin through my beard. I stopped because he began to look worried I may have fleas.

"You want some ice cream, kid?"

He quietly nodded.

"Help yourself. Lord knows I won't eat it." I gestured toward the freezer, directing him to move the frozen dinners out of the way to the carton of chocolate ice cream in the back.

"This carton is all banged up, Mr. Bliss." He read the expiration date on its side. "This ice cream is from 1984. I'll throw it away."

"No." I flipped the flimsy chair back as I stood.

"But it'll make you sick. You've got to let it go." He stepped away with the carton.

"You give that to me. Right now, boy. I said give it to me." I grabbed hold of the carton, trying to yank it from his tight grip.

"Mr. Bliss . . ." He held on.

"Goddamn you to hell."

"Mr. Bliss, no—"

I didn't realize I'd slapped him until long after he left. I stood the lawn chair back up and sat there, holding the ice cream carton to my chest. At first, it was freezing, and burned my skin through my thin shirt in that way all frozen things can. Eventually, the freeze left. The carton was just cold then, until it wasn't cold at all. It sweated and dripped down onto my lap. I must have sat there for hours like that, holding onto all that melt.

"Mr. Bliss?"

I raised my eyes to the boy. "My God, kid. You came back?"

"I just wanted to give ya somethin'." He laid what he had down on the table by the door before leaving.

With the carton still pressed against my chest, I left the chair and hurried to the table. There was a photograph of his smiling face, a saguaro in the background, the sky yellowed by the sun rising behind him.

"Damn kid."

I opened the carton and stared at the melted ice cream. Before I knew it, I was at the sink and pouring it down, some of it splashing on my shirt, little dark drops of chocolate that splattered like blood.

I balanced the carton on top of the pile of trash before going to a wall of photographs. I took down one of the frames and replaced the photograph of the steeple with that of the boy. It felt like maybe I was reaching for one of those hands Sal talked about. That whole second-chance hope sort of thing.

I spent the rest of that night in front of the fan. It was the first time in years I had tried to cool off. I even thought about putting my clothes in the freezer. That was one of Sal's ideas, to put our clothes in the freezer overnight. By morning, they would be crisp and chilled.

Word on the cooling regime hit the town, and freezers became a second dresser for many. Everyone had their own ideas on how to stay cool. Mom kept her lotions and creams in the refrigerator so they'd be cold when she put them on. Most everyone carried little spritz bottles of ice water they could spray on their face or back of the neck, though the ice melted too fast for it to make any real difference. A couple of people even went so far as to paint their roofs white under the knowledge dark colors draw heat in.

Then there was my great-aunt, Fedelia Spicer, who made a habit out of visiting our house in the afternoons to spend time with her only surviving family. Mom was her niece.

Old Fedelia's way to cool down was by licking her forearms. There she'd be, the shades of her eyes pulled half closed, her tongue amphibiously long and aggressive.

"Kangaroos, you stupid boy. Kangaroos." Her amber eyes lit with rage as she shook her forearms at me when I asked why she licked them.

It was Scranton who had made Fedelia so angry. He'd been her husband before running away with a blonde in fishnets. Through their marriage, Scranton was the sound of a motel bedspring squeaking.

I'd seen photographs of Fedelia taken long before Scranton's infidelity. All that beauty and life. Too bad she didn't inoculate herself against the disease that was Scranton. Because of him and the anger she held onto, her features reached home to their bones, causing cave and shadow. Her face thinner than her body where the weight collected in the abdomen, hips, and thighs. She ate the comfort she couldn't find anywhere else. Padding piled upon her as defense for the hard in life. She looked even larger because she wore clothes too big. The woman in bags who wore costume heavy makeup because her face was afraid to go into the world alone, lest she be seen. Lest she have to see herself.

Over the years, her anger piled her hair atop her head in a ratty heap of tangles and frizz. Looking to recapture the color of her youth, she would spray her hair with dye in a can that was supposed to be auburn but left her with an orange that cost all who saw it their respect of carrots. Her roots somehow managed to escape the dye and were such a bright white, they always looked like the start to something holy.

Amongst the orange were tied ribbons, a dozen in all. Each a different color, though faded, and representing a different woman Scranton had shared betrayal of Fedelia with over the long years of their union. She'd tell how the tattered teal ribbon was for the woman who waddled, while the dull fuchsia was for the woman with the feather boas.

She never removed these ribbons, so over time her hair wrapped around them. The way they wove, they could sometimes look like slithering in an undergrowth. It was as if she were the infected Eden, the snake still turning through Eve.

She would reach up to the ribbons, making sure they were still there as if she was afraid they would fall out or leave her like Scranton. On occasion, she'd pull one tighter, just for insurance.

Outside of Scranton, Fedelia's conversations with Mom that summer centered on the heat and that new disease that would come to define the 1980s.

As Grand came into the living room reading the newspaper, Fedelia jerked it out of his hands to read the front page.

"This new goddamn sickness. *AIDS*." She held the word for a long time. "Unusual fuckin' name for a disease. You know, I wonder what it'll do to Ayds? You know, them appetite-suppressin' chocolates I've been eatin'. Goddamn."

Those appetite-suppressing chocolates that did not work. That did not keep the lonely woman from eating the company of food. Bandages on a plate for all the wounds inside.

She continued to read the newspaper. "I wonder if Scranton will get AIDS. They say it comes with the fuckin', you know." She seemed both pleased and distressed by the thought, though it was hard to tell with the heavy black liner she drew across her white brows. "That old rat bastard. If anyone deserves it, he does."

Grand tried to swipe the paper back from her, but she began to bark and growl at him like a dog. He backed, along the way grabbing up his baseball glove from the table.

"I'm goin' to practice." He pecked Mom on the cheek.

He made a last attempt for the paper but this time Fedelia bit him on the left forearm, leaving behind her red lipstick that smeared across his skin like blood.

"Goddamn, Auntie." He grabbed his arm.

"There's more where that came from, you piss-ant." Fedelia rolled and pointed the paper at him, her cruel smile made even more monstrous from the lipstick having been smeared around her mouth, spreading so far from her lips, it reached her cheeks in claw-mark strides.

"Сука," Grand mumbled out the door.

Fedelia threatened that when she found out what that meant, she was going to kick his ass good. Then in a sudden turn of emotion, she looked toward Mom. "Before I forget, have you heard about Dovey?"

Fedelia, the wheel of gossip.

"She's still in the hospital up in Columbus, ain't she?" Mom picked up her crochet hook and yarn, pretending to be more interested in finishing the crocheting of her afghan square than anything else.

"Oh, my, yes. Might lose that baby. Fall really done her in. Or was it a push?" Fedelia puckered her lips, the wrinkles emphasized and parading around her mouth like thorns of flesh.

A push. That was the idea laying pipes through town. Elohim did as he told the sheriff he would, which was to clear Sal's name. Still, the thought was too hard to abandon for some, and once it was said, it became like most gossip, drama that ruins.

As Fedelia kept chatting with Mom, someone knocked on the front door. It was the sheriff come to speak to Dad. While Sal stayed in the living room, staring at Fedelia's hair, I crouched down in the entry hall, at the side of the screen door so I could see and hear the sheriff and Dad out on the front porch.

The sheriff spit over the railing. The glob colored red from his cherry hard candy. He wiped his mouth on his arm before saying, "You know how I've been lookin' into some of the surroundin' counties for missin' boys? Well, now, I've come up with somethin' quite interestin'."

"What's that?" Dad asked.

"An abundance of missin' boys. Not much ruckus has been raised about these disappearances. Furthermore, these vanishin's have happened over the course of years. I can't say they're all related, yet I can't say they ain't. I mean we're lookin' at boys disappearin' at exactly thirteen years of age. Same as the boy you got in your livin' room. Boys from poor families. Judgin' by the clothes he showed up in, he ain't no Rockefeller. I'd say he's some farm pup. Plus, all these kids, they were all black, Autopsy."

Dad wiped his hand over his mouth. "Any suspects?"

"No sir-ree Bob." The sheriff leaned back into his heels, causing his bulbous stomach to lead out. "Most folks ain't gonna pay a lot of attention to a kidnapper if they ain't even aware there is one. These stories of these kids, only two were even mentioned in their local papers. The rest were just police files. And most of 'em was put down as runaways."

"No linking evidence?"

"Nothin' hard. There was one thing. A shirt was found belongin' to one of the boys. Found by a series of railroad tracks. At first they thought the spots on the shirt were bloodstains. Tests proved it chocolate. Better chocolate than blood, I reckon. Gave the momma hope her son was still alive. I imagine the truth will eat her up sooner or later though. It's a thing to eat any parent up. Losin' a child is a thing with teeth."

"Were there photographs in the police files?"

"Some."

"Any of these boys, the recent ones to go missing, any of them look like Sal?"

"A bunch of little black boys?" The sheriff's laugh reminded me of Elohim's. "Sure they looked like him."

Dad sighed and wiped the sweat from the back of his neck. "Be fair."

The sheriff spit over the porch rail and cleared his throat. "Listen, there were three possible cases reported that fell in the timeline of when that boy arrived. One of 'em was that boy Amos. The other two cases had photographs supplied by the parents. They had their likenesses to that boy in there. But they ain't him. Shucks. Never found those green eyes of his in any of 'em. That's not sayin' much.

"I mean maybe the family he disappeared from just never filed a police report. Or maybe they did, but who knows what state they did it in. Maybe the kidnapper ain't just in Ohio. Maybe he's done this all over. I'd like to talk to the boy. First, I gotta tend to some issues over at one of the farms. A shitload of cows have just died.

"These animals ain't built for such heat. We ain't either." He used his sleeve to wipe the sweat from his cheeks. "You know, I could use some help puttin' flyers on cars. Remindin' everyone not to leave pets and children in vehicles. Already had an infant had to be rushed to the doctor with heatstroke or heat rash or some sort of heat sickness after bein' left in his momma's truck."

"I'll help you hand the flyers out." Dad said so without much care. He was still thinking of all those missing black boys.

"Listen, this evenin' is clear for me. Would you bring that boy by later, Autopsy? Not to the station. We'll question him at my house. Make him feel comfortable, at ease. He'll talk, I'm sure of it."

I slipped back into the living room. Fedelia was reading aloud the articles in the newspaper about the fields drying up, livestock collapsing, and the recent infestation of flies. As she got to the article about home remedies for heat rash, Sal sat at her feet and stared up at her hair.

"Can I ask you something, ma'am?"

She folded the paper and smacked it down hard on the table. "Devil gonna ask me a question? Shit, this oughta be good." She sneered, showing how the bright lipstick had smudged across her yellowed teeth. "Shoot, green eyes."

"Do you count your days well spent?"

She batted her eyes, the false lashes about to fling off. "Are you offerin' to buy my soul? Goddamn." The sweat on her face was little beige droplets, colored by her heavy mask of makeup. "Do I count my days what now?"

"Well spent."

"Well spent? Fuckin' philosopher here. Why don't you tell me?"

"You do not count your days well spent. How could you? Not with all the anger you have. Why have you built infinity for your husband's mistresses upon your head?"

The circles of blush bounced as her lips twitched like boiling water. "You little shit. How dare you."

"What else would you call it but a place for them and their damage to live forever upon you?"

"It is none of your damn business anyways, boy." Her roar shook her dangling earrings.

"Have you ever heard of the paradise shelduck?"

"Fuck you," she whispered through clenched teeth, her hand beating at her chest as if she couldn't quite catch her breath.

"The rule is female ducks are less colorful than their male counterparts. The paradise shelduck is the exception. While the male has a boring black head and an even more boring gray body, the female has a head of bright white with a body of chestnut and gold. The female paradise is a rarity in the duck world. She beats the beauty of the male.

"You, Fedelia Spicer, are meant to be paradise. Look at the white hair there at your roots. As white as the head of the female shelduck. But these colors of the other women. They feather you away from paradise. You must let go of them." He reached up to a ribbon, but she grabbed his arm.

"I can't." Her voice tore at the edges. "Don't you understand?"

She sat there in the chair looking so fragile, I thought if I touched her with my little finger, she would instantaneously break like a plate being struck by a sledgehammer. Mom tried to comfort her, doing her best to keep Fedelia's false lashes from falling with the tears.

Dad had long returned from the porch and had listened quietly to the exchange between Fedelia and Sal. Now he placed his hand on my shoulder and said, "Fielding, why don't you and Sal go be a couple of little boys for a while."

I waved for Sal to follow me outside. Dad stopped him with just a finger gently pressed into his chest. "You are unusual, aren't you, son?" He looked down into Sal's eyes, waiting for a big answer. All he got was a small shrug.

"Well," Dad sighed, "don't be gone too long."

We went out the back door, and once we were through the yard and into the woods, I told Sal the sheriff wanted to see him.

"What about?"

"They think you've been kidnapped."

"By you guys?"

"Naw, by kidnappers. Were you?"

"Yes."

"What?"

"I'm kidding. Don't be so serious, Fielding."

With a smile he took off, his head start giving him a lead we traded to the tree house. Granny followed, staying to sniff the trees below as we climbed up the slats into the house.

"This ain't good racin' weather." I swept back the strands of hair stuck to my forehead.

"What are these?" He was over by the pair of handprints on the wall.

"That's my hand on the right, and Grand's is on the left. We made 'em years ago." I felt my finger as I remembered the knife and shoe-laces.

As he continued to stare at the prints, even placing his own over mine, I began to toss through the board games that me and Grand kept in the tree house. Me and Sal never did decide on one of those games. We got to talking about movies instead, and I found myself explaining the plot of *Ghostbusters*. Just when I was about to tell him about the Stay Puft Marshmallow Man, he shushed me.

I didn't hear what he did, but still I followed him down the slats and continued to follow him through the woods, the dry shrubbery and briars scratching my legs. As I stopped to wipe small dots of blood off my shins, I heard the low cries. It was then I saw Elohim's rusty can. A few feet from it lay a pile of gray.

Please, God, I prayed as I ran to her. Already I felt the tearing inside myself, and by fear alone, I knew home would never be the same again.

I fell down by her side, unsure of where to touch her, for she seemed in pain everywhere.

"Oh, Granny. Hey, old girl. How much of the poison you think she got?"

"Enough." Sal gently fell to his knees beside me.

"What do we do?"

Her tremors became spasms that convulsed her whole body. Sal would later tell me I screamed for God. All I really remember shouting for was help.

He stood, wiping his hands on his red shorts as he walked away. I asked him where he was going, but he didn't answer. I tried to soothe Granny by saying all would be fine as I scratched behind her ears, her favorite place. It was hard to avoid the thick saliva dribbling from her mouth. Over and over again, she jerked, and in the sharpness each jerk was the corner of so many things I just kept running into.

"Sal, where are you?" A crackle of twigs. "There you are."

He held up the revolver.

"What you gonna do with that? Sal?"

"She's dying, so it isn't a killing. It's what has to be done."

"No." I threw myself over her convulsing body. "She'll be okay. She just needs to throw it up. Yeah, that's it, throw up the poison." I wasn't sure how to induce vomiting in a dog, so I started to pinch her throat. The sticky saliva clung to my hand. I moved down and massaged her stomach as I pleaded with her to vomit. "Please, Granny. Just throw it up. Please."

All she did was look up at me with the same eyes she had used to beg for table scraps. Now begging for something else.

"Why force her to suffer when you can take it all away?" He held the gun out to me.

"I can't kill her, Sal. She's Granny. Like a real granny."

"You're not going to kill her. Death has already started. You're not initiating anything that isn't already there. If you're waiting for God to take care of it, He won't. He doesn't do that. By letting her suffer, you risk being God.

"People always ask, why does God allow suffering? Why does He allow a child to be beaten? A woman to cry? A holocaust to happen? A good dog to die painfully? Simple truth is, He wants to see for Himself what we'll do. He's stood up the candle, put the devil at the wick, and now He wants to see if we blow it out or let it burn down. God is suffering's biggest spectator.

"Will you wait, Fielding? Will you wait to see for yourself what happens? If you're strong enough to watch suffering without laying down the pain, then you've no place among men, Fielding. You are a spectator on the cusp. You are a god-in-training." He kneeled and wrapped his arm around my shoulder.

"Just give me some room." I shrugged him off. "I need to think."

He stood back, the gun dangling at his side as if the choice were so casual.

"Hey, old girl." I scratched her neck, and her tail wagged as best as it could. Only a dog could show such love in such pain.

If only she could've told me it was okay to pick up the gun, to end her suffering. It's having to make the decision all alone and them not being able to tell you it's the right one. All I could see was the fear in her eyes. The fear of not knowing what was happening to her.

I thought of all the things she had planned for the rest of the day. I could see her almost saying, *I've got to get up from here. I've got to go home. Watch Mom fix dinner. Beg for some table scraps. Watch Dad sit and think. Think with him. Watch my boy yawn and go to bed with him so we can get up in the morning together.*

All the things she always did. Looking in her eyes, I could see these were all the things she wanted so desperately to get back to.

I hated the way she looked at me as she lay there. Out of all the world, she looked at me, and I wanted to say, *Look at the trees. It's the last time. Look at the sky. It's the last time. Look there, at that ant crawl the grass blade. It will be the last time you see it. That you see any of this.*

There was something about her eyes that made me see her death as final. There was no place after, her tears said. This was it. Dying animals have that effect. I think because you never see them in church preparing for an afterlife. You never see them wearing crosses around their necks, or lighting candles in Mass. It all seems so final with them. Their dying is not moving on, it's going out.

I wiped my eyes with my fists before asking for the gun. Sal didn't say anything. Just placed it in my hand. I wasn't sure if distance mattered. I placed the end of the barrel at the side of her trembling skull, beneath her ear, just in case it did.

My hand was surprisingly still. Though I don't know how.

I could no longer breathe through my stuffed nose, so I drew in deep breaths through my mouth. I looked at Sal, so prepared. I hated him for not crying. I closed my eyes and lightly felt the trigger, its slight curve like a smooth tooth, a fang, ready to bite. I flexed my hand. I needed all my muscle. The gun was the heaviest thing I'd ever held up to that point in my life.

When Granny started to whimper, I threw the gun down and ran.

It felt like the only thing I could do. On the way, I tripped over the can and spilled the poison. Even with that, I kept running before stopping by a tree. The sound of the gun made me.

As if I'd been shot myself, I fell to the ground, curling up into myself. I closed my eyes and rocked as I sang an old song Mom sang to me over the cradle.

Down in the hills of Ohio,
there's a babe at sleep tonight.
He'll wake in the morn' of Ohio,
in the peaceful, golden light.

"Fielding?"

I opened my eyes to Sal standing over me, the gun held by the smoking barrel in his hand. "She's still now. Like water healed of its ripples. She's calm and at peace."

"I couldn't do it, Sal."

"It's all right, Fielding." He sat down beside me. I heard the gun plop off to the ground on the other side of him.

When he brought his hand up to his mouth to bite his nail, I saw the blood on the inside of his wrist.

He saw me staring and lowered his hand. "It got on there from when I was checking for her pulse."

"I don't want another dog." I wiped my nose hard on my arm.

"I never said anything."

"Folks always say that. 'We'll get ya another.' I don't want another one."

"All right."

For a long time, the only sound made was that of me finding my way back to breathing through my nose.

"Sal?" I took a deep breath. "Not doin' somethin', am I a god-in-trainin', like ya said?"

He squinted, and I thought how like Dad he looked when he did that.

"No. You're just a boy. A boy holds a gun but cannot fire it, even when he knows it is the right thing to do. A god would never hold the gun in the first place. So you're a man-in-training. And on the day you are asked to hold the gun once more, you will have to decide whether to stay the child . . . or finally become the man."

10

A summer's day, and with the setting sun
Dropt from the zenith, like a falling star
                    —MILTON, *PARADISE LOST* 1:744–745

WHEN I THINK of her as a grandmother, as old as I was young, with gray hair and a shawl around her frail shoulders to keep out the chill, what happened in those woods becomes something much harder to bear. Granny was my first loss, my first emptying. She was the something that matters for eternity.

I haven't had a dog since, though the neighbor boy has his mutt. The other day, I watched the two of them together. The dog did his best to catch the ball the boy threw. I tried to teach the boy to throw better, the way Grand taught me.

I didn't show the boy I framed his photograph, but he saw it just the same and smiled a little too much. I even told him so. He asked if I wanted to drop by his trailer for dinner. He said his mom was making her famous meat loaf and she always made too much of it, he said. I got to thinking about my place at their table.

"Say, kid, I never see your old man around. Where's he at?"

I knew it wasn't going to be a clean answer, the way he slowly dragged his finger across the dirt on my kitchen counter.

"Mom says he's in the jungle, findin' the cure for cancer." He kept his eyes on the counter. "Even though he died of it six years ago."

"Jesus."

He looked up at me. "So you comin' to dinner?"

How the hell could I refuse after that? Besides, it was meat loaf, and I haven't had meat loaf since my mother's, but when I got to their yellow trailer across the road from mine, it was too damn nice. The smell of dinner. The young mother in a dress. The table set and the boy and his dog just smiling away. To tell you the truth, I was a little scared. I don't know how to be in that world anymore. That world of dinner and niceness. So I ran away as fast as I could. I sat there in the dark of my trailer while the light of theirs shined a yellow glow.

A while later the boy came over, carrying a plate of food. I didn't go to the door when he knocked, so he placed it on the milk crate and headed back home. I opened the door before he got too far away.

"Why you like me so much, kid?"

I didn't say it loud, and for a moment I thought he didn't hear me, but then he stopped and stood there. He was looking across the road at his own trailer, at his mother there in the window doing the dishes in the warmth of the light.

"I remember one Halloween my dad dressed up like an old bum." He softly smiled. "He looked like you."

He seemed to be waiting for me to say something. When I didn't, he walked across the road and into his trailer.

I sat down in the doorway of my own and stared into that clear shot of their kitchen, where I could see the boy give his mom a kiss on the cheek. He stayed there by her side, helping her wash the dishes, sharing suds between their fingers.

The mutt, left outside, came smelling the meat loaf. I removed the foil and set the plate on the ground, letting him have the meal that was too nice for me. Once full, he yawned and lay down on his side. I had to look away because it was how we had laid Granny in her grave. I believe that dirt from burying her is still under my fingernails.

We used some loose pieces of sandstone to break up the dry dirt.

It was evening by the time we left the woods. We forgot the sheriff wanted to see Sal. When we got home, we told Dad Granny had been hit by a car. If we'd told him about the poison, then we would've had to tell him about the gun, after which we would've been punished for having the gun in the first place.

When he asked to see Granny's body, we said we had already buried her in the woods by the tree house in a small funeral. We showed our fingernails as evidence.

Sal had grown agitated the whole time we were digging the hole, laying her body down in it. He wouldn't even look at the gunshot wound. I knew what he had done was rubbing at him like little grains of sand scraping his bone. As I sat grieving by her grave, he said something that surprised me. I had to ask him to repeat it.

"You heard me. You make me sick. You didn't even have to do it. I did. So shut up your crying."

We didn't speak the rest of the way home. I was relieved when Dad took him away to the sheriff's. I went up to my room, sat on the edge of my bed, feeling on the edge myself. The sadness like a motor, idling inside me. Idling still. Sometimes *vroom, vroom.* But never off.

"What's wrong, little man?"

Grand stood in my doorway, his dark brow trying to figure out on its own what was making his little brother cry on the edge.

"Granny, she's . . ." I didn't say hit by a car. I told him the truth as he came in and sat beside me. I told him about the poison, the gun, the *bang*, the pile of dirt in the woods.

He put his arms around me and pulled me into him. For seventy-one years I've been trying to find that feeling of being held by my brother. The other day I bought a bunch of those plastic-wrapped bread loafs. Unsliced. Wheat brown like the Midwest. I put them in the oven to warm, and when I took them out, I carried them to my bed and lay down with them, feeling their warmth. Holding that very thing and begging it to hold me back.

Please, Grand, won't you hold me back?

"You know, little man, Sal did the right thing. When somethin's dyin' like that, you gotta end it. If I was sufferin', dyin' a slow death, I'd wanna end it early. Wouldn't you?"

I was quiet. He said that was all right. He asked where Sal was. I told him he was at the sheriff's.

"You let 'im go alone?"

I nodded.

"That's not the Fielding I know. The boy who tiptoes behind. Listenin' to and watchin' all the things we try to hide. You are а тень. A shadow. I know this 'bout you, Fielding. That's why I spray my cologne on your clothes. So I can smell you comin'. Smell you out."

He tousled my hair. "You need a haircut."

"No way. The girls like it. They think I'm a rock star."

He laughed as he ran his fingers through his own short hair. "Okay, rock star. Hey, you been puttin' that sunscreen on I gotcha? The sun's a bastard this summer, Fielding, and you gotta be careful with all them moles of yours. I read in the paper about somethin' called mela—"

"Mom's got moles and you never got her sunscreen."

"She's never outside, little man. Don't be a smart-ass." He lightly punched my arm before saying I should go to the sheriff's to listen in. "Just make sure you're not seen. Dad'll be angry if he finds you sneakin' 'round."

"Where you goin'?" I asked of his leaving.

"Got a date."

"With who?"

"The girl everyone wants."

I used Dad's brown shoe polish and colored my skin before I left the house. Movies I'd seen up to that point, like *First Blood,* had drilled into me that camouflage is needed when embarking on a secret mission.

I stayed out of the streetlights and the headlights of oncoming cars.

I thought I was the shadow Grand said I was. Just as I was a turn away from the sheriff's, I was suddenly tackled from behind and forced to the ground.

"Got you now." The voice was more growl than anything else.

The perpetrator's arms were short but strong. So strong, it was like I could do nothing right to get away from him. He kept me forced down on my stomach, my face pressed against the ground and the prickly blades of dry grass.

I felt something wet and hard embedding in the flesh on my arms. The man was biting me, my skin pinched up between his sharp teeth. He tasted the shoe polish. Spit, cursed, and spit some more.

His hold loosened enough for me to back my head up off the ground and yell for him to get off me.

"Fielding?" The growl was gone from his voice.

"Mr. Elohim? What you doin'?"

"What *you* doin'?" He quickly let me go and moved back. "Walkin' the hours of night. All niggered up."

"I'm camouflaged." I wiped his slobbers off my arm, maybe some of my own blood. "You really bit me hard, Mr. Elohim."

He stood as he used his sleeve to wipe the polish from around his mouth. "I was merely usin' an old army technique to disarm the enemy."

He looked even shorter in the night, all white shirt and white jeans.

"I ain't the enemy, Mr. Elohim."

"Shoe polish makes ya close to it."

I sat there long after he left, maybe a little too long. I felt sore in the toes. Like I had been stretched up on them, looking over a ledge, straining to see what was. Up on toes, raising to the truth. Which was what? I wasn't yet sure. I knew it reminded me of something. Something I'd seen. A tractor breaking cobwebs in a field. Dead spiders on the wheels. That's what the truth I didn't yet know reminded me of. That's what its edge sang to me that night as my toes lowered me back down. Down to the quiet grass. But not for long. I had to pull myself up. I had things yet to hear.

The sheriff lived in a honey-colored brick house close to the center of town. The front of the house was dark, though there was a light in the back. I followed it and peeked through the open windows. The room had a table with three chairs pulled out. There was some hard candy on the table in an offering pile but no empty wrappers. Sal was too smart for that.

I eased down onto the dying grass below the window. I thought they would return to the room, so I sat there and waited so long, I fell asleep.

I dreamed myself, waving. Not hello, but good-bye. The waves falling from my hand in objects. Baseballs. Overalls. Dad's suits, three pieces at a time. Mom's aprons. My own fingers, falling. Me crumbling away until no one's at home. Just a pile of baseballs and aprons.

What was that sound?

The dream getting pushed back behind the reality of a June bug landing on my cheek and its wings buzzing together into a close. I brushed the bug off. It flew away wondering why. It was still night, but the light of the room had been turned off. The lost moment creaked like a door closing.

I headed home. As I was nearing Main Lane, the night filled with crystal sounds. I ran toward those sounds. When I got to the lane, I saw the streetlights were all broken, the lane left in a darkness that allowed whoever was shattering the store windows to do so unseen. I could hear their feet pounding on the brick sidewalks. Sometimes it sounded like one person. Other times it sounded like more.

In the houses close to the lane, lights began to flick on. Porches were lit and screen doors were opened.

Voices called out.

"What's goin' on out there?"

"Sounds like glass breakin'."

"Best check it out."

And so they came, running toward the lane with flashlights and questions. I was illuminated, while whoever was really at fault was running the other way.

"Hey, it's that black boy. He's out here breakin' the store windas."

They charged, bright light with feet, blinding my eyes. They were going to teach me a lesson, they said. I felt someone grab my arm. Someone else on the other. I tried to tell them it was me.

"Kill 'im." A woman's voice. She said it so casual, I imagined her standing there in her housecoat and slippers and hair rollers, one arm around her waist, propping the other up to her mouth, where a cigarette slipped in and out, smooth like a dream.

Someone wrapped their arms around my neck. I was pulled back into a sweating, bare chest. The hair on it as dense as the foliage of a jungle and me straining not to get lost to the jaguars.

"Hey, let 'im go."

Was that Grand's voice?

"I said get off 'im."

Yes. Superman in Levi's. Seeing his blue eyes was like seeing the day breaking the night as he punched one in the face and threatened the others with the same. He grabbed the arms that were holding me and yanked them back, kicking their groins. I felt one of the hands slip away on its own.

"His skin's comin' off," the hand said.

Grand stopped. They all did. Flashlights were turned toward the hand, brown shoe polish showing on its palm.

The other hands let go of me. The light left and made a backward turn to themselves, inspecting the color smeared upon them.

"Do you think it'll make us sick?" one of them asked.

"Don't know. Don't know what it is."

"It's his skin, just meltin' off. Must be the heat."

Even those hit by Grand no longer bent toward their pain. They looked at their own hands to see if they too had the come-off color.

"C'mon, quick, Fielding." Grand bent down. "Hop on my back. You haven't got shoes on. Glass is everywhere."

And so I rode the back of the god across the sky to the safe dark of the woods, where I slid off to the ground. Didn't want to, though.

"You're lucky I was out, Fielding."

"Thought you had a date?"

"She wasn't my type."

"I thought she was the girl everyone wants?"

"I went for a walk instead."

He had layers of sweat. One from the heat. One from the fight. One from his walk. One from the girl he did not want. The sweat making a circle on his shirt at the small of his back like some sort of ripe fruit.

I was about to say something more but the night was speaking my name.

"Sal? Is that you?"

He stepped from the trees.

"You know what's goin' on out there, Sal?" I pointed back. "Some-one's broken the windas and the streetlights. They—" I stopped when I saw what he held in his hand. "Why ya got a rock, Sal?"

He dropped it, and the thud sounded like a window breaking.

"Don't say it was you, Sal." Grand put his arm out in front of me, the way a mother might in a car suddenly stopping.

"Now, hold on, guys—" Sal took a step toward us.

"It was you. You broke those windas."

"No, Fielding."

"You've got a rock."

"Not to break anything, Grand." Sal's hands were up in a way I'd only ever seen on cop shows. "I'm gathering them. That's all. I'll show you." He quickly reached behind Grand to grab my arm, his grip hot and strong. "Please, let me show you."

I let him pull me through the woods with Grand following behind and on the way picking up the rock Sal had dropped. We ended up at the tree house. In the patch of dirt over Granny's body, a pile of rocks were freshly stacked.

"I was just making a gravestone." He let go of my arm, my flesh feeling almost burned.

"Just a gravestone." Grand placed the rock in his hand on the very top.

"Shit. I thought . . ." I walked around the rocks. "I'm sorry, Sal."

He looked down at his hand that had gripped my arm. "What do you have all over you?"

I didn't answer him. I was thinking about Elohim. About how he had attacked me earlier.

"He was just like a damn wolf," I told them. "Or a rabid dog, at the very least."

"Why'd he attack you?" Sal was still studying the shoe polish smeared on his palm.

"He thought I was you."

"Is that why you colored your skin? Trying to be me?"

"Naw. I was in disguise."

"As what?"

"As the night. I was sneakin' over to the sheriff's, see what all they were askin' you 'bout."

"Aw, little man, it's my fault then." Grand sighed. "I'm so глупый."

"I would've went even without you sayin' I should. I'm a shadow, remember?" I turned to Sal. "How'd it go with Dad and the sheriff, anyways?"

"They wanted me to eat candy and be a son from up north. To be something taken. They were upset to take the candle into my night and find I really am just the devil after all. Afterwards, Autopsy went home, but I came out here. I wonder who did it. Broke the windows. Let's go see."

"What?" I grabbed Sal's leaving arm. "No way. They saw the shoe polish on me. They think it was you. I thought they were gonna tear me to pieces. They would've if Grand hadn't stopped 'em."

"Anytime, little man." He lightly tapped my chin with his knuckles and then quickly looked away.

I'll never know how my adoring smiles affected my brother. Were they yellow and nice, like afternoon butter? Or were they pressure? Pressure to be that hero, that god who could be only at the sacrifice of his true self. Sometimes I think older brothers should not be allowed. We fall in love with them too much. They are our everything, all the while, they hurt out of sight for our sake.

"C'mon." Sal started through the woods. "Sheriff is bound to be there by now. They won't do anything around him. He'll stop them."

We hid behind the bushes lining Juniper's, hidden more by the trunks of the large trees in front. From there, we saw the sheriff's car, its spotlight on and reflecting in the broken glass.

Elohim was there, listening as person after person went up to the sheriff, claiming to have seen Sal.

One woman swore she saw Sal actually throwing the rocks. "I tried to take them rocks from 'im, but you know what he did? He picked up one of them glass shards. Cut me good."

The blood on her forearm glistened under the sheriff's flashlight.

"I can't believe they're actually believin' her," I whispered to Sal, watching him scratch his chin. In that gesture I saw the blood trickled down the back of his left hand.

"Where'd you get that blood from, Sal?" Grand saw it too.

"From checking Granny's pulse earlier. Remember, Fielding?"

"But it looks . . . fresh." Its shine was both beautiful and starved of that very thing.

"What they're sayin,' Sheriff, it's all true." Another witness stepped forward. "He threw a rock at me even. He ain't nothin' but a devil, a—"

Sal's interrupting shout, calling them liars, echoed for miles and made them jump as he stood and walked out toward them.

"Liars," he said again, rather hushed this time as he balled his hands up into fists at his sides.

A woman reached into the pocket of her bathrobe, pulling out her most holy ally. "Sheriff, I swear on my Bible that there devil has done this."

Sal dashed toward the woman, snatching the Bible out of her hand as the crowd gasped. He wound up his arm, just as Grand had taught him, and threw the Bible into the last remaining window on Main Lane, that of the butcher's.

Some will say the window did not break. That the Bible was too soft, not hard like the rocks. Others will say the window did indeed break into the sharpest pieces of all.

I say, never doubt the strength of a boy's arm.

II

His crime makes guilty all his sons

                  —MILTON, *PARADISE LOST* 3:290

AT THE BEGINNING of July, Mom turned forty-five years old. Me, Dad, Grand, and Sal baked her a cake. A lopsided, poorly frosted yellow cake she praised as the best ever.

Dad tugged on her tail of hair and made her laugh before giving her a diamond tennis bracelet. Grand's gift was a book of Walt Whitman poetry, the pages with his favorites dog-eared. I gave her a Bruce Springsteen cassette, and Sal gave her the rain.

"But there's been no rain," Grand questioned the water in the jar.

"I hopped a train and stopped at the first town it was raining in," Sal answered.

Mom held up the jelly jar with the slosh of water in its bottom. "A gift of the rain?" She looked through the jar at Sal on the other side.

"You never know," he said. "One day the rain might be just the gift you need."

She thanked Sal, but held the jar fearfully. It was only faucet water. I'd seen Sal fill it up myself. I never did say anything to Mom, so she never doubted its origin from the sky. She even had Dad keep it in his study, just to be on the safe side.

She rarely went into the study during the course of that summer, as it had become a second sheriff's station with the cork bulletin board pinned with papers, notes, and a map of Ohio, upon which more pins showed the locations of all the missing boys. The sheriff came frequently to the house, updating Dad on the investigation, and together they'd look at that board and try to find Sal.

One of the papers had a phone number written on it. It was the number for the Columbus hospital. One day they might say Dovey was better, might even be able to move her out of critical care, they'd say. Then the next thing you knew, there'd been a setback, the baby's vitals weren't looking so good.

Based on the records Dad played, you could tell what days were good news days and what days were not. You knew the baby might make it if Dad put on Louis Armstrong and "What a Wonderful World." But if he played Samuel Barber's *Adagio for Strings,* you knew there is such a thing as infinite slips and falls and high-pitched chaos.

On Mom's birthday, it was the sad latter. Dad did wait until the end of the day, after the celebrating, to put the record on. As I lay in bed, hearing the strings below, I thought about the baby and what work it is to be born.

I wondered if their child would look like a muscled dove, the build of its father and its mother. I prayed for its birth, quietly and in myself. I prayed not to God, but to Dovey's womb to give birth to the son who may serve as the miracle to that summer. A miracle to rest the fray.

"Sal?" I looked over at him lying in the window bed. "When's your birthday?"

"The devil doesn't have a birthday."

"Ah, c'mon, Sal."

"You want me to lie? Tell you my birthday is, I don't know, February second or something?"

"Is that when it is? February second?"

"Do you really think the devil's birthday would be in winter?" He was quiet. Then with his arms behind his head and his eyes upon the ceiling, he told me about a man he once knew who had a wife and a son.

"Every year for this man's birthday he would ask the woman and child to get him a long rope as his gift. A rope long enough to stretch around their house. An easy feat, as their house was so small, just a blur, really.

"When he would wrap this rope around the house, he did so beginning at the porch steps, ending there also with a knot that was like a swarm of brown flies too easily swatted away.

"During the course of his year from one birthday to the next, the man would shorten the rope. He would swat the knot away, and from there, whenever he was the reason for the bruise, for the wound, for the shivering terror, he would take the ax and chop off a piece of the rope. He swore that if ever his evil lunged so far and for so long, making the rope short enough to make a noose, he would hang himself, knowing he had put the sun under the wheel and run over the light one too many times.

"The wife and child thought well of the man's purpose with the rope. That he documented his sins by it and bound himself to the crack of his own abyss. They believed he would one day no longer sweat with the blade of the ax but that he would sit calm and peaceful within the circle of unbroken rope. That is the hope of the abused. That the bruises will leap away and the monster of the man will lift above his person like smoke.

"Then came the year the crops strained. The roots shifted and the dry fields began to constrict like throats too weak even to muster a whisper, all the while the man couldn't stop screaming. Little can be done to mute the roaring monster. Pity too, because up to then, the man had been good. The rope had barely been chopped away. But every day the crops yellowed and the ground cracked, the shorter the rope and the angrier the man.

"The fields were unnerving him at a rate the rope had never known. Perhaps it was the man's fear that the fields would never grow again.

That his American chance would go to the grave in the dirt around him. Whatever it was, it spurred a cycle of fists and blood and screams. The small house felt even smaller. Their bellies felt even emptier. *Bang, bang, bang* went the man. *Chop, chop, chop* went the rope.

"Then came the day the man got so angry at the woman. The reason I forget. I always forget the reasons. They were always such small drops. Burnt meat. Overalls not yet patched. Too lax a look when looking out upon the barren fields. Things that wouldn't be cured by a fist to the cheek but the man tried that day as he beat his wife down to the floor, while the son watched from the doorway but only out of his left eye, as his right was still low and swollen and like peering through milkweed.

"The son knew if he helped his mother, he too would get poured upon by his father's lava and he was still burnt from yesterday. If the boy had it to do over, he would do something to help his mother, but something is hard to come by when you're only nine years old and stalked by the shattering blow. You are so exhausted that to not be beaten is to squeeze into the crevice of light, even if it means your mother is beaten in your place.

"It was a terrible day to be hurt in the kitchen. The sun coming in the windows, the spots of light looking like lemons scattered across the floor. The screen door opening the room to the sweet air and the clothesline outside, where the just-washed dish towels flapped in the breeze.

"All the while, the woman lay there on the floor, doing her best shield. That was her way. To be still. To take it and all its killing. It was like seeing a handkerchief try to cling to a window screen during a tornado. You knew she would lose in the end, and when the blow to her face came, there was no more clinging to the screen for a chance.

"She was knocked unconscious. Her face bleeding like old red rivers from broken ground. The man quickly scooped her up in his arms and ran out the door with her. He was always good when it came to the save, and as he sped the woman to the doctor, the boy cleaned up the blood with a mop, afterwards wringing it out in the dying fields as if the drops of his mother's blood would in some way pay for the crops' growth.

"When the man returned, having left the woman with the doctor, he took the ax and chopped the rope down until it was short enough. He carried the rope up to the porch, where he hung it from the exposed beams of the ceiling. With the loop around his neck, he stood on the stool, checking it back and forth. Without more, he kicked the stool over, grunting as his body jerked down.

"Having not had his neck broken, the toes of his boots dangled just above the porch boards as he hung there with his still arms by his side. Suddenly he started to thrash, though looking more like he was rummaging through some drawers than losing his life.

"The boy would have thought had this moment ever come to pass, he would pull up a chair and watch patiently as his father strangled to death. Instead the boy ran and stood up the stool so it was there for his father's feet once more. The father kicked it back over. Let it be said, the father did want to die. It was the son who didn't want him to.

"Once more, the boy stood the stool up beneath his father's feet. In kicking for the stool, the father kicked the boy, who fell back onto the two-pronged pitchfork they would use when gathering hay from the fields.

"The father used the last of himself to hoist his legs up onto the porch rail, supporting his body as he loosened the rope from around his neck. He smelled of piss and whiskey as he scooped his crying son up. He's always been good with the saving, the boy thought as his father carried him inside and laid him on the bed.

"The father very carefully cleaned and dressed the two large gashes going up the boy's back, along his shoulder blades. As he did so, the father apologized, and the boy reached out to the noose marks.

"'Promise you won't do it again, Pa. Promise you won't let the rope get so short again.'

"The father looked down at his son. 'You'll have to help me. I can't keep it long on my own. You must help me.'

"Later that night, while the father lay asleep beside the boy, the boy got out of bed and went to the porch. He took down the noose and carried it to the yard where the other pieces of chopped rope were piled. Piece by piece, he tied the rope together until it was long enough to stretch whole once again around their house. When the father woke the next morning and saw the rope, he promised his son, in the sober morning light, that the rope would stay together forever. In the world of truth, it stayed complete for seven months.

"While the rope was chopped after that, it was never chopped so short again to make a noose, and the son, while bruised, was always grateful to the father for at least keeping the rope long enough, because if it were to happen again, the son knew he would not prop the stool back up beneath his father's thrashing legs."

When I was twenty-one, I was with a woman with hair like rope. I say *woman* because she was thirty-seven. She had this small cabin by a lake in Maine. During the day, I'd go off to the town to replace the spires of the boot factory I'd been hired at. She'd go to work as the secretary of that factory. All day I'd be on the roof, on top of her, and then at night we'd go to that cabin, and all night she'd be on top of me.

I liked her. But I loved her hair. It was dark and long enough to graze the backs of her calves. During the day at work, she wore it up in a braided bun. But at night, at the cabin, she let the braid go loose, twisting and turning and so much like rope, I named her that very thing.

I remember how she'd stand up out of bed, naked in front of the windows. The moonlight silvering her flesh. She'd take her braid and circle it around her thin waist. It went all the way around, making the trip back to her belly button, where she would gently tie a loose knot.

"My, my." She'd click her tongue and look down, admiring what her hair could do. She'd say her hair was like Samson's and was where all her strength came from. Then I'd pat the bed and she'd come over, her legs around me, her hands on my chest, her rope stretched back. I came feeling like a good man who had not yet picked up the ax.

I stayed in Maine with her that winter, long after I'd finished working on the spires of the factory. I found other work to do in town.

Then, at the end of January, while standing in only a pair of wool socks, she wrapped her hair around her waist. The ends would not tie in a knot.

"It has begun," she whispered.

That night I heard the chop of an ax. As the weeks went on, soon the ends of her hair would make it only to her side. *Chop, chop, chop.*

"Have you been cutting your hair?" I asked her.

"My belly is getting bigger. It's making my hair shorter."

Of course I knew that. I just didn't want to say it. Neither of us ever said it. She just started buying bigger clothes, and I suddenly made a cradle for the back bedroom. There wasn't a plan to make the cradle. I just one day picked up a handsaw and a piece of wood, and next thing I knew, I had a bed for my child in front of me.

The closest we ever got to discussing the baby was the night she asked me what I thought.

"Fielding? I asked what you think?"

I'll say it now because all the years in the world have passed, and I am old enough to know I wanted the child.

I knew I would be no good for it. I would build it cradles, yes, but wouldn't actually cradle it myself. How could I with my sleeves drenched in blood? The snake has had its victories over me. And in its victories I am no longer sweet nor gentle. The very things a good father must be. It's impossible to make a family when your mind spins mad with the old monsters. Isn't it?

The fear of being the horrible father was a noose tightening around my neck. It was why when she asked what I thought, my answer was, "I don't like how your hair doesn't wrap around anymore."

That long rope that in its length meant I could have a shot at a good life. Its length meant I hadn't done anything bad yet to chop it off. But wasn't her growing belly my bad inside her? Wasn't that growth an ax, making the rope shorter, making her weaker? And weaker she'd gotten.

Pregnancy did not give her that glow. It gave her a redness to the cheeks like punches. It drooped her eyes from all the sleeping she did not do. And mornings sounded like sickness being flushed down the toilet. Maybe she was like Samson, the long hair her strength, and I was Delilah, cutting it shorter and shorter with the wielding ax I put inside her.

I suppose I said the wrong thing to her, for shortly after, she began buying castor oil. It was said the oil would help with hair growth, so every night she'd slather it on, staining pillowcase after pillowcase. Even if her hair had grown, it wouldn't have shown, because her growing belly was always outpacing her hair.

Castor oil was everywhere. On the doorknobs, on her clothes, on her forehead from where the oil dripped from her scalp. She was sent home from work because the oil kept dripping onto all the paperwork.

Then came the day she drank the oil. I didn't know, I tell you. I was off at work, trying to wipe the castor oil off my hands. Later in the hospital, she would say she drank it because she thought it would make her hair grow from the inside out, like a big oily vitamin.

"Oh, Fielding, I had no idea it could affect the baby. I wouldn't have drank it. Doctor?" She wanted to make sure he heard too. All the nurses as well. She didn't want them to think she had tried an at-home abortion. "I didn't know it could induce labor. And as soon as the blood and the cramps came, well, I called straightaway for an ambulance. It felt like a kick to my stomach. Oh, Fielding, stop looking at me like that. Please. I didn't do this on purpose. Fielding, I said I didn't do this on purpose."

Later, when she was out of the hospital, she stood in front of the windows, the moonlight upon her flat stomach. She pulled her hair all the way around her waist, just as she always had before.

"Now you can love me again. Fielding? I said, look, the hair goes all the way around, just as before. Now you can love me again. We can start over."

That night, while she slept in her castor oil crown, I went to the back bedroom, picked up the cradle, and threw it into the lake, watching it sink like a ship beneath the dark water.

I never went back to Maine. I did buy a rope. I did make a necklace on a porch one night. I did think of Sal as the stool wobbled. I did make the rope too long, as my toes landed on the porch floor and became the son who saved me, if only for that one, brief moment.

12

THE FLYERS ABOUT him first came as inserts in the vegetarianism pamphlets. By July, Elohim started writing so much about Sal that those inserts became pamphlets all their own. These pamphlets led to meetings held every afternoon in the woods.

When I overheard the sheriff telling Dad he was going to stop by Elohim's to have a chat, I ran through the neighbors' backyards as the sheriff drove down the lane to Elohim's. I snuck up through the side of Elohim's yard, hunkering below his windows, should he be near them. Then I crouched by the lattice, waiting for him to answer the sheriff's knock.

They sat down on the porch in the padded wicker chairs while the sheriff reminded Elohim of how he said he wouldn't speak ill of Sal anymore.

"Now, Sheriff"—Elohim's smile was careful—"I never said that. What I said was I would talk to folks and help 'em understand the possibility of Dovey fallin' on her own. I said I would tell 'em that that car hittin' that boy was perhaps an accident after all. I never said I wouldn't go further. I never said I wouldn't speak ill of him on other issues. Folks have got a right to know about the devil in their midst, and I am merely describin' his flames for them. Now, I ain't sayin' I'm tellin' folks to run 'im outta town. That wouldn't do me no good."

"Do *you* no good?" The sheriff spit between the columns of the porch.

Elohim quickly controlled his disgust as he turned from the spit that had landed on the leaves of the hostas, which were drying and yellowing in the drought, though still relevant and lining the front of his porch.

"It would do none of us any good, runnin' an evil off like we're too weak and too scared to take care of our own problems. As if we zero in bravery and sword. We can't forget, we are the lords of our own 'round here, and we alone hiss back the serpent."

"Now, Elohim, I'm warnin' ya right now to leave that boy alone. I trusted you to do no harm. You waited till the Blisses got custody, and now you're startin' up again. You best get used to that boy. Their custody might not be temporary after all. We're talkin' 'bout a boy that could be part of their family permanently. Every family is part of this town. Don't hurt the town, now, Elohim. You hurt us all, and there ain't gonna be enough bandages to heal every wound."

"Sheriff, I am merely keepin' information and knowledge alive and healthy."

"Shit, Elohim." The sheriff crossed his snakeskin boots at the ankles. "You got more followers than the church now."

"That's 'cause the preacher finds it hard to point the snake out. That preacher has always been on the cautious side of things. Him and his khakis. He's from Canada, for Christ's sake. What the hell is he doin' down here? We ain't his people. He ain't one of us. He ain't got Ohio soil shakin' off his roots, he ain't got hands for squeezin' river mud through fingers, and he sure the hell ain't got the holster that the hills and the hollers put at our hips."

"I ain't got Ohio soil on my roots either. You forget that?"

"But ya got the South on 'em, and ain't that a magnolia closer than anything Canadian? Listen, it ain't my fault if that careful preacher can't keep an audience. Folks come to me 'cause I'm one of 'em. Maybe more than that, they come to me 'cause I don't candy the horns and I certainly don't dignify the demon.

"But don't you worry your badge, Sheriff. We are a refined group, me and mine. We don't force our ideas or pamphlets on nobody, we simply offer them. As I will offer them to you now."

The sheriff accepted Elohim's offered pamphlet with a grunt. As the sheriff started to read it, Elohim spoke more about his group.

"Our meetin's are held out in the woods, far from the town. You don't have to hear or see us if you don't wanna. We are simply a concerned group. I can assure you we are not on hunt. We are merely on guard."

The meetings were held, just as Elohim said they were, out in the woods in that abandoned one-room schoolhouse close to the tree house. The schoolhouse had at one time caught fire, burning the roof away and leaving only the brick shell. Inside this shell, Elohim raised his religion to his followers, which at first was a small group that steadily gained members over the course of that summer. It was a funny thing. One day you'd hear someone warning about Elohim's cult. Then the next day that very someone would be at the meetings like they'd always been there.

Elohim was smart to hold the meetings out in the woods, where there were no fans, no air conditioners, no way of alleviating or escaping the heat. The heat was his partner. It was what connected his words to their sweat, his furnace to their melt.

Those meetings consumed Elohim. Before, he could be gone from Breathed for months at a time as his work took him across the country. There wasn't enough steeplejacking to be done in Breathed alone to be profitable. Long-held travel was necessary.

His obsession with Sal forced Elohim to find other work closer to home, like roofing jobs, burning brush with his propane torch, and patching concrete like what he did in Juniper's.

I hadn't worked with him on a roof since before Sal arrived, so on that day, after the sheriff left, I followed Elohim to a job. When he put all his tools into a small wagon, I knew the roof would be close by.

It ended up being a cinder block house, a few lanes away.

As he stared up at the chimney of pale, beige brick, I went to him with my head down. We hadn't spoken since the night he attacked me. His teeth marks were gone from my skin, but they were fossilized underneath. Branded upon my bone. I have no doubt they would show up on X-ray. I am his walking dental record.

"Hey, Mr. Elohim."

He dropped his eyes from the chimney to me. The way he looked at me was as if he were looking at someone taller, at someone wider, at someone more beast-sized than human. I was no longer the boy he used to know. I was friends with the demon, and in that friendship, I became transformed as such.

"What *you* want?"

What I wanted was the Elohim I used to know. The man who taught me how to repair belfries, how to hold a chisel properly, how to save myself from roofs. The man who once saved me when I wasn't saving myself. When my foot slipped and I was going down, it was him who kept me from falling two stories below. That is what I wanted. The saving hand.

"I just wondered if I could help ya today, Mr. Elohim."

"I'll be needin' your assistance no more. I cannot associate with someone who associates with . . . Well, you know who I'm referrin' to. You have to understand somethin'. We build chimneys and towers and steeples. In essence, we are buildin' and erectin' starts to heaven.

"They may not reach there, but they are the start of somethin' to there. I cannot, in good faith, build with someone who associates with the great antithesis of God Himself. What if one day one of these starts we build together ends up bein' the first step of the devil's climb? And all because I allowed evil to build the beginnin'."

He watched me scratch a scab off my arm until I drew blood. "I really liked steeplejackin' with ya, Mr. Elohim."

I remember the first time I stood on a roof with him. A storm had caused damage to the church's steeple. Of all the roofs I've done, that of Breathed's carpenter church has always been my favorite.

As he assessed the damage to the spire, I sat back on the ledge of the belfry and looked out at Breathed. He came and sat by my side, sighing something like, "Beautiful, ain't it?"

"Yeah," I must have said, and probably nodded.

"You can see the top of everything. Well, not everything, but a lot more than other folks ever see. Look there at the top of that tree. Top of that car. Top of that house. Top of that woman's hat and that man's head. I never see the tops of most things unless I'm standin' on a roof.

"It's funny 'cause the top of my head is the only thing anybody ever sees of me. Folks think when they look at the top of my head, all they're seein' is the top of a short man. But they're really lookin' down at roofs, trees, hills. I got 'em all right on top of here." He tapped the top of his head. "I'll never be a tall man, Fielding, but by God, I'll never be a short one either. No matter what folks may say."

"Listen, Mr. Elohim." I shoved my hands into my pockets as I watched him pick up the tools from the wagon. "I hear ya 'bout the ladders and chimneys and steeples bein' starts to heaven. But, today, well, today you're fellin' a chimney. Right?"

He nodded his head as he examined the end of one of the chisels.

"Then I reckon me helpin' ya today, for one last time, wouldn't be so bad, because we'll be tearin' the ladder down, stoppin' the start to heaven and I suppose 'cause of that it wouldn't be such a bad thing if I helped ya this last time. It'd be like we were tearin' the start down so the devil couldn't finish it. That there's the opposite of wicked work."

It was a slow coming around, but eventually he did see me as the boy he used to know. How could he not? The way I urged him to with my eyes, with my smile, with my begging, "Please."

"I suppose there's no harm in the fellin'." He handed the chisel to me. "One last time."

Before we climbed the ladder, we said the little something we always said:

> Up I go, up so high,
> I pray I do not fall and die.
> But if I should, let it be said,
> I'm mighty missed, now that I'm dead.

It was a chimney easily removed one brick at a time using the single jacks, small sledgehammers, along with tempered steel chisels. By the time we dismantled the portion of the chimney above the roofline, it was late and Elohim said I should go home, that the remainder of the chimney in the house was work he would do alone.

I picked up my shirt I'd taken off to use as a sweat rag. But I couldn't go. Not before I knew.

"Why you hate Sal so much, Mr. Elohim?"

He wiped his forehead with his handkerchief as he sat down on the roof. I think he must have gotten sweat in his eyes from the way he blinked.

"Some folks think just 'cause I set her plate at mealtimes, wash her clothes, wear this weddin' ring that I don't know my Helen is dead. I know she is. Did you know she was an art historian? Yep, sure was. And in 1956, she went to France, to look at a paintin'. I missed her terribly, probably more than I should've.

"One night I had a little too much to drink. I stumbled to the phone and called her hotel room in Paris. A man answered. An American. A nigger."

He bit his fingernail off and swallowed it before saying, "I could tell that's what he was. They got a different sound. Sure ain't the sound of a white man.

"I hung up. Dialed the operator, told her to get the number for God. She never did say nothin', just laughed. I hung up on her too. It wasn't God I really wanted anyways. They say if you wanna get things done, you gotta get hold of the devil.

"So I picked up the phone again, but I didn't dial nothin', I just waited. The dial tone hummed in my ear, then it crackled and I knew. I knew he had picked up."

I shifted beside him. "He?"

"The devil. I told 'im what I wanted. Told 'im I wanted Helen home. He didn't say nothin', but I knew he understood. The next day I got a call from Helen. I asked her 'bout the man who answered her phone. She said it was just a hotel worker, bringin' more towels and for me not to worry 'cause she was comin' home early. Had booked passage on the *Andrea Doria,* she said. Wasn't I happy? she asked."

He fell quiet, and together we watched a hawk go flying by. When it landed, he spoke again, rather low in the chest. "The so-called hotel worker came to her funeral. A tall son-of-a-bitch. I recognized his voice when he came up to me to offer his condolences. I hated the way he bent down to talk to me, like I was a damn child. Told 'im that. Told 'im I thought it funny he would come all that way from Paris for a woman he'd just brought towels to."

The silence that followed was like practicing for death. That lonely silence that describes the dark so well. A fly came and landed on the back of his hand. I shooed it away for him because he just sat there, a concreted form, heavy and still.

"Mr. Elohim? You okay?"

His head seemed unsteady on his neck as he said, "Turned out he was a painter. An artist. I suppose they like that distinction. I saw his work years later in a museum up in Cleveland. He had a paintin' called the *Andrea Doria.* It didn't have the ship in it, though." He bit and swallowed another fingernail. "It had Helen. Beautiful paintin', I'll give 'im that."

His trembling hands gripped his knees.

"My momma, God rest her soul, used to say a black boy is only good till he reaches thirteen. After that, he's man bound, and a black man's no good for nothin', especially since they passed all them laws on workin' 'em.

"I thought of my momma and what she had said as that man shook my hand at Helen's funeral. I thought, gee, if only someone had stopped him from growin' up. Just ate his future away, I would still have mine."

I didn't know what to say. I didn't know what to do, really, except lay my hand on his back and pat like I'd seen Dad do before.

Elohim slowly turned to me. "Don't pat my back like I'm a damn dog, boy. I'm a man, for Christ's sake." He stood, trying his best to make himself taller. "I think you better go on home. And, Fielding, keep all I just said to yourself. I shouldn't even have said it. It's just sometimes you don't say nothin' for so long, you forget why ya shut up in the first place. Oh, and Fielding? You might wanna let that boy know somethin'."

"What?"

"Dovey lost that baby."

He didn't say it cruelly. Nor did he say it as if it were a victory for him and his. He said it like a man tired of describing what *lost* means.

13

I'VE NEVER BEEN married, though when I was twenty-eight, I was close to it. Got the tux and everything. Even went to the church. She was a lovely girl. Maybe a little too much hair. She was always putting this white cream on her upper lip. I'd walk into the bathroom, and there'd she'd be, snow on the face.

Years after we were to be married, I would hear she died in a car crash in Minnesota. They didn't find the accident right away. The state was in the middle of a blizzard, and by the time they come upon the car, only its roof was visible. Windshield was in a bad way. They knew she'd been ejected. They shined a flashlight around. *Beam, beam, beam.* Saw something a few feet out. It was her lips. That was all that was seen. The rest of her was covered by snow.

Snow on the face, and I've hated Minnesota ever since.

I don't know. Maybe I should've married her, but when I got to the church, I found myself staring up at its steeple. I didn't have a ladder, so I had to stand on the outside sill of a window and reach up and grab the gutter. Then I just pulled myself up. I used to be strong like that. They heard my feet walking across the roof, that's what they said when they all came out of the church to stare up at me. Said they heard a noise and came out to see.

"What are you doing up there?" they asked.

"Fixing the steeple," I answered.

I didn't have my tools with me, so I had to improvise. I heard someone down below say I was mad, the way I gripped air and hammered it too. The way I sounded out the sound of steel hitting wood. I had gone temporarily around the bend. Don't we get to at least once in our lives? To go so mad, we survive what it is we are doing. And what I was doing was jilting the woman who loved me. My God, what I must've done to her heart.

I heard someone from below say I had always been good for nothing. I picked up one of my invisible crowbars and flung it his way. He didn't flinch.

I suppose someone told her I was on the roof. She came running out of the church, white dress and all. I heard her mother saying, "Mary, get back inside. He's not supposed to see you yet."

But Mary didn't care. Mary only ever heard what she wanted to hear. It was her fault we got as far as we did to the church.

One day I said *Mary* and then I said something else, I know I did, but ended it all with a *me*. She thought I'd said *Marry me*. I didn't have the heart to tell her that wasn't what was said at all. She was just so excited. I thought, hell, this girl really wants to marry me. Why not give it a try? Maybe her love would be enough to paradise the hell. But then I realized, I couldn't use her like that. Like a shield in the fray. She deserved to marry a man who loved her for all the things she was and not for all the armor she could be.

As she stared up at me that day on the roof, she knew exactly what I was doing up there. I'll always be grateful for her, how she never asked me to come down like everyone else did. She just took off her veil and told her mother she'd like to stop by Denny's on the way home. She was hungry, she said.

That was the last I saw of her, her white dress piling up against her body like the snow I never saved her from.

I waited for them all to leave. I cringed when I heard a woman call me a no-good son-of-a-bitch. Even the flower girl flipped me the bird. I threw an invisible hammer at her. She just dropped her chin to her chest and shook her head as she walked away, dragging her feet while the flower petals fell from her hand.

Before I climbed down, I yanked some of the shingles off the steeple, kicked it in the side, and broke the stained glass in its little window. A week later, I'd drive by the steeple and see it was still damaged.

Some people might call me lonely because all I got are pictures of steeples and towers and roofs. I do have the neighbor boy's photograph, but he's not mine. Like I said before in Maine, I wouldn't have done much good with a kid if I had one. I did have a dream once that I had a son. In this dream, I went out to the woods with him and put a gun in his young hands. I woke up at the bang.

"Just a nightmare," I muttered, reaching for the bottle by the bed. "Just a nightmare."

Maybe I am lonely. Maybe I do hold onto the pillow at night, maybe I have twisted a bread tie around my ring finger just to see what it feels like to have a meaning there. I think of Elohim during these moments.

Him and his Helen.

Too bad he couldn't just let go of what she had done to him. After all, it wasn't the losing of her to the *Andrea Doria* he'd been destroyed by. It was the losing of her to another. It's a gasoline betrayal when the romance of your lover becomes a separate energy from you. It lessens your significance as lover. As man.

Spark, spark, hiss, and burn.

I've been with many Helens. Their legs around me. My head on their husbands' pillows.

Sometimes a husband would come home early. I'd hear his tires crunching over the gravel in the drive. She'd throw my clothes at me, tell me to get out. That the window was the best bet. I'd just lie there.

"What are you doing?" She'd try to pull me up. Fear in her whisper, "He's gonna catch you."

I could hear his keys in the front door.

"Honey, I'm home," he'd call, like a sitcom. I could tell his head was down, looking over the mail he'd just brought in. "Honey?" A step creaking on his way up while she yanks on my arm, telling me he has a gun.

"Does he know how to shoot it?"

She'd shriek and look at me with fear like she could already see the blood and all the cleaning up she'd have to do. Blood is hard to wash out, I knew she was thinking, her eyes rolling like washing machines already starting the job.

Only when the doorknob turned with his hand did I grab my clothes and throw them out the window, me jumping after. I'd wait in the yard, thinking he knew. How could he not? How could he not smell me all over her? All over his sheets? His pillow? But the curtains would close and no guns would fire.

Later the bartender would say to me, *you look like you could use a drink.* Later after that, he'd say I'd had enough and I'd have to use my fists to say otherwise.

I dated a girl named Andrea once. I could feel her sinking under me into the downy comforter. I asked her if she ever heard of the *Andrea Doria.* She said no and said for me not to go so fast.

"Gentle, gentle." She patted my back.

I said, "I'm not a damn dog," and I came and she went disappointed and rolling off to the side, saying I shouldn't stay over anymore and not to call again and if it wouldn't be too much trouble to hand her some fresh sheets from out of the closet on my way out.

I wonder what lovers Sal and Dresden would've been if that summer would've been hot and nothing else. He would've kissed each one of her freckles and moved his hand up her leg. *Spark, spark, fire.* Orgasm is a many-flamed wonder to the thrusting bodies that in their fond collision makes husbands of boys and wives of girls.

I will say conversation was a long time coming between him and Dresden that summer. They first spoke with their eyes. Every look. Every glance. Every long stare and short one.

He would nail a poem to her oak. They weren't his work, these poems. They were Shakespeare, Keats, Whitman, all the old masters and the old standby lure for lovers everywhere.

He'd hide behind one of the other trees and watch her take the poem down from the nail. She'd bite her lip and tuck her frizzy hair behind her freckled ear as she read, sometimes long enough for me to think he'd given her a whole novel. I suppose she was reading the poem over and over again, finding the parts of it that were less Shakespeare and more Sal.

I climbed her tree with him once. She didn't know as she leaned back against its trunk, opening her book and circling its words. I think it was *Gone with the Wind,* but that could just be me going with the wind in my memory.

A few pages in, Sal signaled it was time to press on the branches. We leaned our whole weight in until they swayed. It was hard work, and some of the branches wouldn't move at all. That's an old oak for you. Its long, heavy limbs stretched out more than up to the sky. Limbs that were thick, drooping things like wet rope. One branch was heavy enough to flop all the way to the ground, resting on it as if reaching bottom was the most natural growth for a tree branch.

We stuck to the lighter branches in the middle, and to the even lighter and smaller branches of those branches. The higher you moved up into the tree, the smaller the limbs became and therefore the easier it was to move them.

There was no wind that day, so when she felt the movement of the tree above her, she looked up, frightened. Then she saw Sal and her fear melted away. She never even saw me, and I was really putting my back into it, shifting those damn branches just for her. Didn't even notice. All she saw was Sal.

"What are you doing, you silly boy?" She wrapped her sweater-covered arms around her book and swayed in tune with the branches, her long dress skimming the ground.

"Giving you a breeze on this very hot day." He lazed over a thick branch and smiled down at her as he used his back foot to stir a small twig, all the while I leaned everything I had into a great big bough. She never once looked over and saw. Instead she laughed at him, one of those laughs that's more open mouth than sound.

"Well, all right then. I'll let you get on with it. Silly boy."

She returned to her book and stayed long after circling the words on its pages. It was as if she couldn't bear to leave. She would look up at him, saying she was going to have to go soon, that her mother was going to be home. But then she'd lean back against the tree and stay for a while more.

Meanwhile, my arms and legs felt about to break off like the few smaller twigs that had become casualties of my wind. I told Sal I was going home, leaving by walking down the long branch that lay on the ground.

Dresden suddenly turned, surprised to see me. "Where'd you come from?"

"My God. Didn't you see me? I was half of that wind up there."

Her shrug was limp, and for that moment I genuinely hated her, maybe because I wanted her to see me as much as she saw Sal. I shook my head and kicked a small gravel past her plastic black flat before heading home. Even at the end of the lane, I could see that tree slowly waving one branch at a time. The only tree in Breathed that day in motion.

Sal stayed long after she went inside. By the time Alvernine pulled up the drive in her Mercedes, he was still there. Alvernine wasn't the type of woman to look up in the trees.

As night came, Dresden pulled a chair to her front bedroom window so she could sit and watch him move the branches just for her. It was late and she tried desperately to keep her eyes open. Before she knew it, her head was in her hands. Then it was on the windowsill. And then it was on the pillow in her bed. She apologized to him in her sleep.

Even with her asleep and curled up with her back to him, he did not stop. He was up in that tree until the middle of the night, when a real wind came and made his something special into something everywhere.

He crawled home, hunched and sore. All that for just one girl. I asked him why, out of all the girls in the world, why Dresden Delmar?

He winced from his sore limbs as he told about the time he went on a drive.

"I went with my—" He stopped himself, swallowing what he was going to say.

"With who, Sal?"

"With a man and a woman I used to know. The man's eyes drooped from tiredness. Her eyes drooped for that and more. The two of them together could stunt a chance. Still, the drive looked to be a fine one. The woman even turned on the radio and sang along. I didn't know she knew any songs. I certainly didn't know he did. I certainly did not know they could make music together.

"Everything seemed all right. I even think I sang with them. And then the man lost control of the car and we swerved to a stop by the side of the road. Something had punctured the tire, and we didn't have a spare. The man was angry because it was the woman's idea to go driving in the first place. It was autumn. She had wanted to see the leaves.

"He kicked the tire, said 'Goddamn,' and then punched her. Not the first time. Not the last time. Just another time that would black her eye. The man looked down at his fist, stuffed it into his pocket, and went walking toward the town we'd passed a couple miles back.

"The woman sat down on the ground by the car, her dress her best rag. I sat with her, leaning forward with my arms wrapped around my legs. I could feel her fingers trace the scars on my back under the overalls."

"Your wing scars?" I felt my own back tightening.

He wiped his hand over his mouth, the way an old man might dust food crumbs.

"As she traced them, she said she was sorry. I traced her eye and its coming bruise and said I was sorry. And there, both sorry, we held each other until the man returned with the night and a spare. He smelled like a barstool. Looked like one too, with his wobbling eyes.

"Her hand shook as she held the flashlight while he changed the tire. He yelled at her to stop shaking the damn light like that, so she handed it to me and I held it still. Though I don't know how.

"After the tire was changed, we drove the dirt roads, his anger driving off. He pointed out the windows at the leaves. Told her to look at all their yellow and red and orange. She squinted and really tried, but said she couldn't see them. It was the night's fault, she said, not his.

"He reached over and she flinched. He said it was okay, he wasn't going to hurt her, he said. He was just unrolling her window. She still looked nervous as he reached across her lap. He unrolled the window quick and beamed at her. Now you can see, he said with hopeful certainty. But she sighed. It was too dark.

"He looked at the tears slipping down her cheeks. He caught one on the back of his finger. He was sorry about earlier, he said as he looked down at her trembling hands folded on her lap. When it got later, he always got sorry about earlier.

"She said it was all right. The way she always did. He slowed the car and parked off the road. Without a word, he got out and me and the woman watched as the dark of him was swallowed by the dark of the woods.

"When he emerged from those woods, he carried something. Fallen leaves that he spread throughout the car. Over the seats and floor, the dashboard, the woman's lap, my lap. Then he took the flashlight and shined it on a leaf.

" 'It's not too dark now, is it? Do you see the leaf, Mother?' he asked. 'How yellow it is?' And she answered, 'Yes, Father, I see. I see now.'

"They always called each other Mother and Father even though they weren't that to each other."

"What'd they call you, Sal?"

He did not answer me. He instead smiled and said, "It was beautiful. All them leaves. All that light. The smile on her face. The relief on his that she still loved him. That he hadn't smacked it out of her just yet. He kept shining that light and she told me to come up from the backseat, onto her lap.

"From there I saw orange maples, yellow oaks, red elms. When there were no more leaves to see, when we had seen each and every one he had collected, he patted his lap and said to me, 'Here, prop your feet up here.' I laid my feet there and he laid his hand on top. It was warm. It was nice. And it stayed there the whole way home."

"Sal, is this the same man with the rope? The same woman beaten in the kitchen? The same boy with the stool for his father?" I wanted to ask those questions, but I feared the answer.

"You asked me, Fielding, why, out of the whole world, why Dresden Delmar?" He looked off into the distance and squinted as if what he saw there was quite possibly the brightest thing in the world. "It's because her freckles are scattered like the leaves across the woman's lap. Her eyes shine like the light in the man's hand. Her hair is as red as the red leaf we passed between the three of us, like the love we could not simply say."

14

. . . with a pleasing sorcery, could charm
Pain for a while or anguish, and excite
Fallacious hope

—MILTON, *PARADISE LOST* 2:566–568

THE FINALE OF fear is first neared by small labors of bravery. These small labors will eventually lead to the last laboring of the great defeat of the fear altogether. That is the breathing text of hope anyways, that we branch an escape from fear's trapping circle.

For my mother, her small labor of bravery was learning how to swim. The acoustics of which involved no splashing water, as her swimming was in her fear's circle and therefore in the house. She was nearing the finale of her fear, and though she was not yet there, Sal was tiring her to the nightmare and introducing her to the dream.

Let it be said that my mother didn't always live life inside. Before I was born, she went out into the world quite regularly. Soon after I was born, she refused to leave the house without an umbrella. By the time I was one, the umbrella proved not to be enough, and she found herself fleeing the world and its lack of ceiling.

For a number of years, Dad tried to help her conquer her fear. He brought in therapists and read various psychological books himself to better understand. Ultimately, the therapists failed and the answer was not found in any book.

Dad, as well as me and Grand, accepted that she may never leave the house again. It was Sal who did not accept this. He was calling out her world and letting her know it would win a carpenter a prize, but it'd never be a darling of the universe where the stars commit to the real thing.

Every day, he asked her to go outside with him. Every day, she said no, but he was wearing her down with the way he described what she was missing. Simple things like the new bench outside Papa Juniper's. The Fourth of July parade down Main Lane and its red, white, and blue confetti. The language of the farthest reaching echo shouted in the coal mines, the just-built windmill in the sunflower field outside town, the way the sky looked when standing on the last claim of Breathed land.

His observations and carefully detailed description of the world were making her antsy. Making her wring her hands and suddenly suck in her breath as if for the longest time she'd not been breathing.

I'd find her looking out the windows or craning her neck off the edge of the porch, longing to see beyond the limited landscape her stuck life afforded her.

At the very best, she'd linger on the edge of the porch, reaching her hand out and testing for rain before snapping it back to her chest, swearing she'd felt a sprinkle, when in reality, it was the slight falling from her own eyes.

Melancholy is the woman with ribs like nails and lies like hammers. My mother's lie was that our house could be enough. That its countries could keep her from feeling like she was missing out. What a housebound woman fears is not the knife in the kitchen drawer. It is the outside being better.

"Stella, please come outside," Sal begged.

"It looks to pour any minute." She folded her arms and rubbed her hands up and down her mole-speckled shoulders as she paced in front of the sunny windows.

"You'll never get her outside." Dad was passing by and had overheard us on his way to his study. In his hand was a new box of pushpins.

The bulletin board had gotten crowded with more papers, more pins, more lines zigzagging this way and that. The progressing investigation meant more stacks of interviews with the families of the missing black boys, of eyewitness statements, of theories and speculation. Stacks and stacks of paper that were taller than Sal, but never him.

The phone number for the hospital was still in his study because Dovey was still there. She'd been kept on suicide watch ever since losing the baby. She was also having a psychological evaluation after she took a black marker and drew a staircase on the wall of her hospital room. She had numbered the steps but didn't get to her goal of seven million before Otis and the nurses stopped her.

Otis stayed with her, dividing his time between Columbus and Breathed. Even Elohim was taking the long drive to go see her. His visits were said to be doing a world of good. Of course, that would be thought. It's easy to be the boulder rolling through what is left of the dandelion field when everyone has their backs turned and are looking at the already flattened ground.

"You'll never get her outside," Dad said again before closing the door of his study.

Mom frowned, angry that he'd given up on her and her fear so easily. Not like in the beginning, when he tried so desperately to get her out. *Why didn't he try anymore?* she wondered. *Doesn't he still love me?* Her anger shifted to nervousness, which put her face in a slope to the right that played favorably with the cluster of dark moles on that cheek side.

"Stella, you know it's not going to rain today." Sal held the curtains back even more, pointing out to the brown ground. "We are in a drought."

She winced as if she was full of shards as she lay back onto the wall, closing her eyes. "What if I do go outside, and it suddenly and unexpectedly starts to rain?"

"Why are you so afraid of the rain, Stella?"

"Oh, you don't wanna hear that." She burst away from the wall, patting her cowlick and licking her hand to do the same to mine.

"No, Mom, stop." I swatted her hand like it was an incoming wasp. "I said stop it already."

"Fine. Hey, I know, let's watch a movie." She skipped, feigning cheer over to the cabinet full of our VHS collection. "What movie you boys wanna watch? Hmm? *Something Wicked This Way Comes?* How 'bout *Mr. Mom?* I just love that one. Oh, here's *Psycho*."

"Yuck, Mom." Grand leaned in the doorway, along with his friend Yellch. "Anthony Perkins is in *Psycho*."

"So?" Mom shrugged and we shrugged with her.

"I hear he's a fag."

Mom pulled *Psycho* out of its cover sleeve as she said, "I don't want you readin' tabloid trash, Grand. And what'd your father say 'bout usin' that word?"

"I love that movie," Yellch added his two cents before taking a bite of the peach in his hand, the juices slipping down his lanky wrist and dropping to the rug.

"Really?" Grand turned to Yellch. "You don't mind Perkins? That he's a—"

"Nah." Yellch dragged his gapped teeth through the peach's yellowed flesh.

Yellch was seventeen, soon to be eighteen like Grand. Both of them soon to be seniors in the coming year at Breathed High. While Grand was pitcher on the baseball team, gangly Yellch was first baseman. He was someone I always thought had the profile of Lake Superior looking out to the northeast. He wore these gold-rimmed eyeglasses that were round and old-fashioned, contrasting his dark, curly mullet.

His real name was Thatch. The reason for the change to Yellch was because of one day in 1975, when he was eight and Grand was nine. Yellch and his Jewish family had just arrived in Breathed. When they came, it was thought they would live Jewish lives. Maybe they'd want to build a synagogue, invite rabbis, constantly smell of matzo ball soup. These were the fears of a town that wasn't comfortable with the Jewish identity.

One day a group backed Yellch into an alley and threw stones at him. Grand happened to be walking by. He ran to stand in front of Yellch, shielding him from the stones. Not only that. Grand picked up the stones and threw them back.

"What should I do?" Yellch cowered behind this nine-year-old god who stood fighting for him.

"Yell." Grand did so himself. "Just yell, as loud as you can. Throw stones at them from your throat."

Yellch yelled so loud, Grand had to look back just to see if it was still a boy behind him or something bigger. Those throwing the stones ran away. From that day on, everyone called Thatch Yellch.

Grand and Yellch became best pals after that, and as Mom slipped *Psycho* into the VCR, they went upstairs, most likely to play *Space Invaders* on Grand's Atari.

We weren't even past the FBI warning of the movie before Sal started to beg Mom to tell him why she was afraid of the rain. She ignored his pleas and tried to concentrate on the big knife, the shower curtain, and Janet Leigh's screams. Finally she could stand Sal's pleas no more and muted the movie.

For a moment afterward, she rubbed her neck as if she were loosening some long-held muscle. Then she cupped her cheeks as she slowly told about the night her parents were getting ready for a party.

"My father was in a tuxedo. My mother was in tulle. She spun 'round for me like a ballerina, I told her with giggles. I was thirteen. I remember it was rainin'. Pourin', really.

"My mother went out the door, under an umbrella. My father after her. I called 'im back. I said, 'Daddy, don't you go out in that rain.' He made fish lips. 'I'm a fish,' he said. 'Your Momma too. We'll just swim right through.'

"That whole night I dreamed 'em doin' just that. Swimmin' through the rain, Father in his black tie and Mother with tulle fins.

"When I woke, I did so to Grandfather tellin' me there'd been a terrible accident. My parent's car, well . . ." She turned her head, unable to finish the sentence.

"I thought maybe they'd bury 'em in the tuxedo and gown. I thought my parents would like to be buried in things like that. I don't know what they were buried in, actually. The coffins had to be closed. So I don't . . . I don't know. That's a terrible thing for a daughter not to know."

She cleared her throat and stood, suddenly desiring to straighten the afghan on the back of the chair.

"For a long time, I hated 'em for leavin' that night. Then I realized it wasn't their fault. It was the rain's. The rain was what killed 'em. Not the car. Not the turn in the road. But the rain."

She couldn't get the afghan as straight as she wanted it to be, so she yanked it up and bunched it into a ball that she sat down with in the chair. She hugged it into her stomach as she said with a slight chuckle or something like it, "I don't know how to swim. My parents, the fish . . ."

Her words got lost for a moment as her eyes merged into a darkness that cast her face in shadow.

"They never taught me, and I know the rain is just waitin' on me. Waitin' to get me like it got them. So I stay out of it. How can it ever get me if I'm never in it?"

"I could teach you how to swim." Sal stood before her. "I can't say you'll never drown in the rain, but at least it will never be because you don't know how to swim."

She stared at him until his fish lips made her laugh. He grabbed the afghan from her and tossed it to the sofa.

"Oh, you silly, silly boy."

He gently pulled her hand until she was up on her feet. She tightened her apron strings and giggled like a shy little girl as he swam around the room, performing the breaststroke.

He directed her arms to do the same until she started doing it on her own, swimming around the room after him, soon kicking her heels off so she could swim faster. Her skirt billowed out behind her, the apron strings bouncing as she swam lap after lap, exhaling loudly through her mouth like a swimmer counting off her breaths.

"You too, Fielding." Sal bumped into me as he passed.

I did the doggy paddle when they did, the backstroke, the butterfly, the deep dive, and the surface breach. We swam laughing all through the house like this, one country to another, until Yellch came quick and stomping down the stairs from Grand's room, yelling for Grand to just stay away from him.

Grand followed so closely on Yellch's heels they almost tumbled down the stairs together.

"I didn't mean nothin' by it. Honest, Yellch."

Yellch wiped his lips hard with his sleeve. "What's the matter with you, man?"

"I'm sorry. I thought—" Grand's voice shook, and for the first time in my life I was embarrassed by him. By that fear I'd never heard in him before. That clinging to Yellch like, well, I didn't know.

"You're fucked up." Yellch said it so steady, so grounded in tone that it seemed such a sobering truth.

He was fast out the door, his mullet bouncing in that near run. Grand also wiped his lips as he watched Yellch leave.

"Shit," he muttered to himself. When he turned to see us all watching, our arms raised midswim, he asked us what the fuck we were all looking at before picking up a vase. He wound up like on the mound and pitched it into the wall.

While Mom was yelling at him for doing such a thing, I couldn't help but be in awe at how perfect a pitch it was.

15

Here in the dark so many precious things

—MILTON, *PARADISE LOST* 3:611

SOMETIMES I THINK I see your shoulder. Then I realize it's just a jar of honey. I scream out your name and am certain I see your mole, but it's only the last grape on the vine. I grab hold of your neck, but it's no more than a piece of rope. I reach toward your rib, but it's simply a grain of rice. I hold your hand, sorrowed to find it is my own.

Who you are, I cannot say for certain. Who you are, Grand, I can never find my way to. You are always just something else. No matter how hard I look for you, I cannot find you.

I try. In the dark, I do try because I was once told you can imagine anything in the dark. So I sit here at night in my trailer with all the lights out, with all the sheets drawn on the windows. I sit here trying to find you and I sit here imagining I do until the light comes back on and I realize you're just something else.

A light coming on and beaming through the thin sheet on the window by the door. I get up from the lawn chair, on the way knocking into and rolling an empty bottle across the carpet. I remind myself to make a stop at the liquor store. Not the one by the pawnshop. He never has forgiven me for breaking that bottle against the wall.

I open the door to the neighbor boy and his light in my eyes.

"What are you doin' in the dark?" He lowers the light to my side. "What are you holdin', Mr. Bliss?"

I turn my hand over, the light shining on the white leather and red stitching.

"It's just a baseball." I drop it. He keeps the light on the ball as it rolls across the floor. Once the ball stops, he shines the light in my face again. I squint past it to his eyes on me, quick from thought to smile.

"I'm sorry if I've bothered you, Mr. Bliss. It's just that your trailer was so dark. Not one light. I thought maybe somethin' happened. That maybe you fell."

I look at his young face and wince. "How old are you?"

"Thirteen."

"Damn it."

"What'd you say, Mr. Bliss?"

"I said leave me alone. Wait . . ."

"Are you okay, Mr. Bliss?"

I hold my head and try to remember. "Have you seen Sal?"

"Who, Mr. Bliss?"

"The boy." I shake my hands at him. How can he not know who I'm talking about? "Have you seen the boy? We must get him . . . we must get him away."

"Are you sure you're all right, Mr. Bliss?"

"Oh, stupid man." I slap my head. "Stupid, stupid man. No, no, I'm fine."

"Who's Sal?"

"Doesn't matter. I know where he is. You go home. I'll be okay."

"All right, Mr. Bliss. Hey, I'm sorry about breakin' your—"

I slam the door before he gets to the time machine part. I shuffle back toward the lawn chair. On the way, I scoot my feet over the carpet until I feel the smooth side of glass with my bare toes. I pick up the bottle and tilt it all the way. Not even a damn drop left.

I carry it over to the lawn chair and sit down. Don't turn so much as a lamp on. I'm okay without electricity. During that summer, we often had none for extended periods of time due to them blackouts rolling across Breathed. By the end of July, they became a daily occurrence. The electric company issued warnings for us to do our part in conserving energy, such as keeping unnecessary appliances unplugged.

In an effort to keep cool, Dad ate heat on everything. He made chili and soup, using hot peppers from the garden as spoons. When I asked him why, he said because ingesting heat cools the body from the inside out.

I wasn't convinced as I watched him drip over bowls of soup, unintentionally slurping up his sweat. A few days after eating nothing but heat, he threw his hands up in the air and said, "Fuck it."

Needless to say, he went back to sucking on ice cubes.

Interrupting the heat were the phone calls. Always anonymous, but always voices we knew and who called us *nigger-lovers, devil-worshippers*. Sometimes both at once. These calls sent Dad to the drawer to pull out the newspaper with his invitation in it.

"What's wrong, Autopsy?" Sal watched Dad silently read the invitation.

"If I knew there was going to be this much trouble, I would never have done it." He laid the paper back down into the drawer.

There was a fan on top of the table, and he stood there in front of it, holding his arms out and twisting his body, allowing the air flow to oscillate as best it could through his vest and button-up shirt. As he did this, he spoke over the fan's whir to tell me and Sal about one of his early cases.

"It was when I first started. It was a case involving a fifteen-year-old girl who had accused her father of rape on four different occasions. The father denied the allegations, but there was evidence of trauma to the girl's, well—" He cleared his throat, that too coming just as loud as his voice over the fan's drone.

"Neighbors came forward, said the girl often went around the house in very little clothing. Furthermore, that her father never seemed to mind this near nudity of his own daughter. They said they might remember instances where his hand landed a little too low on her back for their liking. Perhaps a kiss or a hug between father and daughter lingered just a little too long.

"One of the girl's friends, a young boy, gave testimony that he had on more than one occasion walked in on the father naked and sleeping in the daughter's bed. The father was known to drink too much and had in the past been charged with rape. The woman who accused him was an ex-girlfriend who later dropped the charges and said she filed only because she was mad at him. Still, I was certain of his guilt in regards to his daughter's rape.

"I looked at his narrow eyes and said to myself, those are the eyes of a devil. I looked at his hands, his rough hands with their filthy nails, and said those are the hands of a monster. Ignoring they were merely the hands of someone who works construction.

"He sat still through the whole trial, never once batting an eye when his daughter on the witness stand described the gruesome details of being violated by him. Yes, I said, he is no father. He is the devil.

"Everyone cheered when he was convicted on all four counts of rape. Hell, I cheered. I had put the devil through the filter and the world was cleaner for it."

Dad stepped over to the window, where he laid his sweating forehead against the glass.

"Just this last January, the girl—now thirty-three—came forward. Said she falsely accused her father for the same reason the ex-girlfriend had. All that man seemed guilty of was making the women in his life angry.

"The daughter said before she knew it, the case just got out of hand and she was too frightened to say it wasn't true after all. But ever since getting off the heroin and becoming a born-again Christian, she felt it was her duty to set things right.

"As for the boy who testified, he happened to be the one who had caused the trauma that led to the police believing she'd been raped.

Apparently, the two liked things a little rough. And the neighbors who said they saw the father with low hands, lingering kisses and hugs, were actually mad at him for a fence he was putting in, which they said was too far over on their property line."

Dad pulled his head back from the window, leaving a smear on the glass from his sweat.

"I wanted to apologize to the man, but that damn daughter, she had come forward too late. Prison can be a tough place for a man accused of raping his own. Three years into his sentence, a sentence that up to that point had been filled with numerous trips to the prison's infirmary, the man had been fatally attacked in the laundry room."

Dad rubbed the scar on his forehead as he mumbled something to himself before squinting to the bright light outside.

"I had been so certain of his guilt. If I could be so certain and yet so wrong, how many times had I been wrong before? I started to wonder. I looked back on my cases and saw cracks, not victories. I was no hero. I had failed in handling the filter entrusted to me."

Dad was standing, but he looked like he was kneeling. His trousers dirtying at the knee before my eyes. His hands coming together, at his sides, but coming together in front. My father was praying.

"It got me thinking about all the things we are so certain about. Like the devil. I put that invitation in the newspaper, and I thought the devil will show and he will have a pitchfork and horns and be red all over. He'll be mean and cruel and evil. I was so certain of that, and then you came, Sal. Not with a pitchfork but with a heart. I—"

Dad was cut off by the ringing doorbell. He wiped his eyes as Mom answered the door and a moment later showed Fedelia in, wearing a heavy black coat—velvet, of all things—that swept the floor and which she held tightly closed by the collar.

I stared at the sweat glistening above her bare lip. It was the first time I'd seen her face naked. The makeup washed off. Little red marks on her cheeks from scrubbing. White film at her hair line left by the soap.

She rather forcefully pushed me out of the way to get to Sal standing behind me. "Well, you little devil, you've put me in quite a state since last I saw you."

"I have?"

"Every time I look in a mirror now, I see the infinity I have built." She gestured up to her hair. "It is time to be rid of it."

"Oh, Auntie," Mom gasped.

Fedelia nodded as she reached into the pocket of her coat to pull out a pair of hair shears, offering them toward Sal. "Won't you do the honors?"

To avoid a mess of cut hair in the house, we went to the back porch, where Mom brought out a stool. The dark of the evening had laid its way, so she made sure to set the stool beneath the porch bulbs, the lights already preaching to dozens of moths, beetles, and little night flies.

As Fedelia sat down on the stool and checked its wobble, she kept that coat closed tight, her squeeze straining the veins in the backs of her hands. She was quickly tapping her toes. In the tapping, the bottom of the coat slightly fell down across her leg and I caught a glimpse of sequins. She grabbed the coat back and frowned at me as if it'd been my fault.

Sal stood behind her, watching the insects fly the light above, giving him a halo of gnats and moths as he asked Fedelia if she was ready.

"I am ready. Set me free."

As the shears made their initial approach, Fedelia closed her eyes. She winced as the blades cut and the first ribbon fell in that slow-motion elegance of falling things.

I thought she was going to stop him, say she'd changed her mind, but as the tear slid down her cheek, she opened her eyes, and as if all the light were shining there in her irises, the amber shade became diluted by glow to a yellow that took hold of us all.

Each ribbon and clump of hair that fell, she sat a little taller, a little straighter. A drip from her forehead. A drip from her eyes. Her nose. Her cheeks. *Drip, drip, drip.* All sweat and tears, and yet wasn't it the anger melting away before us?

I watched the ribbons fall, their curling and swirling like retiring snakes given the send-off by a woman letting go of the anger that had nearly cannibalized her.

Sal cut so close to her head, all that remained were her white roots. Once he finished, she stood and stepped away from the pile of orange hair and ribbons on the floor. She lowered her head and felt the short rise left.

"Auntie?" Mom reached toward Fedelia. "You all right?"

"All the weight of that hair. You get so used to carryin' it around, you forget how heavy it is." Fedelia raised her head and smiled. "I am so happy it is finally gone."

She threw off the black coat, revealing the glistening chestnut and gold gown beneath. It was cut low in the front and back, fitting to a waist and hips I didn't know she had. No more bags for her. Sequins and fit the rest of the way.

"Just name me Paradise." She struck a pose that called to mind a certain duck in flight.

"You look so beautiful, Fedelia." Mom smiled and lightly clapped her hands under her chin.

Fedelia lowered her arms. "I haven't heard anyone call me beautiful in forty years."

Dad held her wet cheek in his hand. "Then that was our fault, not yours."

He didn't stop staring at her as he said, "Fielding, tell your aunt how beautiful she is."

"You're beautiful, Aunt Fedelia."

She grabbed Dad's hand and squeezed it before kneeling down in front of me. "I haven't been very nice to you, have I, Fielding?"

"You haven't been nice to any of us."

That was the first time I'd ever heard her laugh.

She thanked Sal and was about to say something more to him, but the loud knocking on the front door distracted us all.

We went to see who it was, Mom complimenting Fedelia the

whole way while Fedelia nodded like she'd never been who she was before.

Through the windows around the front door, we could see Otis pacing the porch, pumping his shoulders and cracking his neck.

Dad stepped over to the door, but Fedelia warned him about opening it.

"He's mighty boiled up 'bout somethin'. Might scald us all if ya let 'im in."

Dad quietly slid the end of the chain into the locking track on the door. "We'll just see what he wants. Isn't the man owed that? Isn't he still our friend?"

We weren't so sure as Dad slowly turned the knob. Over his pacing, Otis heard the quiet opening of the door. The whole house shook as he clutched onto the frame to stop himself from overshooting the door in his mad dash for it.

His face was so damp, it looked as if it'd been attached to a water hose. He was squeezing his head in between the door and the frame, his nose pressing against the top of the chain.

"Did you get our card and vine? You and Dovey have our prayers at this most dreadful time." Dad shook his head in that give of sympathy.

"Where is he?" Otis tried reaching his arm through the opening, but his muscles were too wide for the narrow way.

"Who?"

"You know who, Autopsy." Otis leaned into the door Dad was trying to close.

"He's not here." Dad waved for Mom to yank Sal out of sight.

Otis roared with his muscles ready. This was what he had lifted all those barbells for. Why he had done all those squats with a bar digging into his shoulders. The running, the protein shakes, they had not been worthless after all. Him being lost in a gym, escaping the world but only in preparation for it. Preparing for this one moment he would be asked to defend his fallen son. He would be asked to bring the grieving mother a revenge she could read in his fists.

"I told you he's not here, Otis."

Dad's fast push into the door wasn't enough, not against Otis and his great bellowing shove. The chain snapped and Dad was knocked back to the floor. Mom cried out and fell to her knees by his unmoving side, holding his banged head.

She slapped his cheeks, trying to get him to open his eyes. "Come on, love."

I kneeled at his other side, grabbing his limp hand and shaking it. He didn't respond.

I looked up at Otis standing in the busted doorway, the broken chain still swinging against the frame as he clenched his fists. All he saw was the boy hiding behind Fedelia.

"You get on outta here, Otis Jeremiah." Fedelia held one firm hand up, as the other stayed fearfully behind her with Sal. "I said get on. Don't you dare, don't you dare come near here. No, I said no."

Otis gave Fedelia a hard shove into the wall. She slid frightened and shocked down the wallpaper to the floor while Otis grabbed Sal up by the collar of his shirt.

"Fielding?" I looked down to see Dad's eyes finally open. He was weakly clutching my arm, saying, "Save Sal."

I would never have been fast enough. No matter how quick I was. I would never have been fast enough to stop Otis from punching Sal in the face. The punch thrust him back onto the floor, where he curled up so tight, I thought he was going to disappear.

I yelled for Otis to leave as I pounded my fists into his abs. It was like hitting a slab of concrete.

He grabbed me by the shoulders, as he'd so often done before when checking my strength. This time it was to throw me to the floor.

I heard a weak grunt. When I looked up, I saw Dad on Otis' back. Dad wasn't a fighter. He tried, but it was like watching a spider struggling to take down a bear. Long legs and arms coming around, but doing nothing more than irritating the beast beneath him.

Otis flung Dad to the floor. Their wrestling sent them into a roll.

Fedelia, improved from her own shove, grabbed the nearby broom, using its handle to prod Otis, on occasion accidentally prodding Dad, who moaned on impact.

Tall, lanky Dad was no match for square, boxy Otis, and he quickly wound up in the bad position of a choke hold. Otis was really squeezing too. Dad's eyes bulged until I thought the blue was going to burst from his face and scatter like the blue chicories cut up by the lawn mower and spewed out the chute.

I got into the fight, wrapping my arms around Otis' bulging neck. It was like holding onto a wet log.

Grand, who had been upstairs, came running down. He would later say he'd had his headphones on and hadn't heard our fighting over the music, until I started screaming for Otis to let Dad go.

I thought Grand would be the god to save us all, but he became just another spider on the growling bear's back. It was Mom who did the most damage when she grabbed the porcelain vase and broke it against Otis' head.

He just stood there, blood trickling over the tight curls of his perm. Suddenly he threw a confused punch that hit the air. He swung around and threw another. Punch after punch, until his glazed eyes landed on me. Before I knew it, his hands were coming. They are why I am still afraid of skillets. His hands big, round cast iron things of heat that pushed into my chest, sending me back against the wall. Hard enough to make the mirror behind me drop to a shatter.

"Stop!"

We turned to Sal's scream. Otis' punch had lacerated Sal's right cheek, and the blood, while not profuse, had gathered like the blooming flora of his already swollen cheek.

"It bleeds?" Otis dropped down to the floor in a squat. That's kneeling to a muscleman.

"Of course he bleeds." Dad wheezed. "He's just a boy. For heaven's sake, Otis."

"I thought he was . . ." His fingers raked through his blood and perm, trying to rake what he'd thought from his brain, his brain that felt like a pulled muscle.

"You thought he was the devil." Dad was still recovering from the choke hold.

Otis nodded his head slowly before apologizing to Sal. "They said you were what done it to Dovey and our baby. I was just bein' a good daddy, you know. I wouldn't have hurt ya if I'd known ya was just a boy. I mean I don't know you. I didn't—"

"You nearly strangled me to death, Otis, and you've known me all your life. And just look how you shoved Fedelia and Fielding. You could have hurt them beyond repair, Otis." Dad slumped by the front door, wearily motioning with his hand out. "It's time you go home."

Otis stood from his kneeling squat. When before he might have loved the perfection of his strength, he stood before us ashamed by it.

"I said I'm sorry. Stop lookin' at me like that. Didn't y'all hear me? I'm sorry. Hey, I'm gonna pay for that mirror." His finger shook as he pointed toward the pieces of glass around my feet.

"And who's gonna pay for all the years of bad luck?" Fedelia shooed me away as she used the broom to sweep up the pieces. "Seven years, we're lookin' at. You gonna pay that debt, Otis Jeremiah?"

"Shucks, Fedelia." Otis grasped the back of his neck, log to log. "Seven years is a long time for just one person to bear when it comes to unlucky things. There's seven of us here. We could all take a year."

"Oh, no." Fedelia shook her head. "I have just come into an awakenin', and there is no way I'm gonna go through it unlucky. No, Otis, this bad luck will be all yours." She began to pick up the pieces of glass, spitting on each as she said Otis' name.

"What ya doin'?" He took a step toward her but no more. He had already threatened us enough, he knew.

"I'm markin' 'em for you, Otis Jeremiah. So this bad luck knows the name of its victim."

He hugged himself because there was no one else to do it. "I've got bad luck enough. I've just lost my baby, don't ya know? My son is dead. I already had a name for 'im and everything. Not just that but the nickname too. Now what am I supposed to do? This nickname rollin' 'round in my head. I saved it up for all the times I would call 'im that. Now it's just a pile inside me. I can't throw it out. It's not garbage. I can't throw it out. But how can I live with it?"

Fedelia left the glass on the floor, the tears in her eyes glistening for that grieving father who loved the fetus as much as most men love the fully grown.

He had already prepared himself to be a father. Already prepared himself for what his son would be. He would've looked like him. Been strong like him. That's how he pictured him. Truth was, he didn't care. That child would never have to lift a dumbbell into Otis' heart. His love was easy.

He would have praised his son for dropping the football when others booed him for not catching it. He wouldn't have cared if his son was scrawny. Couldn't fight. Didn't know who Arnold Schwarzenegger was. If he was fat. Ate candy bars and television shows and smelled like sofa cushions. Just as long as he came. It was the not coming that Otis couldn't handle. The not having the son to see.

Sal knew this. That was why he went to the pile of broken glass. He picked up one of the larger shards and offered it to Otis with instruction to take the glass out into the night.

"Every light that reflects will be your son."

Otis, the man who would later die at 660 pounds of pure fat, accepted the sliver of glass and went out the door with his head down. It was his sudden shriek that made us run out to the porch.

He was looking into the mirror, the sharp edges of the glass cutting his palm in his tight grip. He was smiling at his son, he said. None of us told him it was just the porch light and always would be.

Long after he left, we could hear him. Seeing his son. Hollering that very thing into the dark for all of Breathed to hear. Sharing it somehow made it more than streetlights, more than house lights, more than cars coming his way.

16

I sung of Chaos and eternal Night

—MILTON, *PARADISE LOST* 3:18

AUGUST WAS. A housewife taken in for heatstroke. A nursing home put on a bus for the next town. A pepper in the mouth. Another cow dead. Another fly landed. A woman cutting her hair—*cuts to get cool,* they called them. A fury. A baby crying but not heard over the fans. Dovey home from the hospital. An air conditioner kicked. Dovey going to Elohim's meetings. Another ice cube melted. Another farmer cursing. Water shortages. Otis staying home and dismantling the crib. Wells going dry. A man throwing up his lunch because it's just too damn hot. August was.

And by the beginning of it, news of our heat wave stretched across the nation like one long sentence looking to never surrender to a period.

"Boiling," said the *Chicago Tribune*, while *The Boston Globe* called the town a "Torrid Furnace." The *San Francisco Chronicle* was a telephone dialed to meteorologists who blamed the depleting ozone layer, while the *Omaha World-Herald* wrote extensively about the barren fields and how farmers kneeled in the loss of their crops.

The Indianapolis Star had a quote from an environmentalist who was certain our dying livestock and infestation of flies were the prologue to the disease in us, while *The Miami Herald* listed Breathed at the top of its list of the ten worst places to spend summer vacation.

Then there were the articles less about the heat and more about Sal and what they called his "devil delusion." *The Columbus Dispatch* quoted a prominent psychiatrist who gave an abridged diagnosis of pediatric schizophrenia while *The Washington Post* gave a detailed description of the therapy and miracles of modern medicine used to treat such a disorder.

The Baptist preacher interviewed by *The Clarion-Ledger* ignored any verdict familiar to the lexicon of the medical and instead said Sal was an energumen, a person possessed. The preacher went further to say that he would be more than happy to perform a Mississippi-style exorcism—for a small donation, of course.

The focus of other papers like *USA Today* was on Sal's race, and their articles were narrations from the NAACP, Southern Christian Leadership Conference, and Al Sharpton. To them, Sal was just a black boy who by calling himself devil was personifying the white man's claim.

There weren't as many journalists to come to Breathed as there were articles written. Most of them phoned it in or relied on their fellow journalists, lifting the common themes of heat and race. Those who did come rarely stayed more than a couple days. The heat got to them. The people who wouldn't talk got to them. Not even Elohim and his followers had anything to do with the newspapers. National news was something Elohim did not want to make.

These reporters especially wanted to speak to the family with the boy. Of course to the boy himself. Every notepad, every big city accent, asking, "Say, aren't you—?" we ran away from. Some chased, shouting they just wanted to talk. We ran faster. They wheezed and cursed over their urban knees. And we ran faster.

Aside from Sal's race, the town got darker that summer, beyond a Midwestern tan. No hat, no shade, no night could keep you pale. The heat had its own sun. Even housebound Mom came away with a cook to her normally rinsed skin.

Much to his annoyance, Elohim was also changed. A browning start surely there. It's why he started to wear white. White shirts. White pants. White everything. He was keeping the white in place. It meant so much to him that it stay in place. That meant a great deal indeed.

As the heat increased, Elohim increased his sermons to an ever-increasing audience. At his feet they sat as lumps of soil. He was their sun. He was their water. He was the Father tugging up their growth, occasionally fertilizing with an Old Testament *amen* and pat on the head, bringing him down from the cloud.

Was he God that summer? There in those woods, he was the only one.

There would be no hollering, no stomping feet, no lectern theatrics. He was the Lord with the soft drawl. Sometimes he didn't even speak. He'd hold up enlarged photographs of concentration camps, of disasters and accidents. There Sal would be, in the sunken stomachs of starving prisoners, in the corpses piled in holes. He would be painted badly by Elohim, whose skill was as splotched as putting a canvas beneath a pan of boiling paint.

In the photograph of the aftermath of the 1906 San Francisco Earthquake, Elohim painted Sal in the billowing smoke of the resulting fires. His face was the rubble of the 1900 Galveston Hurricane and the bodies by the wreckage. He stared out from the debris of the Johnstown Flood and peered from the shattered windows of the Cocoanut Grove.

He was the 1913 Ohio Flood, the Blizzard of 1888, the explosion in the Monongah mines. Train crashes, bridges collapsed, buses of children careening off the cliff. He was avalanches, stampedes, sinking ships, like the *Andrea Doria*.

Elohim had made Sal everything bad. Gone wrong. Gone to death.

And they all sat there, believing it, their common sense melting away one drip at a time. Had it not been the flame's summer, those people would've stood and left Elohim. Probably even called him a son-of-a-bitch.

If only it would've been a normal summer, a summer where the heat was easily alleviated by air conditioners and fans and those cooling stations set up in town for the elderly and those at high risk of heat-related death.

We were all high risk. That heat brought out the throbs in hearts, the fevers, the things that couldn't be let go of. It was a perfect extractor of pain and frustration, of anger and loss. It brought everything to the surface and sweated it out.

Those followers of Elohim all had their own Helens, their own *Andrea Doria*s, their own devils they needed to blame. It was a support group for the wronged. Like the brother of the twin killed in a gas station being robbed by a black man in a black ski mask. There was the father whose daughter had been made a vegetable by the drunk driver who was drunk, black, and very, very drunk. And a wife who'd been raped while coming out of a bar in Toledo. Three rapists, all one color. Black. Black. Black.

That color brought Elohim and his group together. It was the color of their devil, and they needed their devil to have a color so they could find him again.

Elohim became the one they all looked to because he amplified their tragedies and in that addressed their desperation to be heard and to matter. To them, he was the someone who was going to give them the opportunity to take action on what before had seemed to be out of their hands. Elohim placed retribution within their reach, and he was helped by the heat and of all things by Sal himself, who came in the right color, willing to be called devil.

Elohim always ended the meetings by handing out vegetarian recipes. It was because of him the sale of meat was down but that of lettuce was up. The butcher nearly went out of business. We should've known right then and there the control Elohim had. All he had to say was buy lettuce and they bought lettuce. Chuck your bacon and they chucked their bacon.

All around me, madness. Madness in the woods, but madness in the town too. Yes, common sense was melting away. At first people followed the old logic that light colors and light fabric are easier to breathe in when hot. Then I started to see a black T-shirt here and dark denim there. Was that flannel? And a leather jacket and some woolen socks instead of bare feet. Those who had painted their roofs white, climbed back up the ladder to paint them black. Instead of iced tea being ordered at Dandelion Dimes, it was hot tea, sent back because it simply wasn't hot enough.

Would it happen to me? Would I one day wake up, put on mittens, and wrap a scarf around my neck? Go out into the woods and nod trustingly at Elohim? Would I start buying frozen vegetables in bulk? Would I see in Sal what they did?

I frightened at these thoughts. I needed to feel like a boy in the summertime. Nothing made me feel more like that than watching Grand play ball. That's baseball for you. A bat-and-ball cure for any boy lost and looking to run home.

The baseball field was behind the high school. It sounded like wasps that summer because the small shed by the field had a nest of them. I walked past the empty bleachers, a pair of dirty cleats tied to the rail. A fly hovering above them.

I smelled pine tar and sweat as I clung to the holes of the chain-link fence surrounding the ball diamond. The fence was painted the deep, dark shade of purple that represented one half of the school colors. The other being lavender. The color of the dugouts and the main color of the team's home game uniforms.

Though there was hardly, if any, grass left in that drought, the nearby lawn mower gave off its heat and fumes of just-worked mechanics. I moved a little farther down the fence, where the air was less gasoline.

Grand was on the mound, waiting impatiently for the ball to come to him from the outfield. It was a practice in which they wore no shirts. Even the thinnest cotton shirts could feel like parkas. I swear, they dripped like faucets.

I once asked Grand what it was like practicing in that heat. He said it felt like being the only ashtray in the world open for business.

"Imagine that, little man, all them cigarettes dumpin' down their hot ash. And you, unable to breathe. в ловушке."

When it came time for Grand to pitch to Yellch, it was a pitch no doubt given. Their friendship hadn't been the same since Yellch went running from Grand. Grand was trying to take things back with a pitch forward. Make it the same as it always had been, but Yellch wasn't ready. He threw all his anger into the swing, sending the ball in a line drive back to Grand, who managed to duck before it cracked open his skull.

The tail of Yellch's mullet flapped as he ran the bases, eventually sliding into home, with the ball in the catcher's mitt only seconds behind.

As the dust settled and Yellch pushed his glasses back up on his nose, the coach and other teammates gave the usual congratulatory gesture by slapping Yellch on the behind. They were quick slaps like water flicking from fingers. *Slap, slap, slap.* Then Grand and his slap that reminded Yellch why he had run in the first place.

He pushed Grand back. "What the hell you think you're doin'?"

"What?" Grand hugged his glove.

"Don't fuckin' touch me, man. Didn't y'all see 'im?" Yellch asked of his teammates. "He just touched my ass."

"He's proud of ya for hittin' a homer." The coach and his chest-high shorts came in front of Yellch. "The heat is gettin' to ya, boy. Why don'tcha sit in the dugout a bit? Pour a bucket of ice over your head."

"Yeah, Yellch," one of the other boys agreed. "Why ya actin' like a dick?"

"'Cause I don't want no dick." The veins in Yellch's neck popped like long stems. "You hear me, Grand? I don't want no dick. And I don't wanna play ball with someone who does."

Grand looked to be one sweat drip away from disappearing as the team urged Yellch to give further explanation.

Grand tucked his glove under his arm and held up his trembling hands like Yellch had a gun. "C'mon, Yell. Don't. I'm sorry, okay? Please. Don't say anything."

But Yellch had to say it. If he didn't, what would it mean for him? Would it mean he liked what Grand did to him? If he didn't yell it out, if he didn't respond with anger, wouldn't that be what people thought if they ever found out about the time Grand Bliss kissed him on a bed while Anthony Perkins played on the TV downstairs? Yes, Yellch had to say it, for his own sake. *Fuck you,* he must've thought as he pointed at Grand and said without doubt, "He's a fag."

My brother. A fag? It was like seeing American flags impaled on white picket fences. He had been red, he had been white, he had been blue and July Fourth. But now, the mythology of him was over. He who was so handsome, as children all the girls thought they would marry him and leave the earth for the stars.

Yellch's accusation was a lingering echo. A full-bodied thing, pumping and veering like poison-dipped arrows. It was as if the entire, astonished world was right there on a ball field in Breathed, Ohio. Between teammates and coach, the little things of years began to be added up.

The quick peeks in the locker room, the lingering hugs, the slaps on the rear that went beyond congratulations. That was enough for them to see him coiling with the snake. It was enough for him to become something they could not sweetly accept.

"Grand, I think you should go home." The coach squinted behind his 1950s glasses.

"Do you mean go home just for today?"

"Grand—"

"I have a right to know if I'm still on the goddamn team. Whatcha gonna do for pitcher, Coach? Hmm? Use Arly?"

"I ain't so bad," Arly came to his own defense. "I've been layin' off the sodium. Think I took off the drag."

"Your arm's dead, Arly. You see its goddamn funeral every time you pitch. мертвых."

"Arly will be fine." In those four words, the coach stripped Grand of the pitcher mound.

I never thought I'd see my brother defeated. He was always so strong. The boy with the durability of linoleum. On that day, I realized the linoleum was just an accessory for effect, and underneath it, he was just as fragile as us all. My brother. The one I thought was marked for eternity, and yet here I am, and where is he? Maybe forever on that ball field. Forever being revealed and they forever stepping back as if he's sickness between sickness.

It was small use to remind them of how they'd say, *I love you, Grand Bliss,* in the golden glow of a big win. Even smaller use to say he was once their friend. The buddy who bought them all tickets to the Reds game, and drove all the way to Cincinnati and back. The pal who stayed sober when they got drunk. The one who punched the guy who would've punched them.

He was the heart they could all be loved by, and yet not one of them loved him back. I wanted him to shout. To cancel out what they were telling themselves. To deny until he won. To shape back his hero self and put on the cape to become my perfect brother once more. But all he did was squeeze his glove and walk away.

When he saw me at the fence, it was like it was through a microscope against his brow, magnifying me to the point of shocking him into a run that was so fast, I would never have caught up to him had he not stopped to get sick.

"How long were ya by the fence?" He wiped his mouth in one long gesture.

"I just showed up as you were leavin'." I couldn't bear for him to know I'd seen it all.

He turned a cheek to his vomit. "Really?"

"Really. I'm stumped why ya left practice so early."

He looked at me and knew, but the lie offered him a chance. All truth could do then was to tap us on the back. We never turned around.

"Heat's made me sick. Coach said it was all right for me to go home." He lifted his cleats, checking his shoelaces to see if any vomit had splashed.

As we walked home, I knew from far away the trees would've looked nice, the grass would've looked green, and we would've looked like just a couple of boys walking home, armed with Midwest love and Bible Belt morals.

But up close, the trees were scorched, the grass was dead, and the boys were on the verge of tears with the belts of those morals tightened around their necks, threatening to hang them if they dared step off the stool of masculinity.

We didn't speak the whole way. That's brothers for you. A splintering silence. A lonely cope. A quick pace to the house we shared and the home we hoped would always be there.

And this is where so many of my nightmares begin. Walking up the porch steps and finding the man with the notepad. He'd been talking to Sal. Grand interrupted their conversation by asking, "Who are you, Незнакомец?"

"A journalist from *The New York Times,*" Sal answered for the man.

Grand gave a fatherly sigh toward Sal. "Whatcha been tellin' him?"

"We've just been talking about the heat." The man tucked his pad of yellow paper into his back pocket. "You know your shoelace is untied?" He gestured down to Grand's shoes. "What's that on the laces? Chocolate stains?"

"Bloodstains."

"Funny stain to be on shoelaces. Either way, it's a pleasure to meet you, kid." The man offered his hand.

It was unnatural how the man called Grand *kid*. There wasn't enough distance in age between them. I figured the man was in his early twenties. Hair copper like fused pennies. Eyes dark like casual shadows. Lines around the mouth from Marlboro Country.

The way he moved, he was like a human saxophone, with jazz in his step. Of course, it probably had something to do with his skin. Such a glow you'd never think he'd ever been sick a day in his life.

"Aren't you going to shake my hand, kid?"

Grand leaned into the porch rail, the man watching the sweat glistening on Grand's bare chest. Watching the way that strand of damp hair fell across his eye, like a sort of whole world holding.

"Perhaps if I introduce myself." The man kept his hand offered. "I'm Theodore Bundy. Just call me Ted."

This was the type of thing to get Grand grinning. To get him to the man's hand. I wish mine would've been a knife to Ted Bundy right then and there. I wish I would've been bigger than myself, the thing to make him nothing but the slowly bleeding dust.

After Grand introduced himself as Michael Myers, they seemed to hold hands a little too long. Grand was the first to let go. Something told him to. Maybe something that was still being said back on the ball field.

The man looked at his own hand, slender like the rest of him but now sullied from ball diamond dust. Maybe some oil from Grand's baseball glove and pine tar from the bat. This dirt on the man's hand was painful to him. He was so spick-and-span, like he washed in a Maytag, spinning out on gentle cycle.

He wiped the dirt off his hand. "I feel like maybe we should give our real names now."

"Let's not." Grand squinted at the bright sun. "I like our fake names."

"You don't mind being a murderer?"

"It's better than bein' the victim, ain't it?"

The man coughed into his hand. "Who said you had to be either?"

"The day has said it." Grand laid his glove down and didn't look at it again.

"All right, to escape being the victims, we shall continue to be the murderers. But only if you promise not to kill me with your big knife, Mr. Myers."

"If you promise not to kill me, Mr. Bundy."

The man leaned in, against Grand's chest, and whispered like he was whispering to the rest of Grand's life, "I might not be able to help myself."

Grand smiled, and for a moment I thought of dragging him back to his vomit, of dragging him back to the ball field, asking him if he still wanted to smile. I thought if the man was there, he would.

I realize now the man was a suffix to Grand's life, offering something new to the old that had ended on the baseball diamond. His was a test-tube romance upon which Grand could experiment. The man knew this. It was why his eyes looked like sheets being spread on the bed.

"I could take you 'round." Grand offered the man Breathed. "Make our town more than the devil and the heat. Make it серъёзная(ый)."

"Why do you throw in Russian?" The man's smile was a line of clean, white teeth.

"My eyes are Russian." Grand winked at me before asking the man, "You wanna see the real Breathed?"

"I'd like that." The man skipped down the porch steps like a little boy getting everything he wanted.

I grabbed Grand's arm, feigning reasons he must not go with the man. Reasons like Mom would be angry if he went out. Dinner's going to be soon. He's got to clean his room.

"My room is clean, Fielding."

"Then let's bomb the Atari."

"Later, Fielding." He bounded down the porch steps.

I screamed so loud, I felt like I'd broken something in my throat. I wondered if they even made a cast for that.

Grand returned to me in a gentle kneel. "What's the problem, little man?"

"I don't want you to go, Grand."

"Why don't ya want me to go? Why you cryin'? Geez, little man." He pinched my nose the way Dad sometimes did.

"Remember how I used to take the shortcut home from school through Blue-eyed Glen's vineyard? It was winter and all the grapes were gone but one. I thought how great it was to find a grape in winter, so I ate it. Remember how sick I got later?"

"Little man, you didn't get sick 'cause of the grape."

"It was the grape, Grand. I shouldn't have eaten it 'cause it grew outta season. It didn't follow the rules of nature. You've got to follow the rules, Grand, or you'll get sick."

"Hey, kid. We going or not?" The New Yorker wiped his forehead like an experienced Breathanian. I followed his cologne to his beautiful neck, to his strong jaw like something to have. I knew somewhere a billboard was missing its man.

"I'll be back later, little man." Grand stood and tousled my hair.

I regret it—Lord, I regret it—but I said the only thing I thought would make him stay.

"Faggot."

I try to see his face at this moment, but in memory, his eyes, his nose, his mouth, are blurred until they're smears of blue. Like watercolors in the rain. Somehow this makes it worse. To see his hurt as something he's vanishing by, and to know I am responsible for that very vanishing.

"What did you say to me, Fielding?"

What did I say in that one word of six letters, sometimes only three? I suppose I said, *I don't want you to be gay. I don't want you to be happy, and no, it isn't fine that you want to be with a man.* Faggot. Isn't that what that one word is supposed to mean? Faggot? One word that said I was scared. That I didn't understand. That no one ever sat us down and patted our heads and said sometimes a man loves another man and they make something nice together.

Above all else, I said with that one word, *I hate you*. How can it ever be believed I loved him above all others?

"Say it again, Fielding." He grabbed me by the collar. As he shook me under him, one of his tears fell onto my cheek. To have my brother's tear slide down my face cut worse than the world's sharpest knife. He screamed over and over for me to call him a faggot just one more time.

So I did.

Before I knew it, I was down with Grand's fists pummeling into my face and stomach. I did my best to shield against them, but he was Grand and I was Fielding and there was no way I wasn't going to get the shit kicked out of me.

"I hate you, you little bastard." His voice trembled. "I hate you."

I could feel my tears mixing with blood from my nose. This mixture felt old, like something pulled from the past. I suppose I was feeling the tears and blood of every boy before me who had a brother who would never have a wife and to whom no one had ever said that was all right.

It was Sal who pulled Grand off of me, leaving me to curl up into my beaten self and whine like a baby.

"C'mon, kid." The man grabbed Grand's arm and led him away. Led him away from me as I reached and cried for Grand to come back.

"I was comin' up from the basement when I heard the most terrible racket." Mom stood in the doorway. "What was goin' on?"

Once she saw my nose, she went for a wet rag and a bag of ice. Too sore to move myself, I watched the man and Grand get farther and farther away. All the while, my voice echoed for miles. I was calling for my brother. *Please, just come back to me.* He didn't so much as turn his head. He just kept walking until I could no longer see his bare back, nor the yellow shirt of the man beside him.

"What on earth were the two of ya fightin' about?" Mom bent down to wipe the blood from my nose. "Good Lord, I hope it's not broken. Noses never look quite right after they're broken."

"It isn't broken."

When Mom asked Sal how he knew, he shrugged and said, "I guess I've been hit a lot myself. I know when it's broken and when it's just hurt. And that is just hurt."

"It's no good havin' sons fightin'." Mom sat down beside me, leaving me to hold the bag of ice. "Just look at what happened to Cain and Abel."

"My nose is broken." I threw the ice down. "And none of you even care. Let alone that Grand is gone . . . with that man."

"What man?" Mom looked out across the yard like they were still there. "You mean that New Yorker? He was all right. Said he'd give us a free subscription to *The New York Times*. I'm gonna hold 'im to that."

"Your nose isn't broken." Sal picked up the bag of ice and handed it to me. "It isn't even bleeding anymore."

"It still hurts."

"My poor baby." Mom pulled me into her side and sang,

Down in the hills of Ohio,
there's a babe at sleep tonight.
He'll wake in the morn of Ohio,
in the peaceful, golden light.

"Come on, you too." She waited for Sal to sit at her other side. And there the three of us swayed with her soft voice,

The Father will smile in Ohio,
and the Mother will hold you tight.
You will be my love in Ohio,
and fooorrrr allllll time.

My mother always smelled like Breathed River, of wet rocks and gritty sand. Or maybe she didn't. Maybe I just gave that smell to her because her flowing fluid form should've smelled more like a river than a house.

"I remember when we first moved into this house," she sighed. "Me and your dad. I was pregnant with Grand. He wasn't due for another week or so. Your father was off at the courthouse while I stayed home here, takin' wallpaper swatches 'round to the different rooms. As I was considerin' makin' the entry hall blue, my water broke.

"I couldn't call your father, 'cause we had yet to hook up the phone. I tried to make it to the neighbors, but the pain became everything. I delivered right there beside the grandfather clock.

"I thought the worst part was over, but as I held Grand in my arms, I heard growlin'. We had yet to put the screens up, and a dog was comin' through the livin' room winda. A big beast of a mutt. I knew at once it was First, Mr. Elohim's dog. Then I saw the white foam at First's mouth. Bein' a country girl, I knew he was rabid.

"I was far too weak to fight off a rabid dog, so I opened the door of the grandfather clock and placed Grand down inside, just below the pendulum. I thought the dog may get me, but at least my baby will be safe. Before I closed the clock's door, I saw it. A revolver with an ivory handle. I checked to see if it was loaded. Then I took aim and fired. One bullet, that's all it took to take down an entire system of muscles and vessels and organs and bones."

I was quiet for a few moments, and then I asked as if I didn't already know, "What'd ya do with the gun, Mom?"

"Don't you get any ideas, Fielding. I put it someplace safe. I do not want you fishin' for it. Mark my words, Fielding, if I find that gun missin', I'll shoot you with it." She took her arm out from around Sal so she could playfully poke me in the stomach. *"Bang, bang,"* but I couldn't laugh, because my stomach was in the low from Grand's punches.

"Oh, poor Mr. Elohim." She coiled the beads at her neck. "He loved that dog so much. It's why he puts the poison out. It was a coon gave First rabies."

After Mom went inside to start dinner, me and Sal stayed on the porch. We were there when Dad got home. He asked about my bruises.

"Me and Grand just played too rough." I shrugged it off.

Grand didn't come home for dinner. He did call. Told Mom when she picked up the phone that he'd eat with the journalist at Dandelion Dimes and wouldn't be home for a while.

I thought about Grand and this man in the yellow booth with the dandelion wallpaper around them, the little yellow vase of plastic dandelions between them. The waitress who would come in her yellow uniform to take their order on a yellow pad, before walking past the yellow curtains to the yellow kitchen to serve their food on yellow dishes. Everything so yellow. Grand, I'm sure, remembered back to how Sal said there was no yellow in hell. With so much around him, Grand must've thought he was with that man in heaven, forgetting they were merely in Dandelion Dimes.

I stayed up long after Mom and Dad went to bed, pacing the porch while Sal sat patiently on the swing. My nose was still sore and the vision in my right eye was obstructed from my hanging lid. It hurt to stand up tall. It stretched the bruises out on my ribs. I was the beaten boy and feeling it all over. I feel it now. Especially the bruise in my chest, the length of a heart, the width of one too. The pain making me wince.

"You should go up and take a hot bath, Fielding. Help with the soreness."

I shook my head at Sal. "I'm waitin' for Grand."

"What if he doesn't come back?"

This thought frightened me. Maybe he wouldn't come back. Maybe I had to go to him.

I ran down the porch steps and was nearly out of the yard when Sal grabbed my arm.

"Let him come home on his own, Fielding."

"What's it to you? Huh? He's not your brother. This is not your family. Stop actin' like it is." I pushed him back and ran. I could hear his feet pounding behind me. He hollered that I didn't even know where Grand was.

But of course I did. He was with our secrets. Where else would he be?

It had been a few years back when I snuck into Grand's room and took his Eddie Plank card. I only took it to show off to a couple of friends, but I ended up losing it. I turned the world upside down looking for it, but it'd already been given to that place out of reach, so I went to Grand and said I had something to confess.

"What is it, Fielding?" He closed the chemistry book he'd been reading and sat up on the edge of his bed.

"I don't wanna say, Grand. You'll hate me."

"Well, I guess you're a little man now, huh? Kids are never afraid of bein' hated for somethin', 'cause they're still kids and easily forgiven. But men, they're not so easily forgiven and live in fear of bein' hated. I say you're a little man 'cause you're still more kid than man, but you got the fear now, so you're on your way. So what should we do, little man? Should ya tell me and risk bein' hated by me? Or, should ya keep it a secret?"

"Don't I have to tell ya, Grand?"

"I have secrets I haven't told you."

"What haven't you told me?"

"The make of a secret is silence, little man. There is a way we could tell our secrets to one another without really tellin' 'em."

We went downstairs to the kitchen, where he took the cocoa tin and dumped the last bit of its cocoa into the trash. So we could bury our secrets in it, he said.

"But that's not really tellin' a secret," I insisted.

"Sure it is. And one day when we're both feelin' brave, we'll dig up the secrets and promise each other, right now, that no matter what they are, we won't turn on each other. We won't get angry. We will accept the secrets and still . . . I don't know . . . любовь each other."

"What's любовь mean, Grand?" I did my best pronunciation of the Russian word. It came out jarred and mumbled, but I already knew what it meant. It was the first Russian word I had learned. Still I wanted to hear him translate it.

" 'Love.' It means 'love,' little man."

This *love* echoed in my ears as I got closer to the tree house, where we had buried the secrets. I shushed Sal as we moved low through the brush. We heard the moans before we saw them. It was the first time I'd ever seen sex. It took me a moment to realize that's what I was seeing.

At first I just saw Grand standing back into the man's chest. Clothes in piles on the ground around them. Two naked bodies strong and close. The movement was gentle and familiar, like the time I was in Juniper's with Dad. He was going up to the register with a tube of toothpaste in his hand. There was another man already at the register. Along the way, Dad tripped and fell into the backside of this man. They didn't fall down, they just nudged forward, bending in a curve of bodies while that tube of white toothpaste shot out in front.

That's what their sex looked like to me, just two men falling into each other and catching each other at the same time.

I wanted it to be a girl he was with. Grand with a girl wouldn't have frightened me. We had been brought up not religiously but Bible aware. I knew the Bible said thou shall not lie with another man if you are one. I was not wise enough to know that God was more than the Bible. I had yet to know this at thirteen years old for not just Grand's sake but for my own as well.

I was sure Grand was going to the fire in the ground, and even though the devil wasn't so bad when he was Sal, maybe he was terrible when he wasn't. Thinking of Grand being tormented for eternity not only broke my heart, it broke all the surrounding area too. My lungs. My ribs. My everything.

I wasn't ready to lose the fantasy that was my brother, because like his name, he was grand. The grandest damn thing I'd ever known. And yet, I didn't know him at all. I had always thought he was just this traditional American male, and here he was so foreign to me. It was then I realized he'd been telling us he was gay all along, every time he spoke Russian. Not because of the Russian itself. It could've been any language because being gay was what was foreign. It seemed not to speak English and he didn't understand it. He knew no one else who fluently spoke that language. He tried to speak it, learn it, understand it, but being gay didn't feel like home, where all the boys wrapped their arms around girls and kissed them and made love to them because they wanted to.

Grand tilted his nose up. He was breathing something in. I smelled it too. His cologne on my shirt. *Oh, God.* Was that his face turning toward me? I pulled back into the shadows. No, he wouldn't see me. I wouldn't let him. But still he would know. He would smell my shadow and know I had seen who he truly was.

The heat was making it worse. It felt centered on my face. I wished I could just go home like it didn't matter. But of course, it mattered. It was the thing to matter the most.

I was going to scream. I had to get away. I made a mad dash to the river, where I jumped into the water and stayed under. Nothing but the fish hear you screaming underwater, nothing but the fish and yourself.

I think Sal thought I was trying to drown myself, because he swam down after me and pulled me up. I suppose I was under there for a rather long time. I let him swim me out of the water and to the bank, where he laid me down. He lay beside me and in silence, we looked up at the stars.

I saw each small glitter as another Earth. A billion planet Earths. A billion Grands fucking a billion men. And would I be lying at the side of the river a billion times? Frightened. Confused. Lost. Or was I up there somewhere getting it right?

"Sal?"

"Yeah?"

"Is it a sin? What Grand's doin' with that man?"

"Are you asking me as a boy? Or as the devil?"

"As a boy, Sal. I'm askin' you as a boy."

"Then, yes. It is a sin. Isn't that what all boys are taught? To like girls? To fall in love with one and make a life out of it? That's what they say. I don't know, Fielding, it's just what they say."

I shut my eyes. The stars were blurry anyways. "And what if I ask you as the devil?"

"I'd say no. It isn't a sin. And shouldn't the devil know more than a boy? Shouldn't a devil know all the things hell exists for?"

When we got home, Sal went to bed while I dusted off the family Bible. I carried it up to Grand's room and, using his yellow highlighter, followed the lines,

If a man also lie with mankind, as he lieth with a woman, both of them have committed an abomination: they shall surely be put to death; their blood shall be upon them.

I left the page open on top of his pillow so he'd see it when he got home. I thought I was saving him.

When he did finally come in an hour later, I stayed in the shadows. I remember how he was whistling. So happy as he turned on his light. I could hear him walking toward his bed. Then silence. Was he reading the Bible?

Yes, he had read it. Yes, he had thrown it into the wall and slammed his door shut. When he started to cry, it sounded like hail on a roof and I had to leave. I returned to the tree house and dug up the cocoa tin, and under the light of a billion mes, I read his secret:

I'm afraid.

A billion times the stars flinched and screamed, *I'm afraid.*

17

. . . mutual love, the crown of all our bliss

—MILTON, *PARADISE LOST* 4:728

I'VE STOOD ON top of more churches than I've gone into. The last time I was in a church, I was forty-four, and it was my father's funeral. Him and Mom had been living in Pennsylvania, and I came in to stay with them while she was sick.

She died in June. He died in August. Another summer of death. I knew he wouldn't last long, the way he sat at her bedside, eyes squinted, arms folded, legs crossed. For all the sunscreen Grand had asked me to put on, no one ever once asked Mom, not even when she left the house and went to all those places in the sun. Her chocolate chips had melted. I wasn't there to pull her away from the oven.

I remember how Dad would lay his hand on her head as white and as slight as powder on the pillow. She'd tilt her ending eyes toward him and the window. Her breathing raspy and rutted, like a finger-nail scratching across a cotton sheet.

All she wanted to do was to go outside, even in the rain. Especially in the rain.

"Let me go." She'd reach for her feet like that was the first step.

We'd pull her bones back to the bed. It was no longer her keeping her inside. It was us, and that turning of the tables clotted our hearts with an inescapable sorrow until we almost wished she were still afraid of the rain.

"You need your rest," we'd say, and feel her pulse, sounding like closing.

One time as she slept, I held my nose to her cold skin. I thought she would smell like the morphine they pumped into her. I don't know if morphine has a smell, but I thought it would be something metallic, something acidic, most definitely something cold. I was relieved when she still smelled like Breathed River. Did she really? I think I just needed her to.

Our conversation consisted of her saying my name, me saying hers. *Fielding. Mom. Fielding! Mom! Fielding? Mom?*

A dying mother is hard to talk to, especially when she starts screaming about a fire. We told her it was put out.

"When?" she asked.

"A long time ago," we said almost in unison.

I took a wet washcloth and stroked her face. She seemed to like it. She smiled. Said Grand's name.

"He's not here, Mom." I laid the washcloth over her eyes so I wouldn't have to see them.

"Why ain't my boy here?"

"He's with Sal."

With my palm lying on top of the washcloth, I could feel her eyes pushing like tiny hands trying to push up out of rubble.

"Oh." She drew her breath. A faintly sketched line. "My boys."

I went away from her then and thought of Granny, of that suffering we are asked as men to end. As I was packing my suitcase to go to Mexico to buy pentobarbital, the phone rang. It was Dad. He didn't say a word. All he did was cry. I told him it was a bad connection and to call back. I had to hang up first. I tore up my plane ticket and went around the house, turning on all the faucets. The kitchen, the bathroom, upstairs and down. Sinks and tubs and showers. I wanted to hear the water go down the drains so I wouldn't have to hear myself doing the same.

After Mom's funeral, when me and Dad were driving back to the house, he told me to take a turn. Following his directions, I ended up driving to an amusement park off the highway.

"We're going to ride the roller coasters." He grunted into his handkerchief.

"You hate roller coasters. And what about what the doctor said about your heart? No quick starts, remember. No big frights."

He rode every roller coaster in the park that day, as somber as his black suit. His heartbeat escalated, his pulse quickened, but what he wanted to happen did not happen. I've never seen a more disappointed man in my life. Every day he returned to the park, but after a month of roller coasters, he did not have the heart attack the doctor assured him he would have under such stress.

He'd gotten so used to the coasters that there he'd be, his chin propped up on the back of his hand, looking out past the loops and turns like he was just taking a Sunday drive while everyone else screamed around him and gripped the bar for dear life.

When the heart attack did finally come, it did so when he was sitting calmly in the La-Z-Boy. Instead of an obituary, I put an invitation in the newspaper. I sat there in a pew of the church, and for every person who walked through the door who wasn't Sal I took a drink from the flask in my pocket. By the time the preacher asked me to stand and say a few words, the flask was empty. I ended up wobbling on the pulpit while going into the graphic details of what happens when a bullet hits the chest cavity.

The preacher whispered in my ear something like, "I think you should take your seat now."

"Fuck you, man," I might have said. And then somebody punched him. I suppose it was me.

I was never meant to be a violent man. I was meant to be my father's son. My mother's. But in the end, I became the son of that summer. That summer is my father. It is my mother. It is my violence's blame.

Sometimes I feel like I'm still fighting my way through the mob to get to the fire. I have to throw a punch. I have to swing a kick. I have to give everything I am to put the fire out. It's been that fight my whole life.

I haven't been back to Mom's and Dad's graves since. I don't even remember the name of the Pennsylvania cemetery anymore. Sometimes I walk to the cemetery up the road from the trailer park here and pick a couple of graves and pretend they're Mom's and Dad's. I stand over them and chat about this and that. It's always light conversation between us, something a gnat would whisper in their ear, certainly nothing to tunnel into the dark about. They've already got their own huge terrors. Why disturb them any more?

Before I leave them, I always lay a flower down for each and go walking for as far and as long as my aching body will allow.

I've not been happy with aging. My once supple limbs and previously bendable joints are now as stiff as layers of cardboard stapled together. I used to be tall, like my family, but arthritis is a bending demon, and in that, a shortening one. But the worst part is the pain that intrudes and clings like venomous batter being poured until it packs up under my skin in lumps and knots that throb like the heartbeat of thunder.

My hands hurt me the most. You wanna know the hurt? Hang a piece of wood up and punch it from sunrise to sunset. See the sick swells of your knuckles, like balls of tightening wire. Pain is our most intimate encounter. It lives on the very inside of us, touching everything that makes us. It claims your bones, it masters your muscles, it reels in your strength, and you never see it again. The artistry of pain is its contact. The horror of it is the same.

Pain is a thing that speaks, and what the pain is telling me is that I've been irresponsible in resting my body. From the time I was seventeen, I worked every single day at breakneck pace, climbing up and down ladders, dismantling brick and stone while pushing my body to stay agile across the expanses of roofs.

While steeplejacking was my preferred occupation, I was like Elohim and did all kinds of work. I burnt brush, laid concrete, any and all construction I could get—hell, I was even a logger for a bit. I've done ironwork, rigging and welding and working with heavy steel. I took the shifts no one else wanted. I'd go from one job to another. Then there was all the fucking I did, which is its own toll on the body. I was trying to earn my way to sleep. It did not happen.

And thus I am pain in every inch of my mind, in every inch of my body. I am the endless flailing, the endless falling, the endless story of what happens to a man who cannot let go.

I think about my death. I know it is the long hallway of burning doors that awaits me. I know it is the real devil I go to eternity with. I wonder about the body I leave behind. How soon the flies will come. How soon I will be found. They'll put me into the ground, not for respect but to be rid of the smell. There will be no handkerchiefs drying in the horizon. I will go to death without the give of tears. Maybe the neighbor boy will shed something. Maybe he will say my name like I mattered.

I might show the boy my scrapbook. Red leather like Elohim's. Sometimes I think the scrapbook is full of Grand and Sal, Mom and Dad, and even Elohim. It's hard to tell the difference between a picture of them and one of a chimney taken apart. I feel like I've felled them all.

The other day I asked the boy if he'd like to go for a walk. I haven't walked with anyone in thirty years. And suddenly there we were, walking down the road past saguaros and desert. I thought maybe we just might keep walking all the way to Ohio, and it might be all right if we did because I'd have him by my side.

But then we saw it, lying by the edge of the road.

"Poor fella." I approached its lifeless form.

"Mr. Bliss?"

"It's okay, boy. It's just a deer. Been hit, poor thing."

I squinted and saw antlers that by their size made the deer a young buck. Its blood had a breakfast quality to it, like something to be spread on toast.

I turned back to the boy. "It smells like strawberries."

"Mr. Bliss, maybe the heat is gettin' to ya. Maybe we should go back home?"

I looked back down at the deer and saw its belly rise. "My God. It's still alive. What pain it must be in." I thought of purpling organs. Of wounds with brutal edges. Of veins unraveling into rivers on a map to the grave. "We've got to help it on its way. Put it out of its misery. I'll do it. You're still just a boy."

I pulled the small piece of pottery out of my pocket as I knelt down and patted the deer.

"I wish I had the gun," I told it, as if it would understand that.

I dragged the pottery's sharp point across its throat, expecting flesh to open and blood to pour. When that did not happen, I tried again, but the deer would not be cut.

"Mr. Bliss, please stop."

"I can't. Don't you understand? It's suffering."

I began to go after the deer's death rather than help it to it. Over and over, I cut the pottery across its throat. The deer started to resist, or at least I was holding its body down as if it were.

"Mr. Bliss, stop."

I felt the boy's arms come gently though determined around my neck, pulling me back.

"It's not a deer, Mr. Bliss, it's not a deer. It's just a cardboard box. Must've fallen off a truck."

"No, you're wrong. It's . . ."

I looked down at what I thought had been a struck deer but was in reality a banged-up cardboard box. The pair of sticks that could be antlers if you needed them to. Then there was the strawberry jam I'd believed was blood. It seeped from the broken jars, oozing wide and then tapering as if the way to eternal glory is one long, narrow passage. Maybe that's why it's so hard to get there. Our sins widen us until the narrow way is something we can never go through. We have no choice but to languish in the boiling of what's left, as I have been languishing.

Oh, God, just burn me away until I'm all gone.

"Mr. Bliss, look here. One of the jars didn't break." The boy held the miracle up in the sun, the light shining through the jam and blessing each seed.

I took the jar from him and tried to twist its lid off, but these damn hands, shortened by the swelling and the knots. I stared at his long, tall fingers as they opened the jar with ease. A boy opened what I could not. I was suddenly the midget and he the tallest man in the world. For that moment, I hated him.

He tasted the jam, it squeezing out to the corners of his mouth.

"Did I ever tell you I had a brother? His name was Grand."

"Oh, here, Mr. Bliss." He picked up the pottery piece dropped to the ground. "Best put it in your pocket before you forget."

"I won't forget."

I remember too well the day. Me and Sal were in the kitchen, helping Mom clean the glass in the cabinets with vinegar. I could hear the music blaring from Grand's room overhead. Ever since that night, it seemed to be the only thing he did. Stay in his room. Blare music. Tell Mom he wasn't hungry and no he wouldn't be down for dinner. And no, Dad, he doesn't feel like going outside at the moment and would you just leave him alone? Those were the things he shouted through his closed door.

He hated me. It was why he couldn't look at me. Why he skipped meals. Why he shut his door and only came out when I wasn't around.

Then one day, there he was, like a spirit, standing in my room. By that time, my eyelid had lifted and my nose no longer hurt when I sneezed. The pain of the fight lay in the reason for it. Grand was the type of brother to regret such brotherly brawls. I saw this very regret, as if in his mind he would never stop seeing the bruises, even after they'd faded from me.

"Have ya seen the Bible, Fielding?"

He could not hide the crushing he was still feeling from the night I opened the Bible to him. That was what he was asking me, after all. How I could do such a thing.

What would he have said if instead of shaking my head, I told him, *yes I have seen the Bible and I have seen you.*

Cowardice is always too late for the fact that bravery has the better chance. Our better chance could've been understanding. It could've been soaring from that which has too long been believed to be a sin. And yet it's far too easy to be the coward when it requires nothing more than a lie.

"I never touch the Bible, Grand, you know that."

He left without another word. Later that night, I would find the Bible open on top of my pillow. A line highlighted there. Hebrews 13.

Let brotherly love continue.

The sun had broke and I blinked in its light. That was Grand. The first to forgive when he had the right to be the last. I tore out the page and held it to my chest as I left my room. His door was open. It was the first time in days no music was blaring. He was laying across his bed, reading. I think it might've been Langston Hughes. I quietly passed his room and went down to the kitchen, where I placed the page in the back of the freezer.

I wonder about that page. Is it still in the freezer behind the box of frozen broccoli? Or has someone cleaned? Removed the ice and tossed the broccoli and by that found the page only to wonder why Hebrews 13 was in a freezer in the first place. I would say because I wanted to save it from that summer, from melting away. Our love forever frozen and safe in that freezing.

Sometimes I wake in the middle of the night, clutching for the freezer that has been dismantled. The broccoli thawed. The ice melted. The page flying away into the flames. I reach for it but am always, always, too late for the save.

"Fielding?"

Mom was calling my name and saying I was leaving too much lint on the glass. The whole kitchen smelled like vinegar as the three of us wiped the cabinets.

I laid down my rag and picked up the bowl sitting on top of the counter. An image of it holding macaroni salad flashed into my mind. "Sal? Where'd you get this bowl?"

"I got it from Amos."

"When his folks came, they said you didn't. Remember?"

"Maybe it was his mother's." Mom took the bowl from me and looked it over herself. "Is that where ya got it, honey, your mom?"

"He don't have a mom. He said so himself. Ain't that right, Sal?"

He slowly nodded while Mom set the bowl down with a sigh and leaned back against the counter, staring at the pantry. Her eyes caught on the can of Crown Prince Sardines. She smiled as if it were her best idea ever as she grabbed the can and pulled its lid off. She warned Sal not to move as she began to place the sardines on top of his head.

"What are you doing?" He smiled. To him life could get no better.

"I'm makin' you a crown because you are a prince and your momma is a beautiful queen who loves you more than you'll ever know."

After she laid the last sardine down, she set the can on top of the counter and stepped back to see Sal in full. "Yes, you are a prince."

"The Prince of Darkness?" He looked afraid she would call him devil.

"My dear, sweet boy, you could never be anything but the Prince of Light."

"I wish you were my mother." Sal's whisper seemed to echo off the walls.

"Oh, my darlin'." The sardines fell to the floor as she grabbed him into her and held him tight. "I can be her for as long as you need me to, my dear, sweet love."

He deserved to have a mother hold him like that, and yet I found myself not wanting it to be my mother. As if by embracing him she put herself in danger. For a moment I allowed myself to believe Elohim. That Sal's feet clacked like cloven hooves across the ground. That he was the forked tongue, the red demon, hell every day of the week. Something to keep back behind a chain-link fence. Away from hearth and home. Away from those you love the most.

"I don't know why you'd wanna thief for a son."

Mom gave me one of her looks, told me to just hush now.

"What?" I shrugged. "It's pretty obvious he stole that bowl and spoon from somewhere."

"Oh, he didn't steal anything." She let go of Sal and he hated me for being the reason.

As she began to pick up the sardines with heavy sighs, I kept at it.

"If he didn't steal 'em, where'd he get 'em? Hmm, Sal?"

"I can't remember." His anger was making a shadow of him, a sort of cold draft coming in under the door.

"You're lyin'. You're a lyin' thief."

"I'm not a thief." He glared at me as if he could light me up. I believe he might've if Mom hadn't been there to be disappointed in him for doing so.

I was in his path to the counter, so he gave me a hard shove to the side as he quickly grabbed the bowl and spoon, running from the kitchen with them.

"I don't know why ya had to go and start somethin', Fielding. Go after him." Mom shooed me out.

From the back porch, I saw him running up the hill, into the woods. I called his name and took chase. He seemed to run forever. The hills like his own rising world. Maybe he was a prince, and he was running away to his castle. Could I follow him there? Could I keep running after the wild ruler to his kingdom, where a crown of sardines was enough?

He ran faster than me, and I struggled with what I saw. Was it a boy ahead? Or a flame burning through the land, starting quiet fires only we knew?

It was no kingdom, but the train tracks he finally stopped at.

"Why'd you follow me, Fielding?" He caught his breath like a true boy who had just run too far too fast.

I think he'd been crying, but there was too much sweat to see the difference.

"Sal, about what I said back at the house. I was bein' stupid. I've just been pissed off lately. You know, with Grand and everything. I shouldn't have taken it out on you."

After all, that was really what my outburst was about, wasn't it? Seeing my mother and Sal embrace so easily. The way I wanted to hold and be held by Grand. The raw strength of that very thing, revealing something of us. In the best hope, something like pretty honey drizzling from the crooks of our elbows while we apologize and say it was all play in the hills and nothing has changed. But, of course, over and over again, everything has changed.

"Sal? I said I'm sorry."

He looked down at the bowl and spoon still in his hands. "I really don't remember where I got them from. But I could make up a story. Let's imagine that you, you're a boy—"

"I am a boy."

"And you're walking down the railroad tracks. Go on, walk down them."

I stepped over on top of the tracks and, although feeling a bit foolish, began walking in place. I figured I owed it to him for starting the fight.

"Why am I walkin' down the tracks again?"

"Because you want a shot at life." He began to circle me. "Your father is exhausted in his overalls and dirt. You can't sing in the big trees if you're too tired to climb. You can't love the day if you're letting each one pass while you stupidly scream at the life you hate.

"Your father is nothing but a losing old man. Yet he wants you to be just like him. To be tired and losing and to work God's green earth. But it's not green earth. It's the closing of passion. The defeat of zeal. It is ground that ends.

"When you say you want to be more, more than the screaming, more than the father, your mother asks you if you realize just how hard he's worked to get this land? To raise the farm to something that can be passed down to you. *'Do you?'* she screams at you, frightened herself, for she too has many deaths to suffer.

"You say, 'Momma, I just want more. I want to fly like the sudden light. I want to know what it's like to have a reason to dance. I want all the possible love.'

"She says people like us don't dance and we don't fly. People like us, she says, don't get more. We take the life we are given and we say grace and glory be to God who in His merciful wisdom has granted such bliss. You hate her God and His wisdom. You hate her acceptance of that empty life. And out of all the places your father lives in you, you want to hit her, just like he does.

"You hate them both for all the things they are and for all the things they will never be. This is what you scream at her. That you hate how he wears overalls every day and that she can't read or write. You hate how he is called boy, even by those he is elder to. You hate he will never be more than a dumb nigger and that she will never be more than a housewife in a kitchen, a kitchen she has had more bones broken in than pies baking.

"You scream until you think you are of single depth and a holding hate you fear you'll never be able to let go of. That's when your mother gets real quiet. You see her eyes and know it was you who put the pain there. You wait for it, knowing it is coming."

"That what's comin'? Sal?"

When his hand struck my cheek, it felt like the smack of a flame.

"She says you'll never have the godliness of your father. *'Devil!'* she screams at you. So you look at her one last time and run away because horns is all you'll ever wear there, but somewhere else, you may be able to have the halo. Still, you hear her final word as you walk down the train tracks. *Devil.* You think maybe you are, and maybe you always will be. Maybe that is your permanence, your one eternity.

"As if hearing you run away, a man appears and says he has some ice cream you could run away to. You say you don't know. He says he can tell you are the type of boy who needs something to hold onto, so he gives you a bowl and spoon."

Sal shoved the bowl and spoon into my stomach, forcing me to take them just to get them out of my ribs.

"The man says you can go for a drive in his sparkling convertible. How can a convertible be bad, you think. They only ever drive them in advertisements when they're selling happiness, when they're selling a shot at a good life. You still want that shot desperately, so you take the bowl and spoon and ride in his convertible, which reminds you of the 1950s, with its polished chrome and high tailfins. You think this is what you're supposed to do. Ride in a white convertible and drop the shadows of the farm.

"As you get closer to his house, he tells you to bend down and touch the car's floor and count to twenty. He's short enough to see over, so you're not afraid, and by the time you've counted to twenty, you're in his garage and from there, in his house where you see pictures of a tall woman. You ask if it's his wife. Yes, he answers. She's smiling in the pictures, so you think he can't be so bad. You forget it is the camera we smile at, not the life behind."

"I don't like this story." I set the bowl and spoon down on the tracks.

I thought Sal was going to slap me again. Instead he continued the story as if there could never be anything to stop it.

"The man goes into the kitchen, to get the ice cream, he says.

While you wait for him, you read old newspaper clippings in the red leather scrapbook open on the table. See a woman's face in one of the clippings, same face as in the photographs around you. You get a sinking feeling, you feel you might sink.

"When the man returns, he doesn't have any ice cream. He has a white handkerchief. And suddenly, you can't breathe at all."

Sal came up behind me and held his hand over my mouth so forcibly, I thought my teeth would break.

"Just go to sleep now, boy," Sal repeated over and over again as I struggled. His strength surprised me, and only when I elbowed him as hard as I could did he let go.

"What's the matter with you, Sal?"

"It's just a story, Fielding."

A horn blared from the train approaching in the distance.

"That was a pretty messed-up story."

"Hell's full of all kinds of stories like that."

He looked back at the blaring train, its smoke churning up like a way to follow. Maybe in his mind he was following that smoke up to the clouds and to the God too gold to be of any earthly help.

I went to get the bowl and spoon off the tracks, but Sal told me to leave them.

"That's the ending of the story," he said. "Something broken."

Together we watched as the train roared over first the spoon and then the bowl, its broken pieces scattered to the ground.

"You know, Fielding, the thing about breaking something that no one much thinks about is that more shadows are created. The bowl when intact was one shadow. One single shadow. Now each piece will have a shadow of its own. My God, so many shadows have been made. Small little slivers of darkness that seem at once to be larger than the bowl ever was. That's the problem of broken things. The light dies in small ways, and the shadows—well, they always win big in the end."

18

Which way I fly is Hell; myself am Hell;
And in the lowest deep, a lower deep
Still threatening to devour me opens wide

     —MILTON, *PARADISE LOST* 4:75–77

THIS IS ME. Teeth marks here. Teeth marks there. Being eaten one bite at a time. I smell myself on my breath. Feel myself swallowed and plopped to my stomach. Clean myself out from my own teeth with a toothpick.

It was Carl Jung who said shame is a soul-eating emotion. It doesn't eat you in one big gulp. It takes its time. Seventy-one years, it is still taking its time.

I am for my own teeth. I am for my own stomach. I alone eat myself to the dark.

It was the end of August, and me and Sal were in the woods by the tree house. There I saw a metal bucket of stones. I thought maybe Sal was building onto Granny's grave. Then I saw the paint on the stones. I picked a few up. They all had the same image of a boat. More than that. It was a ship given the details of something grand like an ocean liner. Then the name written on the sides. SS *Andrea Doria*.

"What do you think?" Sal came up behind me.

I was stunned at the details of the ships and how the same image could be done over and over again without miss.

"I painted them at night, while you were sleeping."

I dropped the stones back into the bucket. "Listen, Sal, if these are for Mr. Elohim—"

"Shouldn't they be? All his pamphlets and meetings. He has no right to keep on me. I've been good. I mean, I could be bad, Fielding. I could be really bad for him, I could be the worst thing ever. But they always take away the trouble, and I want to stay.

"If only he would just be good. Then we wouldn't have to worry about any bad he's done or could do. You don't have to worry about the teeth if they get filed down. And that's all I want to do. Just file his teeth down a bit, so we can all live together."

"You can't throw stones at 'im, Sal."

"It's not skin bruises I'm after. I want to take him down from the heart. Only the *Andrea Doria* can do a thing like that."

He picked up the bucket. "Would you go to the schoolhouse, Fielding? Where he holds his meetings. I'll meet you there in a few minutes."

Feeling no more argument within myself, I went to the schoolhouse where Elohim and his followers were standing around a contained fire. Hunkering down behind a fallen log, I watched Elohim drop a wiggling burlap sack. The group crowded around as he opened the bag and reached inside, pulling out a garter snake similar to the one Dad had set free in the woods. The bag was full of them, and one by one, the followers grabbed their own.

By then, Sal had come along, hiding down beside me while I stared at the stone in his hand. I wondered if what we were about to do would be something we could never take back.

All eyes were on Elohim as he approached the fire with the snake in his hand, a harmless little black thing that slithered in and out of his fingers.

I've never forgotten the way he looked at that snake with hunger for its death. He started to chomp his teeth at it, biting large chunks of the air before swallowing big with an even bigger smile. All the while, the snake innocently twirled around his fingers, not knowing the flames were for it.

"Good-bye, boy." Elohim tossed the snake like it was nothing.

The others followed. Snakes flying for the first time, landing in flames for the last. I closed my eyes and found another fire. One where snakes weren't writing in pain. One that was warming cold hands on a cold night, lighting the dark. Not one where hisses were cries. Not one that was pain slithering, trying to escape.

You could smell the foul secretion of the snakes. Mixing with that was the smell of their burning. You know the smell.

That car crash you're passing. It smells like garter snakes burning. That airplane falling from the sky. Garter snakes. A husband collapsing heart down. A woman screaming. A child hit by a car called Father. You know it all smells like snakes on fire.

"See what I mean, Fielding? Doesn't he deserve to be punished, even just a little bit?" Sal gripped the stone in his hand until his knuckles blanched.

I nodded, repeated his own words, "You can tell a lot about a man by what he does with a snake."

You could lose your eyes, staring at that group. At their silent twinkling. I am still surprised by the excitement in their smiles.

I was once told writing in a journal could help me. Something about putting the pain on the page. So I got one and finished it in a day. I looked back to see what I'd written. Nothing but little lines, swooping and curving. Not one word. And yet didn't it say everything? The way their smiles did? All the dark, all the hurt, scooped up, carried by curve.

Long after the last snake burned, they continued to watch the flames, in love with fire and so certain of what they wanted burned. It was hurt for them to finally douse the flames. They grieved, watching the smoke of their beloved churn away to the sky.

It was Elohim who called them up from their knees. The meeting was over and he was handing out vegetarian recipes. They quietly received them before glancing back at the fire, wishing it still huge and bright.

When Elohim was alone and humming over the snakes' ashes, Sal stood and announced rather quietly, "I have the *Andrea Doria*. I have your Helen."

Elohim turned and stared at the ship painted on the stone Sal held up to him.

"You little—" Elohim fell into a tirade of profanity as he took chase after Sal.

I went after them, running past the nearby tree house and through scratching briars and dry blackberry bushes while a woodpecker knocked on one of the trees overhead. I didn't know where we were running to, but I wasn't stopping, not even when a flying squirrel glided across the path in front of me.

Flying squirrels were usually seen only in the woods at night. It was as if the squirrel was saying, *Go back, Fielding, before you make a mistake. You don't belong any further, just as I don't belong here in the light.*

At that moment, I didn't care where I belonged. I was all legs running after two souls more entwined than any of us could ever have imagined. Isn't that a scary thing? To be soldered, sword to sword, the battle eternal and the win never had.

I realized Sal was leading us to the river, and once there, he threw the stone into the water as he said, "Best hurry, Elohim, the *Andrea Doria* is sinking. Don't let her. She won't forgive you a second time."

Without hesitation, Elohim threw himself into the water, paddling his short arms up in big splashes to get to the stone that had already sunk. Still he dived down, only to come right back up empty-handed and gasping for air.

"I'll give you another chance." Sal reached into the bucket by his feet. "See if you can save this one."

This was how it went. Sal casting a stone. Elohim splashing to get it. Splashing more to find it before it sank. It always sank. He became stupid-faced. Eyes frantic. Mouth open. Probably slobbering as he turned his face this way and that, his cheeks seeming to bobble in each movement. A slow-motion whale caught in the fisherman's net.

Turning and twisting, trying to be free but only getting further away from that very thing.

"Sal." I grabbed his arm. "I don't know 'bout this."

"I'm doing this so he'll stop. Maybe he'll even move away and we'll have Breathed all to ourselves. You, me, Mom, Dad, Grand . . ."

It was the first time I'd heard him make my parents his own. The first time he'd spoken my brother's name like he belonged to him too. I guess I should've said that was all right, because he looked down like it wasn't. Like he could never be my brother, the third son of Autopsy and Stella Bliss.

"I just mean he's not going to stop with me. You know that, Fielding. He's starting to talk at those meetings about you and yours."

Elohim was still diving below the water, unaware of anything more than the ship and the woman he was trying to save.

"I'm not telling you to hit him." Sal placed the stone into my hand. "Just let him feel a little splash. Let him know you're willing to fight for and protect those you love. That if he drags out this fray, he will not leave it unscathed. It's a battle we are in, Fielding. And if a few stones can end it, wouldn't you rather have them than a war that goes forever?"

Ready the earth for all she can spare, for it was a war, and already we had lost one on our side. Granny. Death by enemy's poison. Wasn't she worth a splash to his face? And what of this war? If it could be ended by a thrown stone, why not? I'd be a fool to hold out for a fire that could dare hell.

I gripped the stone and heard Grand's voice from when he was teaching me the art of the throw.

"Head up, Fielding. Chin pointed to your target. Get your whole body workin' together. Do you feel it now? Let me see your grip. Fingers over the top. Good. Keep it out on your fingertips now. No, Fielding, not in the back of your hand. Keep it at your fingertips. Good. Use your wrist. Don't let it get stiff. That's right. Now you're ready. You're ready, little man. Throw."

It was a beautiful throw. The way the stone sliced through an arch down to a large splash that hit Elohim's face.

"Hey"—I smiled—"this ain't so bad."

Maybe I even called Elohim a dumb midget as he dived, his feet thrashing at the surface to follow him down.

We threw stone after stone, believing with each one we were bettering the war.

But more than this. I was actually having fun doing it. I was laughing even as I said, "C'mon, Mr. Elohim. Can't ya save at least one? Your fiancée sure would be disappointed you can't save her. Hear her screamin' for you, Mr. Elohim? Gosh, I sure do."

I turned to give Sal a high five, but he was just standing there, his hands empty as he looked out on Elohim as if he were someone we should kindly pull from the water and sit with our arms around. It was then I realized I was the only one still throwing.

"When'd you stop, Sal?"

"We've done enough, Fielding."

"He deserves this. Remember?"

As soon as I threw, I knew what big sins can be made from things as small as stones. When it hit his chest, it sounded like melons being ripped apart. I waited for the howl. The scream of pain. Neither came. He was quiet and still. The stone sinking in front of him. He could have saved that one. All he had to do was to reach out and put his hand under it and he would've saved it. But he gave it up, to look at me.

He's still looking at me.

Every morning, I get up and think the sunrise might be beautiful. He's looking at me and I know it's not. Every night, I go to bed, thinking I may get some rest, but he's looking at me and I know I won't. The seasons may still exist, celebrations of life, but I don't know, because he's looking at me. Was that a joke you told? I can't laugh, because he's looking at me. With those gray, broken eyes saying, *I loved you once. Maybe like a son. Why are you doing this to me? Why are you hurting me, Fielding?*

I didn't return to the bucket for another stone. I didn't return to the bucket, but Sal did. He picked up a stone, the largest of them all. He gripped it tight as he moved through the water.

"You've saved her now." He placed the stone into Elohim's hand. "You can stop your crying. You've saved her now. No more sinking today."

I'd never felt more like the devil. I taste the salt of that shame to this day. Teeth marks here. Teeth marks there. This is me.

19

. . . she for God in him.

—MILTON, PARADISE LOST 4:299

ALL LOVE LEADS to cannibalism. I know that now. Sooner or later, our hearts will devour, if not the object of our affections, our very selves. Teeth are the heart's miracle. That a mouth should burst forth on that organ without throat and crave another's flesh, another's heart, is nothing short of a miracle.

To fall in love is our species' best adventure, and when love, in its burgeoning industry, coils sweetly around our soul, we surrender to the heart's fang and we pray—yes, we pray—to the infinite span that all love has its fair chance, its own share of miracles. And yet the miracles seem pushed to the side when the lovers are young, as if in their youth, there seems to be an almost certain prophecy to be had.

Maybe the misfortune of young love is just the *Romeo and Juliet* fragments Shakespeare has left us with, or maybe it really is the voyages of fate that youth and love should burn on contact. What is it the Greek chorus sings? Something like, *Young lovers are tragedy's excuse.*

I ask you now, what was the excuse of the yellow balloon? Did it escape from celebration? Was it the bloated announcement of a birthday, a wedding, a day at the fair? Is a child to be blamed for its wandering way?

Was it God, Devil, or wind that blew it upon release? Was it God, Devil, or tree that decided it should motor between branches, waiting for us in its harmless ruse?

I must first tell of the day that sparked the possibility of Sal and Dresden ending up together, for always and ever.

That day started by me and Sal throwing water balloons. It'd been my idea, but I had to stop. It reminded me too much of that day at the river. It would be throwing the stone's spirit from then on out.

"We shouldn't have filled 'em anyways." I stepped on the remaining balloons until they burst. "Dad would be angry if he knew. We're supposed to be conservin' water."

By the end of August, the heat had made more of a mess. The farmers lost their cash crops due to the drought, and the number of livestock continued to dwindle. Thankfully, the flies had been controlled by a recent spraying of pesticide. While at first the flies were blamed on Sal, they were actually traced to an infestation at an egg farm in the next town.

The rest of the country seemed to have forgotten about Sal and our heat wave, which was a fine relief to us, though Dad and the sheriff were still conducting their own investigation with more theories, more guesses, more places for pushpins to go and lines to be drawn.

I suppose I hoped they wouldn't find out where he came from. He had become my best friend. What boy is ever ready to lose that? It's not like Sal wanted to go back to wherever it was he came from. No boy who wants to go back calls another woman *Mom* or another man *Dad*. He doesn't call the place he's come from *hell* and the place he's at *heaven*.

His stories, his language, his way of manner said a child is not here, and yet there the child would poke its head. When he ran giddy to the tree house. When he sat up all night, telling me ghost stories in the dark, trying to deepen his voice to mystery over the light of the flashlight under his chin. When he wanted to learn how to play the piano in the living room. Or baseball or *Mario Bros.* Mom taught him the piano. Me and Grand taught him the rest.

There was a boy at home. He just wasn't ready to say it yet. And maybe he was afraid. I mean, it was the devil who'd been invited in the first place. Maybe he was afraid that being the devil was the only way he could stay.

Being the devil made him a target, but it also meant he had a power he didn't have when he was just a boy. People looked at him, listened to what he said. Being the devil made him important. Made him visible. And isn't that the biggest tragedy of all? When a boy has to be the devil in order to be significant?

It's not like anyone was coming looking for him. No mother showed up on our doorstep. No father either. Major newspapers from all over the country wrote at least once about him and various media outlets from TV reported on him in their local broadcasts, yet no one came saying they'd been looking for him and that he was theirs. No one came saying they wanted him back. Maybe if they had come and said that, he would've went with them. It was their not coming that kept his staying.

After bursting the balloons, we walked down the lane. When we came upon the Delmar house, Dresden stood up against the oak. I noticed her face right off.

She watched us approach over her book, *Lord of the Flies.* When I asked what was on her face, she answered it was makeup. In truth, it was construction paper, cut, trimmed, and taped into blush, lipstick, and purple eye shadow with long black lashes. The most unflattering was the pair of arching black lines placed over her own faint brows, giving her a sort of exaggerated madness.

She sighed like we were bothering her as she returned to her book and began to circle words.

"Why do you do that every day?" Sal asked.

"One should write in their diary every day." She flipped through the pages, showing how circling a word here and there made sentences like, *Today was not so bad,* and *I hate my leg.*

"I'm no writer, but still I want to record my days. And books have given me all the words I need. I just go through and take the ones that belong to me for the day. I like having my life entwined with literature's great tales. It makes me more—" She closed her eyes and found the word. "—significant."

I tried not to stare at that leg. I couldn't see much of it. She wore a long, flowing dress, one of her many muted floral ones that went below her ankles, but the leg's silhouette was still there. Its unbending form and black flat, which went against the bareness of her other foot.

"There's a pool in the backyard." Her frizzy hair stuck out as if it too had its own life to seize. "You guys could go for a swim."

We walked around the house, which was a large whitewashed brick, the white fading in places to the rusty tinge beneath. It had green shutters and green trim that matched the green bushes of the rose garden.

The heat would not prevent Alvernine's roses from blooming. When the sun's rays were too much, she would shade the roses by setting up tents, the kind used for parties and events. She would drape the bushes with dampened blankets to regulate their temperature, and she used fans, reaching from the house by extension cord, to keep them cool.

Each rose was so perfect and just like the next, they were almost unreal. Like they were machine printed. A garden of wallpapered walls. Later, we would come to learn Alvernine had been siphoning water from the forgotten artesian well at the top of the hill to keep her roses hydrated.

If found out, the well would've been seized by the town, and Alvernine would've paid a fine for breaking regulation. Worst to her, the town would've stopped her use of the well, and her roses would've died like most of the gardens in Breathed.

We still had our cannas, but only because Mom insisted we still water them, which we did so by driving to the river and bucketing it up, though the river too was getting low.

There by the rose garden was a sweeping inground pool with a diving board. Sal was looking down into its clear, clean water as he asked if he could go into the house. He had to use the bathroom, he said.

Dresden looked at the back door and frowned. "Mother doesn't like . . . strangers in the house."

"Is she home now?" I asked.

"No, she'll be gone for the day, but still—"

"Please." Sal stepped closer to her.

"All right. It's, um, just through the back door there and . . . Well, here, I'll just show you."

With them in the house, I went over to the edge of the pool, where I dipped my toe in. The pool had been filled in late spring, before the water regulations would've made such a thing impossible.

"You can get in if you want."

Dresden was back and looking at my bare chest. I couldn't tell if she approved or not. It's hard to be shirtless in front of a girl who may wish you weren't.

The summer had tanned her usually pale skin and given her freckles their own sort of triumph.

"You can swim, can't you?" She laid her pen and book down on top of the patio table. "Mother will be upset if you drown in her pool."

"I can swim." I headed toward the diving board but stopped when she asked if Sal was a nice boy.

"Whatcha mean?"

"I mean is he nice?"

"I'm nice."

Her sweat wet the edges of the construction paper. Even the heat was trying to undress the clown. She certainly didn't look like Dresden, the girl who in her simple beauty could make two boys give her the wind.

I brushed by her, feeling her on the back of my hand. Sometimes the briefest touch is the one that lasts the longest.

"Wanna swim with me, Dresden?"

"I think I might drown with you." She said it softly, the way someone may speak of floating instead of sinking.

"I wouldn't let you drown."

"I don't think you'd be able to help it, Fielding."

I told myself she was wrong. That there was no reason for that sadness in her voice, because no one would ever drown with me. I would be enough to save them all, I said to myself, feeling confident in that great, big lie.

"And what if you swim with Sal?" I asked. "Would ya drown with him too?"

"Girls don't drown with boys like Sal. They live eternity with them."

I walked by her, didn't brush her again, though. I returned to the diving board, not realizing I had said her name until she said mine.

"Yes, Fielding?"

The splashes of my cannonball reached her, but she didn't shriek like other girls would've. She just stood there, a wetter girl than the one before.

I followed the cannonball with a few laps. By that time, Sal had come back, apologizing for taking so long. I climbed out of the pool, my jeans shorts hanging low from the water, the denim's heavy fray splotched and matted against my legs.

"Why don't you take your sweater off, Dresden?" Sal looked at the sweater as if he hated it.

"I'm not that hot."

I could've laughed at her, at her sweaty forehead and hair plastered to the nape of her neck like an attack.

"You're burning up." Sal spoke like the soft spot of a hard truth. "And all because you're trying to cover the bruises she gave you."

"How do you know about the bruises?" She asked in a whisper.

Sal bit his lip with the fear all boys have of the girl they love. "I read your diary. One of them anyways. I didn't have to use the bathroom. I found your room. I went to the shelf and picked a book at random. *Ham on Rye* by Charles Bukowski. A lot of beatings for you to circle in that."

"God, don't you know anything about girls? You should never read what is still their secret. You . . . you . . ." She attacked him with slaps. I tried to break it up but got slapped myself, the happening like getting blood drawn by a thorn.

"I want you to leave this instant. Both of you." She stomped her good foot the way all girls are prone to do at least once in their lives.

He reached for her, but she backed away from him.

"Get away from me." She took a deep breath as if building the courage to say, "I hate you."

Hate, that all-too-willing pallbearer of love, that all-too-eager shovel piling the dirt over the lover's head until the funeral is over only a second after it's started. The boy can go nowhere near happiness when the girl he loves is not willing to go there with him. He may grow up, borrow a tuxedo, a sunrise, a tropical honeymoon, but they'll never be his without her. She was his truth, his wisdom, and he was stupid without her. Just an idiot with a dumb life.

He stood there teetering, knowing full well that without her, it would be the cliff all the time. He tried once more to reach for her.

"I'm sorry, Dresden Delmar."

"I don't care if you are sorry. I want you to leave, and I never want to see you again."

"All right," he whispered.

I don't even think he realized he was walking until we were almost around the corner of the house. It was her shouting for us to stop that made him jump as if being sparked back to life.

"I didn't really want you to go. You just . . . surprised me, reading my diary like that." She kept her eyes on the ground in front of her.

"I wasn't prepared to be revealed like that. I'm sorry I yelled at you. I don't hate you. Not really."

He smiled, and I think the whole world knew it. "Will you do something for me, Dresden Delmar? Take off your sweater."

"Oh, please. If I take it off—"

"You won't be able to pretend anymore," he finished her sentence. "Pretend that your mother loves you."

"She does love me. You just don't understand."

"Every bruise you've ever had, every sharp shade of purple, blue, black, I've had it too. We have had the same boss of pain, we have asked the same question, over and over again, *What have I done to deserve this?*

"There is no lack of understanding between the two of us. We've been part of the same crash this entire time. We just had yet to meet and pull each other from the wreckage. When you take your sweater off and reveal, it is not to reveal you alone, it is to reveal our shared selves. The purpling, black whorls something we can make fine together."

She was quiet as she watched a small yellow butterfly flutter past. As it landed on a rose, she began to unbutton the cardigan as she said, "I've never shown anyone, not even her, and she's the one who gave them to me."

"Her who?" I asked.

"Mother."

She slipped off the cardigan, revealing her strapless dress and her lay of freckles like a beautiful spray of mud. There with the freckles were the bruises. Flat as bruises are, yet piled upon her like things to weigh her, to make her buried beneath blues and violets and colors less terrible than the things they make.

She dropped the sweater to the ground. I walked around to see more bruises at the top of her back.

"Dresden?" I looked away because sometimes you see too much for just two eyes. "You said you haven't even shown your mom, but if she gave them to you, wouldn't she know about them already?"

"She only hits me when she's had too much to drink. I don't think she remembers when she's sober. I always make sure to be covered up so she doesn't have to remember. She wants me to wear long dresses anyways, because of the leg."

"I think I should tell my dad. He's a lawyer, ya know, and—"

"Don't you dare, Fielding Bliss." She sounded so mature saying my full name.

"All right, geez." I looked up at the sky and the God who should've done better. "Why does she hit you, Dresden?"

"I guess because I'm not as perfect as her roses. Everything must be as perfect as those roses. You've seen Mother. Is there or has there ever been anyone more perfect than she? It must be a great pain to her. To have everything so beautiful but me.

"Sometimes, I'll look at the bruises and see petals. I'll see roses. And then I'm no longer sad. How can I be? When my mother has given me nothing but flowers."

Dresden was a girl too in love with her mother ever to see the monster of her. She needed help, so I said as simply as I could, "Your mom's a bitch."

"She isn't. And I'd like it if you never call her that again, Fielding."

That whole time, Sal had been quietly staring at her bruises, like a boy too well depressed to be able to say something large enough. I knew the way he saw her then would be the way he would fight never to see her as again. From that moment on, she had the shield in him. She had the boy who would turn into a man for her and be the one her mother would never be strong enough to go against.

"I could turn your bruises into real roses." He went to the patio table to pick up the pair of scissors and roll of tape left there from when Dresden was putting on her construction paper makeup. With a glance around the garden, he went toward the bush of roses so lavender they were almost certainly blue.

"What is the name of these?" He cupped one of the roses in his hand—so large, it eclipsed his palm. "Do you know?"

"I know all of my mother's roses." She stood so close by his side that the bottom of her dress blew across his calves. "This one is Blue Girl."

He quickly cut the stem of the one he held.

"Mother will kill me," she said in a hushed gasp.

"Isn't she doing that already?" He looked at the bruises. His frown never greater than when he looked upon them. "Let me make the hurt into every other happiness possible. Let me make you the infinity of the roses, instead of the life with the bruises."

She allowed him to cut the bush nearly empty, the roses piling in severed beauty at his feet. He laid down the scissors and asked if she could tie up her hair. She took the hair clip from off the patio table to hold her curls and frizz up in a bun.

And then he began. Rose after rose, taped to her flesh by their short stems. Always directly over a bruise, and always carefully, as he knew bruises and their business well.

By the end of it, she was left with roses upon both her arms, a cluster on her chest, and a scattering on her back. When he went to better the bruises on her legs, she stopped him from pulling up the billowy skirt of her dress.

"Let me cut the dress shorter and—"

"No." She rubbed the leg through the dress.

"We don't care 'bout it bein' fake," I said.

"I do. It's hideous."

"It's a marvel," Sal corrected her. "Look all around this world. A tree loses a branch, no one replaces it. An angel loses his wings, and he'll never have another pair." He turned and showed her his scars. "But a girl loses her leg, and somebody gives her a new one. In this world where so few things are given, how can you not be in awe at what you've got?"

She took a few steps away from us, her eyes slowly widening as if through thought she was coming to defy her own gnawing doubt that she was not something special. When she let the dress slip free from between her fingers, I could see a sort of echo inside her. Broad and far, a glowing thing to flick back the shadows of her own self-hate.

"I didn't lose my leg." She whispered as if what she was saying were too fragile for anything more than a hush. "I never had one to lose. Still, I like what you say. Hand me those, will you?"

She held her hand out for the scissors, and as soon as Sal gave them, she gathered up the bottom of her dress and began to cut through its pale blue cotton. Thinking it too long after the first cut, she made a second and a third even, bringing the hem to above her gently freckled knees.

"I've never worn anything so short." She giggled as if it came from the very small of her back.

Sal took the scissors from her to cut the remaining roses from the bush. These he would gently and softly tape to her legs.

The sun is hot and the boy is nervous as he moves his hand up the girl's legs, toward the thighs that already know his name by heart.

"*Sal,*" she whispered, "*my Sal,*" while I, nobody's Fielding, stood close enough to know I was forgotten.

"Did you know it's my birthday?" She grabbed Sal's hand. "And this is the best gift ever."

"Sal, you swimmin'?" I spoke, if only to remind myself I still existed.

"You go ahead, Fielding." He let Dresden lead him to the bench amongst the roses.

I tried to splash some water their way as I jumped from the diving board. Failing, I hung on the side of the pool, watching the two of them share the same smile as he leaned in and smelled the roses on her chest.

I dived under the water, nearly swam the length of the pool on that one breath. When I resurfaced, I heard Dresden talking about her construction paper makeup.

"Mother would be angry if I got into her makeup. I do it for her. Try to be prettier. I thought I'd put on some makeup and try to be prettier. She blames me, you know. For Father leaving. She says he left because of my leg.

"She hates my leg. She hates that I won't be able to follow in her ballet footsteps. She says I'll never be asked to dance. I think that's the worst thing to tell a girl. That she'll never dance."

Sal began to remove the construction paper from her face. She didn't try to stop him. The tape made soft sounds as he gently pulled it from her skin, the paper falling in a pile of color at their feet. Once every piece was removed, he held her face, his hand perfectly sized to her cheek as if the make of them individually was had in the creation of them both at the very same time

"I hope you're infinity, Dresden Delmar."

She sighed, "You know, I shouldn't even be talking to you."

"Because I'm the devil?"

"Because you're . . . not white." She struggled to say that very thing. "Mother says I am to stay away from you. She says my leg makes me prone to trash."

"I'm trash? But I know Tolstoy and Shakespeare and . . ." his voice disappeared. A frown on his face as if the air was bad. An incident really, entangling him like wire wrapped around his teeth, back down to his ribs.

"I'm sorry, Sal. I didn't mean to . . . it's just, well, I don't think you're trash, but Mother's Old South, you know?"

"I see." He smiled for her sake. "If you're not supposed to be talking to me, then I don't suppose you'll dance with me?"

She looked about to burst at that very question. A golden rise about her as if she could already feel herself being spun around, held, waltzed across a ballroom. Then suddenly she lost her smile as she stared at the white roses in front of her.

"Those are Mother's favorite. But she's the one who says I can't dance with a black boy. It serves her right to lose her roses to my dance."

She grabbed the scissors and without hesitation cut the white roses so quickly and with so much eagerness, she'd be cutting a new one before the old one even had the chance to hit the ground.

Rose by white rose, she taped his dark skin, until he was someone she could dance with. Sal in the white way, but not the right way. And yet it would not lower him, he would not let it. He was going to be dancing with Dresden Delmar, and everything else was outside the heaven of that.

"Fielding?" she called to me. "Would you turn on the boom box? There under the patio table?"

I pulled myself up out of the pool, shaking the water off my hands before lifting the box up on top of the table. I found the local station and turned up the volume. I suppose it could've been any song. In memory it is always Alphaville's witchy ballad of youth. "Forever Young."

Arms around each other, they placed the trust in their feet as they closed their eyes. Her face tucking into the white roses on his. I watched them until she kissed him. Lips on lips and I dived into the pool, staying under until I thought my lungs would burst into bright, turquoise shards.

When I surfaced, I saw the smashed birthday cake dropped on the concrete by the pool. Red rose frosting and cake as white as the white high heels clanking on that very concrete. Alvernine, come with her green polka-dot dress and its silk that clung to her braless form and her sexy-as-hell curves.

And sexy is what Alvernine was, with her full lips and slim cigarettes. She was a woman known to turn an ashtray into a tool of seduction. Her heavy brow made her eyes seem pillowed in a sort of jungle-cat way. I thought, there is where men go to die. There is where they are devoured by the jaguar.

Though it was from her Dresden got the red hair, Alvernine took to dyeing her own a light strawberry blond, ironing it straight and smooth. And while she was covered in freckles just like Dresden, Alvernine lessened her darker freckles and successfully hid the lighter ones on her face with makeup, which she would also apply to the freckles on her body.

What it must've been like to be such a woman's daughter. No wonder Dresden felt hideous and imperfect in the presence of her mother, who by her own guilt had failed to ever call her daughter beautiful.

As Alvernine stood shaking in fury before Sal and Dresden, I didn't know what she was more upset about. The cut roses or having caught her daughter dancing with a black boy.

I pulled myself up out of the pool just as she was reaching for Dresden.

"You stay away from her." Sal raised his fist as if he were willing to use it.

"Don't you dare try to intimidate me." Alvernine pointed her finger in his face, her nail perfectly filed and polished in a spectacular red. "I've dealt with your kind before, believe me. Now, you get away from my daughter. And you get my roses off of you."

She ripped the roses, the white petals tossing into the air and falling around them as the closest thing to snow to have ever fallen in the middle of a heat wave.

"Momma, don't hurt him," Dresden pleaded, her frightened hand reaching through the falling petals toward her mother.

"This is all your fault." Alvernine grabbed Dresden's hand, jerking her. Sal tried to pull Dresden back to him, but Alvernine pushed him away. In the struggle, Alvernine yanked a rose off Dresden's chest. As she clutched the rose in her hand, she stared at the bruise that'd been revealed on Dresden's skin.

"What is that?" Alvernine squeezed the rose in her hand until the petals looked like guts oozing between her fingers. "This boy give you that bruise?"

"No, Momma." Dresden was giving her softest tone. "You did."

"Nonsense."

"When you hit me, Momma." Dresden barely spoke above a whisper, I knew, for her mother's sake.

"A slap here and there. We all have slaps done to us. I did. Nothin' to cause a bruise like that. It was this beast. This devil, he's done this to you."

"They're more than slaps you give me, Momma." Dresden began pulling the roses off herself. "You don't remember because you drink more than you should."

As Alvernine stared at the bruises, she dropped the one rose she held. It landed on the ground like a wadded-up tissue. She blinked over and over again. A robot malfunctioning and desperately trying to get her system back to its perfect way.

"You've hurt me, Momma. You've hurt me and—"

"No." Alvernine spun around, her hands up to her neck and its choker, like a pearl noose. "I would never hurt you."

"But you did." Sal was loud and bold. Unafraid, as she slowly turned to him and his accusation.

When she slapped his cheek, he neither frowned nor retaliated. He merely turned his face up toward hers as if silent hurt was the loudest scream in the world.

She raised her hand again, but Dresden quickly stepped in and took the slap for him.

"You still believe you've never hurt me, Momma?"

Alvernine lowered her hand to her stomach like she was sick. She was a woman coming undone, one perfection at a time.

"Come on, Sal." Dresden grabbed his hand, and together they turned toward the hill behind the house.

"Where are you going?" There was a tinge in Alvernine's voice. Helpless, frightened even. A hard dose of reality she'd been given. A real bang, and I almost felt sorry for her. "Baby, come back."

They were running away from her, though Dresden had difficulty with the leg, they were still running faster than Alvernine as she chased, all the while screaming for her baby to come back. Her arms stretched toward them. Her heels something she went down by. Landing on the side of her face. Her lipstick, an awful smear out to her cheek. Her knees two pink things as she rolled onto her back and held herself at the ears, maybe only to check the jewels dangling there.

Her crying had made her mascara look like a whole herd running from her eyes. Rhinoceros wires stretching down her face. Over the blush and freckles, which were small unlit things. Not like the freckles of her daughter. Her daughter who had stopped running when she heard her mother's falling cry.

Dresden would have returned to her mother, had Sal not gently squeezed her hand and whispered something in her ear. Whatever he said made Dresden turn from her mother.

Alvernine sat up, but did not stand. She merely continued to reach from her fallen spot, crying out to Dresden, to her baby to just come back to her. Dresden buried her face in Sal's shoulder.

Having been left behind at the pool, I slowly walked past Alvernine.

"You." She pointed that perfect nail at me. "I know you. You're the lawyer's boy. Your father will hear of this."

She shook her finger before dropping it back to her trembling lap as I stood over her.

"What?" She sniffled. "What do you want?"

"I just wanna give you a rose, ma'am."

My hand stung after, but I knew her cheek did even more. I wiped the smears of her mascara and tears from my palm onto my shorts. It felt strange to hit a woman like that, but how can you regret bruising the bully?

I left her there, sobbing into her hands as I ran to catch up to Sal and Dresden, who had stood there watching me slap Alvernine. Sal patted me on the back and said I did a good thing, but as I looked at Dresden, I knew she didn't think so.

"That was my mother, Fielding."

"I did it for you. Don't you know that, Dresden?"

"Yes, I know. But I still wish you hadn't."

I think she was about to go to Alvernine, maybe hold her cheek, but she just looked at me and one last time back at her mother, before the three of us ran up the hill.

Together we helped Dresden manage the climb with her leg, and all kept pace until the high land flattened out into a long meadow that we crossed to the dense woods of another hill, which came out on the other side to a fenced pasture belonging to three horses.

There in the pasture, Sal and Dresden removed the last of the roses from each other.

"I like you better without the roses. You know that, don't you, Sal? That I want you just the way you are."

He held her cheek, his thumb lightly brushing over her lips as he whispered in her ear, "I'll be the black boy. You'll be the white girl. And the world will say no. But we'll just say yes, and be the only eternity that matters."

20

Did I request thee, Maker, from my clay
To mould me Man?

—MILTON, *PARADISE LOST* 10:743–744

WE STAYED IN that pasture with the horses long after sundown, doing what three people in a horse pasture do, think about what brought them there.

Funny enough, I thought of Elohim. I suppose because of the night sky above me, so like the one I had lain with him under the previous summer. We were there on his roof ending the day of work, which had been removing the nests of chimney swifts in his stacks.

All day long, the swifts circled us as we used long poles to scrape out and dismantle their nests of twigs and saliva. Some of the birds swooped down upon us. They were more aggressive than usual, and when we pulled out the last nest, we saw why.

"We could fry 'em." Elohim held up one of the five small eggs.

"But I thought you were the type of vegetarian that don't eat eggs."

He met my eyes for just a moment. "I didn't mean me specifically. I meant you."

I looked up at the swifts anxiously circling above. "But . . . the eggs are their babies."

He sighed as he looked up too. "I gather you won't be eatin' 'em then?" He laid the egg he held back down into the nest with the other four before gently picking the whole nest up. "You're too sensitive, boy."

He tossed the nest off the roof, the eggs coming out in the fall to hit the ground before the lighter nest of twigs. They broke on impact, their yolks spilling out like yellow blood.

"Why'd you do that?" I watched the swifts coming down to land on the branches of the tree overlooking the fallen nest.

"You said you weren't gonna eat 'em. And I couldn't have, so there was no other choice but to break 'em open. What'd ya think I was gonna do? Give 'em back to 'em?"

He threw his arms up toward the swifts, a few of which had flown down from the branches to inspect the nest and eggs as if there were some sort of saving to be had.

"It would've just been more good-for-nothin' birds, cloggin' up my chimneys and bein' a pain in my ass, Fielding. Now, come on, help me finish this up."

We continued on in silence, fitting metal screens over the top of each of his chimneys to keep the swifts from building any future nests. By the time we finished cleaning and screening, it was evening.

"Take in the stars with me." He lay down on the roof and patted the shingles beside him. "You're not still angry about earlier, are you? They were just eggs, Fielding. Like the ones your momma fries come breakfast."

As I lay down beside him, he grabbed his pack of cigarettes from the toolbox. I didn't know him to smoke often, but he was on his third cigarette by the time he spoke again.

"You know why I love the sky, Fielding? Because it makes everyone short. There ain't a man tall enough to ever look down on the sky. The sky makes everyone look up, and in that, it makes everyone me."

"Do ya ever wish you were taller, Mr. Elohim?" It was one of those things you ask without thinking. I hadn't meant to be cruel, but when I looked over at him and saw the tear already halfway down his cheek, I knew I had nudged old shadows.

"I'm sorry, Mr. Elohim. I didn't mean—"

"My father was a tall man," he interrupted my apology, never taking his eyes off the sky above him. "My mother was a tall woman. By measurement alone, they were greatly disappointed in me. They were not people who were well prepared to be disappointed, as they so often weren't in their comfortable lives. They didn't much know what to do with it, with me, this letdown and disruption to their comfort.

"They weren't vicious parents, they never screamed in my face that I had failed them in my inability to grow beyond the height of the common armchair. They never struck me, tryin' to get me to swell taller, one bruise at a time. No, they were not violent. And yet, I don't remember my mother ever lookin' at me.

"I like to think she at least did every once in a while when I was still in the cradle, but when I was old enough to recognize whether someone saw me or whether they didn't, I realized she never did. She would speak to me, of course, she was present in my life. I don't want it ever said she was cruel or bad tempered or absent. She was there, she was always there in her absolute lady way. She just never looked at me.

"When she would speak to me, she would do so by lookin' at the things 'round me, but only the short things like the table lamp, the silverware, the string on the shade. It was as if she looked at those short things, she could at least say, my son is taller than that there lamp, that there spoon, than that there four-inch string. There must've been comfort in that.

"As for my father, he only ever spent time with me at night and only in the dark woods. He would say it was to collect fireflies, but I knew the real reason was 'cause my father couldn't bear to be in a room where the light reminded him of his midget son. He had to escape to the dark woods, where in the absence of light I could be as tall as he ever imagined me to be. I was six foot, I was seven foot—hell, I was thirty feet tall, a giant in them woods at night with my father.

"Most people are afraid of the dark, but the dark was the only time I ever heard my father laughin'. There he'd be, my tall, banker father rollin' up his sleeves, and gallopin' through the woods, giddy as a hoodlum, chasin' after the fireflies, all the while yellin', 'I can't see ya, Grayson. It's so dark. I can't see you, son.'

"You had never heard a father exclaim he couldn't see his son the way my father did with such joy."

Elohim himself laughed. He tried to anyways, but the grief gave it a certain defeat.

"I'd say, 'I'm over here, Father.' And he'd tilt his head in my direction, but never down, he never looked down at me in those woods, because in there, I was the son he could look up to. The dark allowed him that. I allowed him that, as I'd stay hidden as best I could as he looked up toward the stars. 'I see you now, son,' he'd say. But of course, he was just like my mother, and never saw me after all, not for a damn second.

"You can imagine anything you want in the dark. You can imagine your father loves you, you can imagine your mother is not disappointed, you can imagine that you are . . . significant. That you mean somethin' to someone. That's all I've ever wanted, Fielding. To matter. That is all I've ever wanted."

Later, after we climbed down from the roof, Elohim went into the house, he said to get something. While I waited in the yard, I listened to the clanking sounds of the train hauling gravel from the quarry miles away.

I leaned against a tree, my hands in my pockets, my head back on the bark, listening to the clanking until it faded and the night was back to its bullfrog and cricket song. When I turned my head off to the side toward the porch, there he stood, watching me. For how long?

"Mr. Elohim?"

"I always wanted to be a father myself." His voice was soft like the moths chattering around the light above him. As he came down from the porch, I saw he had two jam jars in his hands. "I'd be damn lucky to have a son like you, Fielding."

Mostly because I didn't know what to say, I asked about the jars.

"These are bona fide firefly jars." He offered me one. "You up for catchin' some fireflies, son?"

It was the first time he had ever called me son, and I let him do it again in the woods as we ran between the trees, laughing and scooping the fireflies up in the jars, using our hands as the lids we would later open together, releasing that which we had caught for that one brief moment in time.

"Fielding?"

I turned to Sal's voice. He was propped up on his elbow, looking over at me.

"We said your name a billion times." Dresden raised up beside him. "What were you thinking about?"

"Nothin'." I sat up.

They glanced at each other, lying back down while I stayed sitting, looking up at the sky and listening as Sal wished Dresden a happy birthday.

"How old are you?"

"Thirteen. For the first time." She sighed.

He kissed her forehead before standing up.

"Hey, where are you going?" she called after him as he walked toward the rail fence a ways off.

He didn't answer her, so she tried me. "Where do you think he's going, Fielding?"

"I don't know."

The moon was enough to see him standing at one of the fence posts. When he stepped away we saw a small light flickering at the top of the post.

"Oh." She gasped. "Where'd he get that fire from? Fielding?"

"I don't know." I moved closer to her and felt the ground until I found her hand.

"Fielding, don't." She quickly pulled her hand away.

I didn't look at her, nor she at me. Our eyes merely followed his figure moving down along the fence, his back to us as he counted off thirteen consecutive posts that lit in tiny flickering flames.

As he walked back toward us, I helped Dresden stand, her grip tight on my arm as she put her weight on her good leg. She was the first to let go. I only did when I heard Sal stepping closer.

"You like your candles?" He wrapped his arms around her.

"How'd you do it?" I looked at his hands for a lighter or some matches.

"Fire comes easy to me." He winked before kissing her cheek and asking her if she was ready to blow out her candles and make a wish.

She closed her eyes and made her wish, but on exhale the lights still flickered in the distance.

"Deeper breath," Sal whispered in her ear, his lips brushing her cheek. "When I say."

She waited and when he squeezed her arm, her exhale carried across the pasture to the fence, where the flames lay down into the night.

There would be no answer then as to how he'd done it. At that moment, he was the one hugging the birthday girl while I stared off into the dark night.

"This will be a happy diary day." She nuzzled into his neck. "I think *The Little Prince* will be my book of choice. Yes, the *Little Prince* who came from the sky."

"I've read that. Doesn't the prince leave a rose behind?" He held her tighter.

"I'll only circle the words that say he takes her with him."

By the time we left the pasture, the horses were lying down. The moon, still full in the sky, provided light for our walk back through the wooded hills, which sounded like crickets and looked like fireflies.

I again thought of Elohim, as I meandered around the trees, cupping my hands up around one of the fireflies and holding it in my palms like a jar. I could feel its tiny legs crawling on the underside of my fingers as my hands closed in around it. Feeling its space getting smaller and smaller, the firefly took to flight, softly tapping against my skin but not finding the exit.

Its flying got more and more frantic the smaller I made its space. I wondered what it was thinking as its body flattened between the contact of my palms. Did it plead for its life in its own bug-speak?

Please don't kill me, there's still summer left. There was a tree, that one over there, that I have yet to fly to the top of. I really wanted to see what the leaves are like up there. Please don't kill me. There's a star, way up there, I wanted to see if I could reach. I probably can't reach it, but still I want to try. Please don't kill me. I'm not finished yet.

When I opened my hands, the bug's squished abdomen was bleeding what was left of its luciferase enzymes, which had been smeared onto my palms. Yellow like the blood of the chimney swift eggs. But not yellow for long, as it was slowly losing its illumination until all I had in my hand was something I could not take back.

"Hey, what's that?"

Dresden was standing under one of the trees, pointing to the yellow orb up in its branches. By that time, we were in the hills closer to town.

"I can't believe it. A balloon for my birthday. Isn't that something?"

"I'll get it for you." Sal was already halfway up the trunk.

I brushed the firefly's death from my hand and wiped that once-illuminated glow onto my jeans shorts as I stepped through the trees closer to Dresden and the tree Sal was climbing.

"I climb too," I whispered to her over the hoot of an owl.

She sighed, almost irritated. "You're not the one climbing now."

I stepped farther away from her and watched Sal. He was an all right climber, though he had difficulty with a few of the limbs. Nearer to the balloon, he reached out toward its string but was still too far away. A step here and a stretch there brought him closer until he had the string in his hand.

The thing about branches is there isn't much warning when one is about to break. It doesn't groan, it doesn't say, *Look out below.* It simply breaks, and sometimes you don't have time to get out of its way. Sometimes it falls right on your head.

It was an everything bad sound. Think of all the bad sounds. A dropped glass. A 3 A.M. phone call. Hands slipping off the edge of a cliff. That branch and Dresden's head made all those sounds and more.

I didn't see the blood at first, not until I fell down by her side. I asked her if she was okay, but she said nothing. I said, "Move, Dresden. Goddamn you, please move."

I could hear Sal grunting down through the limbs, landing on the ground behind me with a thud. He still held the balloon, so tightly, his nails were digging around the string into the other side of his palm.

I stood and wiped my eyes on my arm. "I'm gonna get help. Are you listenin'? Sal?" I shook his shoulders because all he saw was her. "Don't be here when I get back."

He finally brought his eyes up to mine. I couldn't see his irises or pupils. The water was too deep.

"Go home, Sal. Pretend you were there all along. If they know you were here, climbin' that tree, they won't believe it was an accident. Not with what happened earlier with Alvernine. No matter what I say as a witness, they'll say you hurt Dresden on purpose. So go. I'll say it was just me walkin' her home. We were under the tree. A branch fell. Simple as that. Okay?"

His hand ate down the string until the yellow balloon was at his chest. There, he pressed his nails into it until it popped.

I shut my eyes. "Please, Sal, say you'll go."

"I'll go," he whispered, still holding onto the string, the yellow remains of the balloon dangling at the end of it.

I opened my eyes and looked one last time down at Dresden, at the blood pooling on the ground behind her head. And then I ran. I ran as fast as I could, the fireflies lighting the way.

21

. . . moping melancholy,
And moon-struck madness

—MILTON, *PARADISE LOST* II:485–486

MADNESS. THE COMPASSING violin when in our head, the directionless chaos when out of it. Isn't that what madness is, after all? Clarity to the beholder, insanity to the witnessing world. My God, what madness this world has witnessed. What beautiful, chaotic madness.

Did I tell you that the other night me and the boy went out into the saguaros? That's the closest thing we got to woods around this trailer park. I asked him to bring the jam jar, the one we found on the side of the road. The jam was gone and the glass was clean as we strolled through the cactuses.

"Mr. Bliss? I don't think there's any fireflies out here. I've never seen any. Are you sure you did?"

"I never said I saw any. I just asked you if you wanted to go catch some."

I stopped beneath a particularly big saguaro, not all of its large arms growing up but rather twisting and crossing in front of each other. I looked at the boy, who was peering into the empty jar.

"I guess you can't imagine everything in the dark. Especially not fireflies." I squinted past the saguaros, into the deep darkness. "Listen, kid. You need to stay away from me."

"Mr. Bliss, why?"

Because I would be no good for him. I was becoming his Elohim. He was becoming my Fielding. I did say to myself if I went out there with the boy and we saw a firefly, just one, I said to myself I'll try again. I would go forth in this world, finding instances of niceness and not turn from them. Niceness like the boy. Just one damn firefly, and I'll be his friend and he will be mine.

Life would be all right to happen.

All its comedy and humor and joy I would let live and live with me in the fresh air and in the yard I would let the light color yellow. If only there was one firefly, if only. What was it Sal said about hope? It's just a beautiful instance in the myth of another chance. Yes, a myth it is.

I know the boy won't realize until he's older, maybe not ever, but I'm doing him a favor. Getting him out of my life is keeping him outside the abyss. Without him, I will stay lonely in this long way, with both ends of forever pinning me to the flames. But he deserves better than to be used as the ladder out of hell.

"You make me sick. You irritate the good goddamn out of me, and I don't care if your piece-of-shit dad is dead or if you and that bitch you call a mom are sad. I don't give a fuck about you or your little insignificant life. You hear me?"

I stared at the cactus' thorns. They gave me inspiration.

"I hate you and I want you out of my life. And if you don't stay out of it, I'll burn your trailer down while you and your mom and that damn ugly mutt are sleeping."

I took out the match I had in my pocket and lit it just for scare. I kept it burning all the while he ran away, the jar having been dropped and broken against the ground. I held the match until the flame ate down and burnt the tips of my fingers. I know that's the last I'll see of him. I know that's the last of the wings.

Did I say I went to a psychiatrist once? I suppose she came to me. I was somewhere in my fifties. I woke and there she was, sitting on the edge of my bed. She asked why I'd want to do a thing like that. Then she laid her hand on the bandages on my chest as I watched the cop pacing outside.

"It was an accident." I brushed her hand away.

"I see." She went to look out the window. "And the suicide note?"

I watched the nurse check the IV. "That wasn't a suicide note."

The nurse left while the psychiatrist leaned back onto the windowsill to face me as she asked, "No?"

"I just wrote I was leaving, didn't I?"

"Yes."

"It was just a note for my girlfriend, letting her know I was leaving for the grocery store."

"You signed your full name. Do you always sign notes to your girlfriend like that? Fielding Bliss?"

The cop was now standing in the doorway.

"Am I under arrest?"

The badge folded his arms.

"He wants to know where you got the gun?" She tilted her head at me. "It wasn't registered, Mr. Bliss."

"I don't know where it came from. It came from a grandfather clock, but I don't know where before that."

She gestured for the cop to leave. Once he did, she closed the door. "I am to evaluate you, Mr. Bliss. Make sure you are no longer a danger to yourself or others."

"Do we have to now?"

"You've been here for several days."

"Have I?"

"Why would you shoot yourself in the chest, Mr. Bliss?"

She came to my bedside again and gently sat down. Her fingers slowly ran through the graying sides of my hair, softly tucking it behind my ear. I thought she looked as Dresden might've looked when she got older. A freckled thirtysomething with eyes like light. Her red hair was tied back, but the shorter strands stuck out around her face, in an almost rounded and even frizz, like the tufts of a dandelion seed head. I thought if I blew those wispy strands, they might blow away just like the seeds. So I tried, blowing lightly toward the ones over her ear. They slightly moved, while she kept her head so very still, as if she didn't want me to stop.

"What are you doing?" She asked me so quietly, the question almost didn't exist.

"Giving you some wind. Seeing if I can't blow you away."

"Do you want to blow me away?" I liked the way she whispered things.

"No."

She turned her head away, but I saw her smile before she did.

"You look like a garden." I reached out to the roses on her sweater. "Who found me?"

"The neighbor heard the shot."

"I've always hated my neighbors."

"So close to your heart." She felt the bandage again. "Doctor said just a little more to the left, and you'd not be here. People who choose suicide usually choose their wrists or pills or rope. A gun is so violent, isn't it?"

"I knew someone who was shot once."

"In the chest?"

I nodded. She nodded with me.

"And that is why you shot yourself, Mr. Bliss?"

"I suppose I just wanted to see for myself . . . what it felt like."

"And now that you know, you won't be trying it again, I hope?"

I laid my hand on hers. It was warm and nice. I'd go to bed with her for a whole year, but never love her and she'd cry because of it.

I'd never love any of those women, really. Never like Sal loved Dresden.

Dresden. I thought maybe a really bad concussion. I thought all she would have to do was to stay in bed for a few days. Of all falling things, who knew a tree branch could take so much?

I did as I told Sal I would. I told the sheriff and Dad and anyone else who asked that I alone walked Dresden home. That on the way, a branch fell. Sal wasn't there, I swore. He was already far from there. Of course, there were those who didn't believe me. It didn't help that Alvernine was telling her side of the story.

When asked about the various bruises on Dresden's body, Alvernine said it must've been the branch. The coroner determined the bruises were received prior to the branch and not a direct result of it. Alvernine was charged. She pleaded guilty and received three to five years.

On the wall of her cell, she taped photos of Dresden. She called that wall her rose garden. Within the first year of her sentence, they would find her hanging in front of that garden, slowly asphyxiated by a noose of sheets.

In the days following Dresden's death, Sal had yet to speak. It was as if he had to pull the strength together. He became the boy with the pain in the chest. I wonder what he did that night I told him to leave the woods. Did he go straight home and hide away under the pillows and cushions of the window bed? That was how I found him. Trying to become just another pillow, another cushion, another thing of stuffing that didn't have to feel a broken heart.

I pulled the cushions and pillows off him one at a time. Found him flat, pressed down from fingertips to heart. Looking at me with his eyes that said, *Cover me back. Please, just cover me back up.*

Pillow by pillow, I did.

Dad tried. He went to the window but didn't touch the pillows or cushions. He reached over them and touched the glass instead.

"Things will be all right." He didn't sound so sure as his sweaty fingers smudged the glass. He began to rattle on about his court cases because that's all he had. I shut my eyes. I was sitting on the floor, leaning back against the wall.

The cases sounded like walking through a cornfield. I'm sure they did to Sal too. Walking the tight rows, the tall stalks. So tall, they're mountains in fields and you're climbing through. *Swish, swish.* The sound of trying to make it through so many things in your way. *Swish, swish.* Unable to touch and unable not to be touched. Each corn leaf sharp at the edge. Slapping your arms. Your legs. Hitting your face.

Just when you get away from one, you've got another leaf already there. Another one after that. Everywhere you look, more of the same, all around you. The leaves cut little nicks, carving you one slice at a time. The jungle of the Midwest. *Swish, swish.* You shut your eyes to protect them from all the sharp and all the slicing. You have to walk blind. Listening to only the sound. *Swish, swish.* Feeling the pollen from the tassels falling down. Light particles but heavy enough to start to bury you. *Swish, swish.* That's what Dad and his cases sounded like. *Swish, swish.*

He left the room. Maybe he didn't even see me sitting over there. He didn't look. He just left, a case still falling from his lips.

Later, Mom came in with her spray bottle of vinegar and a rag. She found a cushion Sal wasn't under and leaned down into it with her knee as she reached over and began to spray the glass.

"You know, they call these picture windas." *Wipe, wipe, wipe. Squeak, squeak.* "I call it my *on the way* winda. I always look out it, every mornin' on my way downstairs. I just stand there in the hall and peek in over your sleepin' heads and look out. And then I move on.

"I hope this is just on your way too, Sal. We've got to keep movin', don't we? Sometimes things happen, bad things, *on the way*, but we've got to keep movin'. If we don't, we won't get to the next thing, and it could really be somethin'. It could be the best something of our lives."

The room smelled like vinegar long after she left. When Grand came in, he remarked about the smell.

He stood at the edge of the pillows and cushions.

"I bet Dad was ramblin' off about cases." He glanced down at the cushions, at the slight movement under them. "He used to do that to me when I was in Little League and lost a game. Here he'd come and start talkin' about *So-and-So v. So-and-So.* I guess he don't know what else to do for loss. Whether it's a ball game or a girl. A girl."

He laid his sweating hands on the pane. "Sometimes I wanna break this winda out, don't you? Just break it out. It's the only winda in the whole house that don't open. Just a big square of glass. Out. Out." He pressed on the glass. The cushions moved again and Grand dropped his hands. "Get better, Sal. You can help me break it out one day."

He patted the pillows. They didn't move again. On his way out, he looked down, his blue eyes seeming to be the only color for miles around that dark room. He'd been the only one to notice me. He kneeled and squeezed my shoulder. I wanted desperately to wrap my arms around him, but he stood before I got the nerve.

After he left, I went to the window bed. I reached in under the pillows and cushions until I found Sal's arm, which wasn't as thin as when he'd first arrived. The same could be said for the rest of him. Mom's meals had done him good, though he never seemed to eat the meat. I think maybe he was the only true vegetarian.

"Stop, Fielding." He pulled back, but I didn't let go.

"C'mon, Sal. Come out now."

"I said stop it."

I pulled harder. His face was out of the cushions and pillows now—so close to mine, I could feel his hot breath. "Fielding, let go or I'll burn the house down while you're all sleeping."

I let go. He slowly lay back down as he gathered the pillows and cushions in a great heap, burying himself once more.

That night I lay in bed and watched the pillows and cushions heave up and down with his breathing. I thought of fire and the house burning. I fell asleep into a nightmare of this. At the part in the nightmare when everyone was burning, their skin oozing off like some sort of goop, I woke out of breath and into the middle of the night.

I used a T-shirt to wipe the sweat off my face as I stared at the pillows and cushions scattered on the floor and leading from the window like a trail. Big cushions, little cushions, big pillows, the little fringed ones, all leading me downstairs. I heard a faint sound, one I thought splattered quite a bit.

I went toward the sound and the dark kitchen, where I found Sal crawling on his hands and knees across the linoleum. All around him were circles of yellow. I saw the emptied mustard bottles piled on top of the table.

As he crawled, he slammed his hand down onto each circle he came upon, causing the mustard to pop and splatter.

"Whatcha doin', Sal?" I quietly asked.

"Popping all the yellow balloons," he answered without stopping. "All the yellow balloons in the world so no more will get caught in trees. And no more girls will die because of it."

"You know it wasn't your fault, Sal."

"Wasn't it?" *Pop* and *splatter.* "I stepped on the branch."

"No, you didn't."

What more could I do but lie. What more could I give him but the shortest way to the light.

"I was watchin' you, and you didn't even touch that branch. It fell on its own, Sal. Sometimes branches just do that."

He slapped his hand down on the circle before him, the mustard splashing onto his face. He turned to me with yellow freckles.

"Go to bed, Fielding. You've got the funeral in the morning."

By morning, the only thing remaining of the mustard balloons were the empty bottles in the trash can. The linoleum smelled of Pine-Sol. The mop still wet in the bucket. Sal didn't leave the kitchen all night.

I was already in my black suit when Dad walked into my room, saying it was time to get up and go.

"How's it fit?" he asked of the suit. He'd been the one to buy it for the occasion.

"Fine." My feet shifted under the weight of it.

"You look . . . grown." He felt his tucked tie. "Where's yours?"

I pointed to the black tie draped over the back of my desk chair. "I didn't know how to put it on."

He went over and picked it up.

"Dad?" Grand was in the doorway. "The sheriff's downstairs. He wants you."

"Here." Dad handed Grand the tie. "Help your brother with this."

Long after he heard Dad go down the steps, Grand stayed leaned into the doorframe, the tie loose in his hand.

"You don't know how to put it on?"

I shook my lowered head.

The floor creaked under his steps, and I closed my eyes in broken joy as I felt his fingers come gently under my collar. They lightly brushed my neck, and though his skin was hot, I felt the cold disaster of the wound we called being brothers.

"Inside out. Cross. Over and under." His hands followed his instructions. "Are you listenin', little man?"

I nodded.

"Pull. Tighten. Take this end here and another pull. Behind this loop. Bring it through the knot. Like this. Then just tighten. Gentle, though. There you have it."

His hands stayed on the knot before following the tie down to straighten it.

"Fielding, look at me."

I slowly raised my eyes, but could get no further than his chin.

"What?" Was that my voice that had come out so thin, so vanished in its presence?

He sighed and tilted his chin up, leaving me his neck, glistening with small drops of sweat. "Nothin'."

The room echoed of this as he left. I could hear him softly close his door. He wouldn't be going to the funeral. Neither would Mom, for the obvious reason.

I looked down at my tie and picked up its end, smelling my brother. I laid my lips against the silk and said what I couldn't say to him. *I love you.*

I straightened it back and went downstairs. The sheriff was gone, and Dad was asking if I was ready. I nodded before following him out to the freshly washed Lincoln.

"What'd the sheriff want, Dad?"

"To make sure we wouldn't be taking Sal along with us to the funeral. I told him we already sat him down and explained to him why it wouldn't be wise for him to go."

"Dad? I don't know if I wanna go."

"She was your friend, wasn't she?"

"She was Sal's. I was just . . . someone she knew."

"Look, son, I wish he could go as much as you. As much as him. But emotions are very high at the moment. No one wants a scene at a funeral. Do we?"

Mom watched us from the window as we drove away. The handkerchief she gave me, folded in my pocket.

"By the way, do you know who used all the mustard?" Dad turned the car's air conditioner on high. "Your mother was upset. Someone's used it all. She puts it on her burns."

"What burns?"

"Burns she hasn't gotten yet. If she touches a hot pan handle or something like that. Just kitchen burns. Yellow mustard takes the sting out."

"Dad, look." I pointed to the field, where Sal was running toward the woods. "Stop the car."

"The funeral, Fielding." His hands were sweating on the steering wheel.

"Please, Dad, stop. I wanna see where he's goin'. I'll meet ya at the cemetery."

"Fielding—"

"Dad . . . I just want to see for myself."

He understood those words and stopped the car, looking straight ahead as I jumped out, slamming the door maybe too hard.

As I followed Sal, I could've been as loud as I wanted. I could've screamed his name and threw sticks at his back. He wouldn't have noticed. He was the boy running toward the something he had to do, and everything else was lost to that cause.

When we got to the pasture, the horses seemed to be in the same spot they were in that night we first saw them. They looked at Sal and remembered him. They even seemed to ask where the girl was.

Did they see me?

One did. The black one with the white on its forehead. It kept eyes on me as I fell back behind a tree at the edge of the pasture and watched Sal walk out to the fence. He gathered the candles still on the posts and with them fell down onto the ground, where he held all thirteen candles close to his chest.

I couldn't hear him from where I was and yet didn't I know what he was saying? Something like: You were my favorite thing, and in imagination your death will not exist. It's all *as if* from now on. *As if* you are not gone. You will be the girl beside me. Never more than a heartbeat length away. The woman who will be the hill of my bed. A climb to the top and such views to make little things of. Little us that will be part you and part me and whole in those two things. *As if* you are not gone and will be with me to get the wrinkles, the white hair, the spine shaped like a rocking chair. *As if* you are not gone and so will have the love of going in my arms, warm and with me. Yes, you are my favorite thing. You always will be.

He slowly laid the candles down while he dug a hole with his hands. It was a frantic tearing of the ground. Sometimes I close my eyes and see his body rocking toward that hole, scooping dirt, shoving it up underneath his fingernails. Over and over again, that grave digging has never passed for me.

In this hole, he placed the candles. The burying of them was a shove away, a short task for a life cut short. As he sat there, patting the dirt, I reached into my suit jacket and took the handkerchief out of the pocket. I rolled it like a long white snake I pulled through my fingers as I sat there, staring out at the grave between him and me.

I was the first to leave. I knew he wouldn't for longer still. I left the handkerchief rolled on the ground. I thought maybe it might slither its way out to him.

Hours passed by the time I got home. Dad was already returned from the funeral. He was still in his suit, the jacket pinned back by his hands on his hips.

"Fielding, where were you?" He was sweating even more. God, why hadn't he taken that black suit off yet?

"Fielding, answer me."

His voice fell behind me as I went up the steps.

"I thought you were coming to the funeral, young man."

"I did," I whispered down to him.

"What?"

"I was at her funeral," I said somewhere.

"Fielding—"

"Leave 'im alone, Dad." Grand was standing in the doorway of his bedroom. As I passed him, he reached out to me. "Do you know how to take it off?"

I loosened the tie the rest of the way and pulled my head out.

"Hmm." His eyes had slippery contact with mine. "You don't need me anymore."

He stepped back and I should've reached, but I let him close his door. I dropped the tie somewhere in the hall. Didn't mean to. It just fell out of my hand on my way to my room. I closed the door and leaned against it. What was that noise? That tapping?

"You okay, Fielding?" Mom at the other side of the door.

"Fine, Mom."

"You dropped your tie."

"It just fell."

"Where's Sal?"

"He'll be home later."

"You sure you're okay, sweetie?"

"I'm fine."

I pressed my ear flat against the door, listening to her walk away. I threw my jacket down on the floor and went to my desk, where I grabbed construction paper and scissors. I sat on the floor and took some red, yellow, and orange paper and began to cut. Oak leaves. Maple leaves. Elm leaves. Ohio leaves. A whole big pile I dumped across the window bed. Then I got a flashlight and sat in the pile and waited.

It got dark and Mom came up, asking through the closed door if I was hungry. No, I said. Darker still. Feet outside the door on their way to bed. Dad. Asking if I'm all right. Fine, I say. More dark. A 3 A.M. dark when my bedroom door slowly opened.

"Don't turn on the light."

Sal's hand dropped from the switch. "Where are you, Fielding?"

"Over here, at the winda bed. Come and sit down." I scooted some of the leaves over to make a seat for him.

"What is all this?" His hands moved through the pile.

I turned on the flashlight and shined it on the red leaf between his fingers. "It's Dresden."

He looked at me and I looked at him, but we didn't say anything for that long while. He slowly looked back at the leaf in his hand, twirling it gently by its stem.

"Thank you, Fielding."

And so we were, on into the night, two boys sharing a light and building a way, one leaf at a time.

22

. . . for ever sunk
Under your boiling ocean, wrapt in chains,
There to converse with everlasting groans

—MILTON, *PARADISE LOST* 2:182–184

WE WOULDN'T HAVE known about the stones that summer had Grand not fallen for Ted Bundy. Of course, his name wasn't really Ted Bundy. The journalist. His name was Ryker Tommons.

He left the morning after fucking Grand in the woods. Grand didn't notice how quickly that was. He had felt the connection of another man, and in the clay of loneliness, he shaped it into something he called love. Before Ryker left, Grand asked for his number.

"I have your number, kid. I'll call you," Ryker promised as they stood in front of Ryker's car.

"I thought you liked me." Grand was doing his routine, the same one I'd seen him use on girl after girl.

"I do, kid."

"So, give me your number."

Was that Grand reaching into the man's pocket? Pulling out the notepad and pen?

"C'mon, Ted Bundy, write it down for me."

Ryker had no choice but to take the pad and pen. Grand had forced them into his hands, even wrapping Ryker's fingers around the pen.

It was as if Grand thought Ryker's hesitation was just a continuation of flirtation.

"I sure will be happy to get away from this heat," Ryker sighed, and wrote with such reluctance, the number looked written by a child just learning.

"Call me whenever." He passed the number to Grand. "Well, so long, kid."

Grand stood watching the car drive away. Stood there long after it went, gripping the paper in his hand and the phone number that would dial through to a pizza shop in Brooklyn.

Grand was convinced Ryker had meant to give him the right number. By Grand's thinking, there was only one number not right, so he'd dial over and over again, sometimes changing the very last, or the very first, or one of the numbers in the middle. He called the entire state of New York, but never Ryker.

Finally it occurred to him he could just ask the operator for the number to the *New York Times* office building.

"*New York Times*, how may I help you?" a woman's overworked voice answered.

Grand gave her his name. Said he would like to speak to Ryker Tommons. Said he was a very close friend. Grand waited, curling the phone cord around his finger.

"I'm sorry, but Mr. Tommons is unavailable at the moment, Mr. Bliss. Would you like to leave him a message?"

She would take many messages on behalf of Mr. Tommons, who would never return any of them. It was at some point while on the phone to her that Grand ordered a subscription to the newspaper, as Ryker never lived up to his promise of getting one for us.

When the paper came, Grand would shower, cologne his neck, put on Saturday night type of clothes like he was fixing himself up for a date.

He read only Ryker's articles. Reading them over and over again like they were new each time. Articles about gays in theater, film, and music. Culture coming at Grand full speed in a language he'd been learning to speak all his life. The foreign cutting away to the shape of his America.

He could spend an entire afternoon reading and rereading one article, afternoons previously spent on the baseball diamond. He hadn't been back to the team since that day they ran him off. He was officially replaced by Arly. The team would suffer. Three losses in a row. No playoffs. No championships. You could see the team looking down into their gloves, seeming to ask if they had made the right choice. Was winning worth playing on a team with a fag?

Empty gloves always said it was, but then the ball would come sailing their way. They'd catch it. Say to themselves, *Of course we don't need him.*

Dad tried to find out from Grand why he was no longer on the team.

"I just don't wanna play anymore, Dad." He shrugged. "Is that okay?"

"I thought you liked baseball. I liked watching you play, but if you don't want to anymore, well, sure that's okay."

And then Dad hugged him and Grand sighed in his arms. "Thanks, Dad."

The team stretched the baseball diamond far that summer, and the things said there went to gossip in town.

"Have you heard about Grand Bliss?" they whispered.

"I can't believe it. He doesn't talk like them. Doesn't walk like one of them. How can he be?"

"But he is. I heard he kissed another boy. You just never know who is or isn't anymore. I mean, look at Rock Hudson. There's always rumors about him. I remember watchin' him in the old films. I never would have guessed he wanted anything more than a good woman. You just never know what a man wants. No, you just never know who a man is."

Dad was never caught in the circles of gossip. Mom could sometimes be, but only because of Fedelia, who brought that type of news into the house during her visits. Though in regards to Grand, she brought none of it up. Instead she would sit across from Mom and say Grand is a very special boy.

"Hmm-mmm," Mom would say, not knowing what moved in the deep.

"I'm scared for him, though, Stella."

Mom would make a noise, something like a chuckle. "Don't be silly, Auntie, he's a strong boy."

Fedelia would rub her hands together. "I know."

Ever since that night Sal cut her hair, Fedelia no longer spoke profanity. Her tone was calm. Like thawed-out honey. Her anger had been cut out with the ribbons and was swept up and dumped into the trash. She stood taller. Walked less clumsy. She'd even lost weight and was planning a cruise for the following spring. She would say Scranton's name only to say, "He was my husband. He left me. That is that. I am over it, and I wish him the best."

Unlike the bags she wore before, her clothes clung now, no longer afraid to touch her and her self coming back.

Maybe it was the hard journey to her own identity that made her feel for Grand so deeply. The boy struggling with his own, and she knowing exactly what it feels like to live under the weight of the world.

"I hear Grand is interested in journalism now." Fedelia crossed her slimmed-down legs while she patted a handkerchief above her lip to get the sweat. Her makeup more subtle than before, more becoming, just like that short crop of white hair.

"Yes, it seems that way." Mom chuckled. "Must've been all those reporters comin' here. He must've found that quite interestin'."

Grand didn't want to become a journalist. I knew that much about him. He was just trying to build the connection between him and Ryker, the first man he ever met who was like him. It's hard not to fall in love with the only blanket in winter.

And love, Grand did.

In his mind, he was making sure he was becoming someone who could be loved back. A notepad for a notepad. A pen for a pen. A journalist for a journalist. The boy flitting around town, interviewing about this and that. Notes that would become articles later on the type-writer in his room. He even did an article on Dresden.

And so she is gone, and we cannot put that out of mind, but we can thrill at the joy of knowing we have loved her and that the warmth we go to, shall be her.

Grand's other articles were of fewer stars. He covered everything from activities of the local chamber of commerce to the farmer study-ing drought-resistant vegetation. He wrote about craft exhibitions, quilt bazaars, and the marijuana growing in a cornfield.

About the movie theater renovations, bigger screens, plusher seats. About the local fan drive and the mayor's continued effort to keep the town cool. Boring things he was unable to make interesting, so he'd crumple them into a ball. Gripping this ball like the old ones he used to. Winding up, a slow pitch to the wastebasket. That was his baseball those days.

I went to the wastebasket, unrolled the balls, and found so many ways Sal was being blamed. Grand quoted a man as saying if Sal touches your mailbox, you'll get nothing but bad news.

"I've taken to freshly paintin' my own mailbox every couple of hours," the man said, "that way if he does touch my mailbox, I'll know it 'cause wet paint always saves things."

A woman claimed she'd seen Sal in the middle of the train tracks.

"He was shinin' a small penlight on a ball of foil. A couple hours later, I turned the radio on and heard about that terrible train crash in the next town. So many folks died, and all 'cause the conductor said he was blinded by a bright, white light."

No need in saying there wasn't even a train crash. I crumpled the articles back up as I'd found then. When I turned, Grand was there, standing in the doorway.

He didn't say anything as he walked past me to lay his notepad and pen by the typewriter. I knew something was wrong by the way he rubbed his head, as if there were a drum there, pounding until it'd won.

He looked out the window and I would be reminded of him doing just that years later when I read a line in a book that spoke of water slipping out a crack in the bottom of a jug.

"Grand?"

He looked out at the columns of the Parthenon painted on his walls. His bedroom was Greece, and Mom had made it as classic as Aristotle.

"They're gonna throw stones at the house, Fielding. Later tonight, they're going to throw stones. Yellch told me. I saw 'im just now."

"I thought—"

"That he don't speak to me no more?" He finished my sentence with a look down. "Yeah. I thought him warnin' me 'bout the stones, I thought it might mean we could be friends again. But he said he was just tellin' me 'cause of that time I saved 'im from the stones."

"Why they gonna throw stones? 'Cause of you?"

I thought for a moment he'd ask me to call him a faggot just one more time. The way he looked at me, it was as if family was the point of collapse and all happiness was going, gone, and impossible.

"No, Fielding, not because of me. Not this time, at least. They're doin' it 'cause of Sal."

"What should we do?"

"Stay away from the windas, I reckon."

"We will do more than that."

We turned to Dad's voice and him standing in the doorway. He told us to follow him outside to the cannas. Along the way, Sal tagged on and I told him about the coming stones. His voice cracked when he apologized.

"It's because of me."

Dad said everything would be all right. Then he instructed us to pull up all the cannas. Mom hovered on the porch, yelling at us to stop. Dad said, to my surprise, "Come out and make us."

She placed her foot on the top porch step. It was the farthest I'd ever seen my mother from the house. *"Another,"* I whispered. *"Come on, Mom, just one more."*

She looked up at the sky, yanked her foot back, and shrugged her shoulders, probably said the word *rain*. We jerked up the cannas harder, and she looked away. When we returned to the porch with the flowers, she asked for one. Sal handed her an Alaska.

And then we waited. On the front porch we sat. The flowers were so tall, I felt like I was holding another me. We waited in silence for the danger ahead. No longer ahead, coming around the corner. Marching down the lane. Bare feet slapping dirt and led by a short man in white.

Mom lifted the bundle of flowers from Sal and added them to Dad's. "Best if they not see 'im."

With Sal and Mom under the darkness of the porch, me, Dad, and Grand walked to the edge of the yard. First they came fast, determined to use the stones in their hands. Stones that filled their palms and stretched their fingers into scary bends at the knuckles.

They slowed when they saw us, looking around at each other, uncertain of what to do. They had not discussed this situation. They had planned to see only the brick of our house, the windows, the door. It's easy to throw stones at these things. It is not so easy to throw stones at people they know. People not like the boy and the devil they'd created from that very image.

They met us at the edge of our yard. They were quiet. We were quiet. Somewhere a cricket wasn't.

Finally, Dad spoke. "Who wants one of my wife's blue ribbon cannas? Hmm? All they cost is a stone. One stone for a flower. Sounds like a bargain to me."

He took a step toward them.

"What about you?" He offered a flower to a woman biting her lip and sweating above it. The woman looked down at the stone in her hand, turned it over. She tried to look at the house, but couldn't get past Dad or the flower.

"All right." She let go of the stone and took the flower before hastily moving to the back of the group.

"And you?" Dad was making another sale.

Grand was offering his own flowers. Those in the crowd in front of me stared, waiting to see if I too would be something to stop their throwing.

"A flower for your stone?" I stepped forward.

And there we three were, slowly dismantling the mob that had so wanted to tear us apart. We tossed the stones into a big pile in the front yard. Every click of stone against stone made me flinch, made us all flinch behind petals and stems.

As I was handing a flower over, I saw Grand slowly extend a Russian Red to Yellch. Without a word, Yellch gave his stone to Grand. Because their hands lingered for so long in the exchange, you could from afar have thought they were merely friends, or gardeners at the very least, holding hands and talking flowers.

In the back of the crowd, I saw Elohim. No one had given him a flower yet, so I asked him in my best voice, "A flower for your stone, Mr. Elohim?"

He held up his empty hands. And yet wasn't that whole crowd just one big stone for him?

"Do you remember when you threw stones at me, Fielding? Don't lower your head like that. Look at me. Do you remember?"

I nodded.

He nodded too. "I hope one day you know what that feels like."

He took the flower and turned away, the crowd going with him.

Years later, when I was standing on my last roof, the stones finally came for me. They came sudden and from the sky. They hit cars and dinged. They hit the slate roof and broke the tiles I was standing on. Still, while others ran inside, I stayed.

"Hey, buddy, you're gonna get killed up there in this hail."

But I stayed and spread my arms out, tilting my face up, the wound before the scar and I, dear Elohim, finally knowing what it feels like.

23

These troublesome disguises which we wear

.   .   .   .

And that must end us; that must be our cure—
To be no more. Sad cure! for who would lose . . .

—MILTON, PARADISE LOST 4:740

2:142–151

WHEN I WAS thirty-three, I met a man. My house was burning down and he was the one with the hose, come to save me. I liked that about him. That he put fires out, didn't start them.

Come here, memory of him. I'll make guitar songs out of his eyes. Come here, memory of him. Give me the Sunday in the warm bathtub when I leaned back against his wet chest and he washed my hair. Come here, memory of him, remind me of the morning sun, like good yellow, on his face. Come here, you memory of him, and give him well.

His dark skin was like that of the color of a bird's feather I found beneath my window long ago. I almost told him about that feather. I almost told him about Sal. I almost told him all my baseball-shaped secrets, but I was too distracted by the possibility of happiness with him. Far too distracted by him pulling me in by the loop of my jeans and reading me Langston Hughes.

Heaven was no bigger than a queen-sized bed during those days. Blankets kicked off, pillows even. Just a white sheeted square and us. Chests were pillows. Arms and legs were blankets. Waist deep in each other. A heaven of mounting gasps and sides rising and falling in the same deep breaths, breaths grassy enough to walk on from here to Elysian Fields, where paradise is set in motion by the almost too beautiful connection of one man and another.

Sometimes it'd be him over me like a swinging branch and my mouth feeling that slight curved fruit of his neck until I felt like I was falling away from him and that paradise. I'd almost scream, a fearful grasp on him, "I'm falling away from you."

"I'll never let you fall," he'd promise.

And so the heaven continued like a scurry to eat the last apple before the tree gets cut down.

Yes, heaven is a breathless mouth. It is the core underneath, where two souls meet and give and take little pieces of each other, all the while the light orbits, rippling soft on the edges.

He was mine and I was his. He told me so as he pulled me and my jeans into him on the street, the Empire State Building in the distance.

After the kiss, he asked why I looked about to break. I said I didn't know, but wasn't it because I did know? Because I knew all the great splendor of a man. I knew the heaven of making love to him later. All the splendid, heavenly things Grand would never know.

We caught the eye of an old man passing by.

"Do you think his frown is because we're gay or interracial?" he asked, his dark skin the best part of me.

"I'm not gay."

"What do you call us, Fielding?"

I shrugged. "Just a moment."

That moment lasted eight years, longer than any woman. A moment that saw me saying *I love you* and for the first time meaning it. After I said it, I said I was going out for some shaving cream and never went back. I wonder if he thinks of me every time he shaves? I know I think about him. I feel my beard and know I think about him.

I deserve the vinegar, not the violets. It was why I left that queen-sized heaven and that man who made love like a Langston Hughes poem.

I couldn't bear such a beautiful life, when Grand never got his. Him and Ryker had fucked, but they hadn't loved—and that was what Grand missed out on. That is what Grand paid for.

It was the beginning of September and a few mornings after the unsuccessful stoning attempt, which was a moment that showed us what they were capable of but it was also a moment that showed us we could win. I suppose that's why we didn't pack up and leave. We thought we could win it all with a flower.

We were sitting at the table, having breakfast. Dad was pouring syrup on his pancakes and Mom was sizzling sausage.

"God bless the woman who cooks in such heat," Dad said. Or maybe he didn't. Maybe it was something we just thought.

Sal was sprinkling cinnamon on his buttered toast and Grand was reading the newest edition of *The New York Times*. As Dad talked about the rising prices of gasoline, Grand tightened his grip on the paper until it pleated and the ink smeared in little wisps from his sweating palm.

"Food prices will be rising with all the drought," Dad was saying as the paper began to tremble with Grand's hands.

When he lowered the paper enough for me to see his eyes, they looked like a lot of something gathered in one place. A whole pile that towered too tall and wobbled, about to fall.

"What's wrong, Grand?" I spoke under Dad's voice, but still he heard me and stopped talking about rising prices.

He too saw the wobbling pile in Grand's eyes and reached for the paper. "Bad news in the *Times,* is it, son? Another *Dred Scott v. Sandford?*"

Grand jerked the paper to his chest. I thought he was going to crumple it up the way his hands wanted. Instead he forced himself to fold it and lay it on his lap as he became determined to spread strawberry jam on his toast without shaking.

Dad was about to ask again for the newspaper, but Mom's short exclamation stopped him. Grease had popped from the pan to her arm. She rubbed out the sting, saying she wished she had some yellow mustard. Sal looked down at his toast while Dad shook his head with a smile, the way husbands are quick to do at wives they love beyond measure.

Dad had forgotten about Grand and the newspaper, but I hadn't. I watched Grand as he took a bite of his toast. The strawberry he piled upon it oozed out around the sides of his mouth.

"It looks like blood."

I don't know why I said it. I suppose I thought it would make him smile. But he didn't smile. Instead his eyes fell strange.

"What?" He sounded hoarse as if in the span of those few moments, he had going on inside him an internal dialogue that had drained him of his voice.

"The jam. It looks like blood." I gestured at the sides of my own mouth to mean his.

Mom was at the table by then, dropping off the carton of orange juice. She stopped by Grand and pulled up the dishcloth tucked into the waist of her apron to wipe the jam from his face.

He jerked back and grabbed her wrist.

"Did you get it on ya, Mom?" The angst in his voice is with me still.

"What?"

"This blood." He wiped the red from his mouth.

"Honey, it's just strawberry jam."

"Strawberry jam?" He closed his eyes as he pushed his chair back and stood, the newspaper on his lap sliding down onto the floor and under the table. "I'm sorry. I'm just tired."

What had happened to the well-rested boy we'd sat down to breakfast with? How could that hollowing, a dig away from reaching bone, come so fast beneath his eyes? His tan of that summer seemed to lift up and float on pale water that went nightmare deep. It was as if he would go on emptying, coming to nothing before our eyes. Just collapse or fade or vanish away.

"I didn't sleep last night."

"Oh, I know. I heard the typewriter." Dad feigned typing. "One day, when you are a married man, your wife will say the typewriter is your mistress, so be prepared, young journalist."

"Yes, my wife." Grand said *wife* as if he was almost sorry she would not exist.

"Go lie down, son. Get ya some rest." Mom started clearing his dishes.

He slowly walked out of the kitchen while Mom and Dad started discussing rising prices again. Meanwhile I slid under the table to scoop up the newspaper. I hurried into the hall with it. Sal followed, but not to read the paper. He was passing me to go up the steps. I heard his knocking and then him asking if he could come in. Grand's door opened and closed quietly.

I frantically tossed through the paper until I found Ryker's name written beneath the title, MY COMIC BOOK DREAM, A PERSONAL ESSAY.

> *In Victorian England, it was hypothesized that having sex with a virgin would cure venereal diseases such as syphilis. This came to be known as the Virgin Cleansing Myth. Myth, because that is in fact all it is. There is no truth to the story that a virgin's blood will somehow cleanse the blood of the diseased. Yet, to this day, there are some with HIV/ AIDS who are having sex with virgins in the hope of a cure. In most instances, this sex is not consensual, and the virgin is put at risk of being infected themselves without their knowledge or their permission.*
>
> *I myself have not had sex since being diagnosed with HIV in November of last year. This is a very personal decision and one I made because I do not want to put my fellow men at risk. That being said, I do understand the desire to find a cure. I understand it, yes, but I'd never knowingly infect another person with HIV/AIDS. I just want to make that clear. I do imagine it, though, in a sort of comic book style, if you will.*
>
> *When it's you and HIV/AIDS, you become a superhero, if you want to survive. Your body becomes the city you must protect and the HIV/AIDS becomes every villain ever created. It's the Joker. Magneto. Doctor Doom. And in the fight, some may call themselves Superman or Batman, but I call myself Dr. Michael Morbius.*

Fans of the Spider-Man *series will recognize this name as that of the villain first introduced during those AIDS-free days of 1971.*

Morbius was dying from, funny enough, a rare blood disease. He set out to be his own hero, looking for a cure that ultimately turned him into the villain. A vampire.

I suppose it's because of these similarities between myself and Morbius that I imagine I am him. He suffered, as I am suffering now, from a rare blood disease. And like he was a vampire, I imagine myself to be one as well. I imagine I have sex with a virgin and, by doing so, I am cured.

Of course, this is just me imagining a comic book hero and a comic book villain, a comic book story and a comic book hope. But in this real world, I have to rely on the heroes in the white coats to see me through. We all do. It is the only ethical way.

I read that last line a few more times before I closed my eyes and saw Ryker. I searched for something in his appearance or his mannerism that would've said he was sick, but he was the human saxophone with the golden glow, and he played no laments. Damn that spick-and-span man.

I hated him.

The only solace I had was of imagining him alone in that one life rotting away, smelling of shit and fear on some hospital bed somewhere. Just another lump under the blanket, waiting to be rolled off into the ground. I'd spit on his grave, dance on it, if I knew where it was. Because I don't, I do on occasion suddenly start dancing and spitting on any ground. People passing by may think I'm just a happy, jiggy, slobbering old man, when really I've got a grave in mind.

The grave of that man, not really a man but the devil. After all, we never needed Sal or any devil to come from underground. I learned at that moment that the devil, the true one, is people like Ryker.

I knew I couldn't show the paper to Mom and Dad. Only Grand could do that and he had decided not to, so I started a fire in the fireplace. Even with the heat, I sat so close to the flames. I thought for a moment I might just say *fuck it* and lean all the way in and come out the other side as nothing but ash.

Ash doesn't have to worry about anything, does it? It doesn't have to worry about a sick brother. It doesn't have to worry about what it all means. Ash just turns gray and blows away. That's what I wanted. I just wanted to blow away.

As I watched the paper burn, I remembered the day me and Grand made his shoestrings red. It was a couple years back. We were sitting in the tree house. Grand's shoes were brand new, having just come from the factory.

"Always white shoelaces." He stretched the untied laces out to the sides like bleached worms. "Why you think this is, Fielding?"

"You've got a tongue of the shoe right there, and the laces are the teeth. Teeth are white."

"Bad design, ain't it? Puttin' the tongue so close to the teeth. I'm always bitin' my tongue. You'd think if God was so smart, He'd have come up with a better design."

He took his pocket knife and studied each finger on his left hand like he was determining their value. Deciding that his ring finger was the least valuable, he took the knife and cut deep into his finger tip.

"Whatcha doin'?" I sat up on my heels but didn't try to stop him.

"Since I'm always bitin' my tongue and gettin' blood on my teeth, I reckon it's only right for my shoes to bite their tongue and get blood on their teeth."

"That's the craziest thing I ever heard."

"What is it they say? You've got to be crazy once in a while, or you'll go insane."

He reached the knife to me. "Go crazy with me, Fielding."

I took the knife and looked carefully at each of my fingers like I still had a choice to make. Really it was the left ring finger all along, making for a strange wedding of us brothers and our blood. The initial tear of the knife is what makes you cringe, but the coming blood makes it worth it. That red river, too well ourselves, too well each other.

After the shoelaces were our blood, we made the handprints on the wall of the tree house. It was a moment shared between us when blood wasn't dangerous, it was just the color of us. That was long before Ryker. Long before the blade followed the shine.

It never occurred to me at that time there was even the slightest possibility Grand had not contracted the virus, as I'm sure it did not occur to him. In those early years of the disease, some feared a kiss was enough. Fear is ignorance's first shadow.

After the newspaper burned, I doused the fire and went upstairs, finding Sal in the hall. He looked like something returned to shape after having been pulled this way and that way and almost in two.

"What were you and Grand doin', Sal?"

"Just talking." He seemed to be gnawed at, as if of himself only a sliver remained.

"About what?"

"Comic books." He frowned, not at me but at something bigger than the two of us.

As he went downstairs, he held tight to the banister, his feet careful with the stairs, lest he go to them, lest they fester the breaks.

He'd left Grand's door open, so I looked into his room. I thought at first Grand was gone. But then I saw him, standing woodenlike, with his back straight against the wall, like a grandfather clock off its time.

"Hey, Grand."

He just stood there and I thought for a moment he really had turned into a clock and the only thing he could ever say again was a minute upon minute.

Finally, he spoke as quick as a glance, "Hey."

"Whatcha doin'?"

"Nothin'." He kept against the wall. There must've been comfort in that.

"Wanna play catch, Grand? Like we used to?"

"I'm through playin' catch, little man."

I cracked my knuckles. I didn't know what else to do. "You know the Reds are gonna be playin' the Braves later?"

He looked at me, and it was like something lost looking to be found. "Oh yeah?"

"Yeah. It'll be some game, they say. You wanna watch with me?"

"I don't much care for baseball no more."

"But you're gonna be a Major Leaguer someday."

"Am I?"

"Sure. Everyone says it."

"Funny, no one ever asked me."

"Don't you wanna be a great baseball player?"

He sighed back into the wall. "I want to be a great man, Fielding."

And so we stand, proved of our existence by those who see us. And how did I see Grand, how did any of us, but as the one who would be great at this and that, as long as it was baseball and girls. He always had to be what we wanted him to be first. He existed only by proxy to our dreams of him.

"Grand? Are you okay?" I took a step toward him, but he held up his arm.

"Don't come any closer, little man."

"Why?"

"I'm gettin' a cold. Don't want you to get it." His arm stayed out. I wondered if he forgot about it.

"I won't get it, Grand. I won't breathe in real deep. Just surface breaths."

"Naw, I like ya too much to take the chance."

I emptied of a long-held breath. "You still like me, Grand?"

"Sure I do. I might even love ya." His lowering arm was goodbye falling, and I too stupid to realize.

"Grand—"

"It's time. You're gonna miss the game, little man."

"Ain'tcha gonna watch with me?"

A quiet came and dripped, making the room something drowned, us drowning with it.

Finally, three words rose above the gasping line, "I'm sorry, Fielding."

"About not watchin' the game?"

He looked at me like I was a boy, stinking of stupid.

"Naw, not about the game, Fielding. About hittin' you that day. I know now you were only tryin' to protect me."

"I'm sorry too, Grand. I shouldn't have called you that . . . that word. And I love you no matter what. And it's okay if you're sick, because I'll be here for you. We'll all be here for you, and everything will be okay."

That's what I wish I would've said. Why didn't I? Maybe it would've changed things. Maybe if I would've said *I'm sorry* and *I love you* and *I don't care that you're gay*, then maybe, maybe he'd be living right next door to me now and I could go over there and sit with him and we could watch the game on TV. Or not watch it. Maybe we'd read Walt Whitman or Langston Hughes or something like that.

Maybe there'd be someone in the kitchen making noise and this someone would come out with the food to set the table and Grand would call him his husband and make love to him after sending me back off next door until next time, until the next day I could see him again. Maybe it could've happened that way, but it never will, because I just stood there and he did a half chuckle into his chest and seemed to say, *stupid brother*. And I was. God burn me for it, I was.

"I'm goin' for a walk, Fielding. Tell Mom and Dad in case they ask, would ya?"

He drifted and I wish I would've reached for him. He stopped by my side, giving me the chance. I didn't take it, though. Stupid boy I was. I let my brother leave without a hug. That has never been an easy thing to let go of.

Just before he left I blurted out, "I took your Eddie Plank card. And I lost it. That was my secret I buried."

"I know." He kept his back to me, but I could still see his smile, too small to ever be real. "I know you did, little man. And it's all right. I forgive ya."

"How'd you know? You dig my secret up?"

"I didn't need to. The card was missin' and you looked guilty."

"I know your secret too."

He turned to me. Looked more through me than at me. "You dug it up?"

I nodded. "You're afraid. That's your secret. You're afraid."

He suddenly looked toward the window, and I thought for a moment the rabid dog was coming back through. I tightened in that fear.

He rubbed the back of his neck. A low sound came trying to be a laugh, but it had too much worry to make a real go of it.

"You know the story of the man who went walkin' in the city one day and found he couldn't walk over the manholes, even though they were covered. He was afraid he'd fall down into them and the devil would finish draggin' him down to hell. That's what I'm afraid of. Men. Holes. And the devil."

He strained like he was gathering something up inside him and it was heavy, heavy, and just too much. He buckled in the knees and leaned into the doorframe.

"Hey, listen, when I get back from my walk, I'll watch the game with ya, okay, little man?"

His leaving had the sound of a turning page. *Whoosh, flick,* and he was gone. By seven thirty, the television was on and Grand wasn't home. I tried to concentrate on the game, but it was a bad day for the color red. Cincinnati's ball caps and uniforms, even the stitching on the ball itself, never let me escape what could be in Grand's blood. I shut the game off and stared at the black screen until eight thirty. Nine thirty. Midnight. Grand still wasn't home.

Dad grabbed a flashlight. Looked more annoyed than alarmed. The worry was all in Mom at that time as she called to Dad from the porch, "Find him, Autopsy."

Dad nodded he would as she stood up against the wall of the porch like a second front door, waiting to be opened. Me, Sal, and Dad went up and down the lanes, shining the flashlight on bushes, passing cars, dark porches, and if Grand had been a leaf, a group of laughing teenagers, a napping cat, we would've found him.

Onward we went, shining the light across the baseball diamond behind the school. Up in the stands at the football stadium. It felt like a hundred different places before, after, and in between, but no Grand.

I found myself leading us through the woods. Dad shined the flashlight inside the one-room schoolhouse as we passed it. Nothing but one of Elohim's pamphlets on the ground.

The whole way walking to the tree house, I had that feeling one has when walking toward a difficult decision. I wanted to find Grand, but when I climbed up and saw the tree house empty, I won't lie and say I didn't feel relieved.

By that time, Dad was no longer annoyed. He was worried, painfully worried now. The light in his hand anxiously bouncing from tree to tree.

"I wonder where that boy has gotten to." He sighed. "I wonder—"

His voice fell with the flashlight that banged against the ground.

"Dad?"

It was too dark to see him, but I heard his feet pounding against the ground, running toward something.

I jumped down out of the tree house and picked up the light. Its shine found Sal. The way he stood there, I'll never forget the horror on his face. What he and Dad had seen, I didn't know. But he raised his trembling arm to show me.

I was afraid to shine the light to where he was pointing. I would go slow to the sorrow. Light on tree, another tree. Bark, more bark. Took the light lower and saw dirt. Leaves and more dirt, and . . . the toes of Grand's tennis shoes.

Oh, God, no.

Slowly I moved the light up his laces, untied.

His jeans. Something red drenching the denim up his left side.

More red drenching his hand, his arm. More than more, it was plenty to scream at, as Dad was screaming.

Oh, God, Dad. You on all fours and scooping the blood up from the ground, trying to put it back into the large gaping slash on your son's arm.

With every scrape Dad made of the ground, leaves and debris were brought up too and because of this Grand's arm became Halloween and I had to look away because the scare was no longer subtle and I thought I was going to scream my throat to pieces.

It was then I saw the pocketknife. The knife me and Grand had used to cut our fingers. The knife that had once bled us closer. Now it was the knife that cut us apart.

I looked at Dad's face. His tears didn't drop. Instead they stopped at his cheeks like they were taped there. I tried to remember, did someone come along with clear tape, and if so, when? Were they still around? Would they tape my tears? I wanted them to. I wanted my tears to be always stuck on my cheeks in that particular fall the way I knew they'd always be on Dad's. In ten, twenty, the eternity of years, I knew the tears would still be there. This would be the reason I would never again be able to get close to my father. I'd never be able to make it past the tears.

Dad never gave up trying to put Grand's blood back into his arm, not even when I asked him to. Even when I screamed at him to stop, to just stop it already, he kept going and was so there with it that he never saw Sal. Never saw how he picked up the piece of paper with Grand's words written on it, *Don't touch my blood.*

I'd forgotten about the blood. It was everywhere and I had forgotten it. I almost told Dad to wipe it off his hands. *It could make you sick,* I almost said, but Sal tore up the letter and stuffed the pieces into his pocket and I did the same with my words.

Even if I had told Dad, he wouldn't have stopped touching it. How could he? All that blood was Grand before it was anything else. And I mean *grand* in all the magnificent definition of the word. I fell to my knees at his side and tried myself to put the blood back because, hell, I wasn't finished with my brother. How could I be when I was only thirteen and he was only eighteen.

I would've worn a tie to his graduation. Dad would've made me, but I would've wanted to. Grand would've grabbed the end of it, tugged it until I laughed, tousled my hair and called me *little man*.

I would've gotten the extra boxes needed to pack his things for the dorm, though he would leave me his baseball glove. I'd hold it when I was missing him. Because of this, my chest would start to smell like leather.

He'd study hard at college, though I'm not sure what and that not knowing would break my heart. It breaks my heart still. That I didn't know my brother enough to know what he would study, what he would become. That I didn't know he would be more than baseball.

Goddamn it, I wasn't finished with him yet. I still had to get drunk with him at least once and stumble into a conversation that would maybe heal all things. He'd make me burnt toast in the morning for the hangover. Of course he would. He was Grand.

No, I wasn't finished with him. We were supposed to grow old together, me and my brother. If I was going to grow old with anybody, it was going to be him. Our parents would die. Our lovers would die. Our friends would all go before us. But we, we would be the last on the road.

My brother of mine, I had your white hair and wrinkles all picked out. Now I wear them, along with my own. Twice wrinkled, twice gray. I hate you for leaving me no choice but to go forth into this heat-colored future and its long voyage I no longer want to hold.

I wonder if when we get to the beyond, if we are there what we were here. If so, he'll still be eighteen. A beautiful eighteen. And I will be old, as I am. He'll be like a grandkid to me. What will I do with that?

I wonder if he would ask me for his wrinkles. Even if I handed them over, they'd never fit him, not that eighteen-year-old skin. A boy trying on his grandfather's face, that's all he would be.

I'll never have my brother back even when he is back, because that night he died, he vanished, and vanished things stop becoming more. That is the tragedy of losing an older brother. He stays still. You keep on and one day become the older one. It's unnatural, that reversal. It's the thing that keeps the family from ever being whole again.

I knew we'd never be the same as I listened to Dad's crying screams and watched him frantically search and dig at the ground for every last drop of blood. As if the reason Grand hadn't risen was because the blood wasn't all back in his arm yet.

"Dad, please stop now."

A bawling howl set me back on my heels. Dad's agony was so severe, it was frightening. I didn't have the courage to hold him through it, so I stayed back, letting my father be devoured before me.

Somewhere I heard a crying that compared to Dad's was so small, it almost didn't exist. I shined the flashlight, and there was Sal, coiled up on the ground, face tucked toward his knees. He didn't rise to look at me or the light. The ache had curled him into a circle, rounding him out, like a porthole into a darkness that was taking his place.

I needed the devil more at that moment than the weeping Sal. I needed that comfort of authority. I needed the experienced angel to stand solid and strong, not collapsed on the ground as just another crying boy who could offer me no wisdom nor understanding.

I grabbed the pocketknife and climbed up the tree house. I looked at mine and Grand's handprints on the wall. There was a new third handprint, smaller than either mine or Grand's. I didn't worry about it then. It was Grand's handprint I wanted. It was his that I stabbed.

"I hate you. I hate you."

I spit my powerful fire. I raged against his ghost, so my living hurt could haunt him, the way he was already haunting me. I stabbed until the wood splintered and broke away, revealing the outside and what I had tried to escape. My father crying. My brother dead in his arms. The darkness eating from edge in.

24

Farewell, happy fields

—MILTON, *PARADISE LOST* 1:249

THE YELL IS permanent, the wrong is lasting, the damage is complete, and the *goddamn* is eternal when a young man goes into the woods and in his fray turns the sword inward.

I waited for Dad to ask me why Grand would do it, but he never did. Not even when the morning light began to reveal more of the scene before us. He just stood and said he was going into town to do the things that needed doing. Me and Sal were to wait with Grand's body, he said. And then he left. Me and Sal listened for as long as we could hear him. He was rambling off case after case. Some real. Some not. Like *Man v. God. Boy v. Knife. Bliss v. Misery.*

Me and Sal didn't sit close to Grand nor close to each other. Spaces had already started to form.

When Dad returned with the sheriff, he said he had called Mom and told her the news so we wouldn't have to. Then he told us to go home.

"Dad?"

"I said go home, Fielding."

Then he turned from me. The start of the rest of our lives.

Me and Sal walked home slowly to give Mom enough time to

scream the loudest, enough time to cry the worst. I thought we'd find her somewhere inside the house, collapsed under a pile of tissues. I was surprised to see her standing on the front porch, her hands full of our refrigerator magnets.

As soon as I stepped up onto the porch, she fit the magnets into my hands. The magnets were wet. Her eyes made everything wet.

"You've got to go to him, Fielding. Your Father won't do it. He says it's being silly." Her voiced cracked, and I can't be certain she even said the word *silly*.

"I don't understand, Mom. What do you want me to do with the magnets?"

"Rub 'em all over him."

"Who?"

"Grand."

"But why, Mom?"

"To get the metal out of him." She wrung her hands until I thought she'd twist her fingers off.

"What metal, Mom?"

"His arm got cut, didn't it? That's what your father said on the phone."

"He cut himself."

"He did not cut himself, Fielding." She refused to say the word *suicide*. "He was simply cut. And when he was cut, some of the metal got inside 'im. It always comes off the blade, a little bit. And that extra metal will weigh him down.

"All souls are weighed come death, and the souls deemed fit to enter heaven are light as lettuce. No sins to heavy 'em. We've got to make sure Grand's soul weighs as little as it can. I won't have my baby in hell."

"All right, Mom. I'll do it."

"But you can't." Sal stopped me from leaving with the magnets. "Only the mother can get the metal out of a son."

"But . . ." Mom looked past us, at the world outside the porch. "I know, you can bring the body here, to me. That's how it'll be done. Then I can do the magnets and make sure all the metal is lifted right outta him."

"They're not gonna bring his body here, Mom."

"That's right," Sal added. "You've got to go down there yourself."

"Leave the house? I can't."

"For Grand." Sal moved the magnets from my hands back to hers. "If it makes you feel any better, there isn't a cloud in the sky. There'll be no rain. Even if there is, you know how to swim now. Remember?"

She held the magnets to her chest as she closed her eyes. She counted to ten before sliding her feet in toothpick strides across the porch. She would on occasion whimper and look around as if terror were going to come in on her from all sides. Finally across the porch, she slowly lowered herself down the steps. She seemed afraid of the way they creaked under her.

Sunlight cast on her red painted toes through her hosiery as she stood on the bottom step. The ground below something she looked at as if it held the greatest fault she'd ever seen. She lifted her foot, as though she would take the step, but instead she lowered her foot back down and cried, "I can't. Oh, Lord, help me. I can't."

Sal looped his arm through her left and I looped mine through her right.

"It's okay, Mom. We got ya."

She sighed as she looked down at me. "I don't think I can, Fielding."

My mother's tears always knew how to hurt. They could push you off balance and send you crashing down. Nothing breaks like a body falling. Nothing puts you to pieces quite like that.

"For Grand, you can." Sal tugged on her arm.

"Grand," she whispered as she stood a little taller.

"Your son," Sal matched her whisper.

"My son."

The son she always loved a little more than the other. The son she always held a little tighter. A little longer. The son who would bring her down from the porch and onto the dead, brown ground.

She looked unsure of what ground was. It'd been so long since she'd been on it.

Her first steps were slow and scared. Close things she tested the earth with. But more and more, they became bigger and bigger. And then suddenly she was off. Walking faster than us even. Eventually our arms slipped out from hers and the world found her walking all on her own.

Those out in the town stopped whatever they were doing. Conversation ended midsentence. Handshakes never got to where they were going. Food slid off spoons. Mouths gaped. Babies were left to cry. The mothers were busy watching mine. Everyone busy watching the woman who had not been seen outside for twelve whole years. Here she was, she who had been living like a curtain, never trailing far from the window of the house she was attached to.

"Isn't that?"

"I believe it is."

"Stella Bliss."

"Maybe the world is really about to end."

"It's just beginnin' for her."

If only they knew, it was no beginning for her. It was an end she was walking to. What a day to come out. A rather beautiful day. Did she even see it? Walking hand in hand as she was with magnets and determination. Quick steps to the boy waiting on her. Was she even sure it was trees she was passing or just tall men? Did she look up at the sky, coming blue from the morning's gray?

Pity the child in her path and who was not hers and who she pushed out of the way. Even kicked his ball into the middle of Main Lane. Pity the wasp who flew too close and who she swatted to a concussion. Pity the day she did not see, a day that had been waiting for twelve long years. A day that took but twelve minutes to walk.

The morgue was in the basement of the courthouse. The light dim and like a shedding of clay, dusty and browned. It was a place that smelled of rust and soil, of chemicals and clogged drains. Compared to the heat of every other place, it was cool. Basements are like that. Probably the coolest place I'd been all summer long.

When Dad saw Mom, the only words he could manage were, "What about the rain?"

She didn't say anything, just threw her arms around him. It was like a cold burning between them. Their skeletons joined at soggy throbs. The space they filled before us, like twisted wire, embedding into itself. They were one grasp. One curve of flesh. One heart breaking in startled, flickering cracks.

When they finally separated, you couldn't tell which tears belonged to her, and which belonged to him.

He tried to persuade her not to see the body. Said it was not a way for a mother to see her son. But she held up the magnets and said, "It is the way for a mother to see her son, if it is indeed the only way left."

We stepped into the room with Grand, where he lay on a metal table with a white sheet beneath him. He looked the same as he had lain in the woods. Only the scenery had changed. It was as if no one knew what to do with the body of a god.

Mom approached the table with wary steps, as if she were walking across water and had to wait for the bridge to keep building. The tan nylon of her hosiery was dirtied and clung to by tiny gravels from the walk outside. Every time she lifted her foot, the nylons cased the strain of her toes as they pointed tensely in every step that took her to the table, where she circled his body, as fluid as the ripple around the dropped stone.

There was a wholeness to the silence that followed. A sort of totality that sucked in all sound, save for our breathing. I thought there would be noise. I thought she would sob uncontrollably. That was the mother I expected. The one who roared louder than the father in the woods. The one who banged her infinitesimal fists and screamed,

Why? That was not the mother who circled her dead son in the morgue.

She ran her hand through his hair, the short strands going through her fingers in a rising and falling like the abstract summary of his short life. She smiled that slight smile all mothers give to the child who has always been their favorite.

Her apron pressed against the sheet as she leaned over him. I thought maybe she would hold the magnets down like he was a refrigerator and she was merely posting notes. A sort of up-and-down motion. Instead she slid the magnets across him, a different one for each part of his body. She believed each magnet only had enough strength in it to lift the metal from one body part, and after that, it was spent of its power.

When she got to his left arm, she paused at the wide wound stuffed with the gathered blood and leaves and dirt. She started to pick the leaves out, but Dad gently asked her to leave them. It was as if the leaves and dirt provided a foliage to the wound so he wouldn't have to see the cut so naked and clear. She understood this, and merely moved the magnet around the wound, the drooping tip of one of the larger leaves gliding across the back of her passing hand.

I thought the wound would drop her to her knees in realization of his suicide, but she merely looked at it as if it were just your ordinary difference of no particular sin or exclusive death. She was in such denial, that the wound was just a moment his skin was not at its best.

She removed his shoes and socks and as she slid the magnets over his bare feet, her voice broke as she said, "I know how ticklish your feet are. I'll scratch 'em good once I'm done."

And she did too.

His face was last, and as she looked at the pile of used magnets, she lost that control she had so carefully held.

"There ain't any left. I've used 'em all. I don't have any to lift the metal from his face." Her cries were like a coming of new death.

Sal went to her and held her hands as he asked her, "Don't you know a mother's got ten good magnets at the ends of her fingers? Not enough to take on a body, but a face, yes."

She looked at her hands, bending her fingers as if testing their strength. As Sal gave her room, she returned to Grand, holding her hands high over his face, standing there for a few seconds as if she was unsure of how to begin. Then as if suddenly realizing exactly how to do it, her hands slowly lowered to his chin, where her fingers stroked back and forth.

I was almost hopeful, watching her hands lie next on his forehead as if they could bring him back. As if her fingers feeling softly down his cheeks were the way to resurrection. I thought this until I saw her face and all its hopelessness, and then I knew there wasn't going to be a miracle.

I imagined a series of small falls in the world at that moment. Somewhere the petals of a lilac were falling off. Somewhere a moth was heading straight for the ground. Grains of sugar were rolling off the counter. A baseball was losing its soar. Small falls taking me down with them and to that low where no wings can be found and no rising is ever had.

"My baby," she whispered. "My dear, sweet love of my life. Why did you leave me?"

She waited as if she believed he might rise long enough from the dead to tell her why. When he didn't, it became a kick to the back of her knees. Dad caught her just in time, bringing them both down to the floor in a hold that made them look like one wound of the same deep stab.

I thought maybe she'd fainted, but she was still open in all the places that can be. She'd just lost her legs for a moment, she said. As Dad held her there, beneath the height of their dead son, I ran.

I ran from my brother's body. From the town. From the terrible ripping apart. I could hear Sal behind me. I went faster. Between the trees, and up the high land to the edge of the cliff that gave way to the rock quarry below.

"Why'd you follow me, Sal?"

"Fielding—"

He didn't get to finish what he was going to say because I tackled him to the ground and hit him even before my hands had formed their fists. When they did, boy did they ever mean it. I hated him that moment because I had to hate someone, and Ryker was somewhere too far.

"Why the fuck did you have to come?" I hit and hit until I couldn't feel my knuckles anymore.

When his punch came, it struck me hard across the chin, knocking me back. He held his fists up as if I would charge him again and he was going to have to fight me off. But I just sat there, holding my jaw in my hand and staring at the long tears streaming down his cheeks.

"I'm so tired of being hit. Why is it always me to get it when the fists come out?" He lowered his own fists as he sat back in a great, exhausted sigh.

The ground seemed the safest place to look, so for the next few moments, we both looked there, struggling with what to do in the aftermath of a god's death.

Only a squawking bird was heard for a while. And then his hushed voice, saying, "I tried, Fielding. To save him. I swear that to you."

His tongue reached and tasted the blood from his nose.

"How'd you try to save 'im, Sal?"

"I told him the story of Century."

I closed my eyes. "Well, go on then. Tell it to me."

"We all called him Cen. He had a vineyard, and one winter he found a grape growing out of season.

"He ate the grape, and people said he was sick for doing so. That it was unnatural to eat a grape out of season. That it went against the laws of God. They forgot that God is the great authorizer, and a grape can grow out of season only with His permission first.

"The people, in their fear and ignorance, chased Cen out of the town and into the woods. There he lived alone and unhappy as the sick Cen no one could accept.

"Then came the day the light went out. No sun shone. No flash-lights turned on. No candles would light. God wanted the people to realize who they had chased away, so He left them in darkness to find out.

"After weeks of night, a light suddenly appeared in the woods. The people, desperate and hungry for light, ran to it, surprised to find Cen. They had been so certain of what they thought was wicked. Of what they thought was a sick desire. And yet, in that darkness, Cen was the only light God allowed.

"The light was coming from Cen's blood. He had cut his finger by accident in the dark, and his blood was a bright pouring. That was what eating the grape had done. Light was the gift, the beautiful re-sult of the man who dared not question his hunger for that which grows out of season.

"The sorry people fell to their knees before this very light. They said they were wrong to run him out of town. They had been fools, they cried. Won't you forgive us? they asked.

"Other men would have turned them away, but Cen was a grand man and he allowed them to stay in the light. He would have allowed them to stay there forever, but his finger stopped bleeding and when that happened, the light stopped as well.

" 'It's so dark again,' they cried. 'How will we ever get home?'

" 'I can help you home,' Cen said.

" 'But how? You've no more light.'

"He took out his pocketknife and cut his arm, the light shining them through the woods to town. There were so many people to see home, Cen had to keep cutting his arm in order to bleed more light.

"After walking the last person home, he had to sit down, for he was far too weak to continue. He'd bled so much for them and there was no more to bleed, not even a drop left. He died alone and in the dark.

"The next morning, in the light of the returned sun, everyone saw the body of Cen on the ground. I guess some say he killed himself, cutting his arm like that, and I guess he did. But at least he killed himself on the way to something else. And that's what I told Grand.

"I said to him when you hold the knife, you have to ask yourself will more light come from this than dark? And if the answer is yes, then by all means cut away. If through your death, you can walk someone home, then do it—but if by your death, they lose a home, then think again.

"I guess to him, slicing open his arm was walking someone home. It was walking himself. And how can you be mad at him, Fielding, if he's home now?"

25

Tears, such as Angels weep, burst forth

—MILTON, *PARADISE LOST* 1:620

THE NIGHT BEFORE Grand's funeral, Dad sat on the porch, squinting his eyes, folding his arms, and crossing his legs. He hadn't bothered turning on the porch light. In those dark days following Grand's death, lights were rarely turned on. It was as if we no longer knew how to pull a lamp cord or flip a wall switch. We'd suddenly gone dumb of the way to light.

Darkness was everywhere for us then. A darkness so thick, it was near solid. And it was all over the place, from Dad's silence to the creases of Mom's tissues. Everywhere there were tissues. Some piled, some scattered, some on tables, and some you had to step over on the floor. If you did step on one, your foot would be wet, the snot and tears carried on your heel.

These tissues light as air but denting the ground beneath them. As we were dented. Every time we passed Grand's quiet room. A dent. When we looked at his empty chair at the table. A dent. When we saw all those crumpled white tissues and thought of baseballs. *Dent, dent, dent.* We were scooped out, hollowed in, and pocketing darkness all over us.

Dad stopped shaving. His hair came straight from the bed. His cheeks puffy, a coming swell. In his mouth, you could hear thunder in the distance and his breath came humid and smelled like toothpaste laid aside.

He stopped wearing his suits and wore a T-shirt and pajama bottoms all day and days at a time. He didn't eat. He was trying to get even in the bone with Grand. If you thought it was a shadow passing, it was probably Dad.

Sometimes I'd find him on his knees, thinking at first he was praying, then realizing his arms were out, reaching beyond the wall in front of him. Twitching his fingers slightly as if to say, *Come on, come on back to me, now.*

Mom got thinner everywhere too, especially her fingers, like unraveling spools of thread. While Dad seemed unable to move, Mom seemed unable to survive stillness. Always up, always moving and circling the drain lest she stop and be sucked down it.

She cleaned out closets, cleared shelves, tossed fresh flour out, not realizing she was bringing more emptiness in.

Age had finally found her. The smoothness she once had appeared to have run out of her like water. A lay of wrinkles that would ordinarily have taken years to put down seemed to have come overnight. In her, something had been dimmed. I found myself unable to pull the strength together to look at her eyes, like gashes on her face torn fresh every few seconds.

I saw her once in Grand's room, pacing around his empty bed. She was singing the lullaby.

Down in the hills of Ohio,
there's a babe at sleep tonight . . .

I watched her, unable to stop moving around his bed, hugging his old sweatshirt in her arms. After every verse of the lullaby, she would fall silent. I'd watch her mouth open slowly in that one syllable word, *Why*. Another verse, another *why*. Over and over again, she was trying to figure it out, all the while unable to stop moving.

Fedelia gave Mom something to help her relax. I thought it was working as I looked in at Mom, lying on the bed, her back to me. I tiptoed around her. Her eyes shut. Her fingers in her mouth. I pulled them out and found her nails bleeding. She'd bitten them down to the quick in her sleep, her teeth still grinding. I stayed there, holding her hands away from her mouth while her eyes tossed frantically under their lids, her teeth searching for something to gnaw.

Fedelia never left the house. She slept in one of the extra rooms. We needed her there. She seemed the only one out of all of us capable of continuing. She would ask me if I was hungry and give me something even though I said I wasn't.

She'd sit by Mom and hold her hand and nod out to me as she said, "Don't forget him, Stella. He needs you too, remember that now, child."

She would sit by Dad and hold her hands up, showing him a crack and how it grew. "It's gettin' bigger and bigger, Autopsy. You have to be careful because if the crack gets too big, it'll break your whole world wide open and destroy you. I know something about being destroyed. I know a thing or two about lettin' cracks get outta hand. You can't let that happen, Autopsy. You have got to get up from here. Shave your face. Put your suit on. Fielding needs his father. He doesn't need a great, big crack."

After Fedelia left, I found a pile of tissues beneath her pillow. Never once did she cry in front of us. She knew it would do us no good. We needed her to be the strong one. She could say Grand's name without breaking into a million pieces, and she taught us how to do it one letter at a time. She could walk by his room and not get dented. We tried her walk. We dented less and less. Our faces got drier and drier, and we went from tissues to sleeves, to brief wiping on the backs of our hands before one day finding there was nothing to be wiped, at least not on the outside.

Sal had mourned with the rest of us. He seemed to drink a lot of water during those days as if to replenish what he lost by eye. He thought it was his fault. Grand's death had made Sal's ears sensitive to those accusations. He was finally listening to the people who said everything bad was him. That whole summer of great undoing, of great unrest. This made him unhinged. Loose. As if you turned his nose slightly to the right, you would unscrew the last piece holding him together and all at once he would collapse into a pile of broken bones and broken heart.

"Do you want me to leave, Fielding?" he asked one night, sitting on the floor of our bedroom, leaning back against the wall. The room dark, his voice more of the same. "I'll leave if you want me to."

I eased down and found his side, leaned into it. "I already lost one brother. How can you ask if I'd wanna lose another?"

Losing Grand turned me into the passed-by. Blue skies, they pass me by. Good days, they pass me by. Talk and joy pass me by. The reasons people laugh, the reasons they smile, pass me by. *Whoosh, whoosh,* passing me by.

When I had Grand, I loved forever. Now forever frightens me. Must it last so very long?

I can't spell me without him. I mean that. His full name, Grandfather, takes out every letter of my own except for two *I*s and an *L*. Who am I with those things? I'm not who I once was. I am simply the teeny-tiny remains of him, this Fielding who had a brother and in that had everything.

I thought it'd get better, losing a brother. That's what they say, isn't it? All those books I've gotten, those meetings I've gone to. They all say it gets better. How can it get better for a brother like me who threw out ignorance too late?

Sometimes I throw out my apologies. I go to the store and I get a pack of baseballs. White. Red stitching. I use a red marker to match. I write, *I'm sorry.* And then I throw. I've thrown them everywhere. Down alleys. Off the side of the road. In fields, in parks, in other people's yards. I throw. And then I wait. I wait to see if an eighteen-year-old god will appear and pick up the ball and come walking with it toward me, saying, *It's all right. I forgive you, little man.*

That never happens. It never will. Forever is here, and it's nothing but hurt over and over again.

The night before his funeral, I dreamed of him. It was a transparent dream, like I was looking at him through jars. A bit seedy too, like the jars once held strawberry jam.

He was wearing tennis shoes that instead of having solid rubber bottoms, had lotion bottles affixed. Every step he took squeezed some of that lotion out.

When I asked him why, he said, "To soften the scar."

"What scar?" I asked.

"Why, my scar." He turned and I saw his left arm was gone. It was then I realized we were standing on it. Either we'd shrunk or his arm had enlarged, either way his suicide gash had scarred and it made for a squishy, pink road beneath us.

He jumped up and down, high in the air like the scar had the springs of a trampoline. The lotion shot out from the bottles and onto the scar as he said, "Maybe if I soften the scar enough, it'll just go away, then God won't have proof I done somethin' bad. Won't you help me soften the scar? Make it go away, little man?"

"How?"

He pointed behind me. I turned and saw a vending machine full of the lotion tennis shoes. I went to the machine and with a deposit of my blood, got a pair of the shoes out. I slipped them on and started walking. Grand was ahead of me. By the time I caught up to him, I tried to stay by his side but the walk was full of turnstiles and there wasn't one with room for the both of us.

Our lotion shoes started flattening. We were running out of lotion. We tried to go back to the vending machine but the turnstiles wouldn't turn the opposite way. There would be no going back.

"What'll we do now, Grand?" Even in dreams, voices tremble.

He looked at me and I wished he wasn't crying.

"покаяться, little man."

Upon waking, I couldn't get to the Russian dictionary fast enough to look that word up and its meaning:

Repent.

We had Grand's funeral at the house, holding it in Russia, which was the living room and large enough to allow space for the great grow of mourners. Neither Elohim nor his followers attended.

His onetime follower Yellch was there. He didn't cry, but his eyes were red and swatted as eyes tend to be at the end of wet work. In his squeezing hand was the end of a tissue. So many ends. He was like an end himself. Quiet. Still. Tired and trying to bend back to the beginning to fix a different end. One where his onetime savior and best friend didn't end up in a coffin.

A coffin that wasn't your usual. It was a decision Mom made when she was unable to sit still and found herself dusting and polishing the grandfather clock. She removed its pendulum and clockworks to make room for Grand's body. The clock didn't look that different from a coffin. Both wood, both long and square. The only unsettling thing was how Grand's face showed through the glass where the clock's dial once did.

They dressed Grand in a dark blue suit, a three-piece like Dad's. I worried Dad would attend the funeral in the same T-shirt and pajamas he'd been wearing for days. Maybe if it were left to him he would've, but Mom yanked the T-shirt and pajamas off and pushed him toward the shower, the razor, the toothpaste by the sink.

Though showered, shaved, and suited, Dad did not look like Dad as he placed Grand's baseball cards and glove in the coffin. I made Grand a new Eddie Plank card for the one I'd lost by cutting a small square out of the flap of a cardboard box. Then I drew Eddie on it, even put his statistics on the back. Sal drew Eddie's eyes. I've never been able to do the eyes.

Mom tucked a *New York Times* under Grand's arm so he'd have something to read while waiting in line to have his soul weighed. I didn't have it in my heart to tell her or Dad about Ryker and all the sorry that went with him. I'd let them have the son they thought they did. In that thinking, Grand became the son who hadn't committed suicide. He had simply died. That would be how they would answer for his death in the future if anyone should ask.

"Is Fielding your only child?"

"Oh, no, we had another son. His name was Grand. But he died."

"I'm so sorry. How did he die?"

"One night in the woods, he just died."

"Oh, I see."

I often wondered if they ever discussed it between themselves. They never did with me. Never asked me why I thought he did it. Had they even asked themselves? In the silence, and in the dark, ask themselves why their son would make such a choice?

I think Dad almost asked me once.

It was long after Breathed, and we were sitting on the porch of their house in Pennsylvania. Him on the porch swing, me on the steps. He was looking at me.

When I turned to face him, he said, "Grand was a fine boy."

"Yes, he was."

"Do you know . . . ?"

"Do I know what, Dad?"

He recrossed his legs and picked up the paper by his side. "Do you know if that fella, the one Grand knew . . ."

"Ryker?"

"Was that his name?"

"Yes."

"Do you know if he still works at *The New York Times?*"

"Ryker died, Dad."

"He did?"

I nodded my head. "He died in '85."

"Oh." He shook the paper out in front of him. "Grand would've been a fine journalist. Don't you think?"

"If he wanted to be."

"He would've been a fine baseball player."

"If he wanted to be."

"He would've been a fine husband and father."

"Only if he wanted to be."

"Well, what is it he wanted to be?" Dad hastily folded the paper and smacked it down.

"I'm sorry, Dad. I didn't mean to make you angry."

I got up to leave.

"Fielding? Wait. Do you know . . . ?"

"Know what, Dad?"

It was on the tip of his tongue. That question of why Grand had killed himself. Would I have answered it had he asked me? No. My father was too rid of any muscle by then. He was an old man and he wouldn't have been strong enough to withstand the tragedy that was his son's life. Maybe he saw this in my eyes, that I wouldn't tell him the truth. Maybe that was why he said *never mind* and looked out over the marigolds growing in the nearby flowerpot.

What was he thinking of? Was it how he screwed in handles along the side of the clock so there'd be something for the pallbearers to hold onto? Dad was a pallbearer, as was I. Grand's body wasn't heavy but his death was, and sometimes I thought I'd have to let go of the handle because the burden was just too much.

It was like trying to lift something pouring in a river wideness and spilling out farther than my hands would ever be able to catch. A deep, torrential pouring that swore to drown me in a limitless sinking. Just when I thought my hand was going to break under the strain, we lifted the coffin into the back of the hearse and I could breathe, not freely but enough to live.

As we were preparing to take the short drive to the cemetery, Mom tugged Dad's sleeve to tell him she wouldn't be going with us.

"Why, Mom? Is it because you're afraid to go outside again?"

"I'm not afraid. Today I choose to stay."

"Why?" Dad asked, but I don't think he really cared. He was too busy looking at his son's coffin in the back of the hearse.

She grabbed his hands in hers and patiently held them until he finally turned from the hearse to her.

"Autopsy, my love. When you get home, you'll say to me, 'Honey, the funniest thing happened on the way to the cemetery.' And I'll ask, 'What happened, my love?' And you'll say the door of the clock suddenly opened and Grand jumped out. Said he was never really dead at all, just pretendin'.

"Then he'll run away. Run right away. And I'll ask you, but where'd he run away to? And you'll answer, where all clocks go. The place where time never runs out, the place of beautiful eternity."

I looked out the car window as we drove away, at her standing in the front yard. Her yellow handkerchief was her wave. Sal was the only one to wave back.

I faced front, straightening my tie. Mom had bought Sal a suit as well, and while I wore my tie like a heavy laying on the chest, Sal's was more like a gentle dropping. He looked at home in a black suit. Sometimes when I think of him now, I see him in that suit, a small form crying on a pew out in the middle of an overgrown field. A tractor going behind him. His shoes shiny on dull soil.

On the way to the cemetery, we passed Elohim and his followers. They were standing in the woods, close enough to the edge to see them. I glanced at Dad and Sal. Dad was staring straight ahead. Sal was looking out the other window. I was the only one who saw Elohim, the little garter snake slithering in his hand.

The cemetery was a flat-top meadow on one of the hills. It was called Reflection Hill because if you were buried there, your stone was a full-body effigy of yourself, laid on the ground. Your reflection, hence the cemetery's name.

Once everything was set up graveside, Sal stood before us with Grand's dog-eared *Leaves of Grass* and said a little something about the brother lost to him.

"He existed. Hurrah! He existed, and we shall be each moment celebrating him and singing him and through eternity, we shall hold him with our strong hearts. And strong we must be because we cannot stop in the night, for the powerful play goes on, and you may contribute a verse. The powerful play goes on, and you, dear Grand, have contributed your beautiful verse."

Sal laid the book on top of the grandfather clock. And then Grand's teammates, the very ones who had turned from him, stood in a line by the side of his body. Like the marine gun salute, they tossed balls up into the air and hit them out. It wasn't perfect. I even think there were a couple of the players who failed to hit their ball, but no one noticed. To all of us, the swings were in unison and the balls flew as the same. Two more times they did this. Two more times it was perfect.

I still remember the sound of the dirt hitting the top of the clock. The glass face would break under the weight, and even though I shouldn't have been able to hear it, I did. Under all those layers of dirt, I heard the glass breaking and the dirt surging in onto his clean face.

As the others left, including my slumped father, who dragged his feet toward the car, I found myself unable to leave the heap of dirt before me.

"What are you thinking about, Fielding?"

Sal was by my side. Where were his hands? For some reason, I remember them on top of the dirt.

"I saw your handprint on the wall of the tree house," I said. "I saw it the night we found Grand."

"Are you angry I put it there? With yours and his?"

"When'd you do it?"

"The night the stones were thrown in the windows on Main Lane. The blood you saw on my hand, it was from cutting my finger."

I looked down at the dirt. Thought about digging it up.

"His birthday is next month. I wonder what Mom's gonna do with that cake recipe she's already got out on the counter."

"There's your birthday. She can save it for that. The candles too."

Candles.

"Sal, how'd you light those fence posts in the field?"

He looked across the effigies. We could see the top of Dresden's from where we stood, her beautiful face upturned toward the sky, her dress long and the toes of the one leg stretched out from under it. The dress flatter on the other side below the calf of the stub she'd come into this world with.

"Remember when I went into her house, to use the bathroom, but not really use it?"

I nodded my head.

"Alvernine had already laid her birthday candles out on the counter, along with a book of matches. The fence posts were splintered in their tops. All I had to do was wedge the candles down in them."

"But they blew out when Dresden exhaled."

"Candles always go out when the wind is as soon as whenever."

"Why'd you tell me that, Sal? Don't ya want me to believe you're the devil?"

"You don't believe anymore?"

I shrugged. "A devil don't need matches to make fire."

"Funny, I've never made fire without them."

"Boys?"

We turned to Dad, having reluctantly returned.

"It's time to go now. C'mon."

The ride back home was a quiet one, and while Dad was just as far from me as the front seat, he seemed to be farther away in the low of some deep field.

Come on up from the field, Dad, is what I wanted to say. It's what I should've said, but I left him there. I always left him there. Grand's death had and would always cause little spaces between us all. Between me and Dad, me and Mom. Between the two of them. Little spaces we got good at keeping. Sometimes we'd walk toward each other like it was hard, like we had water up to our waists and it was a fight to move through it. That's how Dad walked toward Mom when we got home. When we got home and she, having been waiting, held her hands hard into her waist, almost like a punch to the gut.

Dad struggled through the water to get to her, his grief leaning back behind a smile to say,

"You know, my love, the funniest thing happened on the way to the cemetery . . ."

26

Must I thus leave you Paradise? thus leave
Thee, native soil, these happy walks and shades?
—MILTON, PARADISE LOST 11:269–270

IT WAS THE last day of summer and only nineteen days since we'd buried Grand. Nineteen days of Dad in T-shirts and pajama pants, of him growing the most beard of his life and of him sitting there in coffined silence. Nineteen days of Mom in a robotic restlessness that saw our house the cleanest it ever was. Nineteen days of Fedelia asking what we wanted to eat, and nineteen days of our not caring and of her making meals of her own decision. Above all else, it was nineteen days of pure, corroding pain.

The florist was always at our door, delivering the latest batch of sympathy and house plant. Even Elohim sent a lily condolence. I don't think it was coincidence it arrived that very morning as I was sitting on the sofa with Sal by the open windows.

Dad was resting in his chair, the strands of his hair like a pile of broken branches. In his mess, in his ruin, in his unkempt chaos, he was more wilderness than the one outside. The groomed father I once had was now like a stain in his almost savage neglect of hygiene. For all the showers and baths he did not take, it was confusing why he wore his bathrobe, slung open though adding bulk to his going frame.

Mom was up and straightening an already straight lampshade. Her apron was like Dad's bathrobe, something worn but not with purpose. Mom hadn't cooked since Grand. Cleaning, sorting, emptying—those were the things she did. It was Fedelia who was in the kitchen cooking meals we wouldn't have the appetite to eat.

As for me and Sal, we were in and out of grief, in and out of quiet talk that made short stretches of the impossible possible. As a whole, we were just a family, just the Blisses trying to get back to it, knowing we never would.

With it soon to be October, the heat had still to break. Some wondered if winter would be skipped altogether. We feared a one-season life, where the fan is always on and the heat boils us in our beds. There are winter dreams to be had when summer makes too good of its time.

"The ice cream will be delivered today," Sal spoke just above a whisper. "Juniper's called here. Said the truck is on its way. They thought I'd like to know because of how I used to call and ask."

He stared out the open window before him. His frown like a red land. A place you can imagine screams echo so well in.

"Funny it took a whole summer to get ice cream to a town in a heat wave." He turned from the window to me and we looked at each other.

Mom on her hands and knees, dusting the already dusted bottom shelves. Dad sitting so still, staring up at the ceiling as if he'd heard someone walking just overhead in Grand's room. Fedelia clanking a pot against another in the kitchen. Amidst all of this and more, me and Sal looked at each other and knew we'd never eat ice cream again.

"Do you hear that?" Dad slightly raised in his chair but did not get up. "I think I hear someone, up there walking." He pointed toward the ceiling and Grand's room above. "I should check, don't you think?"

He asked no one in particular, still Mom was the one to answer as she stood up from her hands and knees, the duster something she used to tap the top of Dad's head with as she passed and said, "It's no one, dear. Just relax back now."

And so he did as she said later she would polish the silver, but first there were the curtains to wash, never mind she washed them just the day before. She climbed the ladder and took them back down, piling them in the middle of the room while she diverted to some other cleaning task. Meanwhile, I reached over to the coffee table and picked up my chemistry book, trying to finish my homework.

School had begun a few weeks back. I was starting the eighth grade. My old friends, who weren't my friends anymore. Flint and the whole gang, who still had their happiness like the whole world laughing. I found myself reaching toward them the way Sal had when they ran past him that first day. They ran by me too, as if I should know better than to think I could ever have youth that way again.

I did have my old locker. Same combination. Who would've thought a combination could make me so happy? But I liked having the same. It was from that old life, and sometimes I thought I could just spin the lock back to it. I could open the locker and find the old Fielding, a summer younger. I could open it to Grand. There he'd be, squeezed inside, and I could just pull him out. Dresden too. Just keep pulling out all the things lost.

Sal took a test to determine what grade level he would function at. According to his score, he'd be in high school already. Apparently, he was some sort of genius. Mom said it wasn't a good idea for him to go to school yet with others. I guess she thought it would be a mad, glistening violence. Bullies and beasts lining up and all that. So a tutor came in and taught him in one of the spare rooms, which Mom eagerly cleaned out for a desk.

When I look back, I now know Grand's death was the final vibration for Elohim and his group. The final fusing of them into a single sword pointed at Sal.

I can imagine Elohim at his meeting, saying Grand's name.

Just a boy, a young god of Breathed who would've made us all proud. But he's dead now. And all because of that devil. How many more gods will we allow the devil to kill?

We Blisses were too busy grieving to see the sword on its way to

Sal. We couldn't see beyond the dirt we felt buried under. I hadn't even seen Elohim since passing him on the way to Grand's funeral. I walked by him, sure. I passed his house when he was out on the porch eating his vegetables, but I didn't see him. I had too many ghosts in my eyes. We all did.

I laid down the chemistry book and my homework.

"I wish it would snow." I reached behind the sofa and laid my arm across the hot windowsill, my fingers dangling to the brick outside. Mom had taken the screens down to clean and the windows were left open to air out the house.

I looked up at the sky. It was like the fur of a coyote, tan in all the places it wasn't gray. A bolt of lightning came in a slender flash. The thunder slipped in a low grumbling hello. In its wild self, it was finally going to rain.

"There's something—" Sal cleared his throat "—there's something I have to tell you all. About me."

I brought my eyes down from the sky and saw Elohim's face staring back at me. How canine his features looked. How his mouth seemed to foam. Just another rabid dog at the window.

"I'm sorry, Fielding."

Elohim looked as though he might have meant it as he reached through the window and grabbed Sal. Dad quite possibly made a leap from the chair to the sofa. Mom quite possibly flew from the lampshade. I know Fedelia ran in from the kitchen, joining Mom and Dad, who each had a foot of Sal's.

Elohim would not let go. For all his life, he would not let go of Sal, of Helen, of her lover. He held tight to all these things and that's when the others appeared. They'd been so quiet, not your usual loud mob. Their silence was worst, stealing away our right to shut the windows and bolt the door. We didn't even have time to scream. It was a silent struggle on both ends. Joining the battle, I wrapped my arms around Sal's legs, pulling back with Mom, Dad, and Fedelia.

"Don't let me go."

Sal was looking at me. If only I were Grand. If only I had his strength. No one ever said it, but I know it was my fault they pulled Sal away from us. I wasn't strong enough, and it was me who let him go.

That was when the screaming started. They were screaming cheers, we were screaming tears, and Sal was screaming fear. A rhyme of the ages.

Dad lost his slippers and Mom lost her heels as they climbed out the window, his bathrobe and her apron flapping as they gave chase. Me and Fedelia were behind them, but she broke off before we got into the woods. She said she was going to get the sheriff. No one had time to tell her the sheriff was in the mob. I suppose he always had been.

Fedelia's parting words were for me to save the day.

I will, Auntie. I tried to believe I could.

Even before we got there, I knew it was to the schoolhouse they were going. The place in which their insanity had ripened and been brought to fruit. There in the middle of the schoolhouse was a wooden post they had newly erected. To this post they tied Sal as quickly as anybody has ever been tied.

Dad grabbed at the rope and punched a guy. Kicked another in the groin, but someone grabbed onto the back of his robe and yanked him to the ground by it. It took three guys to hold him down.

Mom was screaming somewhere on the other side of me. I know I looked at her face, but all I remember is seeing the edges of her dress. Edges turning and flailing under those who held her down.

I myself was scratching, biting, and kicking the shins of a guy holding me against him. It was then I saw Dovey with the gas can. Beside her was the woman in the rhinestone belt who had asked Sal if God was a nigger too. Together Dovey and this woman poured gas on the ground around Sal. They did it so steady, as if they were pouring milk in glasses for their very own dinner table.

I bit down on the man's hand holding me until I drew blood and he let go. I ran to Sal. I almost made it too. I felt the rough of the rope at the tips of my fingers. I saw him smile with the hope I would be enough to save him.

It was Elohim who grabbed me back by my hair and slapped me down. By his orders, two followers came to get me. I hit one in the stomach. He hit me in the face. I bit one on the arm. He bit me on the hand. I wiggled and squirmed, but it only seemed to tighten their grip.

All I could do was watch Elohim light the match like it was the only right choice. I would like to say he was not smiling. I would like to say he was not happy as the match tossed through the air in slow motion like a thing that held all of time. Tumbling and flipping its flame down to the gasoline, where it lit in a bright, painfully beautiful burst.

I was still looking at that burst when I heard Sal scream to me to remember Granny. Granny? The flames were all I saw. But then I did remember. Granny. The suffering. The gun. Yes, I remembered what I couldn't do the first time. Would I stay the child? Or become the man Sal was asking me to become?

The flames burned through the gas trail around him, building higher and higher as they headed for him. He didn't scream, but he did cry. I didn't understand how a boy could have so many tears, yet not have enough to put anything out.

In love with the flames, the two men who held me loosened their grip as they watched the fire they couldn't stop being in awe of. It was enough of a loosened grip for me to break away, to run past them, past Dad, watching me, his teeth gritting under the elbow plastered to his cheek.

I ran past the edge of Mom's dress, to the tree house not far there in the woods. From the crate I grabbed the gun because it was the only water I had to put the fire out.

By the time I returned, the flames had made their way in the circle of gas around the tree, and were now at Sal's feet, burning up his calves. The smell of his melting flesh was so thick, it packed into the nose as something solid. I thought my nostrils were going to split under the strain.

No one saw me with the gun. They were busy cheering the flames.

"Just look at him." They laughed as he struggled to get free of the rope. *"Just look at the devil wiggle."*

Sal never once screamed. I know he did it for Mom and Dad's sake. It's a hard thing for a parent to hear, that of their child burning alive. Sal loved them enough not to let them hear a thing like that.

"I'm sorry. Oh, God, I'm so sorry, son." Dad's crying left little room for his words. He was still being held down. Still fighting to not be.

Mom had a whole different fight. Each of her limbs were held by a person a piece, but her whole middle bounced up and down like she was on a trampoline as she screamed and called them *bastards* and *bitches* and *fucking devils*.

Truth be told, I thought a miracle would come, yellow and soft like a peach. If ever there was a moment for God to appear, it was right then and there. I waited for Him. For Him to save me from the choice of the trigger, because to squeeze it was to risk the wrong decision. A decision I could never come back from. It would tangle me. Follow me, choke me, scatter me, seize me for all sorrows. And yet, if I did nothing, I risked being Him. Just another God. A spectator of war.

The sound was like that of a heavy book falling from the top shelf, just magnified. How could two things so different share the same sound?

It was a sound that stopped all the others. All that remained was the crackling of the fire, which no longer burned a life, just a body, and there ain't suffering in that except for the coffin's loss.

The bullet was as successful as a bullet can be.

People let go of the things they'd been holding tight to. Things like Mom and Dad. Dad just stood there, his fingers like claws digging into his head as he stared at Sal's body. Mom walked slowly, holding her arms out. She got so close to Sal, the fire caught on the edge of her dress.

In her unbelieving daze, she didn't realize the flames at first, not until she felt their heat on her legs. She screamed she didn't want to burn. Dad threw her down onto the ground, told her to roll while me and him threw the dry dirt, trying to suffocate the flames. But the flames continued on. They were eating her dress, they were eating her apron, until the rain fell sudden and strong.

Call it a miracle, or just call it weather. Either way, Mom was put out and Dad fell down beside her.

"Yes," she whispered as he held her in a rocking way.

"Yes, what, love?"

"The rain is just the gift I need." She tilted her face to the drops, thinking of the small jar of water sitting in the study.

The rain carried Elohim's blood from the gunshot wound. It was him, after all, who I shot in the chest.

My plan for the gun was to shoot Sal, to stop his suffering of the flames. But his eyes told me to aim away from him. To aim at the reason for the suffering. And so I did, and Sal heard the bang before he died. He heard the bang and he lowered his head and went knowing what I'd done for him.

As Elohim lay dying, no one cared. No one held his head in their hands and told him to *breathe, breathe, help is on the way.* No one said, *You're a good, good man, and you matter.*

No one cried for him or shouted at me, *What have you done?*

And what had I done?

I had shot a man. A man I once called a neighbor, a teacher, a friend. The best steeplejack in all the world. That's what I told him once, and he'd smiled.

I shot all those things. The man who was the saving hand when I nearly slipped off the roof. The man I caught fireflies with one summer night. The man I'd known all my life. All shot to pieces by me. I shot all the bad, but damn it all, I shot all the good as well. That's something you never quite come back from. That's something that's a fresh pain every day.

Out of all the things to last see, Elohim saw me with the gun as he lay there. Even in the rain, I saw the difference of the tear slipping down his face. His eyes said to me, *I hope one day you know what it feels like. The pain, the hurt, the slow dying.*

Yes, Elohim, I know what it feels like. I have seen for myself.

When he did finally die, he did so to the sounds of the women weeping and the men howling, not for him but for the boy they had burned to death.

They stared at his small, charred figure in the smoldering ash and knew he was no devil. They knew they had melted the skin off a thirteen-year-old boy. The pain of that was etched into his face, the way his mouth gaped open, the way his teeth protruded from the lips no longer there.

The sheriff, careful not to burn his fingers, began to gently untie the remaining rope as me, Mom, and Dad left.

Along the way, we passed Juniper's and the truck delivering the ice cream. Mom couldn't help herself. Her mad laughter caused the man unloading the ice cream to drop a carton. It rolled into our path. It seemed to stop everything, including us. Would we ever be able to move past? That is what I wondered as we stood there frozen before the frozen.

Mom was the first to move. She lifted her foot as if to take a step over it, but she felt the weight of that great task and instead walked around the carton, her head hung in the disappointing realization. Dad followed her around the carton. He didn't even put on the show of any other choice. Their steps said there would be no getting over it, there would only be the living around it. That *it* would always be there. *It* had become the Alpha and Omega, the beginning and our end. I knew this, and yet I wanted to try.

I took a step, but my toe caught on the carton and I fell as if the fall had always been in my nature. Waiting for the right moment of my life. When all my soul, in its smallness and its vastness, would fall face down against the earth from the bliss of my name to the hard crosses I would be handed to bear.

Mom and Dad silently waited for me to stand up on my own. Somehow we knew we could no longer help one another. It was up to ourselves to learn how to survive, and it was because of this, Dad let me carry the gun home. I was no longer the child. I was the man who had yet to have height on his side.

27

They, hand in hand, with wandering steps and slow,
Through Eden took their solitary way.

—MILTON, *PARADISE LOST* 12:648–649

COOLER TEMPERATURES AND regret ultimately equaled the re-covery of the town. Yes, the murderers of Sal really did regret. Some even regretted it enough to hurry to the grave. Brains on the wall. Gun in the hand. That was how they found one of them. Another rolled a cigarette with some cyanide. His whole room smelled like almonds because of it.

Otis hadn't been part of the mob. He found out Dovey had only after the fact. He didn't know what to say to her nor she to him. Those moments after the death of their child, Dovey and Otis were husband and wife unable to come together and heal. That distance between them led her to Elohim. It led to the night she said she was going to take a bath and asked Otis if he could hand her a bar of her homemade soap out of the closet.

Later, in the cold water of the tub, she shoved the bar of soap down her throat. Internal cleansing, I suppose. It's said they didn't even have to use more soap when they washed her body. Bubbles and suds came by just plain water and the friction of her skin. The dirtiest, cleanest woman ever to be buried.

After her death, Otis no longer walked the nights with the mirror, hoping to see his son. Too much had been lost, and the mirror gleamed from the top of a pile in the junkyard while his shorts and shirts got longer and his muscles turned to fat atop the sofas he sat on and the potato chips he ate.

A large number of the mob chose suicide by bottle. The sale of whiskey and its kin bled upward in Breathed.

There were a few of the folks who seemed to manage.

Did we? Me, Mom, and Dad?

Losing Sal was different than it was with Grand. The tissues weren't all over tables, floors, beds. Did we even open the new box in the hall? Sometimes I think not having tears meant we cried even more.

It was all that death. It made our eyes unable to produce the grief we felt. We were shell-shocked. Walking stiffs. If we ate, I don't remember. We must've, though, for none of us died of starvation. If we slept, I don't remember that either. I know both Mom and Dad died tired. As I am dying tired. Maybe that's what got us. The inability to sleep because nightmares and dreams became alike, as we were gladdened by the sight of our ghosts but haunted by them at the same time.

Mom didn't work through Sal's death. There was no cleaning out already clean shelves. Padding already plump sofa cushions. House and home became a place she was rarely in.

She stopped wearing dresses. Too many edges to catch, I guess. There was also the singeing to consider. She was pants from then on out. Polyester, corduroy, denim. Pants, pants, pants. I lost something of my mother when she lost her dresses. That woman in the kitchen. Floating here and there, as light as the flour on her hands.

In pants she got heavier. She stayed thin but got heavier like she was attached to the ground. One grave on her right, one grave on her left, both pulling her down with them. She was veiled, darkened over. The shadow of our family. Of herself. No more guzzling the sweet syrup of the canned pears she'd open like our little secret when it was just me and her in the kitchen. No more kitchen at all. No more aprons.

No more hair tied up in strings. No more Dad pulling on those tails and making her laugh.

Dad.

I don't think he made her laugh again. Maybe he tried. When I wasn't there. When it was just them and pillows. Maybe he wanted to when he sat there, eyes squinted, arms folded, legs crossed. He just didn't know how to be the man he once was. The man who had a son named Grand. A son named Fielding. A son named Sal.

After Sal's death, Dad didn't fall into T-shirts and pajamas, the way he had when Grand died. Instead, Dad looked the part of who he once was. Three-piece suits. Shaven face. Even added a pocket watch. I suppose to have something certain to look at when his uncertainty got too much for him. Something to see for himself in the palm of his hand. Yes, he looked the part, but he wasn't it. Not anymore.

Conversation with him became like dragging something out. You had to put hooks in and keep pulling, pulling until he spoke. And then you wished you hadn't, because his tone alone was like lying down in a coffin and having the lid nailed shut. Talking with him was working with the gravedigger, and sometimes you had to get away from the cemetery, which meant I had to get away from him. I would too, at seventeen. I'd just up and leave my parents.

Or were they just people who looked like my parents? Maybe my mother and father burned that day with Sal, and I walked away with their ashes.

And who was I? Who am I? The boy who met the devil and met hell at the same time. I'm not saying it was Sal's fault. Of course it wasn't.

It was Dad's.

Without his invitation, I would not meet Sal in front of the courthouse. I would not take him home. No journalists would come. Grand would not open his veins and try to bleed Ryker out. There would be no fire. There would be no best friend in its flames. There would be no man I would have to kill.

Yes, Dad, you started it all.

I should address what legally happened to those who took part in Sal's murder. They were rounded up and charged. The devil was put on trial, though there were no horns, no pitchforks either. It was not one strange face indicted, but many familiar ones. The man who sold us all insurance, the woman who ran the church raffle, and the couple whose cake we ate at their fortieth wedding anniversary the previous April.

The man who fixed my tire when it went flat in front of his house, and his older sister who bandaged my knee when I fell. The guy who was said to have the warmest handshake, and his wife who fed the stray cats in the neighborhood.

They were not walking caves of nocturnal demons, scared of the sunlight and fresh air. In fact, the way they all went into court, they looked like cotton curtains of the sunniest, breeziest, most welcoming windows in all the world. They came not from underground lairs but from homes with flowers in vases and cookies in the oven. They were men who held the door open for the ladies who thanked them as they passed through. And in alphabetical order, the jury found each one of them not guilty by reason of temporary insanity.

Dad was not the man prosecuting them. He was the one defending them. When he first told me and Mom about it, I screamed at him. How could he defend them? The murderers of Sal? It's like the man I knew all those years was just one long weekend away from the real man who burned garter snakes Monday through Friday.

For the months of the trial, I let go of my father. Maybe some of it was my wanting to let go of myself.

If I didn't have to be me, then it was someone else who lost so much that summer. Someone else who saw how red his brother's blood was. Someone else who lost their best friend. It was someone else who killed a man—a bad man, but a man nonetheless. It was someone else, and I was okay with being just that.

Take me away from this Fielding Bliss.

To be someone else. Bottle after bottle, I try to be just that. Pill after pill, restless sleep after restless sleep, fuck after fuck. But still I sober to myself, still I wake to the reaching abyss.

The same abyss that reached for us all. For Dad, for Mom, for Grand, Elohim, and of course Sal. That abyss that always wins.

Dad was walking the edge of it during those months of the trial. I knew he didn't want to defend them. I also knew he would do every-thing to see them found not guilty. Because of this, I would never tell my father I loved him again.

The whole situation was made worse by the journalists who came to Breathed, this time not for the heat but to report on the progress of the case. I looked out for Ryker. He never came. Don't know what I would've done if he had. Maybe led him to Grand's grave. Maybe shown him I know how to fire a gun now. What's one more murder on my conscience?

A few of the reporters shoved a mike into my face and asked how I felt. Seventy-one years later, and I'm still answering. Is anyone still listening?

I hated the reporters. I hated their questions. I hated the trial. I hated the smell of melting flesh still in the air. I hated the echo of the gun lasting eternal. Gone were the hills of my youth. Gone were the trees. The houses I had known, the people I had loved. Gone, gone, gone with a town that became a place behind a burning door, down a long hallway, and behind an evermore burning door.

I watched my father walk to the courthouse every day, hated him every day a little more. I needed to see exactly what I was hating, so that last day I followed him to the courtroom and listened to him deliver his closing statement:

"All the little choices we make, what shirt to wear for the day, what to eat for dinner, what movie to watch come Friday night, they are all rehearsals for the bigger choices of our lives, like what captains we will be when the brakes go out and we rocket full speed ahead.

"But even with all the rehearsing, there can come along someone who makes us forget our God-given right to choose. It is the inability to choose by our own will that lessens us all. It is disease to our sanity, which sickens our good sense until we are the victims of choices we would not normally have been in the company of.

"This is exactly what happened during the course of the summer of 1984. These people lost their right to choose, and in that lost their sanity like sweat in hot bathwater. By the twenty-first of September, they were severed from themselves as completely as they were tied to Mr. Grayson Elohim. Like puppets in the master's claws, they twitched when he told them to twitch. They stepped when he told them to step. They growled when he told them to growl.

"Grayson Elohim had the genealogy of a tablecloth, but over the course of one summer, he became God. At first, his ideas tumbled as dry and harmless as bones from his mouth, but somewhere along the way, his words became the great dinosaurs before the fossils. Yes. The form had gotten its function back. And his function was to orchestrate panic through the chorus of fear. Fear of the boy with color in his skin. Fear of the devil in the skin of a boy. He sang over and over again, *fear, fear, fear* like a lullaby laying their sense down in the thorns disguised as roses.

"You may say this level of manipulation would never happen to you, members of the jury. But how many times have you been convinced to buy something on television that you don't need? How many times have you done something you didn't want to do, but did anyways because someone told you to? How many times has your choice fallen second to the choice of someone else?

"This is the year 1984 we're talking about. The year George Orwell said we would be convinced two and two makes five. He proved through story, mind is controllable. These people have proved through reality no different.

"What these poor souls were desperate for was a light. But the thing about light is it all looks the same when you're in the dark, so you can't tell if what powers that light is good or if it is bad, because the light blinds you to the source of its power. All you know is that it saves you from the darkness. That's all his followers knew. They were in the dark of their own private pain, and then this Elohim comes along and he's shining so bright.

"They reached for that brightness, and while the light distracted them, while it comforted them in its false rescue, the dark power behind it did its work, and before any of them knew it, they were not being saved by the light, they were being changed by it. They were being controlled by it. By this Grayson Elohim."

In the gesture of spitting on Elohim's grave, Dad dramatically spit on the floor before throwing his arms up as he boomed, "How can you call them guilty? When they were away from themselves. Temporarily gone. These people, your family, your friends, your neighbors, possibly you under the right circumstances. Away from themselves.

"Haven't you ever been away from yourself? Only to come home and find a mess has been made in your absence? A mess you need help to clean up. Not to be punished for but to be helped with. Won't you help your family now? Your friends? Your neighbors? Yourself?

"Grayson Elohim is the murderer, the real murderer, and he is already gone and buried. Isn't it time we put the shovels down instead of digging more holes? The more holes we dig, ladies and gentlemen of the jury, the less solid ground any of us will have to stand on."

Later that night, Dad came home victorious from the courthouse. You would never have known it. The way his head hung, the way his feet dragged, the way his eyes hardly knew who he was. He went into his study and took down the plain wooden cross from off the wall. With it, he went to the back porch, where he sat down on the steps.

I watched him turn the cross over in his hands. His hair had become more gray than brown, like tree branches covered in ash. His tie was out of his vest, as if he no longer cared if it played noose.

When I sat beside him, he didn't notice. That was Dad from then on out. The man who was sat beside, but was always alone.

It was late spring by then, though it felt wintry. The grass was holding back its green. Flowers didn't know what blooming meant. The trees' bare branches scratched the sky that always seemed to be bright and white, like snow about to come. There was a quiet stillness, even in the moving breeze you wanted to grab a sweater for.

"Dad?"

He didn't answer, so I said his name over and over, putting the hooks in and trying to pull him out.

He let go of a long-held breath. "Yes, Fielding?"

"Why'd you do it, Dad? Why'd you invite the devil?"

He looked at me as if he forgot who I was. And through that, I didn't know if it was me either. I didn't know if I was enough left to be a son. If he was enough left to be a father. Or if we were just two flames, with not enough love to be anything more than reminders of the burn.

Finally, he turned his eyes back out onto the world. "You remember when I told you and Sal about the case I prosecuted? Of the girl accusing her father of rape? I killed that father, Fielding. All because I'd been wrong. I killed him. It wasn't the girl. It wasn't the jury. It wasn't the misunderstanding. But me. I alone killed him because I was the one who was supposed to be certain. I was the one entrusted with the filter. The one who was supposed to do everything right with it. I failed."

He was quiet, as if to allow me the chance to say something or, at the very least, pat him on the back. I did nothing. I sat there and felt the unrelenting crush of that very choice.

"We live each day with thoughts we think are certain to the core, Fielding. But what if we are sincerely wrong? Take a look at this cross. We are told it's a cross, so surely it must be a cross. But what if it isn't? What if we're wrong? What if this whole time we've just been hanging a lowercased *t* on our walls?"

With one swift pitch, he flung the cross. We watched it hit the ground and felt nothing.

He didn't speak for some minutes later.

"I once overheard Elohim ask, 'Would a panther eat us before we could call it black? Or would it not eat us at all?' I thought, of course a panther would eat us. Of course. I was certain of it, and yet what if I was wrong?

"That is what I wanted to do. I wanted to test the validity of the claims. I wanted to meet the devil, and through that meeting I would know for certain if I'd ever met him before in the courtroom, in those men and women I sent away. And if I had, then I would've done some good after all. I would've been right and maybe in all those rights, I would be able to make up for that one wrong when I sent an innocent man to prison and in that sent him to his death.

"I had all my faith in. I was so sure of what was evil, of what was good. But then Sal came, and the panther ate salad, and the devil— well, he turned out to be the only angel among us. And I'm lost. I'm lost now, Fielding. What is good and what is bad?" He tossed his arms weakly in the air. "I don't know. I just don't know anymore. My faith is gone. How can it not be? After all, who was burned at the end of this story?"

The quiet filled in all the spaces between us as we sat there, unsure of not just ourselves, but also each other.

"I don't get it, Dad. You loved Sal, right?"

"He was my son." The world seemed to move a little after he said that. As if it were opening a drawer and putting his words inside for safe-keeping, so should there ever come a day when it was doubted Autopsy Bliss loved Sal as his own son, that drawer could be opened and those words pulled out as the precious proof of a father's heart.

"Then why'd you defend his murderers, Dad? They were the devil. How could you defend the devil?"

He seemed to be asking himself that very question. In answer, he began telling about the time Sal was flipping through one of his law books.

"Sal said to me I might have to defend the devil just once in my life. I said I didn't think I could do that. He said to defend the devil is to defend the broken glass.

"When glass is whole, it's good. When it's broken, it's bad. It's swept up. It's thrown away. Sometimes thrown away too soon. Think of a window, Sal said. Imagine a violence breaking that window. All those shards of broken glass fall to the floor.

"The violence is inside the house now, wrestling you. It could kill you, so you grab one of the shards and stab. The violence dies and you are saved. Saved by the broken glass. Isn't that a funny thing? To be saved by the bad.

"Sometimes, not sweeping that bad up and throwing it away will save you in the end. It just might. So to defend the devil means defending the good of the bad. That's what I was doing, Fielding. Hoping that all those folks are just shards of broken glass and one day in the future, they'll save someone by being just that.

"Furthermore, I am responsible for those people, Fielding. I'm the one who wrote the invitation, and all because I wanted to see for myself. I wanted to see for myself."

The sky, in its white sheet, let loose a heavy, cold rain. Dad stood and stepped into it, stretching out his arms and tilting his face to the drops, as if in surrender to the fall.

The screen door screeched behind me. Mom came, and together we joined Dad. A barely there family, as together as we could ever be.

Shortly after, we left Breathed for good. Dad never stepped into a courtroom again. He went into linoleum flooring. Ended up with a small bliss after making a chemical discovery that allowed linoleum to be nonslip.

"So no more mothers will fall back and lose their faith," he said.

They took his picture for the paper. He did not smile.

Mom became a traveler, going to all the places that was our house. She never forgot that house either, so when she went to these places, she'd bury a piece of us there. Since England was our kitchen, she dug a small hole at the base of Stonehenge and buried there the spatula she once used to frost our birthday cakes. And because Russia was our living room, she buried there the framed picture of our family.

As the years went on and she'd return to these places, she would never say, *I'm going to Egypt* or *to the Netherlands* or *to Vietnam.* She'd simply say, *I'm going into the attic* or *walking down the hall* or *stepping into the breakfast nook for a bit.*

And Dad would say, "Don't forget to turn the lights off when you leave."

It was us she wanted to leave. Going to all those places. She was trying to get away. That's why she always went by herself. Why Dad always sat home alone, wondering when she was going to come back to him.

Dad nor Mom spoke to me in regards to my killing of Elohim. Dad didn't ask how it made me feel. Mom didn't say I'd done the right thing. I was just the one who had a gun, and Elohim was just the enemy shot. Everything else wasn't said. I wasn't charged with murder or put through a trial. It was, dear jury, self-defense. But don't you worry, I have been in prison ever since.

When they went into Elohim's house, they found in his cinder block basement a freezer of ice cream and body parts. There were Polaroids of black boys before they'd been butchered, and more gruesome Polaroids of the various stages of being butchered.

Elohim had said he wished someone would've stopped Helen's lover from growing up. Just ate his future away. Elohim, the vegetarian, was eating black boys before they could become black men.

In the collection of Polaroids was a boy identified by his parents as Amos.

And then there was the Polaroid of a boy in a pair of overalls. It was taken near the basement window. The light streaming through was bright and whitened out the boy's face, which was upturned toward the bars of the window, where birds flew outside.

The boy good at escaping.

Or was it?

No one knew if it was in fact Sal or not. Sometimes I'd look at the picture and think the overalls were different. Too much grass stain, not enough dirt. Was the boy in the picture shorter than Sal? He was shorter than the shovel leaning against the wall behind him, and I remembered Sal always being taller. Maybe it was just the camera angle. Maybe it was that light that blocked out his face.

I'd look at that light, squint into its brightness, and think I saw Sal's eyes looking up at those birds just as he always had. After all, that's how I knew Sal was no devil. Because of the way he looked at the birds. Not as an angel who once flew, but as a boy who so wished he could.

We buried what was left of Sal on Reflection Hill, next to Grand. Grand's effigy saw him carved in his baseball uniform. A ball in his pitching hand. A glove on his left. Sal was carved in overalls. A weed daisy in one hand, nothing in the other. Two stone sculptures that did not represent the boys lying beneath them, but rather our own pure ignorance of who they were. For all the ways we knew them, we knew them not at all. They were deep water, and all we could cling to were the baseball uniform and the overalls floating on the surface.

Fedelia took over the shoe factory from Mom. I sure as shit didn't want it. It would be sold before Fedelia died. Fedelia who had stayed in Breathed for the rest of her life. Eventually remarrying. Happily. Ever. After.

We didn't go to her wedding. None of us ever returned to Breathed again. Maybe it was the same problem that faced Adam and Eve when they lost their Garden of Eden. Breathed was a paradise lost to us.

It was the summer that melted everything, and as Dad, Mom, and I drove out of Breathed for the last time, the puddles splashed beneath us. These puddles were from the rain, but to me, well, I've always thought they were the puddles of everything that had melted.

There were the puddles for all the tangible things like chocolate and ice cream. Then there were the puddles for all those things that lived inside us. Auntie's anger. Mom's fear. Dad's faith. Grand's life.

There was a puddle for Dresden. A puddle for Granny. And one for the boy who would change us all. Sal. A puddle that never would've been if not for the puddle of the town's common sense.

As for that last puddle, the one that splashed the most. That was the puddle of my innocence, the splashes still falling in the past as they are still falling now, as they will continue to fall for that eternal always, in a pooling water, ferrying me back.